RANDOM
HOUSE
LARGE
PRINT

Also by Mary Daheim
available from Random House Large Print

The Alpine Journey

THE ALPINE KINDRED

Mary Daheim

RANDOM HOUSE
LARGE PRINT

*The Library of Congress has established a Cataloging-
in-Publication record for this title*

0-375-43253-1

www.randomlargeprint.com

FIRST LARGE PRINT EDITION

10   9   8   7   6   5   4   3   2   1

This Large Print edition published in accord
with the standards of the N.A.V.H.

THE ALPINE KINDRED

Chapter One

EINAR RASMUSSEN JR. was angry. The deep grooves in his face that reminded me of cedar bark were twisted, and the agate-blue eyes never blinked.

"So Miss Steinmetz told me to be here by noon," Einar Jr. growled, planting both fists on my desk. "It's twelve-fifteen. I've been waiting for her out front, but nobody's there."

Unseen by Einar Jr., a small child sat on my feet. "Carla—Ms. Steinmetz—left before eleven to do a story on a new restaurant," I explained, trying to keep my patience along with my composure. The child was bouncing up and down. "She should be back any minute."

The agate eyes narrowed. "A new restaurant? So you mean that harebrained scheme the Bourgette kids came up with?"

I nodded. "Dan and John. They want to build a Fifties-style diner where the old warehouse burned down by the railroad tracks."

"Dumb," Einar Jr. declared. "Alpine doesn't need a new restaurant. My son, Beau, would never come up with such a harebrained scheme. When it comes to business, those Bourgette kids haven't got the sense to pour sand down a rat hole."

I didn't know the Bourgette kids—who were actually thirty-something—well enough to assess their business acumen. But then I didn't know Einar Rasmussen Jr. much better, and I'd never met his son, Beau.

"It's different here now with the college," I countered as little Brad Erlandson started to squeak like a rubber duck. "Alpine's no longer just a stagnant mill town. You ought to know. You've had a big hand in helping build the new community college."

The flattery wasn't intentional, which was just as well, because Einar Jr. scoffed. "Bull. A few underpaid faculty members and a bunch of hard-up students can't support new restaurants." Einar Jr. scowled, the hard blue gaze raking my little cubbyhole of an office. "What's that noise? It sounds like a pig's loose in here."

I reached under the desk and tried to budge one-year-old Brad. "It's Ginny Burmeister's boy," I explained, gritting my teeth as Brad offered resistance. "Ginny Burmeister Erlandson, that is. Our office manager."

"So I wouldn't think an office would be the place for little kids." Einar Jr. smacked one fist into the other. "What are you running here? A newspaper or a baby-sitting service?"

Einar Jr. had pushed too far. "Look," I said, finally getting little Brad to remove himself from my feet, "I don't need advice on how to run *The Alpine Advocate*. Would I try to tell you how to run your trucking business? If you don't want your picture taken in front of the Rasmussen Union Building at the college, just say so. When I need an outside consultant, I'll take out an ad in *The Advocate*'s classifieds."

At last Einar Jr. blinked. "Okay, okay, Mrs. Lord—you don't have to get ornery with me. So I'm leaving. If your inconsiderate reporter ever shows up, let me know."

"I will. *She* will. Have a nice day. And," I added in an uncharacteristic display of waspishness, "it's *Ms.* Lord. I've never been married."

"I don't doubt it," Einar Jr. shot back. "Who'd have you?"

In my youth, there would have been a dictionary at hand to throw at Einar Jr.'s infuriating head. But in the computer age, there was only software. As with so many other aspects of life, high tech had sucked the drama out of human emotions.

It was probably a good thing. As the editor and publisher of *The Alpine Advocate*, I had no reputation as a prima donna. But Einar Rasmussen Jr. had pushed the wrong buttons; Carla might be a flake, but she was *my* flake.

Einar Jr. ought to stick to supervising his fleet of eighteen-wheelers.

Getting little Brad out from under the desk proved hopeless. I had just unwrapped the tuna-salad sandwich I'd made at home when the phone rang. My former ad manager, Ed Bronsky, assaulted my ear with a jumble of words that I didn't quite catch. "Sorry, Ed," I interrupted, "would you mind going over that one more—"

Ed was exasperated. "Emma, have you got a bad connection down there at *The Advocate*? I repeat, Shirley and I are getting an opergirl, and we want you to meet her."

"That's what I thought you said, and I don't know what you're talking about. What's an op-ergirl?" I winced as little Brad tickled my legs and started to giggle.

A heavy sigh rolled over the line from Ed and Shirley's so-called villa above the railroad tracks. "A live-in, a helper, a . . ." Another sigh followed, shorter and conveying frustration. "It's spelled A–U space P–A–I–R. I think it's French, but she's a Swede."

"Oh. An *au pair* girl." I pronounced the term as well as two years of French class at Blanchet High School in Seattle would allow.

"Right, right," Ed said impatiently, "you got it. She gets here tomorrow, Tuesday, and Shirl and I are giving a little party up here at Casa de Bronska. Friday, May sixteenth, eight o'clock. You and Vida and Leo and Carla and everybody else at the paper are invited. Tell Ginny to bring her husband and their little boy. We'll have a big spread."

The biggest spread at Casa de Bronska was Ed himself, but naturally I kept that thought to myself. Maybe my mean-mindedness was caused by envy at Ed's soft life since inheriting money from an aunt in Iowa. Or perhaps it was little Brad, now shinnying up and down my legs and threatening to bump his head on the underside of my desk. With the boy toddling at my side, I went into the news office, and expressed my annoyance to our current ad manager, Leo Walsh, who had just returned from making his Monday-morning rounds.

"Is Ed as big a dim bulb as I think he is or am I crabby these days?" I asked of Leo.

"Ed's a dim bulb, all right," Leo agreed, his weathered features amused. "On the other hand, you may be crabby because you haven't gotten laid lately."

"That's a really rotten thing to say," I retorted, flashing angry eyes at Ed's successor. "Besides—how do *you* know?"

Leo shrugged. "Ever since you and the Sheriff broke up last fall, I haven't seen you hanging out around Alpine's hot spots with any other guys."

"There *are* no hot spots in Alpine," I said with a straight face. That much was true—in our small mountain aerie in the Cascades, nightlife generally consists of unemployed loggers dumping pitchers of beer over each other's heads at the Icicle Creek Tavern. "Where's Carla?" I asked, changing the subject. "She was supposed to meet Einar Rasmussen, Jr., here at noon for a photo shoot out at the college."

Leo shrugged. "I haven't seen her since I left around nine-thirty."

"Where's Ginny?" I demanded as Brad suddenly decided walking wasn't such a good idea after all and began crawling around on all fours.

"It *is* the lunch hour, boss lady," Leo replied. "She probably went over to the Burger Barn."

"She shouldn't have left Brad," I complained as the boy crawled under Carla's desk. "Ginny is usually so responsible. What if I weren't here? What if you weren't here?"

"But we are," Leo said reasonably, then pulled out his wallet. "Are you seeking male companionship? Bright lights? Fusion cuisine in a sophisticated setting? Look. I got five of six numbers in the lottery Saturday night. Want to drive into Seattle and have dinner this weekend?"

"Wow!" I was impressed. "How much?"

"Six hundred and forty-seven bucks," Leo replied, fingering a half-dozen Big Bens. "What do you say?"

While occasionally Leo and I fraternize in a platonic sort of way, his offer sounded suspiciously like a date. "Why me? Why not Delphine?" I asked, referring to his off-and-on-again girlfriend, who happened to be the local florist.

Leo wrinkled his broad nose. "We don't do it for each other anymore. To tell the truth, I think she's stalking one of the construction workers out at the college."

"Well." I fingered my chin. Invitations to big-name city restaurants didn't come along very often. In fact, invitations of any kind—except for Ed's, which somehow didn't count—were as rare as an environmentalist at the Icicle Creek Tavern. "Okay," I said, diving after Brad, who was trying to pull a desk drawer onto his head, "why not? I haven't been into Seattle for a couple of months."

"Five months." Leo had stood up, stretching and ironing out the kinks in his broad back.

"What?" I stared. "Are you keeping score?"

"Yeah, I am." Leo grinned and ran a hand through his graying auburn hair. "I was only partly kidding when I made that crack about your sex life. You've been spending too much time alone lately, babe."

I despised the nickname, and Leo knew it, but obviously didn't care. "So you're taking it upon yourself to save me from myself?" I asked, my tone rather stiff.

"Something like that. Hey," he continued, leaning on his cluttered desk, "a while back you were worrying about me, remember? I let you. Now it's my turn."

I had indeed fussed about Leo's temporary withdrawal almost two summers earlier, and had wondered if he'd started drinking again. But my ad manager had merely been going through an introspective phase. The life he'd left behind in California looked better from a distance, *was* better, in the sense that he had reconciled himself to his ex-wife's remarriage and resumed speaking to his children.

"Okay," I finally said, pulling little Brad out of Carla's wastebasket. "Saturday it is. But don't forget, you're invited to Ed and Shirley's soiree Friday."

Gazing through one of the small windows that looked out onto Front Street, Leo sighed. "How can I forget? Nobody can forget Ed. Though we try." He sighed again.

My House & Home editor, Vida Runkel, was neither surprised nor dismayed when I told her about Ed's invitation. "I heard he and Shirley had sent for an *au pair*," she said, shrugging out of her new orange raincoat. "Frankly, I didn't think they'd get one. Whatever is the point except that the Bronskys want to show off?"

I had no explanation. The oldest of the five Bronsky children was now attending Skykomish Community College; the youngest was an eighth-grader at St. Mildred's Parochial School. "Maybe," I ventured, "Shirley needs help with that big barn of a house."

"Then she should hire a housekeeper, not an *au pair*." Vida sniffed. "Of course Shirley did hire at least three housekeepers, including Frieda Wunderlich, who told me it was utterly useless to clean the Bronsky house. They litter, like vagabonds. Food, clothes, appliances—they simply drop them as they walk—or waddle, as is the case with Ed."

"Maybe she won't stay," I remarked, checking Carla's computer screen to see what she was working on for the weekly issue due out in two days. The screen was blank. "Damn it," I groused, "Carla and Ginny have both been gone far too long! Little Brad's asleep under my desk. What's going on around here?"

Vida peered at me over the orange rims of her big glasses. She had recently acquired new bifocals, and replaced her tortoiseshell frames with a shade that matched her raincoat. I still wasn't used to the change.

"Something's afoot," Vida said in an undertone, though no one else was in the news office. "Ginny and Carla had their heads together earlier this morning. Buzz-buzz, whisper-whisper. I couldn't believe they wouldn't tell me what they were talking about."

Neither could I. There was scarcely a soul in Alpine who didn't divulge the darkest of secrets to Vida Runkel. She knew everyone, she was related to many of them, she hardly ever missed a morsel of news. If Vida had worked for the CIA, no foreign power's secrets would have been safe.

To prove the point, Vida pounced when Ginny and Carla entered the office ten seconds later. "Well?" my House & Home editor demanded, fists on broad hips and formidable bust thrust forward. "Where in the world have you two been? It's almost one-thirty."

"I'm sorry, I'm really sorry," Ginny Erlandson said, wringing her thin hands. "Is Brad okay?" She turned in every direction, her glorious red hair spraying around her shoulders.

"Brad's napping," I said, gesturing toward my office at the rear of the newsroom. "He's fine, but he'll be hungry when he wakes up."

My office manager rushed to check on her

son. Carla, however, strolled to her desk without looking at Vida—or me. "Was I supposed to get those Rasmussen Union Building pictures today?" she asked in a detached voice.

"You sure were," I responded, waving a finger at her. "Einar Rasmussen Jr. waited around here for twenty minutes and left in a huff. He said you had a noon appointment here."

Carla glanced at her calendar. "No, I didn't. It's tomorrow, the twelfth."

"This *is* the twelfth," I shot back. "Monday. You must have written it down wrong."

"Big deal. There's plenty of time. The dedication section isn't due out for over a week." With a languid air, Carla sat down.

I started to respond, but Vida interrupted: "What have you and Ginny been up to? It couldn't have taken you almost three hours to interview the Bourgette boys. Why would you need Ginny to go with you? It seems more likely that the two of you were out shopping at the mall or ate a very long lunch. No one takes more than an hour break at *The Advocate.* Isn't that right, Emma?" The latter comment was clearly an afterthought. Sometimes Vida has trouble remembering who is in charge. Sometimes I do, too. At sixty-plus, Vida not only can spot me by twenty years, but she has seniority on the newspaper, having been employed for almost two decades by the previous owner, Marius Vandeventer.

I nodded. "It tends to leave the rest of us in the lurch, especially with Ginny bringing Brad to work most of the time." As the boy began to walk and grow more active, I was beginning to think that my original offer of on-premise child care was a bad idea.

"That's it." Carla's pretty face brightened. "We were checking out day care. Ginny thinks it may be time to find a nice place for Brad."

Vida scowled. "Goodness, but you're a poor liar, Carla. You know perfectly well that Ginny's sister-in-law, Donna Wickstrom, has always said she'd take Brad in. *Now, where were you?*"

Carla's olive skin flushed and she hid behind her long, black hair. "It's a secret." One eye peeked out between the dark tresses.

"Nonsense!" There were no secrets in Vida's world. "Come, come, what's going on?"

Slowly, Carla brushed the hair from her face and made an attempt to stare down Vida. "I mean it. Honestly. I can't say—yet."

"Yet?" Vida's scowl deepened.

Carla shook her head. "I really, really can't. Wait until this weekend."

The sigh that Vida uttered could have blown

down a small sapling. "Carla! I'm ashamed of you!"

Ginny was tiptoeing out of my office. She was Bradless, so I assumed the child was still sleeping. "It's true," our office manager put in. "Carla can't say anything just yet. But it's nothing bad."

It seemed to me that Vida looked faintly disappointed. "Well, now. Then I suppose we'll have to wait." She drummed her short fingernails on the desktop. "When, this weekend?"

Carla and Ginny exchanged quick glances. "Sunday?" Carla finally said. "We'll drop by your house in the evening."

Mention of the weekend reminded me of Ed's phone call. As soon as Vida indicated she was partially appeased, I relayed the invitation. Ginny said she'd have to check with her husband, Rick; Carla hemmed and hawed.

"I just can't say," she said at last, then pointed to a news release on her desk. "Now, what about the RUB?"

"Oh—the RUB," I echoed, using the acronym for the student-union building named to honor Einar Rasmussen Jr.'s financial contributions to the community college. The dedication was set for Sunday, May 25. Our special section would be published Wednesday, May

21. The scheduling was awkward, because it meant we had to postpone our Memorial Day edition until after the legal holiday, but at least it would come out before the historical date, May 30. "Leo figures he can sell enough advertising for a four-page pullout," I said. "How much space can you fill with photos and text?"

For once, Carla seemed more at ease discussing business than personal matters. "I've got plenty of photos. I've been taking them ever since construction started. I ran into Mr. Rasmussen on campus last week to set up a photo of him in front of the completed union building. Now I suppose I'll have to reschedule." She sighed, the soul of self-sacrifice. "This is such a pain. I can't find his number in the phone book."

"He doesn't live here," Vida said with a faint sneer. "Einar Rasmussen Jr. lives off the highway on the river, between Grotto and Skykomish." The distance from town was less than ten miles, but Vida's disparaging manner indicated that Einar Jr. might as well reside in the Florida Keys. Though I had lived in Alpine for seven years, I still marveled at the natives' insular attitude.

I literally inserted myself between Carla and Vida by standing in the middle of the news office. "Einar Rasmussen Jr. is originally from

Snohomish," I explained to Carla, though it seemed that I'd already imparted the background information to her a week or more ago, "but he and his father, Einar Sr., have always had ties with both Snohomish and Skykomish counties. Until about eight years ago they owned a sawmill on the site where Einar Jr. built his house."

"It was nine years ago when the mill shut down, before you came to Alpine, Emma," Vida put in, with the usual implication that I was completely ignorant of the town's history before I moved in. "And don't forget Harold."

"Yes . . . ah . . . Harold." I *had* forgotten Harold, and my puzzled expression must have conveyed the oversight.

"Harold," Vida intoned, "is Einar Jr.'s older brother. Harold lives between Monroe and Sultan. Harold has rather peculiar habits."

The Rasmussens, it seemed, covered the route along Highway 2. "Such as?" I inquired.

"He drinks." Vida's face was wreathed in staunch Presbyterian disapproval. "Some people blame his condition on his brother. Very silly of them, of course. I doubt that Einar Jr. opens the bottles and pours the liquor for Harold."

I doubted that, too, but it wasn't Harold Rasmussen who had made generous donations to the college building fund. Until today, I had met Einar Jr. only once or twice; the rest of the family was unknown to me, except as a leitmotif in the history of Snohomish and Skykomish counties.

"Okay," Carla said, still lacking enthusiasm, "I'll look for Einar Rasmussen Jr. in the directory's Skykomish section. I still think the photo session was for tomorrow. He got mixed up."

It was pointless to argue. Though Carla was often wrong, she seldom admitted it. But that was typical of many people, including me.

Vida had turned away and was going through her in-basket. "I need 'Scene' items," she announced without looking up.

"Scene Around Town" was Vida's weekly collection of local human interest, a kind of gossip column that was probably the best-read part of the paper. While Vida's eagle eye usually provided most of the snippets, she relied on the rest of us for help. I'd never been certain if she really needed our input or if she was checking to make sure she hadn't missed anything.

Leo had just come through the door. "Cal Vickers is going to add a new line of tires at the Texaco station," our ad manager offered.

Vida gave a single nod, but didn't make a note. She never writes anything down; it all goes into her brain and sticks, like some cerebral bulletin board.

Ginny, who had finished feeding Brad, came in to check the coffeepot. "Carla talked to Dan and John Bourgette. They really are serious about building a restaurant where the old warehouse burned down last fall."

"That's a front-page story, not a 'Scene' item," I pointed out. "A new restaurant would be big news in this town. Carla, what did the Bourgettes tell you?"

"Not much," Carla said absently. "They're still involved in figuring out who holds the title."

"Keep on it," I urged, trying to come up with something for the gossip column. "Father Den traded in his eighty-five Honda for a ninety-four model," I said, starting to head back to my office. "I saw it Sunday at Mass. It's blue."

Vida nodded again. Having made my contribution, I turned away, but Carla caught me up short.

"I've got one, Vida. I'm pregnant. Does that count?"

I whirled around, Leo fell rather than sat in his chair, Ginny stifled a giggle, and Vida looked up so fast that she knocked her tan beret askew. "You're *what*?" she shrieked.

Carla let out an exasperated sigh. "You heard me. I'm pregnant. Ginny knows. The baby's due in December."

Vida's eyes were bulging. "That's your news? Why didn't you say so?"

But Carla shook her head, the long black hair sweeping around her shoulders. "That's *not* my news. I mean, it's not what I have to tell you this weekend. But maybe it's not right for 'Scene.' You usually don't put baby stuff in the column until after they get here, right? You know—'Sally So–and–so seen pushing her newborn along Railroad Avenue in a red-and-white-striped stroller.' "

"Well . . . I . . ." For once, Vida was flummoxed. "Carla!" My House & Home editor put a hand to her heaving bosom. "Really, I don't know what to say!"

Carla shrugged. "Then don't use it. I know the staff isn't supposed to be mentioned unless it's something really wild."

"This," I said, moving slowly but deliberately toward Carla, "qualifies as wild. Not," I added hastily, "in a *bad* way." After all, I had borne my only son out of wedlock. "How do you feel?"

"About what?" Carla gave me a puzzled look.

"In general. Physically." I waved a hand in an

agitated manner. "You know—remember how sick Ginny was the first few months when she was expecting little Brad?"

"I feel fine." Carla continued to look at me as if I were the one who was acting strangely. "I dialed Einar Rasmussen's number, but nobody answered. How come they don't have a machine?"

The change of subject indicated that Carla had told us as much as we were going to hear. For now. Even Vida held back, sitting up straight and adjusting her beret.

"The Rasmussens—the junior Rasmussens—" Vida began, "don't need a machine, because there's always someone home. I suspect they either didn't hear the phone or they chose not to pick it up."

"What do you mean?" I asked, turning my gaze to Vida. "Why are they always home? I thought Einar Jr. was a busy man."

"He is," Vida responded, taking a sip of the ice water she always kept at hand. "I wasn't referring to him. I meant his wife, Marlys, and their son, Beau." She gave me her gimlet eye. "Surely you've heard people around here say, 'Do you know Beau?'—and chuckle."

If I'd ever heard the phrase, I didn't remember it. But I had heard of Marlys, and was aware of their son, Beau. They also had a daughter, as I recalled. "I don't get it," I confessed.

With a sigh, Vida put one fist on her hip and enlightened me. "Marlys Rasmussen is rather odd. I understand that one of the reasons they built the house along the river was because Marlys didn't like being around other people. She wanted to move out of Snohomish to someplace where the neighbors weren't so close. She appears for certain social occasions, but I must say, she usually acts like a robot. A pity, too, because on one of the rare occasions that I've seen her, she actually smiled, and it simply turned her into a different person. You must wonder what makes a woman so withdrawn and unhappy."

It wasn't surprising that I'd never met Marlys Rasmussen. "What about Beau?" I inquired.

"*You* tell *me*," Vida said in a huffy voice. "To my knowledge, no one has seen Beau in years. Yet his father refers to him constantly. Beau this, Beau that—which is why people ask, 'Do you know Beau?' It's a catchphrase, suggesting something elusive."

"It sounds more reclusive than elusive," I murmured.

"It sounds like a bunch of nuts," Leo asserted.

"Now, now," Vida demurred, with a wave of

one finger. "The Rasmussens are merely different, perhaps a bit eccentric. I must admit, I
don't know the family that well. As I mentioned, they've never actually lived in Alpine."
Her disparaging manner suggested that the
family fed small children to circus animals.

Carla was back on the phone, perhaps trying
to reach the Rasmussens. Leo had turned to his
computer, and Vida, who wouldn't have surrendered her battered manual typewriter for a
one-on-one software seminar with Bill Gates,
began rattling the keys with her two-finger
touch system. I retreated into my office to finish the latest logging-crisis story. The afternoon
wound down, its soft spring sunlight filtering
through my little window. The occasional
rumble of a truck or a train passing through reminded me that there was life outside of *The
Advocate*'s four walls.

Shortly before four-thirty, I'd just finished
conferring with Carla and Kip MacDuff, our
back-shop manager, when Vida hurtled into
my office.

"Honestly!" she exclaimed. "I thought Carla
would never leave! She finally went out to the
back shop with Kip. Now, what is this baby
business? Is it that college dean?"

"It must be," I responded. "She's been going
with Ryan Talliaferro for a year."

Vida began to pace in her splayfooted manner. "Are they living together?"

"I don't know." I felt like adding, *How should I, when you don't?* "As far as I know, Carla hasn't had a roommate since Marilynn Lewis left town to get married to Dr. Flake."

Vida gave a brief nod. "That was last fall," she said, referring to the nuptials between Peyton Flake, M.D., and his nurse. Flake was Caucasian, and Marilynn was African-American. While both had courage to spare, they had felt that their interracial union stood a much better chance of survival in a more cosmopolitan environment. Yet the timing of their departure seemed somewhat ironic: since the college opened the previous year, Alpine was becoming increasingly, if somewhat microscopically, more integrated.

"That's the trouble," Vida groused, "with you assigning so much of the campus coverage to Carla. I really don't know as much as I should about these newcomers. Goodness, I'm not sure where Dean Talliaferro lives! For all I know, he could have moved in with Carla. Tsk, tsk."

I assumed the tsk-tsks were not aimed at the couple's illicit merger, but at their lack of communication with Vida. "I've dropped by Carla's a couple of times the past few months," I said, "but I didn't notice if there was any sign of him living there."

Vida shot me a disparaging look. "That's the problem—so few people notice. Really, Emma, I expect better of you."

I let the remark pass. "So what's Carla's big news?"

"Oh, that!" Vida waved a dismissive hand. "Now that she's told us she's pregnant, I can guess. She and Dean Talliaferro no doubt are getting married. Such a letdown! And how like Carla to do things backward!"

That much was true. Carla often wrote her news stories backward, paying no attention to whether the pyramid was inverted or not. The who-what-when-where-and-why of the classic newspaper lead might get buried in various parts of the story or show up in the last paragraph. Despite a degree from the University of Washington's school of communications and six years of experience, my reporter's professional lapses still appalled me. She was, however, an excellent photographer, which, along with my wishy-washy managerial tendencies, kept her safely employed.

Yet it occurred to me that if Carla was going to have a baby before the year was out, I'd need some fill-in help while she took maternity leave. "An intern," I muttered.

"An intern?" Vida scowled. "We don't need an intern, we need a full-fledged GP. Poor Doc Dewey—he's working himself into the ground since Peyton Flake left."

"I meant an intern for here, while Carla's having the baby. You know," I clarified, "maybe someone from the college. It would only be for a few weeks."

"Oh." Vida made a face. "I thought you were referring to our current shortage of medical personnel. Do you know that Grace Grundle has to wait four weeks to get her bunions off?"

I didn't know, nor did I care. The search for a qualified physician had gone on too long, however. Only the previous week I'd written yet another editorial about the county health department's foot-dragging. Until the influx of college students, Alpine and its environs had one of the oldest populations in the state. Between the longevity of its many Scandinavian residents and the migration of young people to the city, the average age in Skykomish County was almost five years older than that of other, larger counties. But for all my carping in *The Advocate*, Alpine still remained a one-doc town.

If I was temporarily disinterested in the current medical crisis, Vida wasn't concerned about a replacement for Carla. "Plenty of time to worry about that," she said. "For now, we must concentrate on this baby business. Why don't you come over to dinner tonight at my house? I'll fix a nice casserole."

Like most of her cooking, Vida's casseroles were a mixed bag. In fact, they tasted more like she'd used a paper bag as part of the ingredients. "Don't go to the trouble," I said hastily. "We can eat at the Venison Inn."

"Well . . ." Vida fingered her chin. "I do have some errands to run after work. Why don't I meet you there a little before six? We'll avoid the rush."

The rush in Alpine is always a relative term. What Vida really meant was that she wanted to make sure she got a window table so she could keep her eye on the passing parade down Front Street.

"Okay," I agreed. "I'll stick around here and get caught up on a few things."

By five, everyone else had gone home. By five-thirty, I finished going through the handouts and news releases that had piled up in my in-basket. Turning out the lights and locking up, I stepped cautiously onto the sidewalk. I would never admit it, but every time I left the office, I checked to make sure that Milo Dodge wasn't in sight. Maybe that was why I was eating lunch in so much these days. I didn't want to see him, not because I hated him, but because he didn't want to see me.

Strange, I thought, glancing the two blocks down Front Street to the Sheriff's office, how we had agreed to stay friends when we broke up. But maybe not so strange that Milo hadn't been able to keep the promise. It was my idea to stop seeing each other. He had reacted much more bitterly than I'd expected. Maybe he'd cared more than I'd ever guessed. It would have been nice if he'd told me so along the way.

There was no sign of his Cherokee Chief parked in front of the Sheriff's office. I assumed he'd gone home to his TV dinner and his baseball game. I didn't want to think about Milo sitting in front of the set and eating Swanson's Hungry-Man frozen chicken.

I didn't want to think about Milo at all.

But I did.

Chapter Two

ON TUESDAY, CARLA turned into a dynamo. She managed to get a photo of a three-car collision on Alpine Way near her apartment, she turned out a creditable story on the RUB dedication, and she filled the gaping hole on page one with the Bourgettes' restaurant plans. Last but not least, she met Einar Rasmussen Jr. at the college and shot off two rolls of film in an attempt at appeasement.

"He wasn't too awful," Carla said later that afternoon when the paper was almost put to bed. "I think he's more bark than bite."

"Good," I remarked from my perch on her desk where I was proofing the cutline for the accident picture. "No injuries. That's good, too." Two of the three vehicles, all driven by local residents, had rear-ended each other when the first had stopped short at one of Alpine's few traffic lights. Carla had managed to catch the drivers as they'd emerged from their cars and were shaking their fists in anger. I recognized an Olson, an Iverson, and a Swanson.

"I'll get the proofs back tomorrow from Buddy Bayard's," Carla said, referring to the local photography studio that handled our developing. "I hated to do it, Emma, but I told Mr. Einarssen he could have a look."

I glanced up from Carla's copy on the Bourgette project. "You did?" I tried not to let subjects interfere—or censor, as I termed it in the darker corner of my free press soul—with either text or visuals. But sometimes accommodations had to be made. "Well, it shouldn't be a problem. It's pretty standard stuff, isn't it? And by the way, it's Rasmussen, not Einarssen."

"Whatever." Carla shrugged. "Actually, I got him to stand on his head."

My eyes widened. "You did? He could, at his age?"

At her desk, Vida harrumphed. "Einar Jr.'s not as old as I am. Why shouldn't he stand on his head?"

I tried to imagine Vida doing likewise. The vision was awesome.

"I think he got a charge out of it," Carla said, exhibiting her dimples. "Mr. Einarssen has a frisky side."

"*Rasmussen,*" I repeated. I'd definitely have to check Carla's cutline for accuracy. Only last week she'd typed Ku Klutz Klan into an article about Mayor Fuzzy Baugh's youth in Louisiana and his allegedly valiant stand against the KKK.

The Bourgette story read well, however. Dan

and John had nailed down the title, and taken out a loan to buy the property from the city. The terms were generous, since Mayor Fuzzy was probably glad to get the fire-scarred eyesore off his hands.

"Say," I said, finishing the story, "how come Einar Jr. is so down on the Bourgette brothers? He was very critical of them when he was in here yesterday."

Vida eyed me over the rims of her glasses. "Really, Emma! Don't you know?"

I shook my head. "Know what? He said they weren't as smart as his son, Beau. The Bourgettes didn't have business sense."

"Einar Jr. would say anything derogatory about the Bourgettes," Vida responded. "They're his nephews."

I was surprised—and puzzled. "Why is that? A family feud?" The Hatfields and McCoys had nothing on Alpine. Internecine quarrels were as common as gopher holes.

"Of course." Vida stood up, crossed the room, and handed me "Scene Around Town." "Mary Jane Rasmussen Bourgette is Einar Jr. and Harold's sister. She married a Catholic. Naturally, that didn't set well with Einar Sr. and his wife, Thyra. They're Lutheran to their toes."

I frowned at Vida. "You teased me about for-

getting Harold Rasmussen. Now you tell me
there's a Mary Jane, too? Did you forget her
until now?"

Vida looked vaguely sheepish. "Not exactly.
It's just that when Mary Jane and Dick got
married almost forty years ago, the rest of the
Rasmussens cut them off. I suppose I don't
think of them as having anything to do with
the rest of the family, because they don't.
Besides, the Bourgettes only moved to Alpine
two years ago when Dick started working as an
electrical subcontractor on the college construction. Dan and John joined their father, but
now they want to branch out. Dick and Mary
Jane had lived in Monroe until then, and I understand they wanted more space to entertain
their grandchildren. The Bourgettes have quite
a brood."

I realized then that I'd seen members of the
Bourgette clan at Mass only in the past couple
of years. Vaguely, I recalled Vida's story on the
family and how they'd taken up residence in
the old Doukas house on First Hill. But of
course Vida hadn't mentioned the Rasmussens
in her article, so I was unaware of the connection.

"I think the Bourgettes have a great idea,"
Carla said after I'd told her to go ahead and
send the restaurant story to the back shop for

publication on page two. "We could use another place to eat. I get tired of the Venison Inn and the Burger Barn and those fast-food places at the mall."

I agreed. "Let's hope they have better luck than the Californians who tried to fix up the old hotel," I noted, referring to the L.A.-area transplants who had tried to renovate the old Alpine Hotel in the hope of turning it into a bijou hostelry, complete with a gourmet kitchen. Five years ago their timing, as well as their financing, had been dicey. The project had collapsed, and the hotel was currently being considered by the local churches as a battered women's shelter.

Which, it occurred to me, would provide editorial fodder for next week. Like the county health department's slow selection process in hiring a new doctor, Alpine's clergy were taking their time to finalize the shelter project. I understood the locals' resistance to change, but in both cases, I felt they were shooting themselves in the foot.

Or was it feet? I wondered idly, still in my proofreader's mode. But the paper was in Kip MacDuff's hands, and it was time to go home. Once again, I dodged Dodge. Behind the wheel of my aging green Jaguar, I turned off Front Street and headed for Railroad Avenue.

It was about time I took a good look at the future diner site.

The loading dock and the warehouse were located just off Alpine Way by the bridge over the Skykomish River. The structures had originally served the Alpine Lumber Company, which had stood on the site of Old Mill Park just across what is now the main thoroughfare in and out of town. The charred remnants of what had once been the bustling hub of Alpine were flanked on the north by River Road and on the south by the railroad tracks. The fire had started during the night last October while Vida and I were out of town. Except for the sagging wreck of a building, damage had been minimal. The loading dock was rarely used, and the warehouse had been empty for years. Like the rest of Alpine, the structures had been waiting for better days.

Getting out of the car, I surveyed the burned timbers and piles of rubble. Though I'd often driven past the ruins, I hadn't paid much attention until now. The site would be a good location for a restaurant, I decided. There'd be plenty of room for parking, a river view, and proximity to the main thoroughfare in and out of town. Maybe the Bourgette brothers had more business sense than Einar Rasmussen Jr. gave them credit for.

With a nod of approval, I got back in my Jag and headed for my little log house at the edge of the forest. Alpine is built on the steep slopes of Tonga Ridge, with residents nestled among the second-stand evergreens. The Douglas fir and hemlock and cedar are seventy years old, and bare patches on Mount Baldy and other nearby peaks attest to more recent harvests. The old growth, which yielded pre-Columbian giants, had been cut down in the first quarter of the twentieth century to supply the Alpine Lumber Company. For almost two decades, the mill had been the town's economic base. But once the founder and owner, Carl Clemans, finished clear-cutting his stand, he shut down operations. Alpine was faced with extinction until Vida's future father-in-law, Rufus Runkel, and a Norwegian fondly recalled as Olaf the Obese, built a ski lodge. Other mills and logging companies had come and gone since the late Twenties, but environmental concerns put timber towns such as Alpine up against the wall. One local mill remained, with a scant half-dozen cutting areas on nearby mountainsides. Feeling like an endangered species, Alpiners had welcomed the new community college with open arms.

Or almost. As usual, there were holdouts who feared newcomers, especially those whose skin was of a different hue. It was one thing to live side by side with commuters from Everett and Monroe, whose fair complexions suggested Northern European kinship. It was something else to stand in the checkout line at the Grocery Basket with shoppers named Kittikachorn or Kuramoto or Cardenas.

Leaving the Jag in the carport, I went to my mailbox, where I found several bills and a couple of catalogues. Inside, my answering machine revealed a big red zero. On Tuesday nights during the year and a half that Milo and I had been a couple, I often celebrated completion of the weekly edition by making him dinner or going out. Since our breakup, I came home, made myself a bourbon and water, then wondered what dismal concoction I could eat by myself. On more than one occasion, I'd ended up with a bag of microwave popcorn. At least I used the kind that had full butter flavor.

Leo was right. Not only was I crabby, but full of self-pity. Nursing my drink, I wandered back into the kitchen and gazed out to the tall evergreens where a couple of chipmunks were darting among the branches. *A couple of chipmunks,* I thought. Even chipmunks came in couples.

I made another drink.

★　★　★

By Friday, my mood had improved, if only because I was so busy. On the way to work, I'd stopped on Alpine Way at Cal Vickers's Texaco station to get gas. Cal had informed me that the Bourgettes were starting to clear away the debris from the warehouse site. I made a mental note to tell Carla to get a picture for the upcoming edition.

I'd also decided it was time to talk to Ginny about Brad's continuing presence on *The Advocate*'s premises. I hated to do it, but if her sister-in-law would take Brad in free of charge, at least the Erlandsons wouldn't be out of pocket. The wages I paid Ginny weren't exactly prodigal, and Ginny's husband, Rick, worked at the Bank of Alpine, where his salary was modest at best.

Thus I tried to be tactful in making my suggestion to our office manager. "Brad's such a lively little boy," I said, forcing a bright smile. "I was wondering if it isn't time for him to be with other kids his age. What do you think, Ginny?"

Ginny's pleasant, if plain face fell. "You mean—day care?" She made it sound as if I'd suggested a chain gang. "But I'd be away from him all day!"

I winced, but tried to keep smiling. "I'm thinking of Brad," I said, lying only a little. "As he gets older he needs more freedom, companionship, experiences."

"I don't know." Ginny propped her chin on her freckled hand. "I've never thought much of moms who dump their kids on somebody else all day and go off to work."

"I did." My smile grew bittersweet. "As a single parent, I had to leave Adam with a sitter when I worked on *The Oregonian*."

Ginny, who is serious by nature, didn't respond immediately. "Did he mind?" she finally asked. "Did you mind?"

"I had no choice," I replied candidly. "It was either that or welfare."

I'd said the wrong thing. Ginny's skin flushed and her nostrils quivered. "That's not an option for us! Rick's been promoted at the bank. You know he's assistant manager now. If I quit tomorrow, we'd survive."

The idea of losing Ginny was too much. She was very efficient, and not only ran the office, but kept the books. It hadn't occurred to me that in getting rid of Brad, his mother might go with him.

"Okay," I said hastily. "Don't worry about it right now. It was just a thought."

Ginny, however, still looked upset. "If you think Brad's a problem . . ."

The phone rang before I could deny that having a one-year-old toddler bite me in the thigh, throw his diaper on my computer keyboard, spit up apple chunks in my in-basket, and piddle in my purse bothered me in the slightest.

"Don't worry," I repeated, with an airy wave of my hand. "Really." I grabbed the receiver before the call trunked over to Ginny's vacant desk out front.

To my chagrin, the voice on the other end belonged to Ed Bronsky. "Don't forget, tonight's the night," he said, at his most chipper. "Who're you bringing?"

"Bringing?" I was somewhat taken aback. "No one. That is, the rest of the staff will be there."

"Ginny's husband, Rick? The baby? Kip MacDuff? He have a date? What about Vida and her air-force colonel?"

Vida was still keeping company with Buck Bardeen, a widower about her own age. "I'm not sure," I hedged. "Figure on six of us."

"What about Carla and the dean?" Ed could be persistent. I'd forgotten that, since it was not a trait he often displayed while employed as my ad manager.

"She hasn't committed." I accidentally knocked my coffee mug over, spilling cold liquid in my lap. "Hey, Ed, I've got to run. Someone's in my office." It was true: Brad Erlandson was crawling across the threshold, dragging a small stuffed bunny by one ear.

"Oh. Sure, no problemo. By the way, if you get a chance, would you mind stopping at the liquor store and picking up a couple of bottles of vodka and maybe one of Scotch? I'll pay you when you get here."

Like fun, I thought in annoyance. Rich or poor, Ed remained a moocher. "I'll see," I said in a noncommittal voice, and rang off.

I was mopping up my slacks when the phone rang again. This time it was Alfred Cobb, one of the county commissioners, droning on about construction of the new bridge out by the golf course. I listened with half an ear and an occasional murmur of feigned interest. If the crazy old fart had read this week's edition of *The Advocate,* he'd have seen everything he was telling me.

"Alfred Cobb!" Vida sniffed after she'd come into my office and I'd finally gotten rid of the county commissioner. "Such a moron! Did you attend the April meeting when he forgot to put on his pants?"

I shook my head. "That was Carla. I traded her that one for the schoolboard meeting."

"Lucky you." Vida, as usual, didn't bother to sit down in one of my visitor's chairs. Instead, she loomed over my desk, her head and bust thrust forward like the figurehead on an old Boston whaler. "Buck can't come tonight. It's his brother's birthday. He and Heather are giving Henry a surprise party at Buck's house in Startup."

Henry Bardeen was also a widower, with a grown daughter who worked for him in his capacity as manager of the ski lodge. "You're not going to the family party?" I asked with more than polite curiosity. For all of Vida's outspokenness when it came to the private lives of others, she was remarkably reticent about her own affairs.

"I'll join them later," she said without expression. "The rain's holding off, and it's not that far to Startup. But of course I feel an obligation to attend Ed and Shirley's soiree."

But of course Vida wouldn't have missed meeting the au pair girl for the world. However, it meant that we would take separate cars to the Bronskys', which was fine with me, as I wanted the freedom to leave at the earliest opportunity.

Thus, shortly before eight, I found myself weakening as I pointed the Jag east on Front Street. The liquor store was still open, and I would drive right by it. Aware that I was playing the patsy, I stopped to fill Ed's request. The worst that could happen was that I'd be out forty dollars.

I followed Railroad Avenue past the holding pond almost to where the paved section ended, then turned into Ed and Shirley's steep, winding drive. The entrance to their property is across from a dilapidated old water tower, which makes the gilded lions and the grilled gate look a little silly. But Ed and Shirley *are* a little silly, which fits. Or so ran my uncharitable thoughts as I pulled in behind a row of cars in front of Casa de Bronska.

The house is two stories of Italianate design, with a red tiled roof and twin turrets. The tall windows are arched and, on the main floor, covered with more grillwork. The purpose is to evoke the villas of Capri, but somehow the steel girding reminds me of security bars on a pawnshop.

Since the night was mild, the front door stood open. I could see the sparkling Venetian chandelier in the marble entry hall and the rather handsome replica of a sixteenth-century inlaid credenza. I could also see Ed, wringing Mayor Baugh's hand while Irene Baugh handed her London Fog raincoat to the eldest of the Bronsky offspring, nineteen-year-old Molly.

"Emma!" Ed cried, spewing some sort of

crumbs from his mouth. "Glad to see you're here! Come on in, and chow down. Oh—you brought the extra liquor. Thanks a million, I'll get some cash for you in just a sec. But first, meet Birgitta. She's a peach, right, Fuzzy?"

"Um," the mayor murmured, "Irene and I haven't yet met the charming newcomer. But we'll take your word for it, Ed. After all, you're a man of honor." Fuzzy, who occasionally betrayed his Southern roots, pronounced the word *honah* and moved into what Shirley called the salon.

Having handed over the vodka and Scotch to Ed, I gave Molly my lightweight corduroy jacket and followed Irene Baugh. "They've got quite a crowd," I remarked, figuring that at least forty people had already congregated in the so-called salon.

"Oh, you know Ed and Shirley." Irene laughed. "They like to party."

"Yes, indeed," I replied, and wondered if Irene noticed the irony of my tone. Ed and Shirley liked to party, but on their own small-town terms. The Bronskys' idea of a big barbecue was throwing some cheap hot dogs on a grill and asking their guests to bring the buns.

But for this event, it appeared that Ed and Shirley had gone all out. A long linen-covered table practically filled one end of the room, and

was laden with various appetizers, from mari-
nated chicken drumettes to miniature crab
cakes. Tim Rafferty of the Icicle Creek Tavern
was tending bar in another corner. I sidled up
to him and asked how much.

"It's free," he said, and gave me his big grin.
"I know, it's not like old Ed. I guess this night
is special. Have you seen the Queen of
Sweden?"

I shook my head, then Tim nodded toward
the far end of the room. "She's standing in the
middle of that bunch over there, with Doc
Dewey and Scooter Hutchins and some of the
Nyquists. She's pretty much of an eleven on a
scale of ten, huh?" Tim was still grinning.

Birgitta definitely stood out in a crowd. She
was at least six feet tall, and towered over
everyone in the group except Oscar Nyquist.
From a distance, she looked very young, mid-
twenties at most. It was no wonder that Tim
Rafferty's youthful eyes were dazzled.

I accepted my drink from Tim and moved
closer. Ed, who was holding a shrimp in one
hand and a chicken wing in the other, nudged
me with his elbow. "Come on, Emma. I'll introduce you." He chuckled and leered. "See
how all the men are congregating around
Birgitta? She's a knockout, all right."

She was. As Ed jostled his way up to the au

pair girl, I noted the sleek blonde head, the classic features, the clear skin, and the glacier-blue eyes.

"Gitty," Ed called out, the self-importance in his voice diluted by a slight deference, "meet my old boss, Emma Lord, from my slave-labor days. Emma, this is Birgitta—I call her Gitty—Lindholm."

Birgitta—let Ed call her Gitty, I wouldn't—put out a strong, firm hand. "How do you do?" she said with an accent.

Certain that Birgitta had already been asked how she liked Alpine about a hundred times, I searched for a noncliché response. "Is this your first visit to America?" I asked, then realized that she'd probably heard that one at least fifty times.

Birgitta nodded gravely. "It is. I have never been anywhere but Europe before."

I kept smiling, despite her solemn expression. "I toured Europe many years ago, but I never got to Sweden. It must be a lovely country."

"It is very nice," Birgitta replied, then turned to Scooter Hutchins, who owned the local interiors store. "You were saying Swedish flooring is very much wanted here? Why is that?"

Feeling dismissed, as well as old, short, and ignored, I tried to pick my way to the buffet table. More guests had arrived, and the salon was getting jammed. I assumed that Ed and Shirley would have the good sense to herd some of the crowd into the adjoining ballroom, which, in reality, held only a big-screen TV, stereo equipment, and three couches, all offering the deep imprint of Ed's behind.

Nodding to various guests including Edna Mae Dalrymple, the local librarian, and Stella Magruder, whose services I desperately needed to style my hair, I spotted Father Dennis Kelly, our pastor at St. Mildred's. He was talking to the young men I recognized as Dan and John Bourgette. I decided it was time to get better acquainted with Alpine's fledgling restaurateurs.

As expected, Father Den's welcome was much warmer than Birgitta Lindholm's. Our pastor is the kind of man who manages to exude warmth while still keeping his distance. No doubt it's an art he's acquired, not just as a religious minority in a Protestant town, but because he is also an African-American. "Do you think Ed and Shirley will con their latest trophy into attending Mass?" Den asked in his wry manner.

I laughed. "She's Lutheran, I'll bet. Frankly, I don't think Ed and Shirley will be able to con her into much. She looks about six times tougher—and smarter—than they are." I

turned to the two young men who were standing next to Father Den. "Help me out here—
which of you is Dan and which is John?"

The older of the two put out a hand. "I'm
John, number-one twig on the Bourgette family tree. There are seven of us, but except for
our folks and one of our sisters and Dan here,
the rest of the gang is scattered."

Dan also shook hands. The brothers looked
very much alike, with cheerful round faces,
high foreheads, dark hair, and faintly ruddy
complexions. John was maybe three or four
years older, but the easiest way to tell them
apart was because Dan wore glasses.

I told them I'd driven by the warehouse site
earlier in the week, but not since they'd started
clearing away the debris. "Carla mentioned
that you're aiming for an October-first completion date," I said.

John, who seemed to be the spokesman for
the brothers, nodded. "That may not be realistic, though. We haven't put out for bids yet.
Maybe we'll do that next week."

"You'll need an architect," I remarked.
"There're only two in town."

"Our younger brother, Kevin, is a budding
architect," John said. "He's studying back in
New York, but we're letting him have a go
at it."

Father Den smiled at the Bourgettes. "Keep it in the family, guys. There's plenty of you to go around."

"That's why we're doing all the clearing away ourselves," Dan said, speaking for virtually the first time. "We don't want anybody else to get their hands on the buried treasure."

All three men chuckled, but I looked puzzled. "Have I missed something?"

John and Dan seemed a bit embarrassed, but Father Den cocked his head to one side and regarded me with a quizzical expression. "The firemen's discovery? The old steel chest? The gold?"

I still drew a blank. "I don't know what you're talking about."

Den cleared his throat. "It was in the paper, Emma. Your paper." He gave me a bemused look.

The fire had occurred while Vida and I were in Cannon Beach, Oregon. Carla had covered the disaster and come up with some excellent pictures. By the time I got back to Alpine, the only article I'd proofed was a follow-up from the investigators stating that the cause was undetermined, but might have been set by kids horsing around with leftover Fourth of July fireworks.

I was at a loss. "I honestly don't remember anything about a steel chest or—did you say gold?"

All three men nodded. "A day or so after the fire, the investigators found an old metal box buried under the warehouse floor," John said, speaking kindly and somewhat slowly. No doubt he thought I was an imbecile. "They opened it up and found what looked like gold, so they turned it over to Sheriff Dodge. He gave it to Sandy Clay, the assayer, who said it was nuggets, probably from one of the mines that were worked around here at the turn of the century."

Behind his glasses, Dan's eyes were sympathetic. "It wasn't much of an article. I mean, it was sort of buried in one of the fire stories."

Buried treasure, buried news, I thought. Admittedly, I'd only scanned Carla's articles, since they were already printed by the time I got back. My main concern at the time had been for backing an initiative to get a full-time fire department for Alpine, instead of the traditional volunteers. And Vida had remained in Cannon Beach on family matters for another week. Given the distractions that had claimed her attention, I couldn't blame her for not scouring every line in *The Advocate.* But Carla should have followed up on the gold angle. Maybe she'd been too busy making like a mink with Ryan Talliaferro.

"So where did this gold come from?" I asked, unable to keep the annoyance out of my voice.

John Bourgette seemed a bit sheepish. "It's still in Sandy Clay's safe. I think Sheriff Dodge has been trying to trace the metal box, but hasn't had much luck. He hasn't mentioned it to you?"

If I didn't know the Bourgettes very well, they didn't know me, either. I noticed Father Den wince slightly as my chin jutted.

"No. The Sheriff has said nothing to me." Nothing. Not even Hello, Emma. I added Milo to my mental list of idiots and incompetents.

Dan's gaze was somewhere over my left shoulder. "Maybe you should ask him. Here he comes now. Hi, Sheriff."

I didn't turn around.

Chapter Three

IF I HADN'T seen Milo Dodge approaching, I suspect he hadn't spotted me surrounded by Father Den and the Bourgettes. Otherwise, his long face would not have registered such consternation.

"Long time no see," said the Sheriff, who I'd never described as glib even in happier days. Collecting himself, he shook Den's hand and nodded to the Bourgettes. "Nice party. Anybody try the chicken wings?"

"Good idea," John said, a bit too eagerly. "Come on, bro, let's attack the buffet. I'm starved."

The Brothers Bourgette departed, while Father Den, who knew what had passed between Milo and me, looked as if he'd prefer talking to someone in deep spiritual crisis.

"I should be heading back to the rectory," Den murmured, perhaps reading my mind. "I have to put together my Pentecost Sunday homily. So long, Sheriff. See you in church, Emma."

Visions of priests martyred by pagans, infidels, and Nazis came to mind, but I couldn't picture

Dennis Kelly among them. My pastor wouldn't even stand by me in my hour of social and emotional need. But of course I was being too hard on Den. Maybe I was even being too hard on Milo. But I doubted it.

"So what's this about gold at the old warehouse site?" I asked, and heard the harsh tone in my overloud voice.

"What do you mean?" Milo, all six-foot-four of him, was looking as awkward as I felt.

"Just that. Nobody ever told me about a box full of nuggets, and it seems I missed Carla's reference in her story about the fire." My tone hadn't softened, but at least I was no longer shouting.

"Oh, that." Milo scratched at his forehead where the graying sandy hair fell in minor disarray. He was wearing his uniform, though his regulation jacket and hat must have been deposited with Molly Bronsky. "Jeez, I put that on the back burner. So far, it's come to a dead end."

"Is it worth anything?" Finally, I sounded almost normal.

Milo gave a short nod. "Sandy Clay says it's probably valued at around three hundred thousand. Gold's down right now, though." The Sheriff wasn't looking at me, but in the direction of the bar. "I could use a drink. I only got off duty ten minutes ago." He pivoted from one foot to the other, and gave me a quick glance. "You need a refill or are you . . . ?" Milo's laconic voice trailed away.

I knew he wanted me to say that I was fine so that he could leave me. I wanted to say so, too, but the truth was, my glass contained only ice. "I'll go with you," I said, and wanted to kick myself.

One of the things I hate most about small towns is that everybody knows everybody else's business. At least two dozen pairs of eyes followed us as we made our slow, difficult way to Tim Rafferty. I could imagine the whispered comments: "Look, it's Emma and the Sheriff!" "Are they back together?" "Did they make up?" "Do you suppose they'll get into a big fight so we can watch and choose sides?"

Even Tim could barely suppress gaping at us. But he assumed his professional stance, poured our drinks, and then turned to Rick Erlandson, who was requesting two white wines, presumably for himself and Ginny. Since little Brad hadn't attacked me, I assumed that his parents had actually left him with a sitter.

Milo edged away from the bar and took a deep swallow. "I've missed you like hell,

Emma," he said in a growl. "I'd like to know if you're happy these days. You look like birdshit."

"Thanks, Milo. That's what I really wanted to hear." I gave him a fierce look, then caught stares from Edna Mae Dalrymple and the Dithers sisters. "We can't talk here," I said, dropping my voice. "Let's go outside."

"How the hell do you get outside in this place?" Milo muttered. "I don't want to use the front. Ed keeps running out there to greet his latest guests."

I'd been inside Casa de Bronska often enough to know that there was a side entrance beyond the so-called ballroom. "Come on," I said. "We can talk in the rose garden."

En route, Milo tripped over a stack of magazines and I put my foot in an empty pizza box. In times gone by, we would have laughed over our clumsiness, but now we were merely embarrassed. Eventually we arrived out-side, where a cherub spewed water into a marble fountain and the rosebushes showed their first buds of the season.

There was also a stone bench where I gratefully sat down. Milo joined me, but kept his distance, which wasn't much because the seat was only about four feet wide. I marveled that Ed and Shirley could sit there at the same time.

"I feel terrible that you're so angry," I said, and meant it.

"You should," Milo declared. "I'll be damned if I can figure out why you dumped me. We seemed to be doing just fine."

I flashed an angry look at him. "Define *fine*."

"I asked you to marry me." In the light from the three-quarter moon, his expression was truculent, more adolescent boy than middle-aged man. "What else did you want?"

"You were too late." I bit my lip. It was a stupid answer, and I knew it.

A silence spread between us. At last, Milo spoke, his tone weary. "You know what? I always felt like a backup quarterback to a Heisman Trophy winner. It's late in the game, the score's thirty-five to seven in our favor, so I get to come off the bench. I complete a couple of passes for short yardage, but all the glory goes to the big stud. You know what I'm saying?"

I did. "No," I said.

Milo sighed. "Emma, you're the most impossible woman I've ever met. Even my ex, Old Mulehide, couldn't beat you when it comes to kidding yourself. Tom Cavanaugh is never going to ride into town on a white horse and carry you away. Get over it, for Chrissakes!"

To my horror, I felt like crying. But I didn't. I hadn't cried for the sake of love since Tom admitted he couldn't leave his wife to marry me even though I was carrying his child.

"I haven't talked to Tom in two and a half years! For all I know, he's dead!" The anguish in my voice made me cough.

Milo slapped me on the back. "You know damned well he's not dead. Adam would have told you. He talks to his father, doesn't he?"

"Yes." I snuffled and snorted and made other unladylike noises. My son, who was now at a seminary in St. Paul, had kept in contact with his father for the past few years, even though I'd done my best to keep them apart for the first two decades of Adam's life. It was punishment, I suppose, for Tom's loyalty to his wife, Sandra.

Shoulders slumped, Milo cradled his drink in his big hands. "You're right. It doesn't matter. It's not just Tom. It's me. I'm not good enough for you. I'm just a meat-and-potatoes kind of guy. You like caviar. Or pretend you do."

The Sheriff isn't usually given to introspection, but I realized he'd spent the last seven months thinking about our relationship. If the food analogy wasn't entirely accurate, his basic conclusion was probably right. My horizons were broader than his; Milo would call me "cultured," which he'd translate as snobbishness. Yet we'd shared some interests, and more importantly, had been comfortable with each other. I could hardly tell the Sheriff that it hadn't been enough.

"Don't knock yourself," I said with as much vigor as I could muster. "You're a wonderful man. Hey, didn't I fight—and win—to help you get appointed instead of having to stand for election every four years? Would I do that if I didn't believe in you?"

Slowly, Milo turned to face me. A frog croaked somewhere in the garden, and the fountain made soothing noises. The heady fragrance of hyacinths all but eclipsed the pervasive scent of the evergreen trees. Except for the empty Fritos bag and the Coke cans lying on the grass, I could almost imagine I wasn't in Alpine. It dawned on me that therein lay the real difference between Milo and me: he could never think of being anywhere else.

"I appreciate your efforts," Milo said stiltedly. "We broke up just before the election. I never got a chance to thank you. Consider it done."

"It's done," I said tonelessly. "I thought we were going to stay friends."

Milo shook his head, a gesture that seemed to drain him. "I can't do that. Not after . . . not when we were . . ."

"Because we slept together," I put in. "Okay, maybe I understand. But give it time. We were friends for years before we were lovers."

Milo didn't respond. He got to his feet, finished his drink, and stared through the twilight in the direction of a rose trellis. "It's easier to avoid you," he finally said.

"I've noticed." My tone was wry, but my heart sank. "I don't have a lot of friends in Alpine," I admitted. "Vida and you have been about it. I still feel like a stranger here."

"Big deal." Milo paused to light a cigarette. "How many friends have I got? Mainly my deputies, and that's tricky because they work for me. Who else wants to be buddies with the local lawman?"

The conversation was degenerating into a self-pity contest. "Making and keeping friends isn't easy," I said a bit brusquely. "That's why it's stupid to throw away what we had."

Through a haze of smoke, Milo narrowed his hazel eyes. "I'm not the one who did it."

We were back where we started, which was nowhere. "I give up. I can't help you, Milo."

He took a deep drag on his cigarette, then chucked it into the fountain. "You're wrong, Emma. You can't help yourself." With his long-legged stride, he stalked back toward the house.

I decided to go home a few minutes later. No one, least of all Ed and Shirley, would miss me.

But on the drive back to my house, I realized I hadn't seen Vida. It wasn't like her to skip such an event. Usually, she'd be on hand with all her senses heightened and her camera ready to roll.

I called Saturday morning to see what had happened. Vida's explanation was, as usual, sensible: "I chose to go to Henry's party first," she told me after apologizing for any distractions while she gave her canary, Cupcake, a bath. "I knew it would be an early evening, so I left Startup shortly before nine-thirty. I must have just missed you. Ooops!"

I imagined that Cupcake had temporarily eluded his toilette. "What did you think of Birgitta?" I asked.

"Aloof. Private. Cool. A Swede." Vida's comments weren't prejudiced, but the product of her upbringing in a Scandinavian majority. "However, I arranged an interview with her for Monday morning. She was reluctant at first, but I coaxed. Oh, dear!"

I pictured Cupcake flying around Vida's kitchen. "Did you get any pictures of the party? Or did Carla show up with her camera?"

"Carla didn't come. As far as I know." There was a pause and some rather strange noises in the background. Now I envisioned Vida and the canary in a wrestling match. "And yes, I took some pictures. Really, I wish Fuzzy Baugh would try not to edge his way into every frame. He doesn't come up for reelection for another year and a half."

"We need to talk," I said, carrying my cordless phone and my coffee mug out into the living room.

"So I understand." Vida had lowered her voice.

"What?"

Cupcake let out a squawk. No doubt he had been submerged in his tiny porcelain tub. Or were canaries cleansed by dusting? I tried to picture Cupcake in a bubble bath or wearing a shower cap. My knowledge of avian hygiene was very limited. "You and Milo reportedly had a confrontation," Vida said while I imagined her ruffling the bird's feathers with a small loofah. "I've been wondering what came of it."

Exasperated, I surrendered my canary fantasy and sighed. "It wasn't a confrontation," I fibbed. "And that isn't what I was talking about. It's something we missed in a story Carla wrote about the warehouse fire."

"Missed?" Vida sounded aghast. "What could we miss? Oh, drat!"

I wasn't sure if Vida's outcry was caused by Cupcake's latest misconduct or her chagrin at having committed an oversight. "If you have time, drop by and I'll make tea," I offered. "Or lunch, if you come around noon."

"Dear me, I can't today," Vida said with what sounded like genuine regret. "I'm going to Everett with Amy to shop at the mall. One of her girlfriends is getting married for the third time, and she's had the nerve to register at the Bon Marché."

Naturally, a shopping expedition with Vida's daughter would have priority. Amy Runkel Hibbert was the only one of her three girls who lived in Alpine. The other two resided in Seattle and Bellingham.

I left Vida to her canary, and spent the rest of the morning trying to get my garden in shape. The growing season comes later to Alpine. In Seattle, the daffodils would be past their prime and the tulips in full bloom. But here at the three-thousand-foot level, my bulbs were just beginning to unfold. Except for a few early crocuses and one brave yellow primrose, my yard looked barren.

But gardening is therapy for me. After filling two plastic bags and one metal bin, I felt marginally better than I had for some time. I also felt filthy, and was heading for the shower when the phone rang.

It was Leo. "I've got some damned bug," he said in a hoarse voice I barely recognized. "It

came on last night, which is why I didn't go to
Ed's big party. Can we do dinner next week?"

To my surprise, I was very disappointed.
Though I hadn't thought much about the proposed trip to Seattle, I must have been looking
forward to it. "Sure," I said, trying not to sound
too bleak. "But we'll have to wait two weeks.
The RUB dedication is next Saturday, and I
should stick around for that."

"I thought it was in the afternoon," Leo
croaked.

"It is, it starts at three, but there's a reception
afterward, and I told President Cardenas I'd be
there." Now I was wondering why I'd made
the commitment. Carla had the assignment,
and my attendance wasn't required except as a
PR gesture.

"Okay, that's fine. I'm not going without
you." Leo coughed several times. "Sorry. Hope
I can make it into work Monday."

"Don't push yourself," I said, and meant it.
Leo was well organized, and probably could
put the ads together Tuesday to meet deadline.

My mood had plummeted again as I faced
another empty Saturday night. Briefly, I considered checking out the latest offerings at
Videos-to-Go, but somehow that seemed like
running up the white flag on my personal life.
I'd simply stay home and watch the Mariners

on TV. Just like Milo was going to do. Just like the way we used to do together.

The Mariners lost to the Orioles at home.

On Sunday after Mass, I tried to call my brother Ben in Tuba City, Arizona. He was out, no doubt making the rounds of his parishioners on the Navajo reservation. I longed to call my son in St. Paul, but having chosen to follow in the godly footsteps of his uncle, Adam was only allowed a certain number of telephone conversations per month at the seminary. We'd already used up his allotment for May.

Nor did Vida answer her phone. Perhaps she was with Amy again. Disconsolately, I went out into the backyard, but didn't feel like another bout of gardening. Instead, I watched the Mariners. They lost again, a three-game sweep by Baltimore.

The phone rang at precisely nine o'clock. "I was right," Vida said, and sounded disappointed. "Carla and Dean Talliaferro are getting married in November. You'll never guess where."

"Where?" I didn't need to guess and be wrong. I'd had enough of losing for one weekend.

"The Petroleum Museum in Seattle. Now,

who on earth gets married in a petroleum museum?" Vida sounded flabbergasted.

"Carla and Ryan?" I said in a feeble attempt at humor.

"Oh, honestly! Why can't they get married in a church like sensible people?" Vida heaved a heavy sigh.

"Maybe because Carla's Jewish and Ryan's not," I suggested. "With a name like Talliaferro, he may have been raised a Catholic. They might be hedging their bets."

"Ridiculous. Who's going to marry them? An auto mechanic?" Vida was no doubt wringing her hands, at least metaphorically.

"But she came by your house tonight?" I inquired. "Was Ryan with her?"

"No, she came alone. Apparently they'd driven over to Spokane to visit his parents. They wanted to wait to make the announcement until they'd seen Mr. and Mrs. Talliaferro. I gather they've already conferred with her family in Bellevue."

"November?" The date finally struck me. "But the baby's due in December. Why don't they get married now?"

"Because Carla wants a big wedding." Another sigh heaved over the telephone line. "Big is right. Can you imagine? She'll be big as a house!"

"Well . . ." I was at a loss for words. "It's their business, after all."

"A funny business, if you ask me. Carla will announce all this at work tomorrow, so act surprised. Oh, by the way, her pictures of Einar Rasmussen Jr. didn't turn out. Something happened to her camera. They're reshooting at the RUB tomorrow night."

"Why at night?" I asked, now holding my head. "Why not during the day when she can use natural light?"

"Because Einar Jr. is ever so busy," Vida replied tartly. "I must go, Emma. The kettle is boiling, and I definitely need a cup of tea after Carla's visit."

I didn't blame Vida. I could have used a drink. Instead, I made popcorn and added extra butter.

Carla duly made her announcement Monday morning. We all gushed, even Leo, who had managed to come to work despite a hacking cough. Not wanting to spoil the euphoria of the moment, I put off asking Carla about the buried gold she'd buried in her warehouse story. That could wait until Tuesday. Or so I thought at the time.

We were on target for the weekly edition, however, including the special RUB dedication section. I hadn't been in the office when Birgitta Lindholm had come in for her interview, but Vida informed me that the session had gone reasonably well. It was standard fare, my House & Home editor informed me. Birgitta had wanted to see the world, and had decided that being an au pair was a practical way to go.

It had been a busy day, as Mondays usually are, and I didn't get a chance to speak to Carla privately until just before five when I invited her into my office. Since she seemed somewhat subdued despite her big news, I wasn't sure how to approach her.

"I assume you're happy," I said in an encouraging voice.

"Oh, sure," she replied somewhat vaguely. "Ryan's great. He loves kids. In fact, he's one of five, but I figure two's plenty. I still want a career."

It would have been unkind to point out that some might not consider the job of reporter on a small-town weekly as a *career*. Indeed, there were some who would quibble over whether the editor/publisher had a career. But if Carla regarded her employment at *The Advocate* as such, then I would be the last to contradict her.

"Of course," I said. "But you'll want to take

maternity leave. What date is set for the wedding? Maybe we can work it out so that your leave could begin before that."

My reporter shook her head. "I'm not taking a leave. I'm quitting."

Carla retained the power to amaze. "You're . . . quitting?"

She nodded. "November first. The wedding's November ninth. The baby's due December fifth. I'm hoping I'll be ready to start my new job a month later, on January fifth."

"Your new job." I continued to stare at Carla. "Which would be . . . ?" I stopped on a hopeful note.

"I'm going to be the adviser to the student newspaper at the college."

I was dumbfounded. To hide my astonishment, I coughed. "Sorry. Maybe I'm getting Leo's cold." Grabbing a Kleenex from the box in my desk drawer, I dabbed at my mouth. "Well. That's wonderful, Carla. I didn't realize that the college was going to put out a paper."

"They've sort of planned to all along," Carla explained, very serious. "They won't offer any journalism classes for a while, but when they do, Ryan says I'll be first in line to teach them. The advisership is only part-time, so I won't be making quite as much money as I do here, but we'll get along okay. We're thinking of buying a house in Ptarmigan Tract. It's right next to the college."

I felt a bit dizzy. Carla's big announcement of her impending marriage had been the least of her surprises. Now I blanched at the thought of her advising a student newspaper, and, worse yet, actually teaching journalism. Maybe it was just as well that the print medium was becoming a dinosaur. Though *The Advocate* hadn't yet been hit hard, newspaper circulation in general continued to dwindle as TV and computers filled the gap. If technology was killing the written word, Carla could deliver the death-blow all by herself.

I offered to take her to dinner to celebrate, but Carla had to meet Einar Rasmussen Jr. at seven-thirty. She had several phone calls to make, all apparently related to her November nuptials.

At home, I went to the trouble of grilling a steak, slicing a tomato, and baking a potato. Maybe I was out of sorts because I wasn't eating properly. I made a vow to pay more attention to a balanced, wholesome diet.

I was using my laptop to write a letter to Adam when the phone rang around seven forty-five. It was Carla, and she sounded very odd.

"Emma," she said, her tone uncharacteristically clipped, "I've got a problem."

"What is it?" I hit the save key on the laptop.

"It's Mr. Einarssen."

"Mr. Rasmussen. Carla, I hope you're not calling him by the wrong—"

"I'm not calling him anything. I can't." Her voice broke. "He's dead."

Chapter Four

MY FIRST REACTION was to doubt Carla's word. She's been known to exaggerate, and I couldn't take her statement literally. It was only when I perceived the panic in her voice that I began to tense.

"I checked his pulse, I even held my compact up to his mouth," Carla said, her voice now coming in a jerky rush. "He's still warm, though. What should I do?"

"Good God." I tried to think clearly. "Call nine-one-one," I said, keeping calm.

"I can't," Carla replied. "The phones aren't hooked up in the RUB yet. I'd have to leave him alone."

"There's no one else around?" I asked, already grabbing my jacket and my purse. If Carla had called me, she had access to a phone. But I wasn't about to argue with her. "Staff? Students? Anybody?"

"Not in the RUB. It's not open, remember?"

"I'll call nine-one-one," I said. "Then I'll be there as soon as I can."

"He looks awful." Carla sounded as if she were close to tears.

"That's probably because he's dead," I said, and immediately felt remorse. Indeed, it was only then that the potential tragedy hit me. With a sense of urgency, I rang off and dialed nine-one-one. Tim Rafferty's sister, Beth, informed me that an ambulance would be dispatched along with a Sheriff's deputy.

Skykomish Community College's campus is west of town, past the reservoir and the fish hatchery on Railroad Avenue. A mill once stood on part of the campus site, but was torn down to make room for a dorm. The official address is Old Bridge Road, though the bridge itself collapsed long before I moved to Alpine.

The Rasmussen Union Building stands between the library and the administration building. Unlike most of the other architecture, which is what I call modified sawmill with shake exteriors and shingled roofs, the three structures are curved cinder block and form a circle around a sunken pond. Benches have been provided where students can study, exchange ideas, or sell pot, depending upon their personal preference and risk quotient.

Though there were night classes in session, the area around the pond was deserted. I noted a hand-carved sign on a cedar slab outside the library informing users that closing time on Mondays was eight P.M. As I hurried up to the

RUB's double doors, it was now almost eight-fifteen.

Carla was waiting at the entrance to let me in. "Where's the emergency crew?" she asked, her face pale and her tone breathless.

"They're coming," I responded. "Where's Einar?"

Carla gestured toward the cafeteria. "In there. I told him to meet me by the kitchen. I thought maybe I'd get a funny picture of him pretending to serve students."

There was nothing funny about Einar Rasmussen Jr. now. He was lying on his back, one arm flung over his head, the other at his side. His mouth was agape and his eyes—those cold, agatelike eyes—were wide open.

"Do you think it was a heart attack?" Carla asked as she bent down beside me.

"I don't know." The look of surprise on Einar Jr.'s face could have indicated anything. Maybe when the fatal blow was struck, he'd been shocked to discover—too late—that he was mortal.

We heard sirens. "Were the doors locked?" I asked.

"No. I'd called campus security to make sure they'd be left open. Shall I . . . ?" Carla pointed in the direction of the hall that led to the front entrance.

"Go ahead. I'll wait here."

Left alone, I wandered around the kitchen area with its gleaming new cooking utensils and unopened cartons of nonperishable foodstuffs. The long room was crowded with supplies, awaiting the first onrush of hungry students on Monday.

I tried to avoid getting too close to Einar Jr., but my eyes were drawn as if by a magnet. The dead man was lying between a long work space and the service counter. He was wearing dark slacks, a sport coat, and a shirt, but no tie. For Alpine, his attire was almost formal.

Carla returned almost immediately with two medics and Jack Mullins, one of Milo's long-time deputies. "Rasmussen, huh? What happened to him?" Jack demanded, his usual droll humor under wraps.

"See for yourself," I replied, and got out of the way while the medics went to work.

The medics began the futile but required ritual of attempting to revive Einar Jr. "He's dead, all right," said Del Amundson, the heavier and more senior member of the team. "Let's roll him over, Vic."

Vic Thorstensen complied. While Carla fidgeted next to the industrial-size range, I peered over Del's shoulder.

There was blood, soaking Einar's sport coat,

pooling on the pristine tile floor. Carla screamed and I let out a strange, strangled cry. Jack Mullins moved swiftly between the medics.

"What the hell?" the deputy muttered. "Rasmussen's jacket is torn. It looks like he's been stabbed!"

Carla threw herself at me. "I'm going to faint! I'm going to be sick!"

Fortunately, Carla is even smaller than I am, but her sudden weight knocked me off balance. I staggered against the service counter, trying to hold her up.

"Let's get you out of here," I said in a ragged voice. "Come on, sit down at one of the cafeteria tables."

Somehow, I managed to get Carla out into the dining area. She didn't want to be left alone, but I insisted on going back into the kitchen, where I told Del Amundson that my reporter might need some medical attention.

"She's about three months pregnant," I said, my voice low and still unsteady. "I don't want this to trigger a miscarriage. See if you can do anything for her."

Since Del obviously couldn't do anything for Einar Jr., he went out into the main part of the cafeteria. Vic Thorstensen remained with Jack, examining the body. I kept my distance, but began to look around the kitchen area. There were no knives or any other sharp instruments visible.

"Who found Rasmussen?" Jack asked, getting to his feet. "You or Carla?"

"Carla," I answered. "She'd come here to take a picture of him for the RUB dedication issue."

"We'll have to get her to make a statement," Jack said, taking off his regulation hat and rubbing at his curly auburn hair. He gave me his slightly cockeyed gaze. "Did you say Carla's knocked up?"

As rattled as I was by the sight of Einar Jr.'s corpse, I took offense. Indeed, Jack's crudeness helped me find my composure. "No, I didn't say that. But she is expecting a baby."

"Yeah, right, okay." Jack had the grace to turn red, then he stared down at Einar again. "I've called for Doc Dewey, but I don't know how soon he can get here. Now that he's the only MD in town, his job as medical examiner may take second place."

Del had returned to the kitchen, where he motioned to his partner. "I think we'd better take the little mother-to-be to the hospital. She's pretty shook up. That okay, Jack?"

Jack gave a single nod. "Sure. Just come back

afterward so you can haul Rasmussen away. I'm not going to try to stuff him into my patrol car."

Now it was Del's turn to look faintly aghast at Jack's attitude. "I hope not. Rasmussen was a big noise around this county. You and Dodge better play this one close to your chests."

"Right, right, we know our job." Jack, who is usually easygoing, was getting testy. "I called Dodge. He's on his way over."

I turned my back so that Jack couldn't see my grimace. "You don't need me," I said. "I'll go to the hospital with Carla."

Jack scowled. "Better not. One of you should stay around to explain how Rasmussen got here in the first place. You know what a stickler Dodge is for details."

I knew it well. With a sigh of resignation, I went out into the dining area to check on Carla before the medics took her away.

"I don't need a stretcher, honest," she was saying to Del Amundson. "I can walk."

"Hey, sweetheart," Del said in his kindly manner, "we got it right here. Let's use it. Come on, you never know. First babies can play funny tricks on you. You been seeing Doc Dewey?"

To my surprise, Carla shook her head. "No. I've been going to Dr. Conreid in Sultan." As she allowed the medics to help her onto the gurney, she turned a wan face to me. "That's where I was last Monday. Ginny went with me. I couldn't get an appointment with Doc Dewey until this coming Wednesday."

I gave Carla a weak little smile. "I know, he's jammed these days. You do what Doc tells you, though. He may want to keep you overnight, so let him."

Del and Vic wheeled my reporter away. I wandered back into the kitchen area, where Jack Mullins was putting on a pair of plastic gloves. "If you're going to stick around in here, you'd better dress the part," he said, handing me a second pair. "Have you touched anything yet?"

I tried to remember. "No, I don't think so. I know the drill."

Jack nodded. "Where the hell's the weapon?"

"I didn't see one," I said. "Carla and I didn't even realize Einar had been stabbed until the medics rolled him over."

A siren sounded in the background, either the ambulance leaving or Milo arriving. I also heard other noises, then voices. Jack and I looked out into the cafeteria. A half-dozen students and President Ignacio Cardenas were marching into the dining area.

"Damn it," Jack breathed. "We should have

locked the frigging doors. Hey," he called, hurrying out of the kitchen, "this place is off-limits."

President Cardenas, who preferred to be called Nat, stopped halfway between the cafeteria door and the serving counter. "Mullins, is it?" His darkly handsome face looked troubled. "What's going on? I just saw an ambulance leave."

Jack gestured at the students. "Get these kids out of here. There's been an accident. Go on, clear out."

The students, four girls and a boy probably not yet twenty, stared at Jack, then at each other. Cardenas put his hand on the boy's shoulder. "Go on, Angel. Do as Deputy Mullins tells you."

With obvious reluctance, the half-dozen students moved off just as Milo Dodge came into the cafeteria. Seeing the young people, he called after them: "You! Lock those doors as you leave. You got that?"

I couldn't see from my place behind the counter, but assumed that the unmistakable authority in Milo's voice would be obeyed. At last I edged forward and saw both the college president and the Sheriff look at me in surprise.

"Emma Lord," Nat Cardenas said with a shadow of his usual brilliant, if aloof smile.

"What're you doing here?" demanded Milo with a deep scowl.

But the Sheriff didn't really want to know, not yet at any rate. He was through the swinging half doors and into the kitchen with Cardenas at his heels.

"Good God Almighty!" Nat Cardenas cried when he saw Einar's body. "What's happened?"

"Somebody whacked your big benefactor," Jack responded, then softened his stance. "He's been stabbed, sir. Please stand back."

Nat Cardenas looked stricken. "Rasmussen? No! That's . . ." He couldn't seem to finish the sentence. "Who did this?" Suddenly Cardenas was angry, wheeling around to face Milo.

"In case you didn't notice, Nat, I just got here," Milo said, his jaw set in that familiar manner which didn't take guff from anybody. "You got any ideas?"

Nat Cardenas glanced at me, and I could have sworn that I'd become Suspect Number One. The black eyes were hard and the finely etched mouth was set in a grim line.

"Why are you here?" he asked, his tone cold as January ice.

"Good question," Milo said, also putting on plastic gloves. "Go ahead, Emma, explain yourself."

I did, briefly, also relating how Carla had

come to meet Einar Jr. and retake his picture for our special section. "All we know is that he was dead when she got here shortly after seven-thirty. She didn't see anyone or hear anything."

The suspicion was ebbing from Cardenas's eyes, but Milo was still frowning. "Are you sure about that? The body's still warm. From what I can tell, Rasmussen hasn't been dead for more than half an hour. The crime must have been committed right before Carla arrived."

"I only know what she told me," I said, trying not to get impatient. But I had to agree with Milo; Einar Jr. didn't strike me as the sort of man who would arrive early and have to wait around.

"So what happened to Carla?" Milo asked, now bent over the body. "I heard on the emergency-band radio that she was being taken to the hospital."

"She's pregnant," I replied, and heard a sharp intake of breath from Cardenas. "She was pretty upset. The medics and I thought Doc Dewey should check her out."

"Jesus." The word was whispered by Cardenas, who had his fingers pressed against his forehead and was pacing the kitchen. He must have sensed my watchful gaze because he stopped and turned around. "This is a terrible thing. For the college. And for Einar Ras-

mussen Jr.," he added, almost as an afterthought.

Jack Mullins, who had been searching the
work space, called to Milo from the sink area.
"Have a look. I think I found the weapon."

Milo straightened up and loped over to Jack,
who had pried open a big drain cover. "There's
a knife in here, wrapped in a towel," the deputy
informed the Sheriff. "There's blood, too."

"Okay. Bag it." Milo gazed all around him, to
the counters, the sinks, the cupboards, the
floor, and the ceiling. A closed door stood by
the refrigeration units. "What's in there?" he
asked of Cardenas.

"Storage," the college president replied. "It
should be locked."

It was. "You got a key?" Milo asked.

Cardenas made a face. "I don't think so. Not
here, anyway. Where's security? Why aren't
they here?"

"Probably," Milo replied in that semidrawl he
reserved for fools, morons, and college presi-
dents, "because we haven't notified them. Go
ahead, call them in. We can use someone to
keep people away until we're done here."

"Christ." Cardenas threw up his hands.
"There's no phone . . . Christ!" he repeated.
"Can I leave so I can call from my office?"

"Go ahead." Milo didn't bother to look at the

college president, but turned to Jack. "Dustman's on his way with a camera," he said, referring to the county's youngest and newest deputy, Dustin Fong. "He got tied up on the Icicle Creek Road with a couple of campers who swore they got attacked by a bear."

"Poor bears," Jack said with feeling. "They've got nowhere to go these days with everybody building up the place."

Without another word, Nat Cardenas left the cafeteria, his shoulders squared and his jaw set in a rigid line. Milo finally looked at me again. "Prick," he muttered. "I've never liked that guy. He acts like a little king in his kingdom."

"That's what he is," I said, more to annoy Milo than to excuse Cardenas. "On this campus, Cardenas rules."

"Bullshit." Milo watched Jack carefully place the knife and the bloodied towel in a plastic bag. "Ordinary butcher knife, right, Jack?"

"That's what it looks like to me," Jack responded, then pointed to a drawer under one of the work counters. "There's a bunch of them in there, different sizes, but all sharp as hell."

"What are you waiting for?" Milo again addressed me, his manner truculent.

"Doc Dewey. I'm covering this story." I picked Carla's camera up off the service counter. "May I?"

Milo raised his sandy eyebrows. "Isn't this kind of gory for your taste?"

"I want you and Jack to block out most of the body," I said in my most businesslike voice. "The only thing I'll show in the photo are the feet and maybe some leg."

The Sheriff tugged at one ear. "I don't think so. For one thing, this is a crime scene, and I'm in charge. I'd rather not see myself posing on page one of *The Advocate* over a victim. For another thing, I don't think the rest of the Rasmussen family would like it."

I'd been amiable for about as long as possible. "Tough," I said, zeroing in on Einar. "This is news, and I'm in charge of *The Advocate*." I clicked off three shots, but wasn't sure they'd be any good. Unlike Carla, I'm not gifted with camera skills.

"Hey!" Milo made as if to snatch the camera out of my hand. "Stop that! I told you, this is—"

I whirled around and took two more pictures, both of Milo looking angry. Then I backed away, toward the dining area, still shooting off frames. Milo started after me, one fist raised and swearing under his breath.

"Don't you dare touch this camera!" I yelled. "And if you touch me, I'll sue your butt off!"

Stopping at the entrance to the kitchen,

Milo's eyes snapped in fury. "You run any of that and I'll haul you up for interfering with a law officer! Now get your ass out of here before I throw you out!"

"Try it." I forced myself to calm down, to lower my voice. Jack Mullins was standing by the service counter, looking wide-eyed and, I thought, more worried than dismayed.

"Emma." The Sheriff also dropped his voice a notch. "Don't push me."

The rational part of my brain was taking over. If I'd managed to make the camera work properly, I had all the shots I needed. There was nothing else to learn until Doc Dewey arrived, which might not be for an hour or more. Campus security still hadn't showed up, and I doubted that they knew anything. I could interview them later, along with anyone else from the college who might have seen or heard something unusual.

"I got what I wanted," I said, lifting my chin.

"You sure did." Milo turned his back on me, then spoke over his shoulder. "I wish to hell you knew what it was."

Vida was agog. I had called her from the hospital with the news of Einar's death and Carla's departure in the ambulance. She had met me in the waiting room shortly after nine. Despite the fact that half of her gray hair was done up in rollers, she still wore a hat, in this case, a bilious green off-the-face straw number.

"Who called Marlys Rasmussen?" she asked in a whisper that could easily have been heard by the half-dozen others in the waiting room. "Where is Doc? Do you think we could find Carla in the emergency area? Who would want to kill Einar Jr.?"

I sorted through the barrage of questions. "Nobody has called Einar Jr.'s wife that I know of, but I'm sure Milo planned to do it soon. Or maybe he's going to drive to their house and give out the bad news in person. As for Doc, I haven't seen him. I suspect he's in emergency receiving with Carla."

"Hmm." Vida rested her chin on one hand, then gazed quickly around the waiting room. She nodded at a young couple who were coping with a fractious toddler. The other three, also young people, were strangers. "Motive?" Vida whispered. "Who? What? Why?"

"Good grief," I said with a faint laugh, "how should I know? A nut, maybe, prowling around the RUB. A vagrant, looking for food." I noted that the others, including the young couple I recognized as Sue Ann Daley and her husband, whose name I'd forgotten, were staring. "Let's wait to discuss this," I said, and picked up an outdated magazine from the nearby table.

"Einar Jr. could make enemies," Vida murmured. "He's that sort. Cold, abrupt, stubborn. Trucking. Teamsters. My, my!"

"Vida, Einar's not Jimmy Hoffa." I tried to immerse myself in *Sports Illustrated*'s Super Bowl issue.

"Perhaps Marlys is more peculiar than I thought," Vida continued. "Some sort of mania. Then there's Beau. If there really is a Beau. You have to wonder."

"Vida . . ." I hoped my tone conveyed a warning.

"Einar Sr. wouldn't do such a thing—probably. But Harold—so resentful, I'm sure. And drunk. Oh! Mary Jane! Surely she must hate all of her family." Vida poked me. "Who have I left out?"

"The Green Bay Packers," I retorted just as a wan-looking Carla came out through the double doors from the examining rooms.

Vida leaped to her feet. "Carla! Are you all right?"

Carla nodded, the black hair hanging limp over her shoulders. "Doc said I was just upset. I'm supposed to go home and stay in bed for a day or so." Her dark eyes sought mine. "Tomorrow's Tuesday, though. What will you do without me?"

"We'll manage," I replied. "Come on, we're here to give you a ride. We can go in my car."

"Nonsense," Vida huffed. "My Buick is much bigger and more comfortable. Emma, you can come with us."

"Thanks, Vida," I murmured. It wasn't worth arguing over the comparative comfort of our aging full-sized sedans.

"Now," Vida said, after she had stuck me in the backseat and put Carla next to her up front, "tell us what happened at the RUB. You'll have to give a statement to the Sheriff, you know."

"Sure, I'll do that later." Carla still sounded subdued, and very tired.

"Well?" Vida had paused at the intersection of Second and Cedar.

"Well what?" I could see Carla wrinkle her nose as she turned to Vida.

Vida sighed and stepped on the gas. "What happened. You had a seven-thirty appointment with Einar Jr., correct? What took place when you arrived at the RUB?"

"I was a couple of minutes late," Carla said, still in that same dull tone.

"How late?" Vida broke in.

"Um . . . five minutes?" Carla wrinkled her nose again, and I figured that she probably hadn't gotten to the RUB until almost seven forty-five. "Anyway, the doors were unlocked, so I went inside to the cafeteria where I'd told Mr. Einar—*Mr. Rasmussen*—that I'd meet him. The lights were on, but I didn't see him any-where, so I waited a couple of minutes, and then I wandered into the kitchen. That's where I found him, lying on the floor. I thought he'd had a heart attack."

As Vida glanced at Carla, the bilious green straw hat struck the car's roof. "Did you see anyone? Or hear anything?" With a firm hand, Vida jammed the hat down on top of her curlers.

"No." Carla leaned back on the passenger seat's headrest. "Nobody was around. And the phones weren't hooked up, so I had to go out to a pay phone by the Ad Building to call Emma."

At the Alpine Way arterial, Vida swiveled around to look at me. "Where did Einar Jr. park?" She swiveled back to Carla. "Where did you park?"

"I parked in the faculty lot behind the RUB," Carla replied. "I don't know where Mr. Rasmussen parked. Probably in the same place. That's where they send visitors at the gate."

I leaned forward, straining at my seat belt.

"No one was at the gate when I came in," I said. "The little kiosk was empty."

Carla nodded once. "No one was there when I arrived, either. I don't think they have anybody on duty once night classes get under way. There's a sign posted, though, telling visitors where to park."

In my excitement, I hadn't noticed the sign, and had pulled into one of the student lots that was closest to the RUB. Since I'd been there for close to an hour and hadn't gotten ticketed, I began to wonder about the efficiency of campus security.

Vida had covered the six blocks to Carla's apartment building, which stood across Alpine Way from the upscale Pines development and was sheltered by forest land on the other. "We'll come in," Vida announced, shutting off the engine.

"Don't," Carla said abruptly. "I'll be fine."

"Nonsense." Vida opened the door on the driver's side.

"I mean it." Carla's voice was unusually severe. "Doc Dewey told me I was fine, I just needed to rest."

Vida hesitated. "I planned to make you a nice cup of hot tea."

Carla shook her head, very firmly. "That's

nice, but hot tea would keep me awake, unless it was herbal, which I ran out of yesterday. Besides, Ryan will take care of me when he gets home. On Mondays, he's done at the college around ten."

"I see." Vida closed the car door. "Well now. Will he bring your car back?"

"No. He has his own. We'll pick it up tomorrow or Wednesday morning. See you." Carla got out of the car and moved with surprising alacrity to the apartment entrance.

Vida waited to see if she got in safely. Even in a small town like Alpine, danger can lurk in unsuspected places. As, I realized, Einar Rasmussen Jr. had found out too late.

"That settles it," Vida declared. "Carla is indeed living with Ryan. He must teach a class in addition to his other duties," she mused, pulling away from the curb. "So he was on campus all along."

"So were a lot of people," I said, still sitting in the back. "What does Ryan Talliaferro have to do with Einar Rasmussen Jr.?"

"Nothing. But who was there who *did* have something to do with Einar Jr.?"

"That's the most pressing question," I conceded. "Where are we going?"

"To get your car," Vida replied.

We had turned west on Tonga Road. "But

we're going in the opposite direction of the hospital," I pointed out.

"My, my. So we are. I forgot."

It was a lie. We were heading for Skykomish Community College. "Turn around, Vida," I commanded.

"Why? It's not that late."

"Because I said so. I want to go home. If you want to see what's happening at the RUB, you can go to the college without me."

"Oh, dear!" Vida gave me a sharp glance over her shoulder. "This won't do! Whatever occurred between you and Milo?"

I ground my teeth. As a rule, Vida's perceptive powers are much appreciated and admired. But not when she takes my personal life into her purview.

I ignored her question. "Doc probably still hasn't shown up. I did everything I could do while I was there. I'm tired, and I want to go home. Please, Vida."

She slowed the Buick just before we reached the Burl Creek Road. "No one seems to want my company tonight," she said in mock self-pity. "Carla has Dean Talliaferro and you have—what? Managed to somehow further annoy Milo?"

"It wasn't hard to do." I could feel my teeth clamp together.

Vida pulled into the road that led to the ski lodge, then turned around. "You'll have to get over it by morning. Both of you."

"Why?" Now I was starting to get angry at Vida.

"Because Carla isn't coming to work, and you'll have to cover the story for Wednesday's edition. Unless, of course, you want me to handle it."

Hard news was not Vida's forte. "Naturally I'll cover the story. I'm the editor, for God's sake."

"I should think so!" Vida, a usually sensible driver, headed back down Tonga Road at what I considered an excessive speed. "Any story of this magnitude involving the Rasmussen family is bound to be tricky. We'll—you'll—need all the help you can get."

I didn't respond. It passed through my tired mind that I needed help, all right. In more ways than one.

Chapter Five

"WHY THE HELL couldn't they have built a college in Snohomish instead of Alpine?" I overheard Milo say to someone in his office the next morning. "Then Einar could've gotten whacked in Snohomish County instead of here. Hell, they're mostly Snohomish types, not Alpiners."

Toni Andreas, the Sheriff department's receptionist, gave me an apologetic smile. "I'm afraid the Sheriff isn't in a very good mood today. He's filling in his other deputies about last night's homicide. Dwight Gould and Sam Heppner and Bill Blatt were off duty."

I didn't know about Sam and Dwight, but guessed that Bill hadn't been working the late shift. He is one of Vida's numerous nephews, and is trained, under penalty of God-knows-what, to relay any big news to his aunt immediately.

"How long before Milo finishes with his merry men?" I inquired as Dustin Fong entered from the vicinity of the evidence and interrogation rooms.

Toni rolled her big brown eyes. "Who

knows? Do you want some coffee while you wait?"

The Sheriff's coffee is not unlike the current state of our relationship—weak, bitter, and irritating. I declined Toni's offer. Instead, I collared Dustin.

"What's going on?" I asked the youngest of Milo's deputies, a quiet-spoken Asian-American from Seattle.

Dustin gestured at the Sheriff's office. "You mean the briefing?"

I shook my head. "I mean the investigation itself. You might as well fill me in. I gather Milo may be busy for a while." Now that I was on the premises, I wasn't sure how much I wanted to go one-on-one with the Sheriff this early in the day.

Dustin motioned for me to come around to his side of the curving wood counter and sit at his desk. "Did you hear anything about a weapon?" he asked, keeping his voice low.

I told Dustin I'd been in the cafeteria kitchen when Jack Mullins found the knife. "Are they sure that's what did it?" I asked.

Dustin, who is the very soul of discretion, cleared his throat. "There has to be an autopsy. As usual, we can't do it here because of our limited facilities, so the body has been shipped to SnoCo, in Everett. It'll take a couple of days. As usual. We're not a priority in the other county. As usual." He gave me a rueful look.

Despite passage of a bond issue a couple of years earlier, SkyCo still was hampered by lack of adequate funding. Headquarters had been renovated and expanded, a small-scale lab had been added, Dustin had been hired to ease the manpower shortage, and the jail's security had been beefed up so that prisoners couldn't escape by kicking a hole in the wall and crawling out onto the sidewalk across from the Sears catalogue pickup office. Indeed, many years ago an escapee who had been serving time for assault with a deadly weapon had gone directly from his cell to the Sears outlet and tried to order a double-barreled shotgun.

"So nothing definite on the weapon until the autopsy, right?"

Dustin nodded. "Sorry. I know you come out tomorrow."

That was the curse of the weekly. If news didn't break within twenty-four hours of publication, it was stale by the next edition.

"What about witnesses?" I asked, writing *no weapon news* on my notepad.

"Nothing so far." Again, Dustin's manner conveyed apology. "Dodge talked to Carla this morning on the phone, but she couldn't give us anything. I guess she'll make her formal statement tomorrow when she feels better."

"Has campus security reported anything?" I inquired. "Where were they, by the way? I never saw them."

Dustin offered his engaging grin. "At night, campus security is Ron Bjornson. He's been out of work in the woods for a while now, and that farm of theirs isn't enough to make a living, so he caught on with the college. It turned out that he was unplugging a toilet in the dorm when the murder must have occurred. It seems that Mr. Bjornson gets stuck doing more than making sure the doors are locked."

I knew Ron and Maylene Bjornson, who lived out on the Burl Creek Road and had teenagers to support. "The college has a bigger force during the day, don't they?"

"Right," Dustin said, and grinned again. "All two of them."

I seemed to recall as much from one of Carla's numerous stories. But with a faculty of only thirty, and a total enrollment just under five hundred students, there wasn't any need. Until now.

"What's going on at the campus?" I asked, though I planned on heading there next.

Dustin shook his head. "I haven't been out

there this morning. I suppose everybody's pretty upset. Do you suppose they'll cancel the dedication?"

"I don't know," I answered grimly. If that happened, our special section was also canceled. I needed an answer fast. "Look, Dustin," I said, catching a few phrases from Milo in his office, "it sounds as if the Sheriff isn't going to be able to see me for a while. Is there anything else you can tell me that I can use for the paper? What about Mrs. Rasmussen and the rest of the family? How are they taking it?"

Dustin didn't know that, either. Milo had driven the short distance down the highway to inform Marlys Rasmussen of her husband's tragic demise. Dustin guessed that Beau was home when the Sheriff came by. As for the Rasmussen daughter, Dustin didn't know they had one.

"Dodge called the Snohomish County Sheriff's office and had somebody go to Snohomish and tell Mr. Rasmussen Sr. He must be a pretty old geezer."

I hazarded a guess. "Close to ninety, maybe. Einar Jr. turned sixty-four in April." I'd done my homework before walking over to the Sheriff's. "I'll check in with you folks before we go to press," I said, getting to my feet and darting a glance in the direction of Milo's open door. "Right now I should go over to the campus. Thanks, Dustin."

"Sure," the deputy responded, also rising and making what looked like a little bow. "Sorry I couldn't be more help. But we're just getting our feet wet."

"Right." I hoped my smile was encouraging. The truth was that I felt Milo and company weren't even close to the water. I walked back up Front Street, got into the Jag, and drove out to the college.

It had drizzled a bit during the night, and the freshly planted lawns glistened under the morning sun. This time I parked behind the RUB in the designated visitors' place. Then I headed for the Ad Building and Nat Cardenas's office.

The president's secretary, Cynthia Kittikachorn, is an exotic young woman who was born in Thailand but raised in Tacoma. Her languid air doesn't inspire confidence, but I'm told that she's very efficient. When I arrived, she had the phone propped between her shoulder and one ear, and was diagramming what looked like a family tree on a legal pad.

"I've no idea when he'll be free," Cynthia said into the phone, her voice musical but detached. "I suggest you call back around four." She hung up and turned to me. "Reporters, from Seattle and everywhere else. Why don't they stick to their own crimes and leave us alone? The phone hasn't stopped ringing all morning." Her usual air of languor wasn't evident this morning.

Despite the fact that I was inwardly seething over being scooped by the outside media, I gave Cynthia a self-deprecating smile. "I'm a reporter, but at least I'm local."

She made a face. "I didn't mean to knock journalists in general. But this is a really ugly situation for us, especially since we're just getting Sky College off the ground. Einar Rasmussen Jr., of all people." Her face suddenly clouded over. "He did wonderful things for us. I wonder if the state higher-education people in Olympia are ready to cancel our funding."

"They won't," I said. "They can't. This is hardly the college's fault. Murder can happen anywhere."

The phone rang again, but Cynthia ignored it. "I'll let the switchboard take that one." She sighed, her plump figure rippling under a beige silk dress. "But why did it have to happen *here*?"

"If we knew that, we might know who did it," I said, perhaps a bit too glibly. But this wasn't my first experience with violent death. Like most other people, Cynthia was probably a novice when it came to homicide. "Is it possible to see President Cardenas now or is he really tied up?"

Nat Cardenas was busy, Cynthia explained, but he was alone. The college was in the process of hiring additional staff, and he was going over the results of recent interviews.

She tapped the diagram on her desk. "I was just filling in the blanks. We're adding faculty for English, math, and sociology."

"Do you expect enrollment to go up in the fall?" I asked, sensing a second, less dramatic story.

"Some," Cynthia allowed. "Overall, enrollment may be down around the state because the economy is so good. But here in Skykomish County, things are still slow, so we may be one of the state colleges to show an increase." She picked up the phone. "Hang on, I'll see if President Cardenas can spare you a minute."

Apparently he could. Cynthia went through the formality of ushering me into Cardenas's office, a smallish but handsome room with tall windows looking out on a stand of cedar trees, which gave a sense of calm and expansiveness. The walls were finished in unbleached knotty pine, and reminded me of my house.

"Emma." Nat Cardenas looked at me from over black-rimmed half glasses. Though we didn't know each other well, he preferred informality among his so-called peers. "Sit down, tell me how we can make the least of this mess."

The college had no media-relations expert on staff, so the registrar, Shawna Beresford-Hall, who also taught English, produced the necessary handouts. Until enrollment increased substantially, SkyCoCo, as it was sometimes called locally, would ask its faculty to wear several hats.

"I have to tell what happened," I said, sitting down in a comfortable leather-covered armchair across the desk from Cardenas. "It's my job."

Nat sighed. "The college isn't culpable. You must make that understood."

"The facts speak for themselves," I said primly.

Nat didn't look buoyed by the comment. He is in his early fifties, a solid man of six feet with wavy iron-gray hair that was probably once jet-black, deep-set brown eyes, and just enough lines in his olive skin to indicate that the road of life hasn't always been smooth.

"Look," he said, placing both hands on his oval desk, which looked as if it were made of

teak, "Einar Rasmussen Jr. wasn't just a benefactor, he was on the board of trustees, he
helped bring the college to Alpine in the first
place. He had influence not just in Skykomish
and Snohomish counties, but in Olympia. His
father had been a state legislator for twelve
years over in Snohomish. His death is a tre-
mendous loss to the community, as well as to
his family and friends."

Nat couldn't have phrased a statement for the
press better if he'd rehearsed it. But then again,
he probably had. The book on Nat Cardenas is
that he's not exactly a political novice.

"What about the dedication? Is it still on?"
My question was straightforward, with no political strings attached.

Nat sighed heavily. "Yes. I spent over two
hours this morning with the rest of the board
of trustees and our administrators. Half that
time we were on the phone to Olympia, conferring with the decision makers at the state
level. Since the lieutenant governor is already
slated to be on hand, they suggested we go
ahead with the ceremonies, but turn them into
a memorial to Einar Rasmussen Jr."

I nodded. As cruel as Einar's death might be,
there were practical matters to resolve. My
brain began to buzz with changes for our spe-

cial edition. With Carla out, I'd be the one making them.

"Do you have any theories about who might have killed Einar?" I asked.

Nat's face, which is usually quite mobile, shut down. "That's up to Sheriff Dodge to find out. If he can." His tone didn't convey confidence in Milo's abilities.

I was still feeling perverse, not an uncommon trait of mine. "May I quote you?"

The heavy lids dropped down over the brown eyes. "Saying what? That I hope the Sheriff is able to arrest the killer? Certainly."

I hadn't come to play word games. "You were on campus last night. Did you see or hear anything unusual?"

If he wasn't guarded by nature, Nat Cardenas now seemed to withdraw even further. "Other than a tragically murdered man in the RUB kitchen?" There was no hint of humor in his manner. But perhaps there was irony. I couldn't be sure. "No," the college president went on, "I noticed nothing unusual. I already mentioned that to the Sheriff."

"I'm not the Sheriff." I gave Nat a tight little smile. "I'm trying to put together a story. Last night's events landed my reporter in the hospital." I paused, waiting for a comment, but he said nothing. "Then you have no idea who might have been lurking around the RUB when it wasn't yet open to the public?"

Nat sighed again. "I understand that your reporter—Carla—asked security to leave the doors unlocked. Anyone could have entered the RUB. A vagrant, a burglar, a drug addict. If you're looking for theories, my best guess is that someone came in with the intention of robbery. It would be an outsider, someone who didn't realize that because the building wasn't yet in operation, there would be no cash on hand. Whoever it was discovered Mr. Rasmussen, and in his—or her, of course—panic, killed him and fled." He gave a slight shrug of his broad shoulders. "It happens, especially when drugs are involved."

It was a nice, pat explanation. It could even be true, though burglars usually don't kill. "What about staff, students, faculty? Has anyone reported anything unusual?"

Nat shook his head, slowly, decisively. "Not a thing. Oh, I'm sure that security has heard a few wild ideas. There are always individuals who imagine they've seen something of importance. Students, of course, have active imaginations. Sometimes. But if anything genuine had turned up, I'm certain I would have heard about it."

My eyes strayed around the tidy, tasteful room with its framed diplomas and certificates and awards. I knew he had his undergraduate degree from the University of Texas and his doctorate in education from Baylor. He also had a stuffed armadillo in a glass case, which was a rather ugly sight. I supposed, however, that it was better than having a stuffed student on display.

"I'd like to talk to your security people," I said. "Especially Ron Bjornson."

Faint lines appeared on Nat's forehead as he blinked twice. "Bjornson? Oh!" The college president laughed, hitting a false note. "Ron Bjornson. There's also a Bjorn Ronstadt, in social sciences. Even after almost a full school year, I'm still getting acquainted, especially with staff personnel."

I made no comment on his remark. "I understand Ron works only at night."

He grew very serious again. "Yes, that sounds right. You can check with Cynthia. She can give you his home number and address."

"I know where the Bjornsons live," I said, getting to my feet. "They're close by, actually, off the Burl Creek Road."

Nat gave a short nod. "Good luck with your story." He turned his attention back to the faculty interviews.

I left the office feeling like a freshman who had just been put on probation. Nat Cardenas might be smooth, he might be political, he might even be a nice guy—but he didn't exactly exude warmth. According to Carla's feature story of a year ago, Nat had been born in San Antonio to Mexican immigrants. He had grown up poor, maybe tough, but determined to make something of himself. He'd worked his way through college, and as I recalled, it had taken him over twelve years to get his degrees. He'd taught in Texas, then moved to California in his first administrative position. The springboard to Skykomish Community College had been the academic vice-presidency of a two-year school in the Los Angeles area. I suspected that Nat's reserve grew out of his rugged background. I also figured that maybe he was suffering from cultural shock. The only thing that Alpine and L.A. have in common is that they are both on the same planet. I think.

Security was located in the same building, but at the far end of a long hall, with a much smaller, more cluttered office. As I'd expected, no one was around. Apparently both members of the day crew were out checking for student cars parked illegally in spots reserved for faculty

and staff. Or, I thought, with an effort at charity, they were helping solve last night's crime.

I drove past the fish hatchery and the reservoir, then turned onto the Burl Creek Road.
Along with some small older homes, there are
still a few modest farms fighting off encroach-
ment by developers. Alpine's rocky terrain
isn't conducive to agricultural subsistence, but
hearty earth-loving souls like the Bjornsons try
to keep up the pretense.

The two-story white frame house could have
used a paint job, but the surroundings were
tidy. I could hear the clucking of chickens from
a coop near the open garage. In the uneven
pasture where a half-dozen cedar and hemlock
trees had been allowed to stand amid the
stumps of their fallen brethren, I could see two
cows and a horse grazing in peace.

An older-model Ford pickup was parked
midway in the gravel drive. Since I'd seen Ron
Bjornson drive the truck around town, I assumed it was his and that he was home.

Ron took some time to answer the doorbell,
and when he finally arrived, it looked as if his
T-shirt and jeans had been put on hastily.
"Emma?" he said with just enough doubt in his
voice to indicate that I was still sometimes a
stranger to the native-born.

Noting the disheveled fair hair and the need of a shave, I realized that Ron had probably been asleep. He was on night duty, after all. Sheepishly, I apologized.

"It's okay," he said, though he sounded wary. Or maybe just weary. "I got to bed around six, and it's going on eleven now. Come in, I'll see if Maylene left any coffee on."

"Maylene's gone?" It was an innocent question.

Ron, however, didn't seem to take it as such. His gray-green eyes sparked with resentment as he glanced at me across the kitchen counter. "Yeah, she had to go to work. Maylene started part-time at the college a couple of months ago, helping out in the library."

I tried to remain ingenuous. "Does she enjoy it?"

Ron handed me a mug of coffee. "Hell, no." He paused, fingering the stubble on his blunt chin. "Well, maybe she does, in a way. But we need the money. How many eggs do you think we can sell to the Grocery Basket in a month?"

I didn't try to guess, but I got the point. "I thought you were doing some auto repair work here at the house for a while."

Ron sat down on a stool across the counter from me. Even though the kitchen was at least as big as Nat Cardenas's office, there was a sense of oppression. Maybe it was the clutter that had been allowed to accumulate on the counters. Maybe it was Ron's frustration. "I was into repair for a while," he said with a grimace. "But I specialized in trucks, big rigs, mostly, and there aren't many of those left around here. The little stuff all goes to Cal Vickers's Texaco and the local dealerships. We just weren't making it, and with two kids, me and Maylene had to get steady jobs."

Maybe it was the sense of something still young in Ron's unlined face; maybe it was the bad grammar. Whatever the reason, I asked if he'd thought about going back to school and acquiring a new trade.

Ron made a disparaging noise. "I got plenty of trades—logging, farming, driving truck, repair, backhoe—you name it, I can do it. But not around here. Sometimes we think about moving, but prices are still down in Alpine. I wouldn't want to take a hosing like Maylene's folks did on their place down the pike in Monroe."

The coffee was stale, but at least it was hot. We had strayed far from the reason for my visit. Curiously, Ron seemed more interested in his financial situation than in my unexpected appearance on his doorstep. But then again, most former loggers would probably react in the same way.

"It's good, though, that we have the college," I said, trying to lead into my interrogation. "It helps people like you and Maylene by providing job opportunities."

Ron gave a snort, then lighted a cigarette. "Right. We can both pick up our bag of peanuts twice a month."

"But you get benefits working for the state," I pointed out.

"I do. Maylene doesn't." He blew out a big puff of smoke, then coughed twice. "She's only part-time."

I started to comment that Ron's benefits should cover the whole family, but we were still off the mark. "It's a shame the college has to have a tragedy in its first academic year," I said instead. "As you might guess, I'm writing a story about it."

The gray-green eyes again turned wary. "You are? For the paper?"

I gritted my teeth. No, I'm carving it on an elephant's hind end and sending it off on a Caribbean cruise, I wanted to say—but refrained. "You were working security last night. Did anything out of the ordinary happen?"

Ron waved his cigarette in an impatient gesture. "Hell, no! Do I have to say it fifty times? I should've gotten off work at four, but instead I got stuck on campus until almost six. All because that Dodge prick had to ask everything over and over."

I ignored Ron's anger. "Who unlocked the RUB doors for Mr. Rasmussen and my reporter?"

"I did, around seven-fifteen." The query seemed to calm him a bit. "Then I went off on my rounds. Parking lots, building doors, just checking everything out. The grounds have lots of trees and shrubbery, which maybe look pretty, but they make good hiding places, too. Not that we've ever caught anybody hiding. Still, we have to follow the instructions in the frigging manual. It's a damned pain in the ass, if you ask me."

It was also Ron's job, and his rancor indicated an attitude problem. My job, however, was not that of a therapist. "How did you find out about Rasmussen's death?"

Ron stubbed out his cigarette and took a big swig of coffee. "The Chinaman told me."

It sounded cryptic until I realized he was referring to Dustin Fong. "The deputy?" I kept my exasperation in check. "When was that?"

"Sometime before ten. I'd just come across the road from the dorms. They had a plumbing problem. Those dumb girls shouldn't put whatchamacallits down the toilet. They plug up the line. But you can't tell them anything."

I guessed that the whatchamacallits were tampons. I knew they were a problem, but the only time I'd ever suffered from such a backup was when Adam was about three and put mine down our toilet while they were still in the box.

"You were surprised?" I asked in that stupid manner characteristic of journalists in search of a meaningless quote.

"Hell, no. Our own daughter, Jenny, has pulled that stunt a couple of times. That's how I knew what caused the backup."

I was gritting my teeth again. "I mean about Mr. Rasmussen getting murdered."

Ron blinked a couple of times. "Oh. Well, sure. You don't expect that kind of stuff, right? It's really too bad."

I agreed. "Did you know him?"

"Rasmussen?" He gave a shrug. "Sure. Didn't everybody?"

"I guess so. He was very prominent in Skykomish and Snohomish counties." My notepad was blank. So was my mind. But I dredged up one last question. "Did you ever hear anyone make any threats or indicate they wished harm to Mr. Rasmussen?"

Ron laughed, a barking, harsh sound. "You kidding? How about half the population along Highway Two?"

"Why was that?"

Ron leaned forward, elbows propped on the countertop. "Because he was an SOB, that's why. Hey, you run the paper. Don't you ever hear the news?"

I refused to let Ron Bjornson bait me. "Such as?"

Ron seemed perplexed by my ignorance. "Like the way he treated people. Like how he ran his businesses. Like thinking he was God Almighty because he was Einar Rasmussen Jr. Like being the biggest bastard from here to Snohomish." He sat back on the stool and scratched his temple. "Hell, it's no wonder he got himself killed. You asked if I was surprised—I guess I was only surprised that it didn't happen sooner."

Chapter Six

I SHOULD HAVE guessed: Vida had been on the prowl.

"I've known the family for years," she said in a defensive tone. "It would have been amiss if I hadn't called on Marlys Rasmussen. Whatever would she have thought?"

But Marlys hadn't come to the door, a fact that secretly pleased me. Vida might horn in on the family, but she wasn't going to get a piece of the homicide investigation. My House & Home editor handled her own section admirably, but when it came to hard news, her style tended to ramble into homey family ties. Hopefully, writing the obituary and covering the funeral would satisfy her.

"Who was there?" I asked, sitting on the edge of Vida's desk.

Behind the big glasses, Vida looked rueful. "I'm not sure. It might have been Gladys. It certainly wasn't Beau."

"Who's Gladys?" I shifted my weight slightly. The midday sun was slanting right through the small window above Vida's desk and trying to blind me.

"Harold Rasmussen's wife. Gladys would be Einar Jr.'s sister-in-law." Vida still seemed full of regret. "Whoever it was said Marlys was un- available. I sympathize, of course. It did no good to coax. And I didn't want to make a pest of myself."

Vida, no doubt, *had* made a pest of herself. But in vain. I suppressed a smile, then told her about my encounters with Nat Cardenas and Ron Bjornson.

"The college president will be guarded about the situation," she allowed. "As for Ron, he can't be blamed for being bitter. Like so many of our out-of-work loggers, he's had problems adjusting to a different lifestyle."

I understood. For the men who worked in the woods, often following in their fathers' and grandfathers' muddy footsteps, the timber in- dustry was a vocation. It was as hard to tell a logger to quit logging as it was to make an ac- tor stop acting. When the parts—or the trees— ran out, they were utterly lost, displaced, adrift in a world where their services were no longer required.

I slid off the desk just as Leo breezed through the door. "I need a decision, and I need it now. Is the RUB special section on or off?"

"On," I responded. "I'll make the editorial changes. You should contact our advertisers to see if any of them want to add an 'in memoriam' line or some such tribute. Instead of a picture of Einar at the RUB—alive—we'll run the stock publicity shot. Okay?"

Leo was already picking up the phone. "Got it. I'll start making calls. Oh!" He paused with a finger on one of the telephone buttons. "There's something weird going on over at the warehouse site. It looks like a giant Easter-egg hunt, except that these are all grownups and there's no rabbit in sight." Leo resumed tapping digits.

"Damn!" I didn't have time to go on a wild-goose chase. I turned back to Vida. "Can you . . . ?"

Vida nodded once, setting the pink paper primroses on her black straw aquiver. "Of course. It sounds interesting." She picked up her camera and headed out of the office in her splayfooted manner.

Passing Leo en route to my cubbyhole, I gave him a wan smile. "I'm glad you recovered so fast. Where would we be if you were out sick, too?"

Leo, who apparently was on hold, glanced up at me sharply. "Did you think I was faking it the other night? Why would I do that?"

I was aghast. "No, no, of course not! I know

you were under the weather. You've been coughing for the past two days."

Leo automatically looked down at his over-flowing ashtray. "So I was. Okay, forget it. Maybe this damned bug has made me irra-tional. Are we still on for—Jake, it's Leo," my ad manager said into the receiver. "Now that poor old Einar has met his Maker, we were wondering if you'd like to add something to your Grocery Basket ad that would . . ."

I went into my office and started revising Carla's RUB dedication copy. It took me over an hour, and by that time my stomach was growling fiercely. I was out the front door, headed for the Burger Barn, when Vida pulled up in front of *The Advocate.*

"Goodness!" she exclaimed, grappling with her camera, her purse, and her swing coat, which seemed to have gotten entangled in the seat belt. "There's a mad treasure hunt at the new restaurant site! The Bourgette boys had to call the Sheriff."

"What triggered that?" I asked.

Closing the Buick's door, Vida shook her head. "I'm not sure. What's this about a boxful of nuggets?"

I'd forgotten that Vida had never read—and much more amazingly—hadn't heard about the steel chest which had been found by the firemen. "Grab a burger with me and I'll explain," I offered. "I was going to do takeout, but I'd better fill you in."

Vida looked as if she were about to take umbrage; she despised having to be "filled in." "I'm dieting, you know. I brought carrot and celery sticks."

Vida's diets were a sometime thing, and never seemed to affect her weight, which, like the rest of her, remained constant. "Have them for dinner. You look gaunt."

Vida ignored the lie, but surrendered. As usual, her curiosity got the best of her. After returning her camera to the office, she came back outside, and we made the short trek across the street and down one block to the Burger Barn.

Since it was almost one, there were a half-dozen empty booths. I waited until after we had given our orders before enlightening my House & Home editor about the gold stash. Naturally, she was outraged.

"How could I not know about the nuggets? What's the matter with my nephew Billy? Are you sure Milo had possession of this so-called treasure?"

"Yes, according to the Bourgettes. The box is at the assayer's office. But I guess it hasn't been

traced yet. Now, what's going on at the warehouse site?"

Vida didn't answer immediately, apparently
taking a moment to digest my account and the
enormity of her ignorance. "John and Dan
started clearing the property Sunday afternoon," she finally said. "They had most of the
debris out of the way by this morning. Apparently that was the signal for the scavengers
to start digging. I must say," she continued,
"they have enough gumption to dig, but not
to haul."

"How many were looking for so-called treasure?" I asked as our waitress brought my Pepsi
and Vida's hot tea.

"I counted twenty-two," Vida responded.
"Naturally, I recognized everyone except for a
half dozen who may have been college students. Two of them were engaged in a rather
ugly tug-of-war with a faculty member from
sociology. Several of the trespassers had metal
detectors. Really, Emma, I can't imagine how I
could have missed such an incident!"

"As I said, it happened while we were out of
town last fall. You were gone longer than I was,
and I suppose by the time you got back, the
initial gossip had died down." I paused, wondering why the treasure hunters had waited so

long. "Maybe it was too dangerous to dig until now. The place was a real mess."

Vida inclined her head. "That's so. Though I heard just now that the railroad had sent someone to watch the property for a few weeks. I also learned that there had been a rash of scavengers right after the fire, but when Averill Fairbanks was knocked unconscious by a falling timber, the others decided to stay away."

"Averill was hurt?" I said in surprise. Averill was our resident UFO spotter and more inclined to scan the skies than dig the dirt. "It must have happened before I got back from Oregon."

"It was. Indeed, the ashes were still hot. Averill also burned his shoes." Vida made a face. "People are so foolish. And greedy. Sam Heppner and Dwight Gould practically had to resort to force to remove the trespassers. I'm afraid the Bourgettes will have to hire a night watchman."

"Could be." My answer was detached. I was wondering if in fact there really was more buried gold on the warehouse premises. "As soon as Carla gets back, I'm going to have her do some research on the early mining days around here."

Vida stopped blowing on her tea. "Carla?

Why? She's been here only a short time. I'll do it."

I suppressed a beleaguered sigh. "She's been here almost as long as I have," I noted. Which, I was well aware, was also a short time in Vida's opinion. "This is a news story or at least a news feature. It won't go in the House & Home section. Besides," I added ominously, "the mining was done before your time." Vida hated it when an event had occurred "before her time." She considered such past history as neolithic, or at least inconsequential.

"Nonsense," Vida retorted. "I've often done historical features, not only for my page, but for special editions. Besides, I might not have been born while they were mining in the area—goodness, there was no Alpine then, only a whistle-stop called Nippon—but I'm well versed in the background."

I didn't doubt it, so I gave in. At least Vida wouldn't have to start from scratch. "Okay, but even you will have to do some—excuse the expression—digging."

"Certainly. If nothing else, I'll need to refresh my memory." Vida sipped daintily from her mug of tea.

My burger basket arrived, along with Vida's fish sticks. Fish, she assured me, was far more slimming than beef, and never mind that the minnow-sized slices of whatever bottom feeders the Burger Barn bought in bulk were thick with deep-fried breading.

"Okay," I said, after filling my face with food, "enlighten me about Einar Jr.'s reputation in Skykomish and Snohomish counties."

Vida dabbed a fry in tartar sauce. "I thought you knew. His father owned a sawmill, dabbled in real estate, and grew quite prosperous. There were three children—Harold, Mary Jane, and Einar Jr. Harold had no head for business, so Einar Jr. worked more closely with Einar Sr. I believe Mary Jane worked in the mill office for a while as well. But of course that ended when she became engaged to Dick Bourgette. You can imagine what a blow it was to the Rasmussens not to be able to marry their daughter off with a big fanfare. It would have been the event of the season in Snohomish."

I was trying to picture Mary Jane and Dick Bourgette as I remembered them from church. She was a pretty, vivacious, dark-haired woman in her fifties; Dick was a good-looking man about the same age with silver hair and glasses. Maybe it was time for me to do more than merely nod and smile at them in the St. Mildred's parking lot.

"What did they do?" I asked as an RV about the size of my house purred down Front Street.

"Dick was from Everett, so they were married by a priest from his church. Mary Jane became a convert just before the wedding. Thyra was particularly outraged. But," Vida added, with unexpected malice, "she would be. She's a loathsome person."

"Thyra?" The name rang a faint bell.

"Einar Sr.'s wife. She thinks she rules society in Snohomish." Vida all but sneered.

"Good grief," I exclaimed, "the woman must be almost ninety! But of course," I added in a more musing tone, "it was almost forty years ago when her daughter cheated her out of a splashy wedding."

Vida gave a nod, her hat tipping to the left. "Yes, and of course that was before the influx of commuters and growth in general. Snohomish was much smaller then, about the size of Alpine. But Thyra Rasmussen is still the sort of self-centered woman who considers herself the queen bee. Why, when the Clemans family permanently moved to Snohomish from Alpine after Carl closed the mill, Thyra all but snubbed Mrs. Clemans. She didn't want any competition. But Mrs. Clemans was a wonderful woman who didn't let such things bother her. I'm quite sure she put Thyra in her place. Nicely, of course."

A haggard Doc Dewey and Fuzzy Baugh

were passing our booth on their way out of the restaurant. Doc merely nodded politely and continued on his way, but the mayor stopped at our table, his heady aftershave mingling with the Burger Barn's prevailing odor of grease.

"Kid gloves," he murmured, leaning in between Vida and me. "This story about poor Einar must be handled with kid gloves. Consider the family, not to mention the college. I play racquetball with Nat Cardenas." Fuzzy withdrew his hands from the table and followed Doc Dewey out the door.

"Ridiculous old fool," Vida huffed. "Fuzzy wouldn't last five minutes playing racquetball. The only exercise he gets is giving long-winded speeches."

I smiled in agreement, then returned to the subject at hand. "You didn't really answer my question about Einar's reputation. Ron Bjornson said it stinks."

"Of course he would," Vida responded, pouring more hot water into her tea. "The haves are always envied by the have-nots. Though," she continued, jiggling her tea bag up and down in the mug, "I've heard stories about Einar's ruthlessness. Of course his father, Einar Sr., was the same way. It's often the case, with successful people. They don't let things— or other people—stand in their way. Mr.

Clemans was an exception. To this day, I've never heard anyone criticize him."

Carl Clemans had definitely achieved saintly status in Alpine. Perhaps it was deserved; perhaps it was a fluke of memory. But Clemans had been dead for almost sixty years and Einar Rasmussen Sr. was still alive. His son, however, was not, and that was paramount in my mind.

By three-thirty, our deadline loomed before me. Whether I liked it or not, I had to check in with the Sheriff before the end of the day. I trudged the two blocks to Milo's office, aware that the sun was playing peekaboo with some ominous gray clouds. Just as I pushed open one of the double doors to the Skykomish County Sheriff's Office, Milo came through the other.

"Emma," he said, looking startled. "Hi." He kept going.

"Hey!" I whirled around. "Hold it! I need two minutes."

At the curb, the Sheriff hesitated but didn't turn toward me. "For what? I'm busy."

"So am I," I snapped. "I've got a paper to put to bed in about ninety minutes."

"You do that," Milo said, still without looking at me. "You can put whatever the hell you want to bed without me." He yanked open the door of his Cherokee Chief and slammed it shut.

"Asshole!" I yelled just as Edna Mae Dalrymple approached with a shocked expression on her face. She'd heard me, but Milo probably hadn't; he'd gunned the engine and was already pulling out of his diagonal parking space.

"Are you all right?" Edna Mae gasped, her overbite making her look even more like a scared rabbit than she usually does. Edna Mae is not only the local librarian, but a fellow member of my bridge club. Though she and others have exasperated me many times with their lame-brained card playing, I've never actually called any of them an asshole.

"I'm upset," I admitted. "I'm up against a deadline, and the Sheriff isn't cooperating. Sorry. I shouldn't be so . . . irked."

Edna Mae tittered. "You certainly sounded annoyed. Really, Emma," she said, pressing so close that I could smell the baked goods she carried in a bag from the Upper Crust, "is it true that you and Milo are on the rocks?"

"It's been true for months," I said, my irritation returning. Where the hell had Edna Mae been since October? Stuck in the stacks in the library basement?

But Edna Mae was wide-eyed. "Maybe it's just a tiff," she said in her customary nervous manner. "I always thought you and Milo made such a cute couple."

I started to snap back at Edna Mae, but fortunately, my better nature came to the fore. I couldn't take out my frustrations on a poor woman whose only serious fault—besides not knowing a short club bid from a singing telegram—was lack of judgment when it came to her fellow human beings.

"Thanks," I said, "but things just didn't work out. See you soon, Edna Mae." I dashed into the Sheriff's office.

Jack Mullins was laughing. At me, as it turned out, though he tried to hide the fact. "Just missed Dodge, huh?" he said, and made an attempt at turning serious.

I realized Jack had been watching through the double doors. "Yeah, right, I got dodged by Dodge. Your boss is being difficult these days. Can you bail me out on this Rasmussen case? I want to finish my story for tomorrow's edition."

Jack shrugged. "What's to bail? We haven't heard from the ME in Everett yet."

"But you've been conducting interviews, haven't you?"

"Sure." He shuffled some papers behind the curving counter. "No leads, though. Honest, Emma, there's nothing to report."

My shoulders slumped. "That's discouraging." After a pause I narrowed my eyes at Jack. "So now I have to write that the Sheriff has made absolutely no progress investigating Einar Rasmussen Jr.'s violent murder on the campus of Skykomish Community College?"

Jack's skin darkened. "Hey, you don't have to get nasty about it! Hell, the guy hasn't been dead for twenty-four hours yet!"

"I didn't know there was a time line for a homicide investigation," I shot back. "Surely Milo has been going through Einar's business dealings, his financial status, his private life. Are you trying to tell me he's come up empty?"

Jack didn't respond for several seconds. Finally, he spoke again, his tone subdued. "We really don't have much to go on. And frankly, there hasn't been time to dig into every dark hole in Einar's life. Give us a break, Emma. You know how short-staffed we are."

I did know. "Okay." I sighed. "But my readership won't be pleased."

"Luckily, you don't have a readership in Snohomish or Monroe, where Einar had most of his clout," Jack said, all but jeering.

"Actually," I replied with a lift of my short, unimpressive chin, "I do. You'd be surprised how many people over in Snohomish County have ties to Alpine and subscribe to *The Advocate*."

Jack made a disgruntled noise low in his

throat and shook his head like an angry pup. "Okay, okay, I know you're pissed off. It's not our fault your paper comes out tomorrow. By then, we may have something. Right now it's really slow going. Hell, I couldn't even get hold of your reporter today just to find out what kind of lipstick she wears. That stick-up-his-butt boyfriend of hers said she was too weak to come to the phone."

I was lost. "Carla? Lipstick? What are you talking about?"

Jack gazed at me with curiosity. "You were there last night. Don't you remember? Or had you already gone when Doc Dewey spotted the lipstick on Einar's shirt?"

"I'd gone," I said faintly. Timing, they say, is everything. As usual, mine stunk. "What about this lipstick?"

Though Toni Andreas was the only other person in the office at the moment, Jack lowered his voice. "Dodge noticed lipstick on the front of Einar's shirt, just below the shoulder. Sure, it could be Mrs. Rasmussen's, but we haven't been able to check her out either. She's not talking to anybody, which, I guess, figures. The son, Beau, said that his sister, Deirdre, has taken over the funeral arrangements."

"It wasn't Carla's lipstick," I asserted. "She never saw Einar that night. Besides, Einar was close to six feet tall, and Carla's barely five feet. Her mouth wouldn't reach Einar's shoulder."

Jack's eyes danced. "It might. Who said they were standing up?"

I made a face. "You don't really think it was Carla's, do you?"

"Hey, you know Dodge—he never rules out anything or anybody." Jack's eyes were still twinkling.

"Very funny. Have they set a date and time for the funeral?"

"Saturday, ten A.M., Christ the King Lutheran Church, Snohomish." He looked beyond me as an older man I vaguely recognized entered through the double doors. "Hi, Elmer. What's up?"

It was my signal to depart. Back at *The Advocate*, I told Vida and Leo about the lipstick-smeared shirt. "I can't use it in the story," I said, "but it's pretty interesting."

"Five-six," Vida said. "Shorter, with heels."

Leo rubbed his upper lip. "Einar's mystery date?"

"Yes. That's my calculation." Vida adjusted her glasses, which, like her previous pair, had a tendency to slip down her nose. "Which might include Marlys. She's at least average height."

Leo was shaking his head. "Forget Marlys.

I've met Einar Jr. a few times, and he's not the type to go out of the door, especially for a picture shoot, with a dirty shirt."

Vida sniffed. "You just want it to be something sensational."

Leo grinned. "True. But I also want to be realistic. Has Dodge figured out where Einar was before he came to the campus?"

"Dodge," I replied with acrimony, "hasn't figured out what year it is."

Leo wiggled his eyebrows. "Ah. So that's how it's going to be on this one. Adversarial stances between the press and law enforcement. Go get 'em, editor-publisher babe."

"I intend to." With a thumbs-up gesture, I returned to my office and finished up the Rasmussen story. The copy wasn't quite as harsh as my recital to Jack Mullins, but I did write that "According to the Sheriff's office, no one has come forward yet with any information that might lead to apprehension of a suspect" and that "Sheriff Dodge has no substantial leads so far." It was accurate, it was news, and it wasn't as unkind as I wanted to be. *Dunderhead* is a term more suitable to editorials than the front page.

The last thing I did before telling Kip MacDuff we were ready to roll was to read through Vida's long cutline, which accompanied the pictures she'd taken at the warehouse site:

"Trespassers had to be ejected by Sheriff's deputies today when they refused to cooperate and stop digging for alleged buried treasure at the site of last October's warehouse fire where John and Dan Bourgette plan to build a restaurant. The Bourgette brothers are the sons of Dick and Mary Jane Bourgette, who recently moved to Alpine, and are enjoying semiretirement in their home near the golf course."

As usual, Vida had written the caption in her House & Home style. I deleted the last sentence, broke up the first one, and added a couple of minor touches. It was exactly five o'clock when I told Kip the paper was ready. It was one minute after five when I began collecting my things in preparation for ending my day at work. I was heading out when Ed Bronsky literally stumbled into the newsroom.

"What was *that*?" he asked in a surprised voice, glancing all around.

"Your feet, Ed," I responded. "There's nothing on the floor."

"Oh." He shook himself. "Darn. It must be these new shoes. They're Gookies."

"Guccis, Ed," I said patiently, eyeing Ed's expensive footgear that would have been more suited to a bandleader in the Catskills than an ex–ad manager in Alpine.

"Right, gotcha." He beamed at me. "Am I too late?"

"For what?" Ed had often been late when working for me. Shirley was sick, the plumbing was broken, his brakes had failed, their dog, Carhop, was having a liver transplant. Ed had a million excuses, some of them true.

"For this week's *Advocate*," Ed replied, still beaming. "I've got some really, *really* hot news."

Rats, I thought. "What is it, Ed?" I tried to look curious.

"My book. *Mr. Ed* is going into a second printing. Can you believe it? What's more, even bigger, is that Hollywood is showing some interest."

I gaped. "Hollywood? Hollywood, as in California?"

Ed gave me an odd look. "Well, sure, where else? You know, movies, TV. I mean, somebody down there called *Mr. Ed* a *project.*"

A reclamation project, I thought in my uncharitable way. But I tried to smile with some enthusiasm.

Ed, however, needed no encouragement. "Down there, in Hollywood—California— when they talk about a *project*, it's practically a done deal. The book's sold almost ten thousand copies in hardcover, and Vane Press goes back for a run of five thousand more next week. Since the book's only been out two months, it's considered a runaway best-seller in the industry."

I didn't know enough about book publishing to comment. Maybe ten thousand copies in hardcover was a substantial number. But I did know that Vane Press, located in Redmond on Seattle's Eastside, was a vanity publishing house, and that Ed had assumed all the expenses of getting his autobiography on the market.

"Do you have a name of the Hollywood type who's interested?" I asked, reluctantly thinking that maybe we could squeeze four or five lines into this week's edition.

Ed shook his head. "The guys at Vane are the contact. They're handling the subrights and all that other stuff for me. They don't want to say anything until the project is further along. But Skip O'Shea and Irving Blomberg both tell me is that what sells *Mr. Ed* is it's so *fresh*. Oh, there've been a zillion autobiographies lately that have done well, like Walter Cronkite's and Cal Ripken Jr.'s and a bunch of others, but none of them have a story like mine. I mean, rags-to-riches isn't new, but as Skip and Irv point out, I got that way by doing absolutely nothing."

I looked puzzled while Ed seemed very proud of himself. "Yes," I said slowly. "You did. Get that way. By doing nothing." I nodded a couple of times. "That's your style, Ed."

The irony was lost on my former ad manager. "Will you run any pix? I sent you that new one last month of Shirl and me in the trophy room."

The trophy room was where Ed kept his three bowling awards and the first putter he'd used to break a hundred. "I don't have room for a picture this time around," I said truthfully. "We're pretty tight, with the Rasmussen murder."

"Oh, yeah, that. I played golf once with Einar." Ed stroked his chins. "That was a real shame."

"Yes, it was," I said, not sure if he referred to his game or the murder. "Einar was a staunch supporter of the community, at least of the new college."

"Huh?" Ed hadn't seemed to hear me. "Oh—yeah, right." He pivoted on his Guccis. "I meant it was a shame because it really upset Birgitta. I guess she didn't think that a little place like Alpine would have violence like they do in the big city. She said none of the *Advocates* we sent to help her get acquainted with the area had any murders in them. 'Course those were issues from last fall and winter, when things were quiet around here. Now she feels like we duped her, and has been threatening all day to go back to Sweden."

"Will she?" I was starting to twitch a bit in my anxiety to get to Kip in the back shop.

Ed screwed up his suetlike features. "I don't know. Probably not. I mean, we've got a contract and all. Shirl and I figure she'll get over it. By the way, if you use Shirley's name in the article on *Mr. Ed*, make sure it's spelled right. Last time Carla called her Swirley."

"I'll watch it," I said, edging for the door. "I'd better dash, Ed, or your story won't make it into tomorrow's edition."

Ed seemed to recall the exigencies of a deadline, at least when his own ego was involved. He meandered away in his Guccis while I went into the back shop. Kip and I decided we could squeeze Ed's item onto page four if we cut the last graf in Carla's feature about DeeDee and Amer Wasco's trip to Europe. The lines were expendable, since they dealt with the Wascos' cheese purchases in the Netherlands.

"Too much of a Gouda thing?" Kip said, grinning.

I was glad he still had a sense of humor. These days, I wasn't sure that I did.

★   ★   ★

Carla kept to her bed the following day, so I decided to use the customary Wednesday lull to talk to the Bourgettes. I was interested in finding out why anyone thought there might be more gold buried under the old warehouse.

I found the brothers at the restaurant site, with Dan running some kind of digging apparatus. "You're really moving along," I remarked to John, who'd been studying a bunch of blueprints. I had to shout to make myself heard over the sound of the tractor.

John smiled, then wiped his brow with his sleeve. "We have to, since we'll be doing most of the work ourselves. Dad may pitch in, now that his job at the college has wound down."

I nodded. We were standing on Old Mill Street, with our backs to the railroad tracks. Now that virtually all remnants from the warehouse had been cleared away, I could see the Skykomish River less than a hundred yards away, and River Road winding through the trees on the far bank. On this overcast morning in May, the Sky flowed at an unruffled pace in this part of the river, but its color was off. The murky brown current might have been caused by the recent rain, or perhaps someone was actually logging farther up, near the source.

I gestured at the old loading dock which stood between the future restaurant site and Alpine Way. "Is that part of the parcel?"

"No." John lowered his voice as Dan shut off the tractor. "Burlington Northern turned it over to the city along with the warehouse, but Mayor Baugh wanted to keep it in case they ever widen Alpine Way and need right-of-way."

I made a note on my steno pad. "So who's getting the gold? The nuggets in the steel chest, that is."

John grimaced. "Mayor Baugh is playing hardball. He says it belongs to the city. Maybe he's got a point. It was found last fall, before we bought the land."

"That's true." I paused as Dan gave me a friendly wave, then started up the tractor again. "What," I asked, raising my voice, "did those trespassers expect to find?"

"More gold," John replied. "We've gone over the surface pretty thoroughly, though, and haven't turned up anything more interesting than some old tools."

"It must have been a onetime stash," I said, thinking that I should interview the assayer, Sandy Clay.

"There were gold and silver mines here in the

old days," John said. "But you must know that."

"Yes. They attracted all kinds of people, including some of the Japanese and Korean railroad workers."

John's broad forehead creased in a frown. "I thought the railroad workers were mostly Chinese."

"They were at first," I explained. "But some kind of legislation was in force for a while which prevented them from working on the railroads. That's when they brought in other Asians, mostly Japanese. Alpine was known as Nippon back then before the turn of the century, and there was a whistle-stop up the line called Corea. With a *C*, the old-fashioned way."

"Interesting," John said, and looked as if he really thought it was.

Dan stopped the tractor again and jumped down from the operator's seat. I thought he was coming over to join us, but instead, he knelt down to scramble around in the dirt.

John had his back to his brother. "We're bringing a trailer in here as an office, so we thought maybe one of us could spend the night and keep watch," he said. "Maybe we won't have to. Those signs might do the job." He

pointed to the half-dozen NO TRESPASSING—
PRIVATE PROPERTY—KEEP OUT signs that
ringed the site.

"John?" Dan's voice sounded uncertain.
"Take a look, will you?"

I hesitated, then followed John to the spot
where Dan was kneeling in the overturned
dirt. It had a damp smell, the scent of age and
the nearby river.

"What the . . . ?" John bent down. I could
see four charred bones, one larger than a turkey
leg.

"Dogs?" Dan said, taking off his glasses and
rubbing at one eye. "Burying bones, somehow.
What do you think?"

Dan stood up and grabbed a shovel. "Could
be. But this one looks like a rib." He jabbed at
a curving fragment with his steel-toed boot.
"I'm not talking beef or pork ribs, either. I
took anatomy in college, remember?"

"What are you saying?" Dan asked, sounding
breathless.

"I'm not sure." John plied the shovel. He un-
earthed several small bones that looked suspiciously like vertebrae. "Holy Mother," he
whispered. "What's this?"

I thought he already knew. But I said it anyway: "I think you and Dan have found a human being."

Chapter Seven

I WAS PAINFULLY reminded of finding similar remains in the basement of an old house in Port
Angeles a few years earlier. The house had belonged to the daughter and son-in-law of my
old friend Mavis Marley Fulkerston, and the
bones had belonged to a woman who had met
an untimely end. Though Jackie and Paul
Melcher had helped solve the eighty-year-old
murder, that gruesome discovery still haunted
me. Now, at the old warehouse site, I felt a
sense of déjà vu and wandered off several yards
before the Bourgettes noticed that I had been
affected by their discovery.

"Are you okay, Ms. Lord?" John asked, his
manner full of concern.

I gave him a weak smile. "I'm fine. I think.
Are you?"

He mopped his brow again. "I don't know.
This is pretty damned creepy." John put a hand
on his brother's shoulder. "Danny?"

Dan Bourgette was still staring at the bones.
"Maybe this was an Indian burial ground at
some point," he finally said after a long,
thoughtful pause.

That was a possibility, but only marginally comforting, given the alternatives. "If it is, would you have to stop digging?"

John and Dan gazed at each other, their faces showing bewilderment. "I'm not sure how that works," John finally said. "We'd have to get hold of somebody from whichever tribe it would be, and as far as I know, there aren't many Native Americans left in Skykomish County."

I knew about the Wenatchis, but they had lived on the other side of the pass. Regrettably, I could name only a few of the other tribes who might have laid a claim to the area around Alpine.

"What should we do?" Dan asked his brother. "Keep digging to find more bones, or call the Sheriff?"

The brothers agreed that alerting Milo was the best solution. I felt I should stay, but wasn't keen on confronting the Sheriff again. Maybe he'd send a deputy.

But five minutes after John had called the Sheriff's headquarters, Milo drove up in his Cherokee Chief. He looked about as happy to see me as I was to see him.

The Sheriff dealt with my presence by pretending that I wasn't there. "John? Dan? More nuggets?"

"Afraid not, Sheriff," John replied. "Take a look."

Milo looked, bending down in silence, almost as if he were at prayer. I knew better; Milo's religion is fishing, and the only time I've known him to pray is when he's trying to catch a steelhead.

"They look like human remains, all right, " he said, straightening up. "I'll bag what you've got and send it to the lab. I'm no expert, but I'd guess these bones have been here a while. Keep digging. If you collect any more fragments, put them in a bag for us."

"What if it's an Indian burial ground?" Dan seemed disturbed by the possibility.

Milo, however, shook his head. "I doubt it. I was born and raised here, and I never heard of any Indian burial ground. If there had been, somebody would have raised a ruckus a long time ago."

"So what do you think, Sheriff?" Milo's assurances hadn't wiped away Dan's worried expression.

Milo shrugged. "Who knows? My best guess is that since the warehouse was next to the train tracks, some hobo jumped off a freight, hid out, and OD'd on white lightning."

Relief flooded Dan's face, and John managed

a smile. "That makes sense," John asserted, then put out his hand. "Thanks, Sheriff."

As Milo headed to the Cherokee Chief to get an evidence bag, I followed him. "What if you're wrong?" I asked, trying to keep up with his long, loping strides.

He barely turned to look at me. "Then I'm wrong. Why do you care? Your paper's already out this week."

The comment rankled. John and Dan's discovery wouldn't be as old as the bones they'd dug up, but it would certainly be stale by the time the news was published in *The Advocate*.

"Maybe you'll have some answers by next week's edition," I said, acid coating my words.

Milo opened the rear of his vehicle and took out a big plastic evidence bag. "Maybe I will. Don't expect me to call if I do." He loped back to the Bourgettes.

I'd seen enough of the Sheriff. With a shout and a wave, I bade the Bourgettes farewell and got into my old Jag. Five minutes later the car was back in its usual place by *The Advocate*, and I was on the third floor of the Clemans Building, where Sandford Clay holds forth as an assayer and appraiser.

Sandy was already occupied. As I entered the small, jumbled office the assayer was talking to a thin-faced Japanese-American man in his thirties who I recognized as Scott Kuramoto, a part-time math instructor at the college.

"Emma!" Sandy's parchmentlike skin stretched into a grin. "To what do I owe this honor? I haven't seen you up here since you brought in your aunt's 1908 British gold crown."

"It was my grandfather's," I replied, "but you're right. How are you, Sandy? And you, Scott? I'm Emma Lord from the newspaper, and I'm not sure we've been formally intro- duced." I held out my hand.

Scott shook it somewhat diffidently. "I've seen you around town," he said in a soft voice. "You work for Mrs. Runkel."

I grimaced. "Actually, it's the other way around. But an easy mistake to make." And not an uncommon one. "Vida exudes authority."

Sandy, who wears small, rectangular glasses with wire rims and very thick lenses, chuckled. "That she does, Emma. That she does." Abruptly, he frowned. "I don't understand why Vida wasn't more interested in our little mys- tery. It's not like her to be uncurious."

I drew back a bit and stared. "It's not. What little mystery are you talking about?"

Sandy lifted a chamois cloth from a battered metal chest. I knew immediately what he was talking about. But I was still puzzled. "Is this the chest the firefighters found? You say Vida wasn't interested?"

Sandy gave a nod. "That's what I heard. What's her name? Carla? She said it was old news, and nobody at the paper, Vida included, would bother writing about it."

Delicate condition or not, I felt like kicking Carla. "When did she tell you this?"

"Um . . ." Sandy scratched his bald head. "Last fall? That's right, it was just before Thanksgiving, about a month after the fire."

I could imagine Carla, lost in the fresh haze of a new love, not wanting to bother passing on an item she wasn't interested in covering. "What was the information?" I asked, still envisioning my foot planted in Carla's backside.

"This." Sandy tapped the box. "Scott here and I were just checking it out before we turn it over to Mayor Baugh. He wants to use the nuggets to finance a petting zoo by the Overholt farm."

It wasn't the worst idea I'd ever heard, but it came close. "How much? Did someone say the nuggets were worth three hundred grand?"

Again, Sandy nodded once. "Approximately. That's the value I appraised them at. But the thing is, I hate to hand the nuggets over to Fuzzy until we've exhausted all possibilities of finding the rightful owner."

Scott made a lithe movement with one hand, lifting the lid of the metal chest. The nuggets were there, not glittering like pirate loot on a movie set, but dull and lumpy and unimpressive. Only when Scott stepped back out of the direct light could I see a gleam or two of precious metal.

"Sandy asked me to take another look today," Scott explained in that soft, soothing voice. "All I can find is the name Yoshida." He indicated some Japanese characters on the side of the chest. "It could be a first name, it could be a last name. Frankly, it's not much to go on, especially not after all this time."

"How old do you think the chest is?" I asked.

"I can pinpoint it to the turn of the century," Sandy replied, "give or take a few years. It's a McFarland case, and they went out of business in 1906. But there's no trademark on it, just the name, which means it was probably manufactured before 1900, when the government tightened up regulations requiring the publication of patent registrations."

I felt myself blanch. What if there was a connection between the chest and the bones at the warehouse site? What if the chest and its treasure of nuggets had been the downfall of those old bones? I started to tell Sandy and Scott about the Bourgettes' discovery, then thought better of it. There was not yet any official word on whether the fragments belonged to a human being. If I couldn't print the story right away, I certainly wasn't going to spread rumors.

"Who actually found the chest?" I asked as Sandy lowered the lid.

"Um . . . one of the volunteer firefighters. Which one?" He gazed at Scott, hoping for an answer.

"Pat Dugan," Scott answered. Then, though I didn't need elucidating, he added, "Pat teaches part-time at the college, too. That's how I know. He was kind of excited. It was his first fire after he joined up as a volunteer."

I'd seen Pat at Mass, accompanied by a pretty, dark-haired young woman who I assumed was his wife. We had never met, but Father Den had pointed Pat out to me one Sunday and identified him as one of the part-timers at SkyCoCo.

"Is there some way you could advertise?" I inquired, dismissing Pat Dugan from my mind. "You know—a blind ad in *The Advocate* and the other area papers to anyone named Yoshida, saying you have something of interest for him. Or her."

Sandy rolled his eyes behind the heavy lenses. "I thought of that. But there must be thirty Yoshidas in the Seattle directory alone. We'd have a stampede on our hands, Emma. And how could any one of them prove the gold was theirs? Whoever mined those nuggets has probably been dead for one heck of a long time."

I thought of the bones, and guessed that Sandy was right.

Vida was in a snit. "Really! So rude! I'm not sending flowers or a memorial or any such thing to Einar's funeral! Marlys has no manners!"

"What," I asked, barely inside the door of the news office, "did she do—or didn't do—now?"

Vida set her chin on her hands. "She won't even come to the phone. Neither will Beau, the so-called genius son. And it wasn't Gladys Rasmussen who answered, but the daughter, Deirdre. I thought she lived in Mountlake Terrace."

"Maybe she does, maybe she's here because her father died," I said mildly.

But Vida shook her head. "No. She's not in the most recent phone book for the north Seattle suburbs. I checked. She's divorced, so I looked under both Rasmussen and her married name, Nichols. In fact, I checked all the directories west of the Cascades and north of Olympia. No Deirdre of any kind. So I must conclude that she moved in with her parents."

"Or a man." Leo spoke up, having just gotten off the phone. "That's what I'd figure, Duchess."

"You would," Vida snapped. "And don't call me Duchess. You know how I despise nick-names."

With Brad tugging at her slacks, Ginny came through the door to check the coffeepot. "I almost forgot, Emma. That Swedish girl who works for Ed and Shirley came by a few minutes ago to see you. I asked her to wait, but she wouldn't. I think she was upset about something."

"Birgitta?" We'd run a brief story on her in the latest edition, but it hadn't quite yet hit the streets. "If she really needs to see me, she'll come back." I took in the presence of three of my five regular staffers and decided to confide in them about the bones. Ginny looked horrified, Leo seemed bemused, and Vida chewed at her lower lip.

"Human, apparently?" She saw me nod. "It's quite clear, isn't it? Someone was killed over the gold that was found in that chest. If ever murder and motive were linked, there it is."

Leo demurred. "So why was the gold with the victim and not the killer?"

"Fear," Vida said promptly. "Someone was

coming into the warehouse. The killer had to run off and leave the gold."

"And never came back?" Leo was justifiably skeptical.

Vida, however, was undaunted. "Perhaps the killer was also killed. Violent people often meet violent ends."

"When," I asked of Vida, who ought to know, "was the warehouse built?"

"Oh—let me think—in the Twenties, before I was born. It had to be then," she added, "because until a few years after World War One, the only major buildings in Alpine were the mill and the social hall."

I knew she was right. I had a framed photograph in my office of the entire population of Alpine standing on the loading dock, with a huge American flag. They had won it for selling more Liberty Bonds per capita than any other city or town in the state. The residents' pride practically blistered the glass on the picture. But there was no warehouse next to the platform.

"Then nobody was killed in the warehouse because it didn't exist." I explained about Sandy Clay and Scott Kuramoto's research.

Vida made a steeple of her fingers. "Nothing was here at the turn of the century," she said.

"Alpine was Nippon then, and only a whistle-stop on the new Great Northern line."

"But there were mines," I pointed out.

"Yes, but no dwellings. Unless," Vida noted, "you count tents. They probably had tents."

"You're going to read up on all this, right?"

Vida sat up very straight, thrusting her bust. "Of course! Are you calling me dilatory?"

"No." I grinned. "Never that. But now you have a starting place for your research."

Vida looked somewhat appeased. Ginny removed Brad from the lower drawer of a filing cabinet, Leo returned to the telephone, and I went into my office. Half an hour later Ed called. He'd just received his issue of *The Advocate*.

"Six lines on page *four?*" Ed cried. "You buried me, Emma! What's happened to your nose for news?"

"It fell off," I retorted. "Ed, you showed up right at five. You know how tough it is getting an item in the paper after the issue's been sent to the back shop."

"What about page one? What about giving me more space?" he complained. "You could have moved the new bridge story back inside. You're always running a new bridge story. You could have jumped the piece on Einar. The guy didn't even live up here until a few years ago. And what about this picture with Einar's feet sticking out from behind Milo and Jack? Isn't that kind of ghoulish?"

It probably was. If I hadn't been mad at Milo, I might not have run such a shot. But I wouldn't admit that to Ed. "It's news, Ed. That's how it works. You were in advertising, remember? You didn't do news. Not then, not now."

"But I know readership," he countered. "Believe me, Emma," he went on, his tone darkening, "you'll hear about this from other subscribers."

"I'll wait. Look, Ed, when you have more on the Hollywood deal, we'll definitely put it on page one, okay?" I didn't wait for his response. "And by the way, I understand Birgitta came to see me a while ago. Is she around?" I might as well use the au pair girl as a means of getting rid of Ed.

"Huh?" There was a pause at Ed's end of the line. "Birgitta? Hey, Shirl—is Gitty here?"

Shirley's response was indecipherable, so I waited for Ed. "Nope, she's out. She had some errands to run for us. I needed shoelaces and Shirl was out of Band-Aids."

Though it wasn't easy, I refrained from saying anything snide. My priority was getting Ed off the line before he started complaining again.

Somehow, I managed. As I replaced the receiver Vida entered the office, still looking disgruntled.

My earlier misinterpreted remarks weren't the cause of her annoyance, however. "Edna Mae Dalrymple just called from the library. She's volunteered to do a story on Thyra Rasmussen."

"What?"

"You heard me." Vida remained standing. "Edna Mae has been in touch with Thyra in Snohomish. The old bag has quite a collection of . . . well, a collection. Edna Mae has been extending her search for library exhibits to Snohomish County, since she claims to have run out of items from Skykomish County to show off in her tawdry little display case. Of course that's partly because Edna Mae has the imagination of a cedar stump. Now it seems that with Einar's murder, Edna Mae suddenly thinks she's a *journalist*, for heaven's sake, and wants to write the story for next week's paper, because, as she put it in that twittery little voice of hers that sounds like a dyspeptic chickadee, 'Anything about the Rasmussens has extra news value.'" She made a disgusted face, but her mimicry of Edna Mae was dead on.

I, too, reacted with displeasure, but for a different reason. Every once in a while, we have a guest writer or columnist. Usually, it's an expert from the national parks, the fish hatchery, or the forest service. But once in a while we find someone who is semiliterate and can produce an article that doesn't require an editorial hatchet job. In fact, Edna Mae had done a creditable job a couple of years back on how young people could and should use the public library. Putting all these rational facts aside, I demanded to know why Edna Mae hadn't called *me*.

Vida's mouth twitched. "You were on the other line."

"So?" Noting that Vida's mouth still twitched, I clapped a hand to my head. "Edna Mae told you about the small scene with Milo, right? Damn it—darn it—was she afraid I'd yell at her, too?"

"I believe," Vida said, now composing her face into a typical owlish expression, "she did mention the word *uncouth*."

"Rats!" I was having trouble not being uncouth in front of Vida. "To heck with it. What did you tell her about the story?"

"Why, that I'd check with you, naturally." Vida's innocence was overdone.

I slumped in my chair. "What's the peg? Besides Einar getting murdered, that is."

"It's a bribe," Vida responded, her tone and manner more natural. "Frankly, I think the

story would be in poor taste under any circumstances so soon after Einar's death. But apparently Edna Mae wants to write about Thyra
to coax the old bat into loaning her gewgaws to
the library. I didn't hold out much hope for
publication."

I agreed with Vida. No matter how tactful the
slant, it was impossible to run any kind of story
about the Rasmussen family that didn't deal
with their recent tragedy.

"Edna Mae will have to come up with some
other plan to coerce Mrs. Rasmussen," I said,
then added as an afterthought, "How long has
she been needling the old girl?"

"Months," Vida replied. "Edna Mae is many
things—and also isn't—but she's not a ghoul.
Nor am I surprised that Thyra isn't willing to
part, even temporarily, with her so-called collection. The wretched woman has always been
incredibly selfish and given to material excess."

While Vida tends to be critical of people in
general, her attitude toward Thyra Rasmussen
struck me as particularly harsh. I made no comment, however, but though I knew the answer,
I asked if she intended to go to the funeral.

"Certainly. Just because I refuse to send flowers doesn't mean I won't attend the services.
Someone has to cover them," Vida responded,

obviously preserving funerals for her part of the paper. "Are you going?" She looked somewhat dubious.

"I'm not sure," I answered, then fingered the phone. "I suppose I should call to see if the autopsy report came through. Not that we're in any rush, since the paper's already out."

"I can call," Vida volunteered.

It was a tempting offer, but I had to keep on top of the news story. "I'll wait until later this afternoon," I said. Maybe Milo would be gone by then.

Vida returned to her desk and I started cleaning my in-basket with its usual accumulation of news releases, press handouts, and sales pitches. Ten minutes later Birgitta Lindholm stepped warily into my office. Her impressive stature, her long, golden hair, and the glow from her well-scrubbed skin seemed to overwhelm my dingy little cubbyhole.

"Ms. Lindholm," I said, rising to greet her and feeling short, dumpy, and rumpled, "I heard you came by earlier. How can I help you?"

"You *may*," she said, indicating her English grammar was better than mine, "help me by permitting to read your newspapers of old."

The grammar illusion was dispelled, though

not her height, youth, or beauty. "You mean back issues? Earlier editions?" I searched for the proper phrase.

"From the past, yes." She nodded gravely.

I resumed my seat, and indicated that Birgitta should sit, too. She didn't. "How far into the past?" I asked.

"I'm not certain." The glacier-blue eyes roamed around my cubbyhole. I thought she exuded distaste for the meanness and clutter. "Where may I do this? When?"

I shrugged. "Now, if you like. The bound volumes are out in the news office. They go back to the original paper, *The Alpine Blabber*. It wasn't put out on a regular basis, but began publishing around 1916. We also have copies of the Alpine yearbook, which began somewhat earlier." The yearbook was primarily the work of Carl Clemans, and included not only major happenings in Alpine, but the annual Thanksgiving Day dinner menu, hosted by the Alpine Logging Company.

Birgitta, however, was frowning. "How earlier?"

"What? Oh—the yearbook. Um . . . I think the first one came out in 1911."

The frown deepened, then the au pair girl shook her head. "No, that will not suffice." She turned away. "Thank you all the same."

"Wait!" I called after her, getting back on my feet. "There are other papers, at the library. They keep some of the publications from Sky-komish and Snohomish and Sultan. I think at least some of them go back to the turn of the century."

Birgitta glanced over her shoulder. "The li-brary. That is good. Yes. Thank you."

She left, no longer wary. But I was still short, dumpy, and rumpled.

Dwight Gould answered when I called the Sheriff's office around four-thirty. The ME's report had just come in from Everett. Milo was out on a call and hadn't yet seen it. Dwight didn't feel right about releasing any informa-tion until his superior had digested it first. The deputy was mildly apologetic, but firm.

With no deadline looming, I didn't argue. I was about to call and check on Carla when I heard a woman arguing with Vida in the other office. I didn't recognize the newcomer's voice, so I stepped to the doorway to get a discreet peek.

"Look," the woman was saying in a husky, ragged voice that should have inhabited a body much older than what appeared to be some thirty-odd years, "I don't give a damn what you do with this thing, but my grandmother insists you run it." She was waving a manila envelope at my House & Home editor.

"That's not the point," Vida asserted. "We ran a picture of your father today, a formal portrait taken quite recently. Indeed, I suspect it's the same one you have in that envelope."

"It's not," said the woman, who I guessed was Deirdre Rasmussen. "It's different. He had it taken in Seattle."

I had almost sidled up to Vida's desk when both women noticed my presence. "Emma," said Vida, "this is Deirdre Rasmussen Nichols, Einar Jr.'s daughter."

"Deirdre Rasmussen will do fine," the woman said, holding out what I perceived to be a grudging hand. "I took my maiden name back when I got my divorce from Jerk-off."

"I see." I smiled, somewhat feebly. "Let's see the photo, Ms. Rasmussen."

"Deirdre will do fine." She opened the envelope clasp and slipped out an eight-by-ten color portrait. "See? This is much better than that stuffed-shirt shot you ran in your paper today."

That was debatable. Einar Rasmussen Jr. was posed kneeling by a large tree. He was wearing a dark green cardigan, white shirt, and striped tie. Next to him lay a large collie dog with its tongue hanging out. The shot was meant to convey warmth and devotion and all sorts of fuzzy, nice feelings, but my reaction was that the hand Einar Jr. had placed on the dog's neck contained an electric-shock device. Einar was smiling, but he looked far from benign.

"Impressive," I remarked, handing back the photograph. "Vida's right. We've already run a head shot. If you want, you could take out a memorial ad and then we could run this picture, too."

Deirdre recoiled as if I, too, had an electric-shock device in my power. "What? You mean *pay* to run the photo? Are you nuts?"

"That's what people do with ads," I said, my face expressionless. "Pay for them."

"Screw it. I already bought a classified ad for Fluff. Our cat got lost. Again." Deirdre tossed her head, causing the late-afternoon sun to highlight the red glints in her dark blonde hair. "Grandmama can stick it in her . . ." She caught Vida's glare and made a face. "Oh, hell, she might buy the damned ad. Grandmama likes to show off."

"Keep us advised," said Vida. "By the way—" She pursed her lips. "How is your dear mother?"

Deirdre's hazel eyes flickered. "Fine."

"Fine?" Vida appeared shocked. "How unusual!"

"Mom doesn't show her emotions much,"

Deirdre said. She was taller than average, heavier than she probably wanted to be, and her potentially pretty face was made up all wrong, as if she were in a decade-long time warp. I hadn't seen so much blue eye shadow since the Gabor sisters. "Mom keeps things to herself," she added, and looked away.

"And Beau?" Vida now wore a semismile.

"Beau's okay." Deirdre still didn't look at either of us, but seemed transfixed by Carla's empty chair.

Vida gave a single nod. "Then we'll be seeing you all at the funeral in Snohomish."

"Sure." Deirdre's eyes now strayed to Leo's desk. My ad manager was gone for the day, but he'd left an almost empty pack of cigarettes by his phone. Deirdre looked as if she'd like to smoke the remnants all at once.

Her anxious gaze gave me an idea. "I was just heading out. How about a drink at the Venison Inn?"

Somewhat to my surprise, Deirdre looked grateful. "Why not? I'm in no hurry. Thanks . . . Emma, right?"

Vida was miffed. She knew that her disapproval of alcoholic beverages in general and bars in particular excluded her from the invitation. Five minutes later Deirdre and I were turning into the local watering hole on Front Street.

The place was already filling up with the after-work regulars. We sat at a table next to a trio of youngish bearded men in plaid work shirts and canvas pants who gave Deirdre the eye. She ignored them, and saved whatever charm she possessed for Oren Rhodes, the bartender.

"You're not a native," Deirdre said in that husky voice after Oren had taken our orders.

I laughed. "I'm originally from Seattle, by way of Portland. How could you tell?"

Deirdre shrugged. "I don't know. You just don't seem small-town." She let out a big sigh as her gaze traveled to the lighted cigarette machine next to a life-sized cutout of a mini-skirted redhead holding a tray of beer. "I've spent my whole life trying to get away from small towns. I never seem to make it. Mountlake Terrace was as close as I got to the Big City."

Mountlake Terrace was a suburb north of Seattle, close enough that it was impossible to tell where the city stopped and the 'burbs began. Apparently it wasn't close enough for Deirdre Rasmussen.

"I didn't want to come back up here," she

continued with no prompting from me. "But Dad thought I needed to pull myself together after the divorce. That was bull. It was Davin going off that threw me."

"Davin was your husband?" I asked. "I thought his name was Jerk-off."

Deirdre smiled, revealing a single dimple in her right cheek. "His name *is* Jerk-off. I didn't care about him. Davin's my son." She lowered her eyes.

"Oh." My mother's heart melted. "How old?"

"Seventeen, last month. Of course he wasn't around for the party I'd have given him. He left Christmas Eve." Her face crumpled; even the blue eye shadow seemed to slip.

I remembered Adam at seventeen. It wasn't a good age, not for a boy. Too much to prove, unsure of struggling in that cleft between boy and man. My son had wanted to be everything, and felt like nothing. It was an age on the cusp, and very dangerous.

"Do you know where Davin is?" I asked, waiting until after Oren had delivered Deirdre's vodka martini and my bourbon and water.

"No." Deirdre didn't look up, but took a deep sip from her glass. She sipped again, and finally her hazel eyes seemed to bore into my face. "Dad knew. But he wouldn't tell me."

"Why not?"

Deirdre drank again. "Because my father was the biggest prick in the world. He's the reason Davin ran away." Her expression was bleak, like a January dawn. "Who could blame me for hating my father?"

I felt my eyes widen. "Did you kill him?" The words tumbled out.

Deirdre blinked once. "No. But I wish I had." She finished the martini in one big, fierce gulp, and swallowed the olive whole.

Chapter Eight

EVERYBODY HAS A story to tell. Part of my job is to listen. But Deirdre Rasmussen didn't reveal anything else about her father, her son, or Jerk-off. The second martini didn't loosen her tongue; she closed up like a vacated house. It was if she'd had a statement to make, and having done it, details were irrelevant.

We sank into chitchat. The funeral arrangements, suburban living, the uncertain spring weather. I'd paid for the first round, but she bought the second. And then she took her leave, a graceless, yet vulnerable figure, making her way between the tiny round tables with flickering candles stuck in old mason jars.

I was now staring at the cigarette machine. I'd quit several times, once for five years. But the urge remained. I was still struggling with my inner demons when Leo sat down in the chair Deirdre had left empty.

"Drinking alone, boss lady? Bad idea." My ad manager shook his head in mock dismay.

I explained about Deirdre Rasmussen. Leo seemed mildly interested. "Nobody liked this Einar much, I take it."

"He sounds typical of many successful men," I replied as Oren Rhodes nodded at Leo, then looked inquiringly at me. Wisely, I decided to skip a third round. "They work their tails off to make money, they interact just fine with their peer group, but they stink when it comes to personal relationships."

Leo chuckled, somewhat ruefully. "Hey, I could qualify—except I've never been a success at much of anything."

"Don't say that, Leo," I said. "You've done a great job for me. I'll bet you did just fine for most of your other employers over the years."

"Yeah, maybe, except when I was drinking booze out of a two-gallon bucket under my desk." Leo sighed, then lighted a cigarette. "Since you brought it up, I might as well tell you."

"Tell me what?" Maybe Leo's arrival in the bar hadn't been coincidental. He'd probably returned to the office, where Vida had told him of my whereabouts.

"It's no big deal," he said, making a dismissive gesture with one hand. "I got a job offer this week. I was damned near tempted, but I've decided to say no."

"I'm relieved," I admitted. "My God, I can't lose two staffers in the same year!" Then, from some dark corner of my brain, apprehension surfaced. "What was the offer?"

Leo accepted his Scotch rocks from Oren, joshed a bit, and finally turned his attention back to me. "I don't know if you remember the guy who recommended me for *The Advocate*, but he just bought up some weeklies in Napa and Yolo counties, north and east of the Bay Area. He wanted me to oversee the advertising for all four of them." He exhaled, then spoke through a cloud of smoke. "Tom Cavanaugh. Remember?"

Remember. The problem was, I couldn't forget. "Sure," I said, sounding unnaturally chipper. I was fumbling in my handbag, my head ducking down under the table. "You got together with him a while back in Seattle, right?"

"Yeah. He talked then about the possible acquisitions, trying to get a feel whether or not I'd be interested in coming back to California," Leo said, his voice normal, neither curious nor suspicious. "You looking for a cigarette?"

"No." I was emphatic, overloud. "Were you interested?" I sat up straight, having caught my breath and gotten a grip on my composure. Still, my eyes strayed to Oren Rhodes behind the bar.

Leo grimaced. "As I said, I was tempted. The money was better. No offense." My ad manager gave me a rueful smile, then acknowledged two of our advertisers, Scooter Hutchins and Lloyd Campbell. "But I'm not ready to go back to California," he went on as Scooter and Lloyd sat down at a table behind us. "I'm going to call Cavanaugh tonight and let him know."

"He called from San Francisco?" I hoped the question sounded innocent.

"Yeah, Monday night." Leo sighed and stubbed out his cigarette. "I've given it almost forty-eight hours. It doesn't feel right. But I thought you ought to know."

"I appreciate it." I winced as Oren, interpreting my glance as a request for a refill, appeared with another bourbon. Meekly, I thanked him. "It doesn't seem like a good time to be buying up weeklies," I said to Leo. "The newspaper business isn't very good these days."

"Northern California's growing," Leo explained. "People moving up from L.A., newcomers who want to live in the state, but avoid earthquakes and riots and brushfires and mud slides. Cavanaugh's got a good business head, and plenty of money. Besides," Leo added, lighting another cigarette, "he doesn't have anything else to do with his time since his wife died."

I lost it. The full glass went flying onto the floor, my mouth dropped open, and I think I actually let out a small scream. Or maybe it was a groan. Leo stared, and so did Scooter, Lloyd, and the three workingmen at the next table.

"Emma!" Leo gaped at me, then grabbed my wrist. Oren Rhodes hurried over to collect the glass, which, fortunately, hadn't broken. The bartender volunteered to mop up the spill while I sat mutely in the chair and shook all over.

"What the hell . . . ?" Leo was still holding on to me, now looking more worried than startled. "Hey, come on, tell me . . ." He gave a shake of his head, as if he were trying to come out of a bad dream.

But the bad dream was mine. "I'm okay," I said thickly as Oren swiped away at the carpet. "Can we get out of here?"

"Sure." Leo let go of my wrist, gulped down the rest of his drink, and tossed a twenty-dollar bill on the table. "Let's go." With a protective arm around my shoulders, he called a thank-you to Oren and hustled me out of the bar.

It had begun to rain while we were in the Venison Inn. Soft, sparse drops fell from darkening clouds that had settled over the mountains. The cool damp air cleared my head as we walked the short block to our cars, which were parked in front of *The Advocate*. Leo said nothing until we reached his Toyota.

"Where to?" he asked, his face still masked with concern.

I wanted to go home. I wanted to call Ben. I needed to talk to Adam. But I owed Leo an overdue explanation. His apartment on Cedar Street was only three blocks away. I could drive that far without killing myself or anyone else. Maybe.

Leo didn't agree. "I'll drive you to my place," he said, opening the door on the Toyota's passenger side. "We can come back later and collect the Jag."

I hadn't been in Leo's apartment for some time. It was an older two-story building with a bleak brick exterior and an entry hall that hadn't yet been swept clean of its autumn leaves. But since my last visit to his second-floor unit, my ad manager had made some improvements. He'd painted the walls, added some decent furniture, and installed an elaborate stereo system. The small living room conveyed a sense of comfort which had been markedly lacking a couple of years earlier.

"I should have guessed," he said, after I was seated on the blue fabric-covered couch and he'd started up the coffeemaker, "that you knew Cavanaugh. You asked if he'd called from San Francisco."

The whole story came out, the fatal meeting

at *The Seattle Times*, where I was a student intern and Tom was a copy editor, Tom's unhappy marriage to a wealthy but unstable woman, my pregnancy, her pregnancy, my flight to Mississippi, where Ben was working in the home missions, Adam's birth, and my pigheaded decision to keep Tom forever out of our lives.

"Then," I went on as the rain came down harder against the windows, "one day a year or so after I bought the paper, Tom showed up. It was strained at first, and I thought he only wanted to meet Adam. I finally allowed it, and they've been in contact ever since."

Leo's brown spaniel eyes were direct and not without sympathy. "What else did he want?"

"Oooh . . ." My hand flapped at the air. "Me, but just once, over at Lake Chelan, where there was a newspaper conference. We tried to make some other plans, but they always fell through, usually because of Sandra. He'd never leave her, though he said he would. Tom was riddled with guilt." I blinked several times at Leo. "Good God! I didn't ask you what happened to Sandra! You must think I'm one selfish bitch."

Leo patted my knee. "One upset little kitten. Actually, I'm not sure. I think she may have OD'd on all that medicine she took. The only times I ever saw her—twice, maybe—she was pretty cranked up on something. But Tom rarely talked about her."

I felt sick. "OD'd?" I could picture Tom, in the hillside mansion I'd always envisioned, finding his wife lying on the elegant bathroom tiles. "An accident?" Sandra was known to threaten suicide.

"I don't know." Leo shrugged. "As I said, Tom kept that stuff to himself."

"When?" Why hadn't Tom told me? Had he let Adam know?

"Ah . . ." Leo scanned the ceiling. "I think it was around the holidays. I only found out when he called Monday night."

The sense of nausea was beginning to pass. Five months ago. Maybe Tom was still grieving. Maybe he was in shock. Maybe he was ashamed.

"I wonder how their kids took it," I said. The last I'd heard of the Cavanaugh son and daughter, they were living away from home.

"I never met his kids," Leo remarked. "Did you?"

"No." I had started to shake my head, but stopped abruptly. "Yes. Adam. It's odd how nobody—including me—seems to remember that Adam is Tom's son."

Leo fell back against the couch cushions. "Hell, I should have guessed! He looks like

Cavanaugh! But I never . . ." Uttering a stunted little laugh, he shook his head.

"Call him now." My voice had an unfamiliar imperious ring.

"Now?" Leo regarded me curiously. "It's six o'clock, he might not be home."

"Where would he be?" I asked with bite. "On a date?"

Leo waved a hand. "He could be anywhere. He travels quite a bit. Hell, he owns papers all over the West, even British Columbia."

"Call him."

Leo started to resume his protests, then slumped against the armrest. "Okay. Why not?"

But Leo had judged correctly; Tom wasn't home. Only an answering-machine message came across the line. It was Tom's voice, and I shut my eyes as Leo held up the receiver and I heard the faint, familiar inflections.

"I'll call back later," Leo said, hanging up without leaving a message.

Neither of us spoke for a couple of minutes. The rain was splattering the old, wavy glass, and the light was dying in the west. Leo got up to fetch coffee. I didn't feel like drinking it, but hated to turn down the offer after my host's kindness.

"Don't do anything just yet," Leo cautioned,

handing me a mug which bore the logo of a California department-store chain.

"I didn't intend to," I replied stiffly.

"Yeah, you did." Leo chuckled and sat back down next to me. "Let me do a little detective work."

"Like what?" I was skeptical.

"Like where Cavanaugh is emotionally." Leo sipped his coffee. "Maybe he's nuts, too."

"Maybe he always was." I couldn't keep the edge out of my voice.

Leo didn't respond immediately. When he did, he turned around to stare into my face. "I've wondered who he was. I felt I was fighting a phantom."

"What are you talking about?"

"Adam's dad. My competition." He put both hands on his knees and wiggled his pinkie fingers. "There've been times when I thought you and I might have something going for us. But the minute I got a little bit close, you put up the 'No Vacancy' sign. Then that goofy Sheriff made off with you, at least for a while, and I couldn't figure it out. Dodge wasn't your type. He's about as exciting as garden mulch. Now it all makes sense."

"It does?"

"Sure." Leo took another drink of coffee.

None of it made any sense to me. It never had.

But oh, how I remembered.

Half an hour later after two cups of coffee and three cigarettes, I was capable of driving. I got home around seven, but wasn't hungry. Instead of eating, I called Ben in Tuba City.

My tale of woe evoked a laugh. Predictable brother, typical Ben. "You're a priest," I practically shouted. "You're supposed to comfort me."

"No, I'm not," Ben responded in the voice that always seemed to crackle around the edges. "You don't want comfort. You just want to talk about it and act like a love-crazed martyr. Hey, Sluggly," he continued, resurrecting his childhood nickname for me, "what would you do if Cavanaugh called right now and asked you to marry him?"

"I . . ." My hand strayed to the glass of Pepsi on the end table next to my sofa. "I don't know," I admitted.

"Of course not. Marriage would ruin it." Ben continued to sound quite jocular. "This is your greatest role. If I were a priest to the stars, I'd call it *Hopeless . . . and Damned Glad of It*."

"Drop dead, Ben."

"Hey—neither of us was suited for the married state. Haven't you figured that out by now? I can manage being celibate, so can you—most of the time. Why fight your single vocation?"

"Are you saying I should have been a nun?" The snarl in my voice wasn't pretty.

"No. You'd have made a crappy nun. You can't do math, so you couldn't have gone into medicine, you haven't the temperament to teach, you've got too much common sense to be a counselor—except when it comes to your own problems—and you won't shut up for more than two minutes at a time, which nixes a contemplative order. You're fine just as you are—single mother, career, independent, all that stuff. And once in a while you can beat yourself up over Tom Cavanaugh because somehow you think you should have been legally wed. Go ahead, wallow around for a couple of days. Then take up with some twenty-year-old stud from your new college campus. Or whatever. Sorry to give bad advice. But I know you, Sluggly. You like living out a romance novel. It adds panache."

"You're hateful," I asserted, but the words packed no punch. "Have you ever considered I might be lonely?"

"Who isn't?" Ben sounded wistful.

"Okay, I know, I'm sorry. Have you talked to Adam in the last few days?"

"No, not since just after the Ascension." It was typical of Ben to speak not in terms of dates, but feast days.

"That was almost two weeks ago," I noted. "Do you know if Adam had spoken with Tom recently?"

I was aware of Ben's hesitation. "Adam saw Tom in St. Paul a couple of days before Lent started."

I felt my face stiffen. "Did Adam know that Tom's wife had died?"

"I don't know."

Was Ben lying? Did priests ever lie? Of course they did. They were human. And Ben was more human than most. Or maybe that was because I knew him so well.

"You're lying," I said. "I can always tell. In fact, you're a lousy liar, Stench." I tacked on the old nickname for retaliation. "Why didn't you—or Adam—tell me?"

Ben sighed. "Tom asked Adam not to tell you. Not yet, anyway. He needed time."

"Time? The sonuvabitch has had twenty-five years!"

"During which time he was married to a woman who has recently died." Ben's voice was so dry that it not only crackled, but seemed to shred. "Come on, Sluggly, give the guy a break. I don't know what happened to Mrs. Cavanaugh—Adam didn't say, maybe he doesn't know, either—but whatever it was, you can be sure Tom is blaming himself. Haven't you told me he's got guilt etched on his manly chest?"

"Shut up." I had leaned back on the sofa, with a hand over my eyes. Of course Tom would feel guilty; of course he'd blame himself.

My doorbell rang. It was working again, after a long hiatus. Milo had fixed it. The Sheriff was good at such things. Irrelevantly, I wondered if Tom could fix doorbells.

"I've got to go," I said to Ben. "Someone's here."

"Okay. But whoever it is won't be riding a white horse," said my brother. "God bless, Sluggly." Ben rang off.

My caller had arrived in a white Chrysler LHS, which was parked in the driveway. Nat Cardenas was wearing not shiny armor, but a tan windbreaker over a pale yellow sport shirt and brown corduroy slacks. His usually aloof expression had been replaced with a self-deprecating smile.

"May I come in, Emma?" He placed one tentative foot on the threshold.

"Sure. Can I get you something to drink?" I waved at my glass of pop on the end table.

"No, thanks. I just ate dinner." Nat seated himself in one of my two matching armchairs. "I'm afraid I wasn't very helpful when you came to see me yesterday. I want to apologize. I was still very upset."

"That's understandable," I replied, my mind not quite focused on Nat, but still lingering over the phone conversation with Ben.

"You handled the college's part in this tragedy with great tact," Nat said, his black eyes level with mine. "I appreciate that. So does the rest of the faculty and staff."

Concentrating, I tried to remember exactly what I'd said about the college. Not much, which was probably why Nat had complimented me on my "great tact."

"At present, the college's role is incidental," I said. "Einar could have been murdered anywhere." It might not be true, but it sounded comforting.

"Of course," Nat agreed. "Though I still think he got caught in the middle of something. Attempted robbery, most likely." The college president paused, his finely etched mouth working slightly. "There's bound to be talk, there always is on a campus and in a small town. That's why I thought I should come to you before you hear a distortion of the facts."

"Talk about what?" Now I had completely zeroed in on the present.

Nat sighed and placed his hands together. "Einar Rasmussen Jr. and I didn't always see eye to eye. Don't take me wrong, he was a wonderful benefactor and his business advice was sound. But when it came to academic matters, he was . . . well, out of his depth."

"Ah," I remarked, more as a prod than in understanding.

"Einar was dead set against hiring two of our part-timers," Nat continued as darkness enveloped the room and I turned the three-way lamp up a notch. "There were some heated discussions at our private board meetings, and at least one of his fellow trustees went along with Einar. Fortunately, the other three followed my lead. In the fall, both instructors will become full-time faculty members."

"This is official?" I asked.

"It will be, at the next board-of-trustees meeting," Nat said, his gaze taking in my cozy living room with its stone fireplace and pine-log walls. "We hope to have word from the governor on a new appointment by then."

"I'll be there," I said, though Carla usually

covered the public sessions. "Which faculty are involved? Why did Einar oppose them?"

Nat hugged himself and laughed softly. "Small towns. They're always a hotbed of hostility and internecine rivalries. You may know the instructors. They're Scott Kuramoto and Pat Dugan."

I nodded. "I know Scott, but I've only seen Pat at Mass." It occurred to me that with a name like Cardenas, Nat might be Catholic, too. But I'd never seen him at St. Mildred's.

"Then you probably know why Einar didn't want Pat on the faculty," Nat said with a twitch of his lips.

I was ignorant. "Because of his religion?" I said, making a wild guess.

"No, no." Nat frowned. "I hope we're beyond that sort of thing, even in Alpine. It was because Pat's married to one of the Bourgette daughters, who, of course, is Einar's niece."

"Oh." I'd never made the connection between the Dugans and the Bourgettes, let alone the Rasmussens. "And Scott? Is he . . . ?" The query trailed off. I'd gotten the impression that Scott was single.

Nat hung his head. "Scott has been seeing Deirdre Rasmussen since her divorce. It strikes me as an odd pairing—he's a very serious young man, and she seems . . . well, a bit flighty. You never know about people, though, when it comes to romance."

No, you didn't. *Some people marry nuts.* "Why didn't Einar like Scott? Her first husband sounds kind of dismal, according to Deirdre."

Nat cleared his throat. "I mentioned that I hoped we were beyond religious prejudices. I'm afraid we haven't reached the same point when it comes to race. Einar didn't believe in intermarriage, if that's what you want to call it. He was, to put it plainly, a racist."

It shouldn't have surprised me. If Einar was typical of some Alpiners, intermarriage meant a Norwegian marrying a Swede. "I don't even know what Einar was."

"Danish," Nat replied, "and very proud of it. His family came from pure Danish stock, which he seemed to think gave him some sort of bragging rights."

"Did Deirdre marry a Dane the first time?" I didn't know that "Jerk-off" was a nationality. It had a universal ring to me.

"I don't know." Nat smiled, the brilliant public smile he flashed to woo supporters and benefactors. "I should get home. But I wanted you to hear about our little controversy before someone else told you and exaggerated it into a downright battle. It was nothing of the sort," he went on, getting to his feet. "Just a disagreement among the trustees which would eventually have been resolved in favor of Scott Kuramoto and Pat Dugan."

In other words, I thought, *not worth killing a man.*

Which, I guessed, was what Nat Cardenas wanted me to believe.

Chapter Nine

CARLA RETURNED TO work the next day, looking none the worse for her experience Monday night. I disliked calling her shallow, but the immaturity she often displayed may have protected her. Or perhaps it was the pregnancy. While expecting, women tend to isolate themselves from anything that occurs outside the womb.

That morning, Leo seemed to keep his eye on me, as if he anticipated another emotional outburst. I held back telling Vida about Sandra's death. I already knew what she'd say: now everything will work out, just give Tommy, as she called him, some time. Vida was usually so sensible, so hardheaded—except when it came to my peculiar nonrelationship with Tom. If, as Ben had said, I was living out a romance novel, Vida was avidly reading it and rooting for a happy ending.

Dwight Gould gave us the official autopsy report over the phone. Einar Rasmussen Jr. had died from three stab wounds in the back which had penetrated the heart and lungs. A massive

hemorrhage had ensued, though Einar probably had not died immediately. Death had taken
place some time between six-thirty and seven-
thirty, the latter parameter set by Carla's discovery of the body.

"He looked surprised," I said to Vida after I'd
relayed Dwight's information. "Didn't you
think so, Carla?"

Carla looked up from her computer screen.
She had plaited her long black hair into pigtails
this morning, which made her seem even more
girlish than usual. "He looked dead. That's all I
remember."

"What about the weapon?" Vida asked, her
glasses far down on her nose.

"It was the knife Jack found," I answered,
"which belonged to the kitchen cutlery set. It
was big, new, and extremely sharp. I figure you
could butcher a cow with it."

"Einar was more of a bull," Vida remarked.
"Have they found fingerprints?"

In my anxiety to make sure I got the ME's report before Milo interfered, I'd forgotten to
ask. "I'll call back now," I said, and hurried into
my office.

To my dismay, Toni Andreas put me through
to the Sheriff. "I asked for Dwight," I said as
soon as I heard Milo's voice.

"Dwight just left." The Sheriff's usual laconic voice was harsh.

"He gave me the ME's report, but . . ." I hesitated, not wanting to admit that I'd forgotten to inquire about the weapon. "I need confirmation regarding prints on the knife."

"What do you mean, 'confirmation'? What did Dwight tell you?" Milo sounded irritated.

"Not much," I said, skirting the truth. "Why don't you tell me?"

"Because we're not releasing anything about the weapon," Milo snapped. "What exactly did my deputy say?"

"Skip it." I banged down the phone. Only then did I realize that the lab must have turned up some prints. Otherwise, the Sheriff wouldn't have been so touchy.

"Damn!" I exploded, hurtling into the newsroom. "Milo's withholding information! That's wrong. He's acting like a big brat!"

"Watch your language," Vida said in mild rebuke. "If there's a personal element involved here, you'd better let me handle the story."

"Hey!" Carla's head jerked up, making the pigtails sail around her shoulders. "The college is *my* beat! If you're going to hand the assignment over, Emma, you'd better give it to me."

Maybe, just maybe, Carla's six years of experience had provided sufficient grounding to tackle an important homicide case. I was caught between Carla's snapping brown eyes and Vida's narrowed gray gaze.

"Carla," I began in my most soothing voice, "I don't want you overtaxing yourself at this stage of your pregnancy. You've already had one bad scare. Take it easy, I'm keeping this one."

"Nonsense!" Vida had pushed her glasses back up on her nose and was sitting with her fists on her hips. "Your feelings—and Milo's— are already getting in the way. He's not angry with me. Besides, I have my nephew Billy."

"I have Ryan," Carla countered. "He knows plenty about the college. I have an *in*."

I struck an adamant stance. "I'm keeping the story. You got that?" My head swiveled first in Vida's direction, then Carla's. "I wouldn't mind help from both of you, though," I added in a placating tone. "Carla, could Ryan meet us for lunch today or tomorrow?"

"Us?" Vida put in. "Or are you going to drink your meal in a bar?"

"We can all eat up at the ski-lodge coffee shop," I said. "It's close to the college. How about it, Carla?"

"Fine." She was almost pouting. "But Ryan can't do it today. He teaches a sociology class at twelve-thirty. He can probably come on Friday. He doesn't have class."

As it turned out, Ryan had a division meeting, so I invited everyone to dinner at my house Sunday evening. I was anxious to speak with Ryan for more than journalistic purposes. While I'd seen him around town, I hardly knew the man, and he was about to take my sole reporter to wife. I felt a certain responsibility for Carla, though I knew she would scoff at the idea.

And while Carla seemed marginally appeased, Vida was not. She was, as she'd put it, "huffy" with me for the rest of the day, until I asked her just before five if she'd like to have dinner at the Venison Inn. With a hint of regret, she turned me down, saying that she and Buck Bardeen were meeting his widowed brother, Henry, and Linda Grant, the high school PE teacher, for dinner at Café Flore out on the highway.

Carla and Leo had left for the day. Ginny was packed up and ready to go, except for Brad, who had escaped once more into the news office and was pulling discards out of Leo's wastebasket. As soon as his mother completed her rescue operation and had bid us a frazzled good night, I told Vida about Sandra Cavanaugh's death.

"Goodness!" Vida exclaimed, a hand to her cheek. "An overdose! How dreadful!" Her gray eyes suddenly narrowed. "Foul play was ruled out, I suppose?"

"Foul play?" The idea jarred me. "I don't know anything except what I've told you. *Foul play?*"

Vida blinked innocently. "Well . . . Sandra was a very wealthy woman who must have made many people's lives unpleasant. You scarcely knew her. What if she left all her money to one of the servants or a pet chinchilla?"

That sounded about right. If Sandra had owned a chinchilla, she might have been goofy enough to put him in her will. But I still found Vida's suggestion outrageous.

"It's a wonder," I said, doing a bit of my own huffing, "that Sandra hadn't killed herself years ago. She took about a zillion kinds of medication."

"Poor thing." Vida's eyes seemed to glisten with tears.

"Who? Sandra? Tom? Me?" Her surprising reaction annoyed me.

"Sandra, of course." Vida took off her glasses and dabbed at her eyes. "Such a tragedy—to be tied to a man who loves another. No wonder she killed herself."

"Oh, good grief!" I literally spun around in

the middle of the newsroom. "You're taking her side! Nobody said she killed herself! And I don't think she ever knew I existed!"

"Of course she did." Vida sniffed a bit and put her glasses back on. "Wives always know."

"Not when they're totally caught up with themselves," I argued. "Sandra Cavanaugh was self-centered, self-absorbed, and, in case you've forgotten, crazy as a bedbug."

"I don't believe that's the medical term for her condition," Vida said primly.

"Whatever. It comes down to the same thing. Look," I went on, returning to stand by Vida's desk, "I'm sorry she's dead. Really, I am. Hers was a wasted life, in my opinion. And frankly, Vida, I thought you'd have a far different reaction."

Vida gave me an unusually helpless look. "I can't help how I feel, Emma. I honestly think it's a terrible thing to have happened. Whatever will poor Tommy do now?"

"I've no idea." Vida's lack of concern for me was making my temper rise. Rather than quarrel with her, I started for my office. "I thought you'd want to know. I'm going home now. Good night, Vida."

She didn't respond. When I left, Vida was still at her desk, seemingly lost in thought.

I was still mad.

★   ★   ★

The next morning, Edna Mae Dalrymple tip-toed up to my office before I could finish my first cup of coffee. "Knock, knock," she piped in her birdlike manner. "May I?"

I'm not really a morning person, and seldom feel anything like jovial until I've downed two mugs of coffee. "Yeah," I said, my voice raspy. "What is it, Edna Mae?"

She ducked inside, but didn't sit down. "Are you . . . feeling better, Emma?"

"Better than what?" I sounded ungracious, then remembered my outburst earlier in the week. "Oh. That. No, as a matter of fact, I'm not. The Sheriff is behaving in a most unpro-fessional manner over the Rasmussen homicide investigation."

My formality seemed to fortify Edna Mae. She approached the nearest of my two visitors' chairs, touched the back as if it might bite, and then awkwardly angled herself down upon the seat.

"That's what I wanted to discuss. With you or Vida. But Vida's not here." Edna Mae glanced over her shoulder to confirm the statement.

"Vida's attending the May Madness breakfast at the Congregational church," I said. "What about the murder?"

"Well"—Edna Mae gulped—"it's not exactly

about the murder itself. Did you hear about the article I proposed for *The Advocate*?"

I assured her that Vida had kept me informed. Edna Mae proceeded to explain all the background anyway, including the paucity of display items available in Skykomish County. She had become particularly discouraged when Darla Puckett had refused to let the library exhibit her collection of dead grasshoppers which Darla had dressed in the national costumes of France, Italy, Austria, Latvia, and Finland.

"Pity," I murmured, wondering where Tom Cavanaugh was at this exact moment.

More background ensued, mainly concerning Edna Mae's futile efforts with Thyra Rasmussen and her knickknacks. "Such a difficult old lady," Edna Mae lamented with a shake of her short salt-and-pepper curls. "But I thought that if I went over to Snohomish and offered my condolences on Einar's very tragic demise, her mother's heart might be softened." She paused, her small, birdlike face contorted with frustration.

"Get the old girl in a weak moment?" I remarked.

Edna Mae's head jerked up. "Oh! No! Nothing so crude. I merely thought that she might be looking more to posterity. That is, if her son was dead, and she herself being ninety or thereabouts, she might want to . . . to make a gesture."

I'd never met Thyra Rasmussen, but given Vida's description of the family matriarch, I could well imagine the "gesture" she might make to Edna Mae. But I let the librarian continue.

"Mrs. Rasmussen didn't seem the least bit moved by Einar's death. At first I thought perhaps she'd become senile and couldn't take it in. But then she mentioned—quite off-the-cuff, as it were—that Einar Jr. probably goaded someone into killing him. That struck me as . . . unnatural."

It struck me, too, in several ways. "Did she mention anyone in particular?"

"No. Indeed, I was so startled that I sort of glossed over the comment, and changed the subject." Edna Mae hung her head. "That was probably foolish of me, wasn't it? I mean, as awful as it sounds, I'm rather intrigued. Human nature is always so fascinating, and in my line of work, I'm often restricted to reading about it instead of actually encountering it. Am I making sense?"

I supposed it depended on how one defined *sense*. Edna Mae meant well; she was a kind-hearted woman. But if common sense could be equated with card sense, then my sometimes bridge partner was a washout. In answer to Edna Mae's specific question, I said yes.

"What about Einar Sr.? Was he as harsh about Einar Jr.'s murder as Mrs. Rasmussen was?"

Edna Mae sighed. "Quite the contrary. I never saw Mr. Rasmussen. He'd taken to his bed, apparently much affected." As usual, Edna Mae had fallen into the vernacular of her favorite dated literary works. "He's way up in his nineties, poor old trout, and his health is failing. Or so rumor has it." She rolled her eyes in apparent dismay.

I waited for her to go on, but she didn't. Her silence forced me to ask what happened next.

Edna Mae's eyes grew wide. "Why, nothing. Mrs. Rasmussen couldn't be moved to part with her collectibles, so I took my leave."

"That's what you came to tell me? And Vida?" I couldn't keep the puzzled curiosity out of my voice.

"Well . . . yes. That is, I thought you should know about this impasse. Vida had mentioned that perhaps later, after a decent passage of time, you might print my article about Mrs. Rasmussen's gold pieces."

One word clicked in my brain. "Gold? Her collectibles are gold?"

Edna Mae nodded solemnly. "Yes, and most interesting. Each piece is fashioned from crude nuggets, and woe upon the critic who despises them! Artful things, and such a glow!"

I gathered that Edna Mae had been reading Dickens. But English classics weren't what intrigued me at the moment. "Where'd she get them?"

"The Klondike," Edna Mae answered promptly. "Her father had been a prospector."

I was disappointed. Somehow, I'd hoped that the mention of gold wasn't coincidental to the nuggets discovered at the warehouse site. However, souvenirs from the Gold Rush a hundred years ago were common in the Northwest. I had inherited a gold cross made out of nuggets from my mother, who had, in turn, received it from a great-uncle who had prospected in the Klondike.

"There's one other thing," Edna Mae said shyly.

"Yes?" I was twitching a bit, anxious to get my second cup of coffee.

"As I mentioned, I find this situation most intriguing. When I first arrived, you said that Sheriff Dodge wasn't being cooperative. Is it possible that you'd like someone to . . . um . . . sleuth for you?"

I pushed back in my chair. "In what way?"

"Well . . . now that I've established some kind of rapport with Mrs. Rasmussen—precarious as it may be—it occurred to me that I might be of help. Family secrets, and all that. There are bound to be some, correct?" Edna Mae glanced over her shoulder again, apparently making sure that Vida hadn't returned. "I'm well aware that Vida knows everything about people in Alpine. But the Rasmussens are Snohomish residents. Surely she isn't as well-grounded in Snohomish County lore."

Edna Mae was probably right. I couldn't see what harm she might do in pestering Mrs. Rasmussen. As a librarian, she was schooled in research. The exercise in social intercourse would be good for Edna Mae. To my knowledge, it was the only kind of intercourse she had ever experienced.

"Go ahead," I said. "We'll appreciate whatever you can find out."

Two pink spots appeared in Edna Mae's usually pale cheeks. "Oh! Thank you! This is so exciting! Just like a book!" She started to rise, then stopped. "You don't think I'm a ghoul?"

"No," I replied truthfully. "Curiosity is very normal. It's a huge part of my job."

Practically walking on air, Edna Mae went off. I was pouring coffee when Vida returned from the May Madness event.

"Such drivel! Really, even after four hundred years, those silly women don't know whether they're Presbyters or Congregationalists! *We* certainly don't want them crossing over!" she declared, marching around her desk as if she were ready to do battle to preserve the purity of First Presbyterian. "Nor will I ever do the Tea Cup Trot again!"

Leo looked up from a layout for Francine's Fine Apparel. "Huh? What's that got to do with religion?"

"Never mind," Vida retorted, but elucidated all the same. "It has to do with posture as a virtue, an arguable point, and those cheap, ugly saucers ruin my hair." She patted her gray curls, which didn't seem any more disheveled than usual. "I'm lucky I didn't spill orange pekoe all over my new blouse!"

Briefly, I tried to envision Vida doing the Tea Cup Trot. The image brought the first smile of the day, but my House & Home editor hadn't finished her tirade. "Then, on the way out of the church hall, I ran into Averill Fairbanks. Instead of UFOs in the sky and his backyard, he's seeing ghosts on the ground. Really, that silly old fool should be locked up!"

"Ghosts?" Carla was intrigued. "What kind? The ones with white sheets or the specter type?"

Vida sat down with a rather loud plop. "I've no idea." Removing her glasses, she rubbed frantically at her eyes. "And Billy—my nephew Billy—my own flesh and blood—refuses to tell me about the knife!"

Such insubordination was unthinkable. No one, especially her kinfolk, ever dared refuse Vida information. "How come?" I asked.

Vida removed her palms from her eyes and gazed at me with a venomous expression. "Because Milo ordered him to hold his tongue. Now, I ask you, why is that? Mere orneriness, or is there a reason?"

"There might be a reason, Duchess," Leo said mildly. "If there weren't any prints, they might as well say so. But if there were . . ." My ad manager held his hands palms up.

"That's what's so annoying," Vida said. "I think there were prints, I think they know whose prints, I think they have a serious suspect."

"Okay." Leo shrugged. "Then they'll make an arrest, and when they do, they'll have to tell us. So why sweat it? We're still four days from publication."

"We don't have much choice," I pointed out. "But I'll be damned if I'll ever let Milo forget how shabbily he's treating us."

"Who?" Vida barked the word.

I turned in her direction. "Who what?"

"Whose prints, of course." She didn't add the

words *you ninny*, but I knew she was thinking them.

"We can't begin to guess," I said reasonably. "So we wait."

Vida harrumphed. I returned to my office. And waited. For many things, including for the phone to ring.

On Saturday morning, I decided to accompany Vida to Einar Jr.'s funeral in Snohomish. It was a cloudy day, with showers that felt more like November than May. I'd half expected Vida to resent my intrusion on what she considered her journalistic territory, but she seemed grateful for the company.

There were two Lutheran churches in Snohomish. Zion Lutheran was much older, and its worshipers were mostly of German descent. Einar Jr. was being buried out of Christ the King Lutheran, whose flock was Scandinavian. The church was situated in a hilly section of town, not far from the new version of old St. Michael's Catholic Church. It was a fairly modern brick building, probably dating back to the Fifties, with tall cedar trees shielding the back of the church. When we arrived at ten to eleven, the only parking left was on the street. Vida and I trooped a full block to the church, where the crowd was already standing-room-only.

"I should have guessed," she murmured, elbowing her way past some elderly mourners. *"Press!"* she hissed, practically bowling over a young couple with a babe in arms.

Vida's aggressiveness carried us only so far, to the back of the last pew, to be exact. She is tall, and I am not, so the advantage was hers. I would be able to see only what was going on up front when the congregation sat or knelt.

"Family room," Vida said in a stage whisper as she nudged my arm. "Drat. It's curtained. We can't see them."

At last, the minister, wearing long white robes, appeared on the altar. The organ played a doleful hymn I didn't recognize as the casket was rolled in. There was no center aisle, and the procession came through the double doors, skirted the standees, and continued up the side aisle on the right.

"Pallbearers," Vida said, again in the stage whisper that was making a few heads turn. "Harold Rasmussen, with the peculiar hair combed over his bald spot. Fuzzy Baugh? Oh, really! Surely they could have found someone more appropriate! Somebody-or-other Jorgen-

sen from Monroe, with the pigeon toes. A
shirttail relation of Thyra's, I believe. Dear me,
I don't know the others."

The service was uneventful, except for Vida's
running commentary. Einar was eulogized by
the pastor, the current mayor of Snohomish,
and Mr. Jorgensen who turned out to be
named Victor, and was some sort of cousin to
the deceased. Forty minutes later we were back
in the Buick, headed for the Grand Army of
the Republic Cemetery at the edge of town.

"I know it's raining, but how else will we be
able to view the family?" Vida demanded after
I'd issued a mild protest. "The reception is private because—I'm sure—that old beast, Thyra,
insisted on having it at their house."

It was only then that I remembered to tell
Vida about Edna Mae's proposal to help us
sleuth. Vida was annoyed.

"That mouse? What could she possibly find
out that we couldn't?"

"Vida," I said in mild reproach, "we haven't
found out anything. How could Edna Mae do
any worse?"

We had pulled into the cemetery, following
the long, slow line of cars, vans, trucks, and
sport utility vehicles that formed the procession. With Memorial Day at hand, the fresh

green grass was already covered with flowers, both real and artificial, as well as numerous small American flags.

"I intend to call on Thyra myself," Vida declared. "I can't go on letting the past keep me away."

"The past?" I turned to Vida, my attention diverted from the large, time-worn monuments that sat beside the narrow road in the older part of the cemetery. Snohomish clung to its own past with a stubborn insistence on keeping up the original buildings, including the many fine old houses that predated the century. Though the outskirts grew and sprawled and congested, the heart of Snohomish beat true to the early days, when timber was king and farms flourished.

"Thyra was unkind to my mother." Vida's lips pressed together. "There was an incident, at Klahowya Days, Snohomish's annual summer festival. Thyra Rasmussen embarrassed my mother in public. I detest speaking of it."

"What did she do?" I asked, undaunted by Vida's grim aspect.

"She . . ." Vida paused, as if unable to go on. "She tromped on my mother's gourds."

I succeeded—barely—in not laughing. "Really!"

"That's not all." Vida gripped the steering wheel with her gloved hands. "Thyra caught her heel in the stem of a very beautiful green-and-orange specimen. The heel broke off her shoe, and she had the nerve to insist that my dear mother buy her another pair. Imagine!"

I was biting the insides of my cheeks. "Did your mother accommodate her?"

"Certainly not! Those silly shoes were very expensive, and unsuitable for Klahowya Days. Besides," Vida said sadly, "Mother felt that she should be recompensed for her gourds. They were not only handsome, but unique."

"Why did Thyra do such a thing in the first place?" I inquired, getting my mirth under control.

"Because my mother's gourds were superior to hers," Vida responded, switching the windshield wipers to high as the shower grew more intense. "Thyra, as I've mentioned, couldn't stand competition."

"Goodness." I tried to sound appropriately aghast. But there was no more to be said: the procession had come to a halt, and we got out of the car.

Being far back in the line of vehicles, we had to walk almost a full block to the grave site. It seemed that most of the mourners had also come to the cemetery. Once again, our viewpoint was obscured. Vida was jockeying for position when someone tugged at my sleeve. I turned around and saw Edna Mae Dalrymple, attired in a baggy black raincoat and plastic rain bonnet.

"I saw you at the church," she whispered, "but I was far back, in the vestibule. Such a crowd! Mr. Rasmussen must have been very popular."

That wasn't the impression I'd gotten so far, but the grave site wasn't the place to argue over the dead man's reputation. Vida acknowledged Edna Mae with a tight little smile, then craned her neck to see around the two young men who stood in front of her.

"The Bourgettes," I murmured. "Dan and John."

"Ah! Yes." Vida nodded. "I'm surprised."

So was I. The two young women standing on each side of the brothers were, I guessed, wives or girlfriends. I scanned the gathering for Pat Dugan, but couldn't find him. The senior Bourgettes, Richard and Mary Jane, were on the opposite side of the grave, just outside the shelter of the canopy. Their usually pleasant faces were set, and they held hands.

As the coffin was lowered into the ground my attention turned to the Rasmussens. Vida's gaze followed mine, and she made a hissing noise.

"Veils! Who do they think they are—the Kennedys?"

The Rasmussen women were definitely heavily veiled. Only Deirdre had removed hers so that her face could be seen.

"The widow Marlys, leaning on Harold," Vida noted, nodding once at the figure swathed in a long black coat and wearing a pillbox from which descended heavy flowing net. "Gladys, clinging at his other side."

More black, more veils. The fourth woman in the family grouping stood apart, ramrod straight and head held high. "Thyra?" I asked.

"Thyra. Showing off, as usual. Black pearls, black fox boa. I'll bet they're both seventy years old. The fox has probably lost its glass eyes."

I hid my amusement as I regarded Thyra's funeral finery. The hat from which her veil hung was a black toque. She reminded me of Dowager Queen Mary at George VI's funeral.

As the rain thrummed on the canopy like a dirge, the pastor intoned prayers for the dead. Just behind Thyra, I saw an old man huddled in a wheelchair. "Einar Sr.?" I mouthed.

Vida nodded. "The rest are Jorgensens and Malmstroms and whoever."

"Where's Beau?"

Vida snorted. "Who knows? Whoever knows about Beau?"

Harold Rasmussen helped Marlys as she threw a handful of dirt onto the casket. He was taller than his late brother, but very thin, and seemed to have none of Einar Jr.'s self-possession. In fact, he appeared almost as wobbly as his sister-in-law.

The graveside service concluded. Several people—but none of the Bourgette contingent—clustered around the family. Only Deirdre chose not to escape. Two men in dark suits, presumably from the funeral home, gently shooed away the would-be offers of condolence. Leaning on Harold, Marlys Rasmussen got into the limousine, followed by Thyra and Gladys. Einar Sr. and his wheelchair were put in a second limo. At last, Richard and Mary Jane Bourgette approached Deirdre.

Vida tugged my arm. "Closer," she whispered. "We must get closer."

"Vida!" I exclaimed. "This is a private moment!"

"Of course!" She gave me another tug; I had no choice but to follow.

Victor Jorgensen, pallbearer and distant cousin, had also edged closer to Deirdre. He hung back just enough for tact's sake, but his blue eyes were vigilant.

There would be no scene, however. Mary Jane Rasmussen Bourgette held out both gloved hands and Deirdre reluctantly took them. "You don't know me, Deirdre," I heard Mary Jane say, "but I'm your aunt. And this," she added, turning to her husband, "is your uncle Richard. We're both very sorry about your father. Is there anything we can do?"

Deirdre seemed nonplussed. "Aunt Mary Jane?" She allowed the other woman to squeeze her hands before drawing back. "No. We're okay. But thanks."

Scott Kuramoto had quietly inserted himself between aunt and niece. I hadn't seen him until now, but he had approached from the vicinity of a tall cedar not far from the grave.

"Deirdre has to leave," he said in his soft, quiet voice. "The car's waiting."

"Of course," said Mary Jane, her usually vivacious face somber. "Remember, if you ever need anything, anything at all, call us."

Deirdre murmured something which I couldn't hear. Along with the two young women, Dan and John Bourgette joined their parents.

"Let her go," John said in a vexed tone. "I don't know why we came in the first place."

Richard Bourgette, a handsome, white-haired man near sixty, put an arm around his wife. "Your mother wanted to do this. It meant a lot to her, John."

John and Dan exchanged glances. There was neither sympathy nor understanding in them. But I had a feeling that their anger wasn't with Mary Jane, but with the man who had just been laid to rest in the GAR Cemetery.

Chapter Ten

WE STOPPED FOR lunch at the Dutch Cup in Sultan. Vida was full of surmises. "Marlys is clearly upset by Einar's death. I must speak with her. Thyra is showing the world she's indestructible. I wonder if I could stand calling on her? It was very kind of the Bourgettes to attend, but the boys only came because Mary Jane asked them to. Did you think Harold was drunk? Gladys is a waste of time. Why would she be so upset and need to lean on Harold? Maybe she was drunk, too. Deirdre *seemed* all right, but you told me she was angry with her father. No sign of her son—what's his name? Davin? But of course I didn't expect him to show up if he's run away. He probably doesn't know his grandfather is dead. As for Beau— well, he's a recluse, and that's that. *Do you know Beau?* as they say. I suspect he's mental. Which might mean he killed his father, except that he never leaves the house. It would be much easier for him to have murdered Einar at home. So convenient. What do you think?"

My head was whirling. "As I said earlier, I think Milo knows who killed Einar. Maybe he was waiting until after the funeral to make an arrest. If," I added, putting salt and pepper on my green salad, "the murderer is actually a member of the family circle."

"I don't know," Vida mused. "Again, why follow Einar to the college to kill him? On the other hand, it's neutral turf. Maybe we were meant to think it wasn't a relative just because the murder occurred elsewhere."

I heaved a sigh. "Einar Sr. is too feeble. Thyra wouldn't come all the way to Alpine to kill her son. She expects to be waited on, hand and foot. According to what you've told me, Marlys is almost as much of a recluse as Beau. Besides, she seemed genuinely distraught."

"It could be an act," Vida noted between mouthfuls of coleslaw.

"It could," I allowed, "but you already mentioned that she rarely goes out. Harold is another matter. Didn't you say he resented being overlooked by Einar Sr. when it came to running their business ventures?"

Vida made a face. "His resentment took the form of drinking gin out of milk cartons. Half-gallon size, I believe. Why wait forty years?"

"Good point. The same argument holds true for his wife, Gladys. I'm counting them out."

"Mmm. Perhaps." Vida beamed as the waitress delivered her stuffed pork chop. "Deirdre.

She was angry with her father. She blamed him for her son's disappearance. Except that he didn't really disappear. Didn't you say she told you that Einar Jr. knew where Davin was?"

I nodded. "Still, I don't see Deirdre as a killer. With Einar dead, how could she ever find out where Davin was?"

"People are unpredictable," Vida observed. "Her anger may have boiled up. But there's that lipstick on Einar's shirt. I trust—I hope—it wasn't Deirdre's."

I'd forgotten about the lipstick. "I wonder if Milo has traced that to anyone," I said, biting into my beef dip. "Did you ask Bill Blatt?"

"Yes," Vida responded, her quick glance taking in the latest arrivals at the restaurant. "Nothing so far." She bobbed her head. "Harold and Gladys Rasmussen. Why didn't they stay at the private reception?"

The Rasmussens had seated themselves across the aisle from us and several booths away, near the door. Gladys had removed both hat and veil. I caught a glimpse of her puddinglike face for the first time. She now seemed composed, even docile. All I could see of Harold was his comb-over.

"They live around here, right?" I'd lowered my voice, though the restaurant was busy, and I doubted that the Rasmussens could hear us.

"Just the other side of Sultan," Vida responded, still trying to discreetly ogle the newcomers. "Toward Monroe. Do you think they're drunk?"

"How should I know?" I grumbled. "Quit harping on booze. They drove here without killing anybody, didn't they?"

"Don't be flippant," Vida admonished. "Really, I should speak with them. Condolences, you know." With a hand to her black straw with its twin black birds, Vida slid out of the booth and made for the Rasmussens.

It took at least a full minute before she finagled an invitation to sit down next to Gladys. I ate and observed. The birds on Vida's hat dipped in sympathy, tilted with interest, and swooped with curiosity. I had finished my meal when she returned to our booth.

"They're not drunk," Vida announced in a voice that might have carried to the Rasmussens. "They didn't go to the private reception because Gladys is terrified of her mother-in-law. But guess who did."

"The senior Bourgettes?" It seemed like a logical guess.

Vida looked disappointed. "Yes. I was surprised. Just Mary Jane and Richard. None of the others."

Admittedly, I didn't know Mary Jane and her

husband. But I had seen their faces at the cemetery, and if not steeped in sorrow, they had shown regret. It was too late for Mary Jane to reconcile with her brother, but perhaps she could come to terms with her parents.

"How are Harold and Gladys reacting to Einar's murder?" I asked as a pair of fishermen sat down in the booth across from us.

"Well . . ." Vida paused in devouring her pork chop. "Harold expressed great sadness. Gladys said little, but indicated a sense of loss. Form, I thought, rather than genuine feeling. But I could be wrong."

"At least they weren't malicious," I remarked. "Even if Einar drew quite a crowd, I wonder how many of the so-called mourners were actually sorry to see him go."

"Yes." Vida lapped up the sage stuffing. "Pretense, hypocrisy, social obligations. That's what I sensed."

The fishermen were grousing about the lack of steelhead in the Sky, an old refrain that I'd often heard from Milo. We paid our bill and left, with a nod to Harold and Gladys Rasmussen. It was still raining, with a stiff wind blowing across the highway. We went through Startup, where I was amused, as always, by the small white church with its long-standing sign which read FOR SALE BY OWNER. We passed the road into Buck Bardeen's house, and I asked Vida how dinner had gone Thursday night at Café Flore.

"Fine," she said. "I think Henry Bardeen and Linda Grant are courting."

Henry, who was manager of the ski lodge, had been widowed for many years, and had a grown daughter who worked for him. Linda had been teaching high school PE long before I arrived in Alpine. Like Edna Mae, she was a member of our bridge group.

"That's nice," I said. "I get the feeling that Henry would like to marry again." Then, because I couldn't resist the puckish question, I asked Vida if Buck was also so inclined.

"Buck is very satisfied with his present situation," she answered in an even tone. "His wife has only been dead five years. Their four children are nicely settled in various parts of the country, and because Buck is retired from the air force, he can fly for free and visit whenever he wishes. Not all men—or women—leap from one marriage to the next after a spouse has passed away."

Vida's message was hardly subtle, and the retaliation was deserved. I didn't respond. During the rest of the journey, we spoke of other things, including her proposed trip to the college library.

"I've gone through everything at the public library," she explained, "which is virtually what's always been there, and isn't news to me. However, I have yet to visit the library on campus. I've been remiss, and now I ought to see if they have more historical information about the area than Edna Mae and her cronies have been able to acquire."

I volunteered to go with Vida. I'd used the college library a couple of times, seeking material for editorials. Its business-and-public-affairs collection was impressive, and partially donated by the Doukas family, whose members were some of Alpine's wealthier citizens. In fact, Simon Doukas, who was an attorney, served on the college's board of trustees. I wondered if he had been the other member who had gone along with Einar Jr.'s rejection of Scott Kuramoto and Pat Dugan. As I recalled from a family tragedy several years ago, Simon had prejudices of his own.

The rain had dwindled into a drizzle by the time we pulled into the parking lot. Inside the library, we found Maylene Bjornson at the main desk. Vida hailed her with a wave and a yoo-hoo which caused some of the dozen students to look up from their reading materials.

"I heard you were working here," Vida said, not bothering to lower her voice. "How nice.

I've always thought libraries would be a pleasant environment."

"It's okay," Maylene said in a flat voice. "It beats hustling toilet plungers at Harvey's Hardware."

"My yes," Vida agreed. "I see you're here on a Saturday. Does that mean you've gotten on full-time?"

Maylene shook her head, which was covered with tiny corkscrew auburn curls. "I put in thirty hours a week, usually on Mondays, Wednesdays, Thursdays, and either Friday or Saturday. This is my week to pull Saturday duty. It's a pain. The whole weekend is blown."

"That is hard," Vida agreed, at her most sympathetic. "Especially with teenagers at home. Does Ron have to work weekends, too?"

"Not usually, the lucky stiff." Maylene rested her plump elbows on the counter. "I've been trying to get him to do some car-repair work on his off days, or even in the afternoons when he doesn't go to work until five or six. But he says he needs to do stuff around the house, which is true. The only trouble is, he never does much of anything."

As often happens, I felt like Vida's stooge. "Ron told me that the repair business had gone south," I put in, just in case Maylene thought I'd become invisible as well as mute.

Maylene's hazel eyes widened. "He told you that? When?"

"The other day," I said, hoping to sound casual.

Maylene gave a little snort. "Well, it's not what it used to be, with all the rigs going out of business. But there's still plenty of work, if only because he undercuts Cal Vickers and the dealerships. Ron won't admit it, but he's lazy."

A student wearing army fatigues came up to the desk to check out some books. Maylene's attention was momentarily diverted. When she got back to us, Vida asked where we might find material on early Skykomish County history. Maylene directed us to three different sections, including periodicals.

"I'll take those," Vida said, bustling between the stacks. "You look at the books in the Pacific Northwest section."

"Thanks, Vida." But my sarcasm was lost; Vida had already turned a corner and was headed for the microfiche. I found a handful of volumes which dealt primarily with railroad building, mining, and timber. Sitting at an empty table, I checked out the indices. There was nothing I hadn't seen before at the public library.

Discouraged, I returned the history books and selected some biographies. There wasn't

much, at least not on local personalities. Alpine
has produced few people worthy of biographi-
cal fame.

I was flipping through a work on James J. Hill
when Vida hurried over to my niche. Her hat
was askew, and the birds looked as if they were
trying to commit suicide.

"Oh, my!" Her voice had finally hushed. "I
can't believe this! I never knew, truly I didn't!
No one—*no one*—ever mentioned such a thing
to me!"

"What?" I couldn't imagine the cause of
Vida's consternation.

She held out a scrap of paper, apparently bor-
rowed from the library. Since Vida never took
notes, I was even more surprised. "Cathouses,"
she whispered. "Five of them along Highway
2, between Scenic and Skykomish, which
means they were just below Alpine. *Cathouses!*"
she repeated.

I suppressed a smile. "When?" The scrap of
paper showed only the names, which included
the Onion Patch and the Mouse's Ear.

"In the early part of the century, while the
railroad was being built and then maintained.
Supposedly," Vida went on, sinking down into
the chair next to mine, "they were for the
pleasure of the railroad workers. How could I
not know?"

Over the years I gathered that Vida's parents, Earl and Muriel Blatt, were prim and proper people, so it didn't seem strange that they'd keep such a seamy secret. The reputation of Alpine itself, especially under the beneficent aegis of Carl Clemans, was of a town steeped in old-fashioned virtues.

"So what have brothels got to do with gold?" I asked.

Vida chewed at her lower lip. "Nothing, I suppose. Still, reading about Scenic and the other towns along the Great Northern route reminded me of the Japanese workers who came here in the 1890s. Some later became section hands. I'd forgotten until now, because by the time they left, I was still a child."

I wasn't sure where Vida's reminiscences were leading. "So you're talking about—when? The Twenties—the Thirties?"

"Both," Vida responded. "A group of a half-dozen or so Japanese railroad workers lived at Tye, just up Highway 2 from Alpine. Very nice men, my father always said, and excellent base-ball players. But I wonder if they might have known a man named Yoshida."

"They might have known fifty Yoshidas," I noted. "According to Sandy Clay, it's not an uncommon name. Besides, if they were here in the Thirties, they must have returned to Japan or been interned during World War Two."

"Maud Dodd," said Vida, seemingly from out of nowhere. "Maud lived in Tye as a girl. Now she's in the retirement home here in Alpine."

I still wasn't following her train of thought. "Maud Dodd would remember a Japanese section hand with a good glove at second base who just happened to know the Yoshida with a metal chest full of gold nuggets?" My skepticism was obvious. "Vida, we're going back a hundred years."

"Oral history," Vida said, patting the tabletop. "I should expect that strangers in a foreign land would pass on tales of their fellow countrymen. Besides, it's all we've got. I found nothing specific about a gold strike involving a Japanese man named Yoshida. Of course I imagine that not all prospectors would broadcast their discoveries."

"Probably not." Especially, I thought, foreigners whose skin was a different color. While greed doesn't recognize ethnic diversity, Asian immigrants might have been more vulnerable to chicanery and extortion, if only because of the language barrier.

Frustrated, we left the library. Vida asked if I'd like to accompany her to visit Maud Dodd in

the retirement home, but I declined. It was going on four o'clock, and I hadn't given my
house its weekly dose of cleaning.

Naturally, the first thing I did was check the
phone messages. The call I'd hoped for wasn't
on the recording. Instead, there were two
other messages: one was from Edna Mae, asking what I thought about Einar Jr.'s funeral; the
other was from Leo.

"Why wait to go to Seattle to blow my lottery loot?" his voice said on the tape. "How
about dinner tonight at Café Flore?"

Why not? I didn't feel like sitting home alone.
I returned Leo's call. He'd pick me up at six-
thirty. As if to earn my right to a free meal, I
rushed around the house, vacuuming, dusting,
and washing the insides of windows. By six
twenty-five, I'd slipped into an orange linen
dress, taken a deep breath to fasten the wide
brown belt, and squeezed into brown pumps
I'd bought before my feet started to spread.

"Looking good, babe," Leo said in greeting.
"How was your day off?"

I explained about the funeral and the visit to
the library. Then, because I felt I owed Leo a
compliment, I told him I liked his tie.

"Nordstrom's," he replied, heading onto
Alpine Way. "The after-Christmas men's sale. I
saved it for a special occasion."

"I'm flattered," I said, and meant it.

Just before Old Mill Park, we saw the red lights flash and heard the warning bells clang. Leo pulled to a stop as a doubleheader freight moved west through town. The sun, which had finally come out from behind the clouds, cast a golden glow on the hills above the railroad tracks. As several empty flatcars passed I could see the old loading dock and the warehouse site where the Bourgettes had now brought in a trailer.

"Hey!" I poked Leo's arm. "Am I nuts? It looks like crime-scene tape over there."

But a long line of freight cars blocked Leo's view. At last, when the train had disappeared and the guards had been lifted, I poked Leo again. "Take a right on Railroad Avenue. Let's see if my eyes are deteriorating along with the rest of me."

"It's probably construction tape," Leo said, though he humored me and turned off Alpine Way. "Or maybe it's some kind of warning to trespassers."

It was definitely crime-scene tape. A couple of kids on bikes had stopped to study the site. Leo and I got out of the car and approached them.

"Hey, guys," Leo called to the boys. "Do you know why this tape's been put up?"

"Uh-uh," the taller teen responded. "Isn't this where they found the gold back around Halloween?"

"Right." Leo was rubbing his chin. "Do you know how long it's been here?"

"Uh-uh," the boy said. "We just seen it now."

"It wasn't here this afternoon when Vida and I got back from Snohomish," I put in. "We'd have noticed it. At least Vida would."

Leo's brown eyes were fixed on my face. "So?"

I grimaced. "We've got to contact the Sheriff's office."

"And hope he's not there?"

"That's right." I sighed. "Maybe you had something there—it could be just another way of warning off vandals and treasure hunters."

The boys took off on their bikes. From across the tracks and beyond the vacant lot, we could hear the river. On the opposite bank, where ferns grew almost five feet tall and second-growth timber had come to maturity, shafts of sunlight sifted through the trees. It had turned into a perfect spring evening. Except for the crime-scene tape.

"Okay, let's go." Leo seemed resigned, and I knew he wasn't referring to Café Flore.

"Don't worry, I can face Milo if I have to," I asserted, getting back into the car.

"Oh, I'm sure you can. I just don't want to get in the way when it happens." Leo gave me his lopsided grin.

The Sheriff was in. He was standing behind the curving counter when we arrived, talking to Dustin Fong and another deputy, Sam Heppner. Milo looked up when we entered, and it was clear that what he saw didn't please him.

"We're busy," he said.

"We're busy, too," I replied. "It's called news gathering. What's with the crime-scene tape at the warehouse site?"

Milo's gaze was steady, though it seemed to be focused somewhere between Leo and me. "We're not releasing any information at this point."

"Milo!" I actually stamped my foot, forgetting that I was wearing pumps. I was lucky I didn't break a heel, like Thyra Rasmussen with the gourds. "Don't be a jackass!" Before he could respond, I dove for the police log. It was on the other side of the counter, about six feet from where the Sheriff and his deputies were standing.

To my chagrin, there was nothing new, except the usual stolen bicycles, prowler reports, a two-car accident at Fourth and Cedar, and a cougar spotted just west of Cass Pond. Then I

realized that the lack of information was mean-
ingful. No crime had been reported, which
meant that something else was afoot.

"Those bones," I said. "The crime-scene tape
is because of the bones the Bourgettes found
the other day. You've been doing more digging. What did you find?"

"Look." Milo leaned on the counter, his long
face more serious than incensed. "We're not
letting anything out on this until we know
what we're talking about. Stop taking this personally, Emma. Check with us next week."

The rational response took me aback. I was
about to tell Milo that I wasn't the one who
was taking things personally when I felt Leo
nudge me in the ribs.

"Let's eat," he said, lowering his voice.

"Do that," Milo said, not sounding so rational. "You two look like you're going out for
a big night on the town."

"How observant," I said, and turned my back
on the Sheriff. Deliberately, I put my arm
through Leo's. "Come on, darling, we're going
to be late."

Leo chuckled all the way to the car, but once
we were seated at Café Flore and had been
served our cocktails, he grew somber. "It's
none of my business, but I don't understand
you," he said. "You've got this thing about

Tom Cavanaugh, and yet you and Sheriff Dim Bulb act like a couple of feuding teenage lovers. Dare I ask what's going on?"

The query irked me. "You dare, but it should be obvious. It's not me who's causing the problem. It's Milo, acting like a . . . dim bulb." Usually, I didn't care much for Leo's disparaging remarks about the Sheriff. I still didn't, but I refrained from making an issue of his attitude. "We've kept our distance since we broke up, but this Rasmussen case has brought us head-to-head. He's been obstructing our news gathering at every step of the way. That's not fair, and it *is* personal."

"In other words, it's none of my damned business." Leo looked annoyed.

I didn't want to spoil our evening. "I just explained the part about Milo," I said, putting my hand on his. "I can't explain Tom, because I don't understand it myself. For the past two or three years I thought I'd gotten over him. Finally. But when you told me about Sandra, I realized I'd been kidding myself. It isn't going to be over until he tells me it is." I swallowed hard and asked the question I'd put off since Wednesday night. "Did you call him about the job offer?"

Leo's weathered face softened. "Yeah, but he still wasn't home. I tried again last night and today. This time I left a message, figuring he's out of town."

"Will Tom call back?" My voice sounded overeager.

"Probably. He's got decent manners. As I'm sure you recall," Leo added dryly.

"Oh, yes. Tom's manners are excellent." I removed my hand from Leo's and drummed my nails on the linen-covered table. As usual, the restaurant was packed, drawing customers from as far away as Seattle. "Why don't you just come right out and tell me I'm an idiot?"

"You're an idiot." The lopsided grin reappeared. "Feel better?"

I laughed. "Yes." And then I added in an unusually candid confession, "You make me feel better, Leo. I don't know why, but you always do."

Leo picked up the big, handwritten menu. It almost looked as if he was hiding behind it. "You'll figure it out someday. Maybe."

Chapter Eleven

"IF," VIDA SAID when she arrived early for dinner Sunday night, "I had included Billy in my will—which I have not, with three daughters and five grandchildren—I would write him out. He has failed me yet again. Whatever is the matter with that boy?"

That boy was now over thirty, and, as I tried to point out to Vida, was undoubtedly following Milo's instructions. "I told you when I phoned earlier today that for once, Milo might not be acting like a complete jackass. He *may* have a reason to hold back. Anyway, he said we could check with him tomorrow."

"Perhaps someone broke into the Bourgettes' trailer. Tools are always tempting." Vida gazed around the kitchen. "Let me help. What can I do?"

"Nothing. Just sit." Vida was not a competent cook, and the table in the dining alcove was already set. "I think there's something odd about those bones. For one thing, I noticed at the time that they were charred. Couldn't that indicate they weren't buried very deep and had been burned in the fire?"

Vida hadn't accepted my invitation to sit, but stood with her back to the refrigerator. "Meaning what, precisely?"

"The metal chest wasn't charred," I said, sautéing onions in butter. "I suppose it was found on a fluke, maybe while the firemen were digging out some of the timbers. Thus I'm assuming it was fairly deep in the ground. But the bones must have been closer to the surface. I guess," I went on, putting the onions into a mixing bowl, "I'm saying that the bones weren't as old as we assumed. Milo was really quite cavalier about them."

"Hmm." Vida stroked her chin. "That's most intriguing. Awful, really."

"Perhaps. But that may be why Milo won't talk. He's waiting for more lab results, probably from Everett." I stirred ricotta, Parmesan, and Romano cheese into the onions. "Now tell me about your visit to Maud Dodd." Vida had cut our phone conversation short when her grandson, Roger, turned up the sound on MTV so loud that she couldn't hear.

"Futile," Vida replied. "Maud's mind is very sharp, and her memory is excellent. Goodness, she's not all that much older than I am. But she only recalls how sweet the Japanese men were, such good workers, and always bringing those lovely little oranges to the other people in Tye. The only helpful information she had to offer was that all of the men except one returned to Japan before World War Two broke out. The fellow who stayed on moved to Seattle, where he had a fiancée. I suspect that they were both interned in that sorry episode authorized by that tyrant, Franklin Delano Roosevelt."

Vida is Republican to her toes, and any defense of FDR was useless. Though I had been brought up in a working- class family of Democrats, I really couldn't defend Roosevelt's panicky reaction toward Japanese citizens after Pearl Harbor. Indeed, I had frequently heard the story of one of my father's Nisei neighbors, who had been hauled away while listening to a University of Washington–Washington State football game. At the time he thought he was being arrested for being a Cougar fan in a city where the Huskies reigned supreme.

"Did Maud remember the man's name?" I asked, adding cooked spinach to my mixture.

"No." Vida finally sat down at the kitchen table. "She said everyone called him Joe. Whatever kind of concoction are you making, Emma?"

"Stuffed chicken breasts," I replied, aware that Vida's idea of exotic cooking was macaroni and cheese. "There's a yogurt-and-red-wine garnish, and I'm serving roasted red peppers and rice pilaf with it."

"Goodness! That's enough to trigger Carla into a miscarriage. Wherever do you get such peculiar recipes?"

"From your House & Home section," I said. "You ran this one last March."

Vida merely raised her eyebrows. She knew that I knew she almost never read the recipes, which she obtained from a news service in Los Angeles.

"So Maud Dodd is a dead end," I said, filling the chicken breasts with spinach-and-cheese stuffing.

"I'm afraid so." Vida looked defeated, her chin resting on her hands. "Maybe Milo will make an arrest in the next day or so. He must be gathering evidence to make his case."

"Could be." I put the chicken in the oven. "You know how meticulous he is. Whatever he does, it won't be impulsive."

"Plodding," Vida said. "That's the word that comes to mind. But of course he's thorough. I must give him that."

Since I'd decided to skip the RUB dedication, I asked Vida if the event had gone off well. She said it was very low-key, with Nat Cardenas and George Engebretsen and someone from the state office of higher education eulogizing Einar Jr. The lieutenant governor had canceled, due to illness.

"Carla tried for some different angles with the speakers," Vida said, examining a pair of salt-and-pepper shakers I'd bought on my last visit to Ben in Tuba City. "Hopefully, they'll perk up the front page a bit."

"Was there much of a turnout?" I inquired.

"So-so. The mood was very subdued."

The doorbell rang. Since I had my hands full of red peppers, Vida volunteered to welcome the other guests. By the time I reached the living room, she had taken Carla and Ryan's jackets, and was insisting they sit on the sofa.

I offered wine, which Carla and Vida declined. Ryan, however, accepted. For the first time I got a close-up look at my reporter's fiancé. He was in his late thirties, just under average height, and a bit on the chubby side. His dark hair was already receding, but his face was pleasant, and his brown eyes conveyed kindliness. He had a faintly boyish air, and if not exactly shy, he seemed self-effacing. *Cute* was the word that described him best, and I could see the attraction for Carla, especially when he referred to her as Little Mother.

"Little Mother tells me I'm about to be grilled," Ryan said after I'd served him a glass of

Chardonnay and brought Diet 7UP and ice water for Carla and Vida.

"Dear me," said Vida. "That's an unfortunate phrase. What we're interested in are your impressions of Einar Jr. and his relationship with people at the college."

Ryan's round face grew thoughtful. "I didn't usually see Mr. Rasmussen interact with people from the college. Once, I saw him come out of a board meeting, and he was pretty angry. That was a couple of months ago. But the only other times I ever saw him were public occasions. The opening of the college, a faculty tea, events like that."

Carla edged closer to Ryan. "Tell them about the sugar bowl."

Ryan chuckled, a light, charming sound. "Oh, that. It was at the library, a couple of weeks ago. You were there, Little Mother."

"Of course I was," Carla said, sounding petulant. "I covered it for *The Advocate*. But I didn't include the part about the sugar bowl. We don't need to get sued."

The mere idea of a lawsuit always sends off alarm signals in my brain. Although *The Advocate* was insured through a group that handled other weeklies and small dailies, the ugly threat of libel is always with us. "What happened?" I

asked. "I don't remember you mentioning anything unusual."

"It wasn't," Carla answered. "It was just sort
of . . . dumb. Go ahead, tell them, Ryan."

A bemused smile on his face, Ryan cleared his
throat. "Cynthia Kittikachorn was pouring
coffee at one end of the table and Shawna
Beresford-Hall was in charge of tea at the other
end. Mr. Rasmussen was standing behind Maylene Bjornson in the coffee line, and Maylene
knocked over the sugar bowl, which contained
cubes. Mr. Rasmussen bent down to pick up
some of the cubes that had fallen onto the floor,
and he . . ." Ryan paused, revealing dimples as
he smiled at Carla. "He dropped one down
Maylene's dress, which was rather low-cut."

"Right in her cleavage," Carla said. "I was
about to take a picture, so I got a good view. I
couldn't believe he'd do such a gross thing. But
both Einar and Maylene laughed their heads
off. Cynthia and Shawna didn't think it was so
funny."

"Did you take the picture?" I asked, remembering my editor's role.

"No." Carla made a face of remorse. "I was
too startled. If I had, I could have blackmailed
Einar."

Ryan laughed uproariously at Little Mother.

"Isn't she something?" he said, hugging Carla's shoulders.

"Yes, she is." Vida's voice held a touch of irony. "This is most intriguing. Does anyone else here feel that the incident implies a certain intimacy between Einar and Maylene?"

Ryan leaned forward on the sofa, his expression now quite serious. "Possibly. But nobody knows for sure that Mr. Rasmussen was having an affair with Maylene. We just assumed it."

Vida's jaw dropped. "What?" She whirled on Carla. "Did you know about this?"

"Ummm . . ." Carla looked more vague than usual. "I guess I forgot. I've had other things on my mind."

Surprisingly, Vida clamped her lips shut. Perhaps she remembered her own pregnancies, and was not without sympathy. Or maybe she was wondering how such a juicy piece of gossip had eluded her. In her defense, the college often seemed more like a world of its own than part of the town.

"Has the alleged affair been going on for long?" I asked.

Carla and Ryan exchanged glances. "A few months?" Ryan finally said. "Maylene didn't start working at the library until January."

"What gave rise to these rumors?" Vida inquired.

Ryan looked sheepish. "A couple of faculty members live out on the Burl Creek Road. They saw Mr. Rasmussen's Cadillac parked at the Bjornsons' a few times when Ron was working the night shift at the college. They couldn't figure out what he'd been doing there unless . . ." He lifted his hands. "You know."

"Does the Sheriff know about these rumors?" I asked, getting up to head for the kitchen.

Ryan shrugged. "Somebody must have told him. Dodge and his deputies have been going around asking all sorts of questions."

I glanced at Vida. "Someone must have mentioned it."

Vida nodded. "There's always one tattletale. Dear me, this doesn't look well for Maylene."

Carla's black eyes grew wide. "That was her lipstick on Einar's shirt?"

"Possibly," Vida said. "She'd be the right height."

I let them speculate as I put the rice-pilaf water on to boil and slid the pan of peppers into the oven. Upon my return, I refilled Ryan's wineglass and added a splash of bourbon to my highball.

The conversation had expanded to include other evidence of Einar's philandering. Ryan pleaded ignorance; Carla said she'd once heard something about Einar and Amanda Hanson, who worked at the post office; Vida pooh-poohed that notion by saying that when Walt Hanson was out of town, Amanda carried on with Dave Engebretsen and Earl Haines, though certainly not at the same time. Amanda had no morals—her skirts were far too short and must be in violation of the U.S. postal workers' code—but she wasn't weird.

"However," Vida continued, sucking on an ice cube from her water glass, "I wouldn't put anything past Einar Jr., if only because his wife is such a dud."

I recalled that Vida had mentioned her intention of visiting Marlys. "Have you paid your condolence call yet?" I asked.

"Too soon," Vida responded. "Tomorrow evening. That makes two days since the funeral, but before the family realizes I didn't send a memorial. I wouldn't want them to think me a piker. They might not let me in."

I'd resumed my seat in one of the two matching green armchairs. "You were teaching Monday night, weren't you, Ryan?"

Ryan dimpled at me. "Is this an official inquiry, Ms. Lord?"

"Hardly. And please call me Emma." I gave him a self-deprecating smile. "Carla mentioned that you taught a class on Monday nights. I was wondering if the Sheriff had asked if you saw or heard anything unusual."

Ryan had turned quite grave. "It was one of the deputies, Jack Mullins. He interrogated me"—he paused to make a face—"Tuesday morning. It was perfunctory. It's a five-credit sociology class, once a week, which goes from five-twenty to ten-twenty, with two ten-minute breaks."

"When are the breaks?" I asked, trying to sound casual.

Apparently I failed. Ryan made another face and squirmed a bit. "There's no set time. I call them when I come to the end of a lecture segment or if a discussion period bogs down. On Monday, the first break was just before seven-thirty. The second was a little before nine." He leaned forward, hands clasped on his knees. "I told Jack Mullins all this. During the first break I went to my office to get some notes I'd forgotten. At the second break I didn't leave the classroom. Two or three students had questions for me. But some of the ones who had gone outside to smoke or stretch their legs said they thought something was going on at the RUB. They didn't know what it was, except that there were several emergency vehicles parked outside. Later I kicked myself for not checking it out, but I'd forgotten that Little Mother had a photo assignment there. You can imagine how I felt when I heard she was at the hospital." He gave Carla an apologetic look.

Vida was looking leery. "You didn't check on the vehicles when you left the classroom? Some of them must have still been there."

"I don't go out that way," Ryan explained. "My class is in Building B, which is quite a way from the RUB. I leave through a rear exit, cut across the main campus road, and circle around the gym to the faculty parking lot. There's a well-lighted trail by one of the bike racks." Again, he turned to Carla. "I was anxious to get home to Little Mother. I always am."

Carla made kissing motions with her mouth. I suppose it was cute, but I had to check my peppers. In my absence, Vida apparently had backed off from questioning Ryan further. The talk turned to the baby, the wedding, and Ryan's background. Though he was from Spokane, he somehow had a tenuous connection to Vida through a neighbor whose late husband had once been pastor of the Presbyterian church in Alpine.

My guests didn't stay late. Carla said she needed a back rub, and Vida had to put her canary, Cupcake, to bed. "He gets so confused this time of year when the days are so long," she explained. "Cupcake still hasn't made the adjustment to Daylight Savings Time."

Carla looked stricken. "What do babies do? How can they know? Are their schedules totally disrupted? Or do we stay on regular time?" She addressed all these questions to Ryan, who seemed struck dumb.

"Babies," Vida said with authority, "are surprisingly adaptable. You mustn't worry so much, Carla."

"But you can't train to be a parent," Carla asserted. "It's not like journalism, where you spend years studying and then applying what you've learned so that the job's a breeze."

That wasn't the way I'd have described it; with Carla, it was often more like a blowout.

As usual, Monday was busy, despite the fact that it was officially Memorial Day. While my staff was forced to work, I felt obligated to pay them double time, as well as giving a paid day off at some other point in the year.

Carla was out covering the parade, which consisted of a couple of dozen veterans, mostly from World War II and Korea, a fire engine, the Dithers sisters riding their favorite horses, the high school band, and a couple of logging rigs that were still in service. Sometimes Milo or one of the deputies joined in, but I understood the Sheriff's department wouldn't be represented this year. I assumed it was because they had more pressing matters on hand.

There was no mail delivery, which allowed me time to write my weekly editorial. By eleven o'clock I'd finished the call for action on the battered women's shelter. It dawned on me that Brad Erlandson wasn't around. Going into the front office, I asked—hopefully—if Ginny had sent him to day care.

"Oh, no," she said, sounding horrified. "The banks are closed, so Rick doesn't have to work today. He took Brad to the parade and then they're going to Old Mill Park to play on the Small Thing."

With a civic contribution of soup labels and some matching funds, the city had recently acquired two play structures. The smaller one, which was suitable for toddlers, had been dubbed the Small Thing; the larger, and more dangerous apparatus was referred to as No Small Thing. I kept waiting for some audacious kid to break his neck on the latter. Specifically, someone like Vida's odious grandson, Roger.

"That's nice for both Brad and Rick," I said, "but I still think your job would be easier if you let your sister-in-law take him in at her day care."

"Donna's really overloaded," Ginny said, at her most serious. "They need a day care at the college, and I guess one is in the works, but meanwhile, students with kids have to find other facilities. In fact, Donna's got a waiting list."

Great, I thought, wondering how early little ones could start preschool. With my luck, we'd have Brad screwing around in the office until he was accepted at Stanford.

I turned to go back into the newsroom, when Averill Fairbanks came through the door. "Them horns," he said. "I hate horns. They send signals from outer space."

Everything came from outer space as far as Averill was concerned. As far as I was concerned, *he* came from outer space, and I kept wishing he'd go back. "Good morning, Averill," I said with what I hoped was a pleasant smile. "Aren't you enjoying the parade?" Even now, the high school band was passing down Front Street, playing its signature tune, "Fight On You Buckers."

"Naw." Averill dug a finger in one ear and gave his head a vigorous shake. "Too damned loud. Like I said, them horns send signals from purple people with six eyes. Where's Vida?" He pronounced it *Veeda*, though he'd known her since she'd been born.

"In there," I said, gesturing toward the news office. "Do you have an item for her?"

"You bet." Averill hooked his gnarled thumbs in his overalls. "I tried to tell her before, but she wouldn't listen. What's wrong with that woman anyway?"

"I'm sure she'll be glad to see you," I lied, sinking to a new low to get rid of our resident UFO sighter and general pest. "Nice to see you, Averill."

He took the hint, and I lingered with Ginny. But Averill was still at Vida's desk when I finally felt forced to return to my office. I tried to slip by unnoticed, but it wasn't possible. Vida was on her feet, fairly shouting at Averill.

"Try—at least try—to get your story straight," she demanded. "Exactly when did you see this apparition at the warehouse site?"

Averill, who is small and brown as a nut, shrank back in Vida's visitor's chair. "Now don't get huffy. I already told you this a long time ago. But as usual, you wouldn't listen. Don't you want stuff for that gibberish you run on the front page or not?"

"It's not gibberish," Vida responded, sitting back down. "It's news items, featuring local personages. We call it human interest. You, of course, would call it alien visitations."

"Not always," Averill said, suddenly coy. "Sometimes it's real people. Like that Cardents from the college."

Vida narrowed her eyes. "Cardenas? The college president?"

"Is that what he is?" Averill rested his hands on his slight paunch. "I thought he was one of them morticians."

Despite myself, I couldn't leave Vida alone with Averill. I was afraid she might do him bodily harm. But to her credit, she was making a monumental effort to rein in her temper.

"What about President Cardenas?" she asked through gritted teeth.

"That's what I came to tell you." Then a puzzled look passed over Averill's face. "I think." He pulled out a rumpled red-and-white handkerchief, and blew his noise. "He was digging, just shovel after shovel."

"At the warehouse site?" Vida took a long drink of ice water from the glass she kept at her desk.

"Did I say that?" Averill stuffed the handkerchief back in his pocket. "Nope. Never said any such thing. Don't go putting words in my mouth."

Vida looked as if she'd like to put her fist in

Averill's mouth, but she kept her voice down. "Start from the beginning, please. You mentioned the warehouse, the fire, some sort of apparition, and President Cardenas. Let's start with the warehouse. What about it?"

I had sat down in Leo's vacant chair. Averill wiggled around, then seemed to concentrate. His face was so puckered with the effort that his eyes all but disappeared.

"It was right around Halloween," he began, his voice deepening and distant. "You behold some mighty strange sights around that time, but this one was real peculiar. I was there on the marge of Lake Labarge—"

Vida held up a hand. "Stop. I've read the poems of Robert Service. Lake Labarge is in the Yukon, not Alpine. Go back to Halloween."

Averill stood up. "You can't go back, unless you get in a time capsule. I've tried that, but I never get further than last week. Thanks for the sandwich."

Averill Fairbanks left. "What sandwich?" I asked.

"There was no sandwich." Vida tossed a pencil in disgust. "The man is mental. Why did I think he might actually have something for 'Scene'?"

"Vida," I said, scooting Leo's chair closer,

"didn't Averill have a ghost item for you earlier?"

Vida retrieved the pencil and tapped it on her desk. "Yes, last week. I met him coming from May Madness."

"He's usually not so persistent, is he? I mean, he comes in or calls maybe once every six weeks. There must be something on his mind," I ventured.

"Absolutely not," Vida snapped. "Or rather, what's there isn't real. It's all imaginary, like the spaceman who wore high-heeled shoes of patent leather."

Of course Vida was right. But something about Averill's garbled report niggled at my brain. As lunchtime drew closer I let it go and headed for the Alpine Mall.

The parade had been over for some time, but a few of the veterans and both of the logging trucks had lingered in the mall parking lot. I saw Ron Bjornson talking to the Peabody brothers, and wandered over in their direction. I wasn't sure what I intended to say to Ron, but I thought I'd try a little subterfuge to see if I could get an inkling about the possibility that Maylene was cheating on him with Einar Rasmussen Jr. Mine is a dirty job, but someone's got to do it when Vida's not around.

I never got the chance. Milo Dodge and Bill Blatt pulled into the parking lot just as the Peabody brothers started to walk away. Before I could take a step, Milo marched up to Ron and cuffed him.

"I'm arresting you for the murder of Einar Rasmussen Jr. Read him his rights, Bill." Milo nodded at his deputy while stunned onlookers gaped in shock. I was one of them. So was Ron Bjornson.

Chapter Twelve

AFTERWARD I WONDERED if Milo would have made the arrest if he'd seen me standing there. He hadn't, and his jaw dropped as I hurried over to the squad car where Bill was reminding Ron to watch his head getting into the backseat.

"So you've closed the case," I said lightly. "That's great. You have evidence, I take it? And motive?"

Milo didn't say a word. He got into the driver's seat, slammed the door, and screeched out of the parking lot. Several people gathered around me, apparently assuming that as the local publisher, I would know all the latest news. One of the Peabodys—I can never tell the two huge, hulking brothers apart—asked what the hell was going on. It seemed self-explanatory to me, and I said so.

But a voice from behind me didn't agree. "Ron's no killer," said Scott Kuramoto. "I've had several talks with him at the college. Under that rough-hewn exterior, he's a gentle sort of man."

"He's got a temper, though," said Cynthia

Kittikachorn, who was probably with Scott on lunch break from the college. Though newcomers to Alpine, they'd already shed some of their city ways. Like the other onlookers, Scott and Cynthia didn't try to keep their distance and disassociate themselves from the rest of humanity. "I've seen Ron get real mad and throw a hammer across the room," Cynthia said.

"But why would he kill Mr. Rasmussen?" Scott looked genuinely perplexed.

Put in an aggressive mood by Milo's silent rebuff, I edged between Scott and Cynthia. It wouldn't do any good to rush off to the Sheriff's office; nobody would talk until Ron was booked and interrogated. "Maybe I should discuss this with you two," I said. "Were you going to have something to eat here at the mall?"

"We were going to get some Mexican food," Cynthia replied. "The RUB's still not open because they weren't able to put the final touches on the kitchen until Sheriff Dodge was finished."

"Mexican's fine with me," I said.

We headed for Dos Señores, one of whom happened to be a Swede, and the other, a German. The tiny restaurant is mainly for takeout, but can accommodate about twenty people on the premises. Cynthia grabbed the last table, and told Scott to order for her. I joined him at the counter, where we all ended up with soft chicken tacos. Instead of a side of refried beans, there was a scoop of red cabbage. Food will be integrated before people in Alpine.

"Poor Ron," Scott said as we sat down. "I suppose I should call Deirdre."

"Why bother?" Cynthia said with a faint sneer. "She won't care who gets arrested, as long as it's not her."

"Cynthia . . ." Scott was pained. "Deirdre wants to see justice done. Don't be so hard on her."

"I barely know the woman," Cynthia said, then looked at me. "Sorry, Emma. You must think I'm awful. But I have this sisterly thing about Scott, and what little I've seen of Deirdre hasn't made me sympathetic. She's the kind who's always leaving for a party that's going to be better than the one she's already at."

"Cynthia . . ." Scott repeated, this time in a peevish tone.

But Cynthia wasn't easily silenced. "I don't want to see you hurt, Scott. I know it's not easy for minorities like us to find romance in a town like Alpine. But you can do better than Deirdre."

Scott didn't look as if he agreed. However,

the conversation wasn't going in the direction I'd hoped, and I couldn't afford to waste too much time with my lunchmates.

"Speaking of romance," I said, "have you heard any rumors involving Einar Rasmussen Jr.?"

"Sure," Cynthia replied. "Einar and Maylene. Another odd couple, if you ask me."

Scott, who seemed relieved that we'd changed the subject, waggled a plastic fork at Cynthia. "That's just gossip. You don't know for certain, and neither does anybody else."

"Ha!" Cynthia laughed out loud. "I know Maylene, and she hasn't kept their affair a big secret. At least not from *some* of us. Why do you think Ron killed Einar?"

"Did he?" Scott gave Cynthia a baleful look.

"The Sheriff says he did." Her tone was dogged. "Dodge doesn't strike me as the type who jumps to conclusions."

"He's not," I allowed. "He's a very cautious person."

"If I had a vote," Cynthia said with a smirk, "I'd put my money on that weird son of Einar's. Assuming, of course, that he really exists."

Given the fact that nobody had seen Beau in a very long time, I thought it was a fair assumption. Maybe Beau was a phantom, like

George and Martha's son in *Who's Afraid of Virginia Woolf?*

But this script wasn't being written by Edward Albee, and the scene was going nowhere. I finished my taco and excused myself. Five minutes later I was at the Sheriff's office. Vida was already ensconced, standing behind the curving counter and badgering Bill Blatt.

"Admit it, Billy," she commanded. "The fingerprints on the knife belonged to Ron. The motive is Einar's affair with Maylene. It was her lipstick that was found on his shirt. Really, it's all quite simple. Why not say so?"

"Because we've got a trial ahead of us," Bill replied, his fair complexion turning red. "We can't give out information like that, Aunt Vida. You know better."

"Better?" Vida glared at her nephew as Toni Andreas cowered at her desk. "I always know better. That's why I'm here." She turned slightly, acknowledging my presence for the first time. "I really can't imagine why I had to find out about Ron's arrest from Leo Walsh"— the glare now included me—"but this isn't the only matter that this so-called law-enforcement agency is holding back on. Now tell me about the warehouse site, Billy, or I'm going to have to speak to your mother."

"Vida," I began, "I was going to tell you as soon as I could, but—"

"Not soon enough," she interrupted. "Ron was arrested half an hour ago."

"It's not your story." I made a feeble gesture with my hands.

"It's an orphan of a story," Vida declared. "You knew Ron was arrested? Or were you shopping at the mall instead of tending to business?"

There are limits to what I will take from Vida. She had overstepped her bounds by mouthing off in front of other people. "That's it," I said grimly. "I'm covering this story, and you know it. I was following another angle at the mall, which we won't discuss now. Please come around to this side of the counter and stop berating your nephew, who is simply following instructions as well as legalities."

Vida was aghast. "Are you giving me orders?"

"Yes. I'm the boss." My stern expression felt a little shaky.

Vida stared at me. Then, with one last, dark look for Bill Blatt, she tromped through the swinging half-door in her splayfooted manner and exited the office.

"Whew!" cried Bill, wiping his brow.

"Gosh," breathed Toni, leaning back in her chair.

"Damn," I muttered, then offered them both a pitiful smile. "Vida will get over it. So will I. But we still need some answers here. What's going on with Ron and the Sheriff?"

Bill's face was returning to its normal pinkish hue. "Ron's being interrogated by Dodge and Jack Mullins."

"Ron hasn't admitted he killed Einar?" I asked, leaning on the counter.

Bill shook his head. "He insisted he wasn't guilty on the ride from the mall. Is it true that Mr. Rasmussen and Mrs. Bjornson were having an affair?"

I blinked at Bill. "Didn't Milo tell you that?"

"No." Bill bit his lip. "Sheriff Dodge doesn't always tell us everything. He's really been kind of tight-lipped these last few months."

"Great." Was I to blame for that, too? "What about the crime-scene tape at the warehouse, Bill? Has it got something to do with the bones the Bourgettes dug up?"

Bill looked miserable; his glance flitted from the interrogation room off to his right and back to me. "I honestly don't think I should say anything about that. Maybe Dodge will let you know."

"Maybe." I bit off the word. "If not, *The Advocate* is going to be rife with speculation this week. In fact, I'm thinking of doing a second editorial, on the lack of cooperation from this office."

Bill looked helpless. "That won't make Dodge very happy."

"I'm not very happy." It dawned on me that I hadn't been happy for quite a while. Even before I'd heard about Sandra Cavanaugh's death.

Milo came out of the interrogation room. "Ron's in the holding cell," he said, then noticed my presence. "Yes, he's being charged with first-degree homicide. He's pleading innocent. Maybe bail will be too high for him to post. We'll find that out tomorrow at the courthouse."

The sheriff's flow of information didn't really surprise me; he was bound to make such facts public. But since he'd volunteered, I decided to meet him halfway. Maybe it was impossible for me to be angry with Milo and Vida at the same time; they had been my two closest friends in Alpine.

"Thanks, Milo," I said, trying to sound pleasant. "How did you come to the conclusion that it was Ron?"

Milo ran a hand through his graying sandy hair. "The usual. Motive, opportunity, et cetera. Although there'd been an attempt to wipe the weapon clean, we found a partial print. Ron had gaps in his schedule that night. In fact, he let Einar into the building. My guess is he followed Einar inside, and they got into it. The charge may drop to second degree, but we'll see about that once Ron admits he's guilty."

"The motive," I said as Dwight Gould and Dustin Fong entered the office from the rear, "being the alleged affair between Einar and Maylene Bjornson."

Milo nodded at his deputies, then turned to face me over the counter. I noticed how tired he looked, especially around the eyes. His face seemed to sag, making it even longer and more melancholy than usual. It was as if he had grown old overnight, while I wasn't looking.

"I can't talk about that," he said, passing a hand over his forehead.

Jack Mullins came out of the interrogation room, presumably having secured Ron in the holding cell. "Who'da thunk it?" Jack mused. "I hated to lock him up. Ron's a good ol' boy if there ever was one. We were in high school together, we played football for the Buckers."

Milo didn't comment. "Are we through here?" he asked me.

"One more thing." I held up my index finger. "What's going on at the warehouse site? Don't blow me off. I know it has something to do with that bunch of bones the Bourgettes dug up."

Milo sighed and reached for his cigarettes, despite the "No Smoking" sign posted on the counter. "Tomorrow's your deadline, right?"

"We haven't changed it," I deadpanned.

"I'll let you know then," he said, turning his back and lighting up.

I wasn't going to get any more out of the Sheriff. The morning clouds had cleared and the sun was shining when I got back outside. The afternoon's brightness seemed to mock my mood, as did the generally cheerful attitude of passersby, presumably buoyed by the holiday.

Leo was on the phone when I returned, Carla was just leaving to drop her film off at Buddy Bayard's, and Vida had her head bent over her ancient typewriter. I hesitated to see if she'd look up, but she didn't, so I went into my office. Ten minutes later, when I went out to check the wire service, Vida was the only one in the newsroom. She still didn't look up.

Resignedly, I went over to her desk. "Vida," I began, "I'm sorry about what happened at the Sheriff's office earlier. But sometimes you sort of tend to take over, and it makes me feel . . ."

She finally met my gaze. To my astonishment, she'd been crying. "You humiliated me," she declared. "In front of Billy."

"Oh, Vida!" I sat down in her visitor's chair and put my arm around her. I couldn't remember the last time I'd seen her cry. "I'm really, really sorry. Look, I've been in a bad mood myself lately. I've been crabby and snappish and impatient with everyone."

"The change," Vida said in an ominous voice.

I gasped. Menopause had never entered my mind. I was still in my forties, if not by much. But of course that's usually when it happens. Maybe Vida was right. Maybe it was a more realistic explanation than having Leo tell me I hadn't been laid recently. Maybe it was both.

"I'll make an appointment with Doc Dewey," I said. "Hopefully, I can get in to see him before I'm too old to care."

Vida dabbed at her eyes with a floral-print handkerchief. "How will I ever face Billy again?"

I hung my head. Keeping up appearances was so important to Vida. "You knew I was covering this story," I said, keeping calm. "I felt as if you were trying to take over."

"I thought you'd given it back to Carla." Vida sniffed. "It seems that the college is her beat."

"It usually is, but not this time." I forced a smile. "She can't handle it, and you know it. Even if she weren't pregnant, I wouldn't let her cover a big story like this."

"I was only trying to help." A piteous note had crept into Vida's voice.

"I want you to," I insisted. "I always want your help. But that's not the impression I got. Do you want me to explain all this to Billy?"

"It's too late," Vida replied. "It happened. It can't be undone."

I supposed that was true. There was only one way out of this mess, and I had to take it or risk losing Vida's friendship. "We'll cover it together. It's that big. We'll both write the stories."

Vida's eyes grew wary. "That will be awkward."

"No, it won't. I'll do the hard news, you do the sidebars." I could probably edit the House & Home style out of them without too much trouble.

"Well . . ." She fingered her chin. "You'll let Billy and Milo and the rest of them know I'm assigned to the case, too?"

"Of course. In fact," I said, so relieved to see Vida softening a bit that I went a step too far, "Milo is going to have some news for us tomorrow on those bones at the warehouse site.

You handle that while I take care of the charges against Ron Bjornson."

"That's another thing," Vida said, receding back into gloom. "Ron's arrest upset me. Not merely the fact that I had to hear it from Leo, but that Milo thinks Ron killed Einar. It's not possible. Ron has his faults, but he's not a killer. Why, I've known him since the day he was born."

I couldn't claim such knowledge of Ron Bjornson. From my chance encounters with him over the years, I'd gotten the impression that he was a decent sort, but embittered by the timber industry's decline. If, however, the latter adversity could turn a man into a murderer, then half of Alpine would be wiped out and the other half would be in jail.

"You know Milo," I said. "He's very cautious. He wouldn't arrest Ron unless he had a good case."

Vida didn't comment. She put her handkerchief back in her purse and squared her shoulders. "I shan't disappoint you," she asserted.

"You never do, Vida," I said, and reached over to give her a quick hug.

"Do you want to go with me tonight when I call on Marlys Rasmussen?" she asked.

I didn't, actually, but I dared not turn the invitation down. "Sure. What time?"

"Sevenish. I'll pick you up."

"Great." I smiled, much more brightly. "Are we still friends?"

Vida had to think about it for a moment. "Yes. Yes, I believe so. Friendships, like hearts, are hard to break."

And even harder to mend, I thought as I walked over to the wire service. Maybe it wasn't my uterus that was bothering me. Maybe it was my heart. It had hurt for a very long time.

I had to stop feeling sorry for myself. There were other stories besides Ron's arrest and the breaking news on the bones. As usual, timber legislation would take up at least fifteen inches on the front page, along with Carla's Memorial Day parade pictures. The photo that she'd taken of the state official at the RUB dedication was better than the one of President Cardenas, but Nat was local, and the other man was from Olympia. We'd go with Nat, and put the state official and George Engebretsen inside. I'd try to squeeze in an article concerning a rumor about the proposed Icicle Creek Bridge. After all the hassles and delays, the college was lobbying to move the span west of town, by the campus. Leo informed me that Deirdre Rasmussen had called to say that apparently Marlys and the rest of the family were willing to pay to run the portrait of Einar Jr. She'd drop the photo off in the morning.

We could pick it up when we called on the Rasmussens, said Vida, who was in a subdued mood for the rest of the afternoon; but at least she wasn't hostile. As usual, she sought items for "Scene."

"Buddy Bayard bought a hedgehog," Carla volunteered. "He's got it at the studio, and its name is Pope Pius the Twelfth. I don't know why. It's not much of a pet, if you ask me. It just sits there, and you can't really see its eyes. If I had it, I'd call it Poopy."

"Somebody over on Fourth Street between Spruce and Tyee put an American flag on their garbage can for Memorial Day," said Ginny. "I think it's the Gustavsons' house."

"Is it blue with white trim?" asked Vida.

Ginny frowned. "No, it's sort of cream with brown."

"That's the Olsons," Vida said. "Anything else?"

"I saw Principal Freeman feeling up Debra Barton outside of the Elks Club last night," Leo offered.

Vida made a disgusted face. "I can't use that." Then she gazed more intently at Leo. "Is it true?"

Leo shrugged. "That's what it looked like to me."

"Goodness!" Vida clucked her tongue. "Emma, you're not contributing."

I wasn't concentrating, either. It had just occurred to me that I should call the Bourgette boys to see what they knew about the bones. "Huh? Oh—let me think. What about Birgitta Lindholm doing research on the early days of Alpine?"

"That'll do," said Vida. "Keep your eyes and ears open, everyone. We've still got one more day to go. I also have Dolph Swecker locked out of his truck and another cougar sighting, this time by the Overholt farm."

In my office, I called Directory Assistance to ask for the number at the restaurant construction site. A phone hadn't yet been installed, but the operator gave me the listing for the brothers' cell phone.

John answered, sounding frazzled. I asked him if the crime-scene tape was somehow related to the bones he and Dan had found.

"Yes," he replied, "and now we've got another delay. We'll never make our opening date at this rate."

Surprised by his candor, I sucked in my breath. "What's the problem with the bones?"

"I don't really know," John replied, still

sounding out of sorts. "Dodge showed up Saturday afternoon after we got back from the funeral in Snohomish. We'd just started getting the trailer organized when he said we had to stop work. Then he brings out the tape. I told him we hadn't reported any new crime, so what was going on? Dodge insisted we had to clear the area so he and his men could do some digging. He'd let us know when it was okay to start up again. Dan and I haven't been back since."

"Do you know if the Sheriff found any more bones?"

"Hell, no. We don't know squat." John paused. "Sorry, it's just that we're pissed. First, the hassle over the gold, then the vandalism, and now this. We're giving up on the gold, it's not worth the trouble. Especially now that What'shername has gotten in the act."

"Who?" The conversation was going off on a tangent, and I was lost.

"That girl from Sweden. You know, the one the Bronskys threw the party for a week or so ago."

"Birgitta," I said, filling in the gap. "What about her?"

A big sigh came through the receiver. "She showed up downtown to file some kind of claim on the gold this morning. But the courthouse wasn't open because of the holiday. Being a foreigner, she didn't know that, and I guess she raised some kind of fuss."

"Birgitta Lindholm filed a claim?" I was astonished. "How? Why?"

"I don't know," said John, who also sounded as if he didn't much care. "Dan was downtown at the parade. He told me about it when he got back. Jeez, Ms. Lord, do you think our property is jinxed?"

"Of course not," I said. But I was beginning to wonder.

I arrived at Casa de Bronska shortly before four. I could have called instead of going in person, but I felt it would be better to talk to the taciturn Ms. Lindholm face-to-face.

Ed, naturally, was face-to-face with a pile of sandwiches. "Gitty made them," he said from his place on the patio. "Have one. Try the Norwegian lox."

I did. It was delicious, with much to recommend it, including the fact that it had not been made by anyone bearing the name of Bronsky. "I'm here to see Gitty, as a matter of fact. Is she in?"

"Sure," Ed replied, pointing to the sandwiches, which apparently justified her presence. "You thinking about another story on her?"

"In a way," I hedged. "Where will I find Gitty?"

"Try the ballroom," Ed suggested, swiping at the mustard on his lower lip and missing. "We got the big-screen TV in there and she likes the soaps. If she misses one, she records it for later."

I'd finished the sandwich. "Thanks, Ed." I started for the side door, which led directly into the so-called ballroom.

"Hey!" Ed called. "I may have something big for you tomorrow."

Big as you? I wanted to say, but didn't. "What?" I turned slightly, shielding my eyes from the sun.

Ed leaned back in the white wrought-iron lawn chair. "Some kind of word from Steve."

"Steve? Steve who?"

Ed chuckled indulgently. "Spielberg. Irving and Skip tell me he usually makes all his calls in the evening, when things quiet down in L.A."

"Spielberg, huh? Okay, let me know." I went into the house before I lost my straight face and my snack.

Birgitta was curled up on a soft leather couch, glued to big images of beautiful people who may or may not have been working from a real script. They certainly had nice clothes. Like most of her generation, Birgitta had the sound on way too loud, and I had to stand in front of her before she noticed I was there.

"Mrs. Lord," she said, looking none too happy with my arrival. "Mrs. Bronsky is at the . . ." With the TV blaring, I couldn't tell if she said *tennis* or *dentist*. It didn't really matter, though I assumed Dr. Starr wasn't working on a holiday.

"I have some questions for you," I said, trying not to shout.

"Some what?"

"Questions," I shouted.

"What questions?"

I waved at the huge screen, which had now switched to a commercial that was even louder than the soap opera. "Can you turn that down?" I bellowed.

"What? Turn which way?" She swiveled around in her cushiony seat.

Spotting the remote on the arm of the leather couch, I grabbed it and found the mute button. "There." I sighed, and gave Birgitta my friendliest smile. "I'm sorry, I couldn't hear. And this is rather important."

Birgitta looked as if I couldn't say anything important, know anything important, *be* of any importance. "You want what of me?" There was definitely belligerence in the set of her wide shoulders.

"As I mentioned," I said, perching on the soft arm of the couch, "I had some questions. I understand you went to the courthouse today to make a claim on the gold that was found in Alpine some months ago."

"The courthouse was not open." Birgitta lifted her head, and the sun that was coming through the long windows turned her hair to a much brighter gold than the nuggets I'd seen in the chest at Sandy Clay's assayer's office. "It is very stupid not to have government at the job on Monday."

I wasn't going to get into an argument over American holidays. I'd already spent seven years trying to get Vida not to call Memorial Day by its older name, Decoration Day. "What about the gold?" I persisted.

Birgitta shrugged. "It is mine. I want to take it home with me."

"How," I asked, holding on to my patience, "can it be yours? You've only just arrived, and that gold was buried for many, many years."

"It is mine because it belonged to my great-grandfather, Ulf Lindholm. I have read many things in your library. I know it is mine." She gave a toss of her head, and sent the golden hair sailing around her shoulders.

"Your great-grandfather," I repeated. "He lived in Alpine?"

"For some years, long ago." The belligerence hadn't quite faded, but Birgitta's face had taken on a softer look. "He was a logger man."

"Was he also a miner?" I noted her blank expression, and made digging motions with my hands. "Did he dig for gold?"

"No. It was a gift." The commercial segment was finished, and Birgitta's eyes traveled back to the TV.

"A gift from whom?" I asked.

Birgitta drew back on the couch. "Why should I say to you? It is the courthouse persons I must tell. Don't ask more questions. I must watch my program."

I've never understood the lure of soap operas. Most people are living one of their own, and rarely seem to realize it. Birgitta and her great-grandfather and the chest filled with nuggets and the newly discovered bones were far more fascinating than the contrived lives of the pretty people in their pretty clothes on the pretty set which dominated the so-called ballroom.

"I assume your great-grandfather is dead," I remarked, wishing I hadn't set the remote down by Birgitta.

"Yes, he died before I was born. My grandfather is dead, too. But he never came to

America, nor my father. Only great-grandfather—and me. He came back to Sweden, to Malmö. I will also come back. With the gold." She picked up the remote and turned the sound back on.

"What," I practically yelled, "did the books say about your great-grandfather?"

"That many Swedish men come to Alpine." Birgitta turned the sound up yet another notch.

"Did the books mention his name?" I'd get hoarse if I had to keep on shouting.

"Many Swedish men. He was of them. I know." She hit the volume one more time.

I was defeated. But I wasn't stupid enough to go out via the patio. Another round with Ed would completely do me in. With my ears ringing, I left the ballroom through another exit and slipped down the hall and out through the front entrance. Carla would have to park herself at the courthouse tomorrow. Maybe we could make more sense of the potential story then.

I related my visit to both Carla and Vida. Neither was impressed by Birgitta's so-called claim.

"Gold digger," said Carla. "Those big, blonde foreign women usually are, aren't they?"

"Well . . . not all of them," I said.

"This Ulf was not mentioned specifically?" said Vida.

"Not as far as I could tell," I responded. "Between her sometimes sketchy English and the blasted TV, I'm not sure I got everything exactly right."

Vida adjusted the big bow on her polka-dot blouse. "The name Lindholm isn't familiar to me. But if he came here in the early part of the century, I might not have heard of him. He certainly didn't stay, but then some of the foreigners didn't. They'd earn a decent wage, save up, and go back to the old country to make a better life for themselves and their families. Like the Japanese at Tye."

Carla was gathering up her things. "I'll be at the courthouse when it opens at nine," she said. "See you."

Vida was also ready to go. "Sevenish," she reminded me. "I'll honk."

It was after five. Leo and Ginny had both left. I checked my messages, but there was nothing of importance. It was too late to call Doc Dewey for an appointment. I, too, might as well go home.

There was nothing there for me, either.

Vida had an easily identifiable way of honking: *Toot-toot-pause. Toot-toot-toot-pause. Long toot.* I was waiting for her when she arrived, but hadn't ventured outside. When I reached the Buick, I noticed that she seemed more like her old self. Maybe she had recovered from this morning's debacle.

"You've never met Marlys," she said as we headed out of town. "Don't be put off by how dreary she is. The woman can't help it."

"Which, you figure, explains Maylene Bjornson?"

"Maylene and forty other women as far as I can tell. Not that I *know*," she added hastily, "nor do I condone adultery. But Marlys is always in the dumps. I used to think she didn't go out much because she drank. Then I decided that if she did, she ought to be a bit perkier."

It took less than ten minutes to reach the Rasmussen home near Skykomish. I could see the house through the trees. We turned off by a half-dozen mailboxes and wound down a dirt road for some twenty yards before we arrived at a paved driveway. The large one-story stone-and-cedar house with its arched windows and at least three chimneys was built not far from the river. I sensed that Einar Jr. had spared no expense. Maybe he had tried to cheer up Marlys.

We pulled up to a three-car garage which had all of its doors closed. "Do they know we're coming?" I asked.

"No. I thought it best to surprise them." She

got out of the car, then hissed at me over the Buick's roof. "Remind me to get that portrait of Einar. It'll save Deirdre a trip tomorrow."

We went up the walk, which was lined with daffodils and tulips and primroses. The double doors had handles instead of knobs, and a replica of Hans Christian Andersen's Little Mermaid sat by the steps. The doorbell chimed the first ten notes of "Wonderful, Wonderful Copenhagen."

Deirdre answered the door. She wore no makeup and seemed startled to see us. "What's going on?" she asked in a suspicious voice.

Vida put out a friendly hand. "We came to call on your dear mother. Do you think she'd mind receiving us? We'll only be a few minutes. Oh, and we'll be glad to take that picture of your father in to the paper. It will save you making the trip."

Deirdre gave a faint nod. "Sure. Thanks. I'll go get it. I might as well cancel the lost-cat ad I called in the other day. Fluff's never coming back. Cats are indoor animals, they shouldn't be allowed to roam, especially out here in the woods. You'll want a check for the photo, right?"

Vida glanced at me. "Do you know the rate?"

I smiled at Deirdre. "Hold the check. Leo Walsh will let you know how much it is."

"Okay." Deirdre started back through the entry hall, which was paved in large polished stones.

"Deirdre," Vida called after her. "May we come in? We want to see your mother."

Deirdre turned around. "I'm afraid she's not feeling well. This has been a terrible strain. I'll get the picture. Wait here."

"This is ridiculous." Vida fumed, rubbernecking around the entrance. "Marlys should be able to cope by now. Einar's been dead a full week."

I expected her to stomp right into the house, but she held back. "You know," I said, "it's not fair to count the days in terms of shock and grief. Einar's death was not only a shock, but brutal. I can see why Marlys is still upset, especially if she's a shy, sensitive person."

"Perhaps." Vida was frowning at the Little Mermaid. "She certainly looked like a mess at the funeral."

"When was the last time you saw her before Einar was killed?" I asked, keeping my voice down. "How was she then?"

"Let me think—it was last September, at the Labor Day picnic. Marlys was very quiet. She kept to herself, tending hot dogs at a grill in Old Mill Park."

Deirdre returned, carrying the same manila

folder she'd brought into the office earlier. "Here. Grandmama felt it would be the thing to do. She's also having it run in the Snohomish paper."

"Thank you." Vida accepted the envelope and offered Deirdre a tight little smile. "Please have your mother phone me when she's better. I simply wouldn't feel right if I didn't call on her."

Deirdre nodded, but said nothing. We trooped off the porch and down the walk. Vida stopped when she heard the doors close. "This way," she whispered, hurrying past the triple garage.

"What are we doing?" I asked, though I knew the answer.

"I just want to make sure," Vida replied. "I can't help but wonder if Marlys is malingering."

"Vida . . ." I didn't finish; it would do no good. Obediently, I trooped behind her as she approached the side of the house and the tall windows that looked into a living room.

"Nothing." Vida kept moving. I could hear the river rushing by the back of the house. "Ah! The kitchen. There's Deirdre, opening the refrigerator."

"It's still light," I protested. "She can see us."

"She's not looking this way. Don't hop about

so much. Someone else is with her. She's talking to whoever it is."

I froze and kept quiet. Birds chirped in the evergreens overhead. I could smell the damp and feel the soft ground beneath my feet. Young rhododendrons and azaleas separated us from the house itself. I admired the landscaping while Vida watched and waited.

"My goodness!" she breathed. "Look!"

I saw a young man with long fair hair move into view. He wore a sleeveless T-shirt and was taking a soda out of the refrigerator. "Beau," I said in a low voice.

"Not Beau," Vida whispered. "Much too young."

"Then who is it?" I asked.

Deirdre and the young man disappeared out of our range of sight. The river rumbled on. "There's only one person it *could* be," Vida said, reluctantly moving back toward the driveway. "It's got to be Deirdre's missing son, Davin. Now, why in the world has he shown up now? More to the point, where has he been?"

Chapter Thirteen

WHEN THE DIRT road ended at the turn onto Highway 2, Vida surprised me. She went west, instead of east to Alpine. "What are we doing now?" I asked, and immediately knew the answer. "Calling on the senior Rasmussens in Snohomish?"

"Correct," Vida responded. "The timing is right, for several reasons. Thyra won't yet have realized I didn't send a memorial. She and Einar Sr. ought to be at home, though you never know with her. I understand that despite failing eyesight and arthritis, she's still quite the gadabout. However, I suspect that she's officially in mourning. The social conventions are very important to Thyra. They always were. Obsessive, really."

"And?"

"And what?"

"That's only two reasons."

"Oh. Yes. Well, the third is obvious. If anyone knows about Davin, it'd be Thyra."

"What about Harold and Gladys?" I asked. "Don't they live around here somewhere?"

"About a mile west of Sultan," Vida replied,

slowing down behind a large truck. "But I'm not sure they know anything about anything. Still . . . we'll see, on the way back."

We followed the truck and the setting sun. There was quite a bit of traffic, no doubt owing to the three-day weekend. Late May is a beautiful time on the western slope of the Cascades. The maples and alder and cottonwood have all leafed out, and the trilliums are in bloom. At the higher elevations, rivulets of melting snow trickle down the moss-covered rocks, forming little creeks that run like an escort to the passing cars. Everything is green, including the river itself, which flirts with the highway in places, then disappears among the trees. I rolled the window down just enough so that I could sniff the evergreens and the permeating damp that signifies decay in the autumn, but rebirth in the spring.

"She'll be rude," Vida said. "Be prepared."

"Maybe she won't let us in, either," I remarked, taking another deep breath.

"Maybe." Vida paused. "Thyra likes to show off, though. You've never seen the inside of her house. She'll want to impress you."

"Is it impressive?" I asked as we passed the turnoff to Index.

"It was to me the last time I saw it," said Vida, finally able to pass the truck which had been keeping us and a long line of traffic well under the legal speed limit. "Of course I was still in my teens, a most impressionable age."

"Before the gourd incident, I take it?"

"Just before," Vida answered. "Mother, who knew how much store Thyra placed on protocol and decorum, went to see her to make sure it would be all right for someone not from Snohomish to bring her gourds to the summer festival. I went along, because Mother didn't like to drive any distance alone. Thyra was gracious, in a condescending manner. She assured Mother it would be proper. But of course she only said that because she thought Mother's gourds would be inferior to her own. They weren't, which is why Thyra was so infuriated."

"So you and your mother never visited the Rasmussens again?"

"Never," Vida said, then uttered a mirthless little laugh. "My, my. We were all teenagers then—Harold, Einar Jr., Mary Jane. No, Mary Jane was younger, still in pigtails. How time flies."

I kept silent, perhaps a tribute to those who had since died, to the different world of the midcentury, to Vida's adolescence. It was hard to think of her as a teenager, harder yet to conjure up the child called Vida Blatt. She had probably always been big for her age, or at least tall. I had seen her wedding pictures, and the satin gown with its three-quarter train had covered a statuesque figure even then. I tried to recall Ernest, her groom, but his face was a blank. Even then, Vida had possessed the power to overwhelm whoever entered her circle.

We had passed through Monroe and were headed for Snohomish on Highway 2. "It's grown so," Vida said almost mournfully. "The last time I was at the Rasmussen Sr.'s house, Snohomish wasn't any bigger than Alpine. The only businesses were the mills and the cannery. They're all but gone now. Creeping commuterism has taken over, and I find it rather sad."

Certainly the town sprawled, with new developments all around the edges. Snohomish, like all the other bedroom communities within fifty miles of Seattle, had spread out to take in the commuters who found big-city housing too expensive. Single homes, town houses, and condominiums flourished on the town's outskirts. But as we drove into the old residential section, the streets were lined with beautifully kept-up homes and stately trees. Vida had turned off onto Avenue B. It was still light, and the sun glinted like gold off the big windows of the Victorian houses.

"There, on the right," Vida said, pulling into

a parking space. "White, with the wraparound porch."

It was one of the larger homes, in the middle of the block. Several concrete steps led up to the walk. The front door seemed massive, and the porch curved around the right side of the house. When Vida hit the doorbell, it played a vaguely familiar tune.

"The Danish national anthem?" I murmured.

"Perhaps." Vida tapped her foot.

Just before she could press the bell again, a gaunt woman of about sixty answered the summons. "Yes?" she said in a voice as suspicious as Deirdre's had been when we'd called on Marlys.

"Mrs. Runkel and Ms. Lord to see Mrs. Rasmussen," Vida announced in formal tones. "Of Alpine."

The woman's washed-out blue eyes narrowed. "Is Mrs. Rasmussen expecting you?"

"No," Vida replied. "This is a surprise visit."

The woman didn't appear to like surprise visits. She hesitated, then went back inside. The door remained open just enough so that we could see her ascend a wide staircase with a carved banister.

"Good grief," Vida muttered. "Can't she just yell?"

"Is she the housekeeper?" I asked.

"I suppose. The Rasmussens have always had help." She resumed tapping her foot.

Five minutes must have passed before the woman returned. "Mrs. Rasmussen wants to know why you're here."

"To offer our condolences," Vida said, though she didn't sound very sorrowful. "And to make sure this is the right picture." She flourished the envelope with its photo of Einar Jr. "We're press."

"Press?" The presumed housekeeper made a face. "What do you mean, *press?*"

"Newspaper people. We think Deirdre might have made a mistake." The lie tripped off Vida's tongue.

"Deirdre?" The name seemed to make some sort of impression on the woman. "Come in, wait here. I'll ask again."

She headed back up the staircase while Vida and I rubbernecked around the spacious entry hall and into the living room. The furnishings were all spare, but handsome, no doubt inspired by Danish craftsmen. There were flowers and plants everywhere, tributes, no doubt, to Einar Jr.

The woman came halfway back down the stairs. "Mrs. Rasmussen will see you. Don't stay long and tire her. Come this way. I'm Mrs. Steelman, the house manager."

"Couldn't have just a housekeeper," Vida whispered. "My, my."

On the first landing there was a large picture of Helsingor's Kronborg castle. *Hamlet's Elsinore,* I thought, and tried to picture Einar Jr. in that role, with Thyra as Gertrude. It didn't play. But of course in real life, it was the son, not the father, who had been murdered.

We followed the scent of freesia down the long hall. Sure enough, there were more flowers, including a four-foot tree azalea in brilliant pink. The master bedroom was big, and obviously served as Thyra's sitting room. In addition to the double bed, there was a couch, several curving wooden chairs, and a TV. Mercifully, it was turned off. I didn't want to have two shouting matches in one day.

"Vida Blatt," Thyra said in a bored voice. "What are you doing here?"

"It's been Vida Runkel for almost fifty years," Vida responded, and sat down in one of the curved wooden chairs without being asked. "Emma Lord and I are here to offer our condolences. We were at the funeral."

"Who?" From her place on the deep blue couch, Thyra peered at me. "Do I know you?"

"No," I replied politely. "I work with Vida at *The Advocate.* In Alpine," I added, in case Thyra was so insular that anything or anyone outside of Snohomish wasn't worthy of her attention.

"What's your name?" Thyra didn't wear glasses, and I doubted that she used contacts. Vida had mentioned that the old lady didn't see well. Certainly, she was squinting. With her eyes practically disappearing and her face thrust forward, Thyra's sharp features reminded me of some ancient bird of prey.

Despite Vida's attempt at an introduction, I said my name and stepped forward to take Thyra's hand. To my surprise, her grip was strong. Maybe the arthritis plagued other parts of her body.

"Emma," Thyra repeated. "That's a nice, old-fashioned name. Not at all like these crazy names they give kids nowadays. Madison. Brewster. Parachute. What next?"

"My son's name is Adam," I said, as if I felt a need to win Thyra over. "That's about as old-fashioned as you can get."

"Very nice." Thyra sat back among the cushions, her rather large feet propped on a leather footstool. Even sitting down, she seemed tall, and now that she wasn't squinting, I could see that she had once been a handsome woman. The bone structure was there, though the skin that covered it was flaccid and deeply lined.

"We tried to call on Marlys," Vida began as I joined her in a matching chair. "She's too unwell to receive visitors."

"Leave her be," Thyra snapped. "Marlys needs privacy."

Somewhat to my surprise, Vida didn't argue. "I spoke with Harold and Gladys in Sultan after the funeral. They seem to be coping."

Thyra seemed uninterested in her elder son and his wife. "Gladys went to pieces at the services. I can't think why. She hardly ever spoke to Junior. Always acted like she was afraid of him. Maybe she was. Gladys is a goose."

"But Einar—Junior—and Harold had mended their fences, I gather," said Vida.

"They had to." Thyra's face hardened. "I told them to make up. It's not right for brothers to quarrel."

"Or sisters?" The words seemed to slip out of Vida's lips, like a snake let loose.

Thyra glared. "You mean Mary Jane. That's different, and nobody's business."

It takes more than Thyra Rasmussen to daunt Vida. "But Mary Jane and Richard were at the funeral and the reception. I thought that showed evidence of goodwill."

"Evidence of greed, you mean." Thyra compressed her lips.

"Greed?" I said in a meek voice.

Thrya's eyes, which I realized were as deep a blue as the couch she sat on, sparked. "Junior's dead. Those Catholics figure Senior and I are on our last legs. Why else would they come to a Lutheran funeral? I didn't think it was allowed by their stupid pope."

"That's not true," I said calmly, no longer amazed by the ignorance of some non-Catholics.

"How would you know?" Thyra retorted.

I was about to say that I knew because I was one, but Vida intervened, probably to prevent Thyra from booting me out of the house. "When did Davin show up?" she asked in a matter-of-fact voice. "Before or after the funeral?"

If Thyra was surprised, she didn't show it. "Before," she said, fingering the nubby gold cross at her neck. "He didn't sit with us in the family room, but he was there all the same. Why do you ask?"

"Because," Vida explained, "Deirdre gave us to understand that she didn't know where he was."

"Deirdre!" Thyra sniffed. "She doesn't know much, does she? All that makeup, you'd think she was a tramp. She's not. Not really. She just uses poor judgment."

"But Davin is with her now," Vida went on calmly. "Where was he until today?"

"What do you care?" Thyra looked belligerent, her hands clasped in her lap and her face again thrust forward.

"Deirdre seemed so upset," Vida replied. "I was merely curious. Besides, I have a grandson just about his age."

Roger had barely entered his teens, which made him at least five years younger than Davin. He was the only boy among her grandchildren, however, which I supposed was why she doted on him, despite his many, blatant flaws. He was also, unfortunately, the only one who lived in Alpine.

"Davin wasn't far," Thyra said, now enigmatic. "Not far at all." Her faulty gaze traveled around the room, to the azalea tree, the potted freesia, the red and white chrysanthemums, the tidy bed with its sky-blue spread, and finally, to a breakfront I hadn't noticed before.

It was filled with gold objects: the gewgaws, the knickknacks, the baubles Edna Mae had wanted to show off at the library. I got to my feet and went over to the glass-fronted cabinet.

"These are lovely," I remarked, wondering if I could do any good for Edna Mae by lauding the objects.

"So they are," Vida chimed in, apparently giving up on learning more about Davin's mysterious disappearance. She also got to her feet and came to join me.

There were all sorts of items, including a small Buddha, a deer, various pieces of jewelry, and what might have been a representation of Mount Pilchuck. Each piece had a nubby appearance, like the cross that Thyra wore. Like the cross I'd inherited, the cross made of gold nuggets.

"Wherever did you get all these beautiful things?" I asked, hoping to sound awestruck.

"From my mother," Thyra replied.

"Your mother," Vida echoed. "Oddly, I don't recall her. Who was she?"

"My mother," Thyra said. "I'm tired now. You'd better go. Have Steelie come up. It's time for my medicine."

I assumed that *Steelie* was Mrs. Steelman, house manager. Vida hesitated, then started for the door. "Again, our condolences. Your son's loss is deeply felt by many." I noticed that Vida didn't necessarily include herself among them.

"Thank you," said Thyra, but there was neither gratitude nor graciousness in her voice. "By the way," she added as we headed for the hall, "how's your mother, Vida?"

Vida turned, her head seeming to swing as if on a stiff hinge. "My mother has been dead for almost twenty years."

"Good," said Thyra.

Vida's eyes bulged. "Better if it had been you," she retorted, and with a swish of her swing coat, stomped off down the hall.

Thyra's laughter followed us practically to the bottom of the staircase.

We did not bother to seek out Mrs. Steelman.

"Wretched old harridan." Vida fumed as we got into the Buick. "Can you imagine what *her* mother must have been like?"

"You didn't know Thyra's mother?" I said, vaguely surprised.

"No. They were Snohomish people. Anyway," Vida continued, pulling out into Avenue B, "Thyra's mother might have been dead by the time I met the witch. I don't recall anything about her. Maybe she didn't have a mother. Maybe she was hatched by a vulture."

"All that gold," I mused, wanting to get Vida off the subject lest she burst a blood vessel. "Does it remind you of anything?"

"Certainly," Vida retorted. "But that doesn't mean much. There are plenty of gold trinkets around this area, either from local mining or the Klondike or the Yukon or Alaska."

"The Buddha caught my eye," I said.

"Hmm. Yes, I did see that. Really, Emma—you aren't trying to draw farfetched conclusions, are you?"

"Sure. Why not?" My tone was glib, but I was serious. "Doesn't all of this go beyond coincidence?"

As we headed for Monroe, Vida grew thoughtful. "Last fall, a chest of nuggets was dug up at the old warehouse. The chest itself bears a Japanese name. The land is purchased by John and Dan Bourgette, who are the nephews of Einar Rasmussen Jr. Einar is murdered a few months later, at the college campus. Bones are found at the same site where the gold was discovered. Birgitta Lindholm suddenly shows up, claiming her great-grandfather was the rightful owner of the gold, though he left Alpine many years ago for Sweden. We visit Thyra Rasmussen and see her collection of items fashioned from nuggets, which she says were handed down by her mother." She paused as we slowed to comply with Monroe's speed limit. "The question is, why did Birgitta show up now?"

"That's not the only question," I remarked. "But certainly her employment with the Bronskys was calculated. Word of the gold stash had been passed down to her by her father and grandfather. If the gold really belonged to Ulf—I think that was his name—why didn't he tell his descendants where he'd hidden it?"

Again, Vida was silent, this time almost until we passed through Sultan. "Because," she said with a sense of triumph, "he didn't know where he'd put it. Didn't Birgitta come into *The Advocate* looking for newspapers from around the turn of the century? If so, there was no Alpine. The whistle-stop, which is all it was at the time, was then called Nippon. I doubt that there was much to mark a specific spot, and can only assume that Ulf Lindholm intended to dig up his stash, but for some reason, he didn't come back."

It was growing dark as we began the gradual climb into the mountains. Since we'd already gone through Sultan, I assumed that Vida had scuttled any plan to call on Harold and Gladys Rasmussen.

"So Birgitta ends up in Alpine shortly after the gold has been dug up," I said. "I'll admit the coincidence is a bit too—wait!" I swerved around as far as I could in the confines of my seat belt. "Ed mentioned that he'd been sending Birgitta copies of *The Advocate* to acquaint her with the area. What if one of those issues contained the story about finding the chest of nuggets?"

"Hmm." Vida sounded bemused. "Yes, that's quite possible. I wonder how that works, getting an au pair. I assume there are agencies who match the would-be employers to the applicants. Now, how many Europeans might select Skykomish County? And who around here but Ed would be extravagant enough to want an au pair girl in the first place?"

"Maybe," I said in a musing tone, "Ed didn't."

Vida turned so swiftly that she lost her grip on the steering wheel and almost sent us over the center line. "You mean that Birgitta contacted Ed and Shirley?"

"She may have, knowing the general vicinity of the gold," I replied. "For all we know, three generations of Lindholms have been angling to get over here somehow."

"How did she find Ed?" asked Vida, again paying strict attention to her driving. "Did she look him up under *Ninny*?"

"The Internet, maybe," I suggested. "His stupid book came out not long after the fire. Or maybe she wrote to the chamber of commerce, asking who was rich around here. There are ways, with so much information available worldwide."

"That part makes sense," Vida conceded. "But I don't see how it ties in with the Rasmussens."

"Maybe it doesn't, except for the Bourgettes now owning the warehouse site," I said. "Unless . . ." My voice trailed off.

"Unless what? Come, come, don't hold back," Vida urged.

"A wild idea," I admitted. "What if Einar—or any of the Rasmussens—had let on that they had an interest in the gold?"

"Why would they do that?" Vida responded with a frown.

"Maybe to spite the Bourgettes?" I offered. "Maybe because they actually have gold nuggets, and Thyra wanted to add to her collection? Maybe because she's a greedy old woman?"

"Not impossible," Vida admitted. "But how would Birgitta hear of it?"

"Ed," I said simply. "He told me he played golf with Einar Jr."

"And Ed is a blabbermouth," Vida said. "Yes, I can see all that. Especially the part about the Rasmussens wanting to annoy the Bourgettes. But none of this has anything to do with Maylene and Ron Bjornson."

"No," I responded in a dejected voice. "It doesn't. The way Milo sees it, jealousy is the motive, and it's always a strong one."

"True," Vida agreed. "Yet I have to wonder.

I've known Ron forever, and somehow I don't see him as a killer, not even in a jealous rage."

I knew what Vida—what Jack Mullins and all the others—were thinking. Ron was a native son, and couldn't possibly commit such a heinous crime. Never mind that it had happened before, with some other lifelong residents knocking off one of their own. The idea was still hard for Alpiners to swallow.

For the rest of the journey, Vida and I speculated, but found ourselves going around in circles. Just as we crossed the bridge over the Sky, I remembered to ask her where she thought Davin had been before he'd showed up at Einar Jr.'s house.

"That's not difficult," Vida declared. "The senior Rasmussens live in a very large house, as I'm sure you noticed. There's plenty of room for a teenager to hide."

"But why?"

"Didn't you say that Einar Jr. was responsible for Davin's disappearance?"

"Not exactly," I said, trying to recall what Deirdre had told me. "I think she alluded to the fact that Einar knew where he was."

"The same thing," Vida said, turning off onto Fir Street, where my log cabin was located. "Who else would have brought the boy to live with his grandparents? Who else could have convinced Thyra and Einar Sr. to take Davin in?"

Vida had a point. But her argument brought something else to mind. "Where was Einar Sr. when we called on Thyra? I saw no sign of him."

Vida snorted. "Probably in the basement. Even when he was hale and hearty, I heard that she kept him down there. Einar Sr. was never allowed to smoke abovestairs."

I had a vision of the old man, huddled in his wheelchair, sitting among the water pipes and the abandoned coal bin and the other musty relics of the past. It would be cold and damp, with spiders and cobwebs and maybe a mouse or two.

On the other hand, it might be better than living upstairs with Thyra.

I had just hung up my jacket when someone came to my door. At nine-fifteen, it was a bit late for a casual caller. I peered through the peephole before responding.

"Ryan!" I exclaimed, after recognizing his plumpish form and opening the door. "Come in. Is something wrong?"

"Not exactly," he replied, looking sheepish. "I felt I owed you an explanation."

I frowned. "About what?"

"Carla," he said, hands deep into the pockets of his windbreaker. "I didn't want you to think I wasn't a morally responsible person."

If we were going to discuss morals, I needed to sit down. A drink wasn't a bad idea, either. I insisted that Ryan make himself comfortable while I poured him a glass of Chardonnay and made myself a weak bourbon and water.

Ryan began after a certain amount of fidgeting and clearing his throat. "Carla thinks a lot of you, Ms. Lord," he said. "She's worked for you quite a while. In fact, this has been her only job since she graduated from college."

I knew Carla's history, and while she wasn't a demonstrative sort when it came to showering affection on her own sex, I sensed her feelings. Giving a nod, I let Ryan continue.

"I tried not to show it when I was here last night," he went on, "but I was very embarrassed. You see, Carla has a rather casual attitude toward being pregnant and yet not quite married."

"Not quite," I repeated with a smile.

Ryan grimaced. "When I found out she was going to have a baby, I wanted to get married right away. But Carla has always dreamed of a big wedding."

The biggest thing about the wedding will be Carla

herself, I thought, and kept smiling. "Women often have that kind of dream," I noted. I had, a long, long time ago.

"Carla wouldn't budge," Ryan said, holding his wineglass in both hands. "Her parents seemed okay with it, but when we went over to Spokane to visit mine, there was an awful ruckus. My family's Catholic, and very conservative."

Washington is virtually two states, divided by the Cascade range. The western half is rainy and mild, with the majority of the population living in its bigger cities. Early on, timber dominated the economy, then Boeing, and now Microsoft. Between the working class and the intellectuals, the Democratic party has held the majority at the ballot box. On the other side of the mountains, the terrain is almost Midwestern, and agriculture has always been the key. The weather is more extreme, with hot, dry summers and cold, snowy winters. Voters tend to be Republican, which means that the state is also divided into liberal and conservative camps. Ryan Talliaferro obviously came from a typical eastern Washington family.

"My folks tried not to let Carla know how upset they were," Ryan explained, "but she knew. Being Carla, she doesn't hold it against them. She has such a good heart."

That was generally true, despite her sometimes self-centered attitude. Motherhood
would probably soften her.

"Anyway," Ryan went on, "when I found out
you were a Catholic, too, I felt I had to let you
know that it wasn't my idea to wait so long to
get married. I'll admit I don't usually go to
church, but I'm hoping that someday we can
get our marriage blessed."

"How does Carla feel about that?" I asked.

Ryan frowned. "I don't think she cares one
way or the other. Between the baby and the
wedding itself, she's got plenty on her mind.
Carla's Jewish, but she doesn't really practice
her faith. Her folks don't, either. I'm hoping
that when the time comes, it won't be an issue."

"The time will come when the baby gets
here," I pointed out. "You're going to want to
have him or her baptized."

"I know." Ryan was silent for a moment. "I
could wait, but my folks would have a fit. As I
said, they're already upset."

It seemed to me that Carla's indifference
would play into Ryan's hands. Still, I hated to
see anyone enter marriage with extra burdens.
"Since you're not getting married in the
Church," I said slowly, "Carla may agree to
compromise by having the baby baptized. If
religion doesn't mean that much to her—and

I've never seen that it has—she may give in quite easily. Baptism doesn't change a child's ancestry."

An uncertain smile broke out on Ryan's face. "Put like that, it makes sense. Thanks, Ms. Lord."

I shrugged. "I'm only guessing. And please, please call me Emma."

Ryan had finished his wine. "I'm glad I stopped by," he said, getting to his feet. "I was afraid I'd made a bad impression on you. I didn't want you to think I was one of those cads who gets a woman pregnant and then has to be hog-tied into doing the right thing."

The old-fashioned word *cad* would have been endearing in another context. Under the circumstances, it didn't amuse me. I was kind and gracious as I ushered Ryan out of the house. It wasn't his fault; apparently, he didn't know. Maybe he thought I was divorced, or widowed, like Vida.

Or maybe he knew, and was simply being brutally frank.

The phone still didn't ring.

Chapter Fourteen

TUESDAY, BLOODY TUESDAY, as I sometimes referred to deadline day, was upon us. No matter how hard we try, there is always the possibility of a last-minute change in an ad or a story, late-breaking news, or mechanical failure. For those of us who live with that kind of pressure, there is also the reward. The paper is printed, it's delivered, and it's read, especially in a small town where the weekly is the sole source of local information. Thus, there is a sense of accomplishment, a raison d'être for our lives. Some people in the business procrastinate and then thrive when deadline draws nigh. They not only do their best work, but probably couldn't function without the warning tick of the clock. I'm not like that, I prefer being ahead of schedule, but the deadline is always there, like home plate or the finish line. Carla once misspelled the word, and it came out *deadlive*. I almost didn't correct it. There is nothing dead about deadlines, but meeting them lets you know you're alive.

Around eight-thirty, Carla had stopped in long enough to drop off a dozen muffins from the Upper Crust, and drink a cup of coffee. Now, shortly after nine, she was at the court-house, hoping to intercept Birgitta Lindholm. Vida was adding items to "Scene," Leo was out corralling last-minute advertisers for the Memorial Day section, and Ginny was putting the classifieds together. I'd decided to forgo my vilification of the Sheriff's office. Maybe Milo would actually come up with some helpful in-formation before five o'clock.

He called a few minutes after three. The usu-ally laconic voice was formal and glum. "Ron's not posting bail," Milo said. "It was set at three hundred thousand dollars, and I don't know if he can't or won't. He's sticking to his guns, says he didn't do it, and he intends to sue the county."

"Wrongful arrest, huh? Have you talked to Maylene?"

"Yeah." The Sheriff didn't elaborate.

"Do you think she believes that Ron's inno-cent?"

"So she claims."

This was not an easy conversation. "Does she admit to having an affair with Einar Jr.?"

"No. She denies it."

"She does?" Somehow, I was surprised. I shouldn't have been. Even a cheating wife can still stand by her man. No affair, no motive. I made a note to myself: "Talk to Maylene ASAP." I asked if a trial date had been set.

"No, but he's been formally charged. We'll get a date later this week. My guess is July or August."

Milo's sudden spurt of verbiage gave me heart. "What about those bones?"

I could hear him sigh. "I don't want to talk about them. We still don't know everything."

"Damn it," I said, though I tried not to sound impatient, "the bones were found. That's a fact. We're going to print the story. Can't you give us anything other than 'We don't know'? It makes you look bad."

"So why do you care how I look?" Milo retorted.

"I care about the office. You're law enforcement for SkyCo," I said, aware that I'd flunked tact. "That's important."

There was a long pause at Milo's end of the line. "The reason I don't want to talk about the bones is because we're still trying to identify them."

I let out a little gasp. "What? Does that mean they're not a hundred years old?"

"Probably not." The glum, formal tone had crept back into his voice.

"How recent?" I was scribbling notes, sitting on the edge of my chair, excited and expectant.

"A year, maybe less."

"Do you have a complete skeleton?"

"Just about."

Naturally, it was impossible to shake Milo over the phone. I took a deep breath instead. "Do you think it's someone local?"

"Can't say just yet. Remember, the old ware-house was right next to the train tracks. We've got a whole new generation of people who ride the rails, and some of them are scum, especially the ones who claim to be FTRA."

Trains, both passenger and freight, always slowed down upon reaching Alpine. I knew that men—and sometimes women—who bummed rides occasionally were mere thrill seekers. They took off from their jobs as CPAs, housepainters, attorneys, and medical techni-cians for a couple of weeks each year just to soak up that sense of freedom and adventure that trains offer the American soul. But there was also the FTRA, the Freight Train Riders Association, a vicious gang whose one thou-sand or more members preyed on those inno-cent vacationers. The FTRA usually rode the Burlington Northern Santa Fe High Line be-tween Seattle and Minneapolis; Alpine was on that route; I'd grown accustomed to seeing the gang's initials painted on various buildings near the tracks.

Yet there was one flaw in Milo's hypothesis. "Don't the bums or whatever they call themselves these days just dump the body? This one was buried."

Milo exhibited patience. "Sometimes the trains stop for another train that has the right-of-way. They'd have time to bury a body. This one wasn't deep."

It was pointless to argue. "Can you tell if the bones belonged to an adult?"

"Yes." Milo paused again. "Probably female."

Again, I was startled. "Female? Doesn't that rule out an FTRA connection?"

"Not necessarily. Equal rights, and all that crap."

It was also pointless to get mad. "Did you find anything identifiable, like jewelry or belt buckles or a watch?"

"Nope. My guess is that the body was naked."

I racked my brain for more pointed questions, but came up empty. "Is there anything else you can tell me?"

"Nope. That's about it. For now."

I thanked Milo, and hung up. For once, I didn't rush out to report to Vida. I wanted to write the story while it was still fresh in my mind. Finishing the six inches it would fill, I hit the print key, then took the piece out to my House & Home editor.

She was on the phone. "No, Ella, it wasn't blue, it was green . . . Yes, of course I was there . . . Come, come, whoever heard of a blue pear? . . . Well, that's why you got a stomachache . . . *I said*," Vida continued, raising her voice and making a face at me, "that's why you got a stomachache. The pear was too green. I must go now, I'll talk to you later."

She put the phone down with a clatter. "Honestly! Ella Hinshaw is not only deaf as a post, now she's going blind! A blue pear, indeed! She wants to sue Jake and Betsy O'Toole for selling blue fruit at the Grocery Basket."

"Maybe it was a plum," I suggested, recalling that Ella was an aged shirttail relation of Vida's. "Here, take a look at this." I pushed the bones article across her desk.

Vida is a swift reader. "My word!" she exclaimed when she had finished. "What does this mean?"

I sat down in the visitor's chair. "The bones were charred, so they—that is, the body—was put there before the fire. You see where I quote Milo as saying 'a year, maybe less'? What does that mean to you?"

Vida frowned. "Naked. Charred. A woman. Hmm. I suppose it could mean that there might still have been hair attached to the skull. You didn't see that, did you?"

"No," I replied, wincing a bit. "Just bones. I imagine Milo's waiting for dental records."

"No one's turned up missing around here in the last year," Vida said thoughtfully. "Oh, one of the Gustavsons ran away, but she came back. So did one of the Lucci girls, who'd moved in with some awful boy in Seattle. Then there was Mrs. Iverson, who disappeared from the retirement home, but I heard she'd gone to live with her daughter over on the Olympic Peninsula."

"That *is* odd," I remarked as Carla entered the office. "If someone else is missing, Milo would know." I swiveled in the chair. "Carla, what's up at the courthouse?"

"Birgitta would hardly talk to me," Carla said in an annoyed tone. "Sometimes I hate being short."

Since I'm barely average height, I thought I knew what she meant. "Birgitta loomed?"

"Loomed and gloomed," Carla replied, settling in at her desk. "When I spoke to her, she literally talked right over my head. I was so annoyed. Birgitta answered in monosyllables, long-faced and dry as a bone. I could hardly get two words out of her."

"But you persevered," Vida put in, her tone suggesting that evasion wasn't acceptable.

"Yes, sort of." Carla sighed, then turned in her chair to reach for one of the muffins she'd brought from the Upper Crust. "What she did—and I found this out from the county clerk—is file a claim on the nuggets. She's supposed to provide proof of ownership, but she has none that I can tell. Hearsay isn't good enough. I gather that Birgitta didn't understand that part. Anyway, I figure she's screwed."

Vida made a face of displeasure at Carla's terminology, but I intervened before we could get sidetracked. "Did Birgitta tell you anything of interest?"

Carla finished chewing on her muffin before she answered. "Bottom line—believe me, I really tried—Birgitta said that some Oriental man gave her great-grandfather the gold to thank him for saving his life. Her grandfather had told her the man was called 'Yo.' That much figures, since you said the name on the chest was Yoshida. But Birgitta didn't seem to know the full name, and I don't think we've ever run it in the paper, have we?"

If Carla hadn't put the name in her original article, then it hadn't appeared in print. The nickname of Yo was certainly suggestive. "So why did her great-grandfather ditch the gold and never retrieve it?"

"Ulf Lindholm had to flee, Birgitta said. It sounds like he fled all the way back to

Sweden." Carla ate the last bite of muffin and reached for the coffee.

"That's sort of what I gathered," I said, trying to piece our scraps of information together. "Maybe some of the other loggers or miners knew Ulf had the gold. They might have threatened him, and he feared for his life. Maybe they'd also threatened Mr. Yoshida. Or worse, tried to kill him, and that's how Ulf saved his life."

Vida was sitting with her chin on her hand, looking thoughtful. "I found nothing about such an incident in the old papers from SkyCo and SnoCo at the college library. Confrontations of that sort didn't always make the news. They happened in remote, isolated areas, and if there was no arrest or trial, the general public never heard about them."

"Very likely," I agreed, turning back to Carla. "Is that it?"

Carla wiped her mouth on a napkin. "Just about. Birgitta mentioned a girl named Christina. I couldn't quite track on that one, but it sounded as if Ulf might have given her some of the gold. Christina may have been her great-grandmother, but I honestly couldn't figure it out, Birgitta was so vague and unclear. Then she took off."

"Christina," Vida repeated. "Very Swedish, as in Queen Christina. Ulf must have kept enough gold to take home, perhaps even to pay his passage."

"That makes sense," I said. "Go ahead, Carla, write up your story, and be sure to include the county clerk's statement about Birgitta not having proof. Attribute it directly. We don't want local resentment built up against her, especially when she's a foreigner."

Briefly, I considered combining my bones article with Carla's piece, but the two didn't really go together. In any event, it would be better to tuck Birgitta's claim inside the paper than to have it go on page one.

Shortly before eleven, I drove out to the Bjornsons' place on Burl Creek Road. If memory served, Maylene didn't work on Tuesdays. She ought to be home alone, with the kids in school and Ron in jail. Given the circumstances, the family probably felt like they were all in purgatory.

The house had a deserted look when I arrived, though Ron's truck and Maylene's car were in the drive. When I stood on the front porch, I realized that the curtains were gone from the windows. Maylene, however, came to the door, her corkscrew auburn curls in disarray and a spot of high color on each plump cheek.

"Emma," she said, and immediately grew wary. "Really, I don't think . . . I don't know . . ."

"Relax," I said, smiling broadly. "I want to hear your side of the story before we go to press."

She allowed me to come into the living room, which was also in disarray. "I'm spring-cleaning," she said on a note of apology. "I'm washing the curtains and cleaning out drawers and then I'll shampoo the carpet. I have to keep busy, or I'll go nuts."

"I don't blame you," I said, sitting down on a floral-covered couch. "This is a hard time."

"It's stupid," Maylene declared, collapsing into a rocking chair. "Ron didn't kill Mr. Rasmussen. I can't think why Milo arrested him. He knows Ron, he knows better."

"Milo's usually very cautious," I remarked. "But that's why I wanted to talk to you. From what I gather, he made the arrest based on discrepancies in Ron's log, and because he was told that you and Einar were having an affair."

Maylene picked up a dust cloth from the arm of the rocker and threw it on the floor. "That is so dumb! Why would I have an affair with that old fart? Einar Rasmussen Jr. was so full of himself that I could hardly stand being around him. Mr. Pompous, I called him. And that lipstick evidence! That's so stupid. Stella sold a case of those lipsticks at half price last month at the beauty salon, and I'll bet four dozen women in Alpine are wearing that shade. Stella ordered the wrong color, and got stuck with them."

Stella Magruder, who owns Stella's Styling Salon, wasn't the type of woman to take a loss. I vaguely recalled seeing the half-price display when I got my last haircut, but lipstick is one of my vanities. I have two favorite colors, which are only carried by Nordstrom's in Seattle.

"Then how did the rumors get started?" I asked.

Maylene shook her head. "Who knows? People in this town love gossip."

"Was it something to do with sugar cubes?" I gave Maylene an ironic smile.

"Oh, that!" Maylene curled her lip. "Dumb. But typical. Einar thought he was God's gift to women. I was as surprised as anybody when he dropped that sugar cube down my front. Think about it, Emma," she went on earnestly. "I could have gone one of two ways. I could have been outraged, and yelled 'sexual harassment.'

That would have created a big stink, which I definitely don't need when I'm trying to get on full-time at the college. So I played it cool, and laughed it off. I suppose I thought I could win some points with Einar."

Maylene was making sense. "What about the people who said they'd seen his car parked outside your house when Ron wasn't around?"

"Who said that?" Maylene's eyes sparked with anger.

It had been Ryan Talliaferro, and I was reluctant to mention his name. Indeed, he had been repeating what someone else had told him. "I heard it secondhand," I admitted. "But my source was quoting at least two other people."

The anger turned to gravity. "Einar did come by once, to ask about Diane Henderson, the head librarian. He'd heard that she was doing something strange with the budget. I don't think it was true, Diane's not like that, but I hadn't worked at the library long enough to know. Einar considered himself the expert trustee on money matters."

"Did he make a pass?"

"Ohhh . . ." Maylene ran an agitated hand through her curls. "I think it was on his mind. He kept stringing out the visit, asking unnecessary questions. But finally the phone rang, and he left."

Maylene was still making sense. I had only one question left. "What about Ron's discrepancies in the log?"

"That's bilge," Maylene asserted. "The log's a joke. Ron can't keep track of every minute he's on the job. He writes down what he did and where he did it, and the general time, but he's not exactly precise. If he were, he'd spend half his working life figuring it all out. That's not what the log's for in the first place. It's to show what problems he's run into and what he's done about them and any unusual occurrences."

"There weren't any that Monday night?"

Maylene shook her head. "Not that he knew of. He opened the door for Einar, then he went to check out the rest of the building. Then he . . ." Maylene blanched. "That's the part he didn't originally tell the Sheriff. He was scared."

I leaned forward on the couch. "Why was that?"

"Ron went back via the RUB dining room. He thought he heard someone leaving. When he didn't see Einar, he went into the kitchen. That's when he found him. Ron rolled Einar over and saw the knife. He pulled it out, because he wasn't sure Einar was dead. When he realized he was beyond help, Ron panicked and ran out of the building. He washed up over at one of the dorms, where the toilet was plugged. The whole thing scared the hell out of him, and he didn't tell Milo."

"That was a mistake," I said, with a shake of my head.

"Of course it was! I told him so when he came home." Maylene looked angry, as if she were reliving the encounter with Ron.

"So Ron actually ditched the knife?"

"Ditched it?" Maylene frowned. "He couldn't remember exactly what he did with it. I think he tried to wipe off his prints, and then put it somewhere. Ron's kind of . . . what's the word? Erratic, maybe? He panicked when he found Einar with the knife stuck in him, then after he got out of the RUB, he had time to calm down before the Sheriff came looking for him. I guess he held up pretty well during the rest of the night, even when Milo or whoever questioned him. But when he got home, he fell apart all over again."

I recalled talking to Ron later that morning. Admittedly, he hadn't seemed like himself. "Can you think of anything else that would support your husband's story?"

Maylene drew back in the rocker. "Why? Are you starting a campaign for him at the paper?"

"No. But I need background," I explained. "I want to be fair to Ron. In fact, I won't print most of what you just told me. Not now. It will all come out in the trial."

"Trial!" Maylene jumped to her feet and began pacing. "There shouldn't be a trial! Why do Ron and the kids and me have to go through all this when he's innocent?" She stopped abruptly and whirled on me. "Know what? When this mess is over, we're moving. I'm not from here, I'm from Monroe. I've never liked Alpine that much, especially after the logging business went down the toilet. I told Ron we ought to settle in Marysville. That's where my folks ended up, after they sold the family home. Maybe Ron and I could get on at the college in Everett."

Marysville, like Snohomish, was another burgeoning town filled with commuters. I couldn't blame Maylene for wanting to escape Alpine. I felt particularly sorry for the Bjornson children, who, as teenagers, were no doubt suffering at the hands of their peer group.

I started to head back into town a few minutes later, leaving an angry and desolate Maylene on the front porch. Briefly, I thought of stopping at the college. I'd been wondering all along why Nat Cardenas was still on campus when Einar's body was found. The Administration Building had been dark that night, so he wasn't in his office. But many people had been around at seven-thirty. It wasn't really strange that the president should be one of them. Maybe Cardenas had been about to leave when he saw the emergency vehicles. I kept driving.

Lunch was a burger and fries from the Burger Barn. Vida, who had been gone when I left to see Maylene, joined me with her carrot and celery sticks. If she was annoyed because I hadn't waited until she could accompany me to the Bjornsons', she didn't show it. Her proprietary air didn't extend to days when we had a deadline to meet.

"That's rather odd," she said. "I don't know Maylene very well, but she doesn't strike me as a liar. Of course I expect any woman would lie to protect her husband from the gallows."

I opened my mouth to agree when an idea struck. "Vida," I said, trying not to get too excited, "wouldn't a man lie to protect his wife?"

Vida knew exactly what I was thinking. "If Maylene killed Einar, certainly Ron would want to shield her."

"The library was open that night until eight," I pointed out. "Maylene works on Mondays. What if she was still there, what if Einar asked to meet her at the RUB? What if he made advances, and she tried to ward him off with the knife?"

Vida twirled a celery stick. "Defending her virtue. Why not say so?"

"Because the lecher was Einar Rasmussen Jr." I liked my own reasoning. "The courts are still wishy-washy about a woman's rights when it comes to defending herself. Maylene was afraid she wouldn't be believed, especially with those rumors afoot. And Einar was a trustee, a big gun in the community. She'd never get hired full-time if she killed Einar, self-defense or not. Ron would probably get the sack, too. In fact, I imagine he'll be fired anyway."

"Hmm." Vida's mouth worked as she thought through our little scenario. "Ron lets Einar in. Maylene may have already alerted him about the assignation. He lurks in the background. But Einar pounces, and Maylene has to act quickly. By the time Ron arrives, Maylene has stabbed Einar. Next, they try to cover her crime."

It made sense. At least for thirty seconds. "Why? Why there, why in the RUB, when Einar knew that Carla was on the way to take pictures? Carla was a few minutes late. What if she'd been on time? And why would Maylene agree to meet Einar in the first place?"

"To seek a full-time position?" Vida suggested. "We don't know what Einar may have told her."

I chucked the Burger Barn containers and napkin into my wastebasket. "I don't know. It sounded good at first, but now it doesn't make much sense."

"But it's not impossible," Vida said, getting up from my visitor's chair. "We'll discuss it later. I'm off now to see Marlys. And Davin. My section is all locked up."

"You're going to Einar's house now?" I said in surprise. "Can't you wait until I can go with you?"

"Not and make deadline," Vida declared. "This time I won't be denied." She hesitated at the door. "You *are* tied up this afternoon, aren't you?"

I was, at least for most of the afternoon. But Vida wasn't going to one-up me. "I can spare an hour," I said. "Let's go."

Vida did her best to hide her disappointment.

Chapter Fifteen

IN THE MIDDAY sun that filtered through the vine maples and evergreens, the Rasmussen house should have looked even more attractive. Instead, the shafts of light created eerie shadows on the cedar roof and long arched windows. Maybe my imagination was playing tricks on me, but I sensed something sinister about the house. Maybe it was Einar Jr., haunting his handiwork until his killer was brought to justice.

Vida had tried to ensure her entry by stopping at the Upper Crust Bakery to buy a peach pie. Once again, Deirdre came to the door. She didn't look quite as careworn as before, but she definitely wasn't pleased to see us.

"Look, Mrs. Runkel," she said, directing her words at Vida, "Mother isn't seeing anybody. I don't mean to be rude, but—"

"You're not rude, you're merely good-hearted," Vida said cheerfully, and barged right inside, nearly knocking Deirdre off balance. "I'll take this out to the kitchen; I know where it is. My, my, what a lovely carpet."

I couldn't help but follow, and Deirdre no longer barred my way. "Vida is very determined," I said. "She's extremely strict about duty calls."

"She could have written a note," Deirdre said in a sulky voice as we trekked through the living room and dining room to reach the kitchen.

Vida had placed the pie on the dark granite countertop. "Peach," she said with a bright smile. "I considered apple, but everyone does apple. I thought peach would be a special treat. Now, where is Davin? I do so want to meet him now that you two have been reunited."

Deirdre slumped against the refrigerator. "Who told you?" she asked in a faint voice.

"Why, your grandmother, who else?" Vida's eyes had grown very wide behind the orange-framed glasses.

"Grandmama!" Deirdre sounded aghast, then rallied. "Okay, why not? I'll go get him."

"She wants to appease us," Vida whispered after Deirdre had left the kitchen. "As long as Marlys and Beau are under wraps, she'll offer Davin as her sacrifice."

"To be honest, it's Beau I'd like to see," I said. "At least I got a glimpse of Marlys at the cemetery."

"True. I wouldn't mind seeing Beau myself." Vida nudged me as we heard footsteps approaching from down the hall.

Deirdre entered the kitchen with the young man we'd seen through the window on our previous visit. His long, fair hair was now tied back in a ponytail, and he was wearing a flannel shirt over his T-shirt. I saw no resemblance to Deirdre in Davin's angular features and slight build. I assumed he took after his father, Mr. Jerk-off.

Deirdre, however, was giving her ex no credit of any kind. "This is my son, Davin," she said, apparently unwilling to mention the boy's last name.

Davin put out a long, thin hand, but to my amazement, Vida enfolded him in a suffocating embrace. "Davin! How wonderful to finally meet you! Your dear great-grandmother has often sung your praises to me!"

Neither Vida nor Davin could see the surprise that registered on my face and Deirdre's. I knew Vida was lying; Deirdre may have guessed as much.

Davin looked goggle-eyed as Vida released him. She stood there examining him, hands on hips, one foot firmly planted, the other resting on the heel of her sensible shoe. "Did you enjoy staying with your great-grandparents? They live in such a lovely old house in Snohomish."

Davin glanced uncertainly at his mother. "I . . . it was okay. I had my own room."

"Yes, so many bedrooms," Vida rattled on, "even a ballroom on the third floor. Are you very crowded here?"

"We're fine," Deirdre interrupted. "This house has three bedrooms."

"How nice," Vida enthused, then moved closer to Davin. "That was very naughty of you not to tell your poor mother that you'd gone to live with great-grandma and great-grandpa. I hope you two have everything sorted out by now. Your grandfather should have told your mother where you were. I'm sure his intentions were the best, but I couldn't see what harm it would do to let her in on your whereabouts and not worry her to death."

I had seldom heard Vida spin such a tale, especially one based on guesswork and conjecture. But Davin seemed taken in, and Deirdre was beginning to look somewhat credulous. I, however, felt lost in Vida's maze of supposition.

"I think Dad was afraid I'd interfere," Deirdre said, moving to stand by her son. "Maybe I would have. But only because I wanted the best for Davin."

"Mothers are like that," Vida said, oozing empathy. "We always want to keep our chicks under our own wings. How long were you gone, Davin? Before you joined your great-grandparents, that is."

"Um . . ." Davin scratched behind his ear. "Four weeks? Something like that. It wasn't all that bad, at least not after the first few days."

"But so beneficial." Vida was nodding wisely. "Your grandfather knew what was best for you. Under the circumstances."

Davin also nodded. "Gramps said it ran in the family. Both sides, for me."

"It can be hereditary. Your grandfather was very smart to notice your propensities." Vida patted the boy's shoulder; Davin flinched only slightly. "Now, you must follow up. That's terribly important, I'm told."

"I know," Davin replied. "I should have gone to a meeting last night, but I was still kind of upset."

"Understandable, but all the more reason to attend," Vida said. "Now we must go." She beamed at both Davin and Deirdre, then started out of the kitchen. "Oh!" she exclaimed, turning around in the doorway that led into the dining room. "I meant to ask—were you here or with your great-grandparents when you learned the dreadful news about your grandfather?"

Davin exchanged a swift look with Deirdre. "I was still in Snohomish. I moved in with Mom after the funeral."

"So thoughtful," Vida murmured.

Deirdre accompanied us to the door, but Davin remained in the kitchen. "Grandmama talks too much," Deirdre said, though the wary expression I'd first seen in her hazel eyes had now returned. "That's not like her."

Vida clasped Deirdre's hand. "Your grandmother and I go way back. You can't imagine the memories we've shared."

I could, and marveled that Vida kept a straight face. "We appreciate getting to meet Davin," I put in, then realized that no one had introduced me.

Apparently the oversight had gone unnoticed. "Thanks for coming," Deirdre said, giving me a small smile. "Thanks for the pie, Mrs. Runkel. We'll have it for dessert."

"Excellent," said Vida as we started to descend from the porch. "My regards to the rest of the family, especially your dear grandparents."

"Sure," Deirdre said, standing by the Little Mermaid. "I just wonder how long we can live with them without going nuts."

Vida turned, the swing coat fluttering around her sturdy calves. "You're going to move in with Thyra and Einar Sr.?"

Deirdre nodded. "We're putting the house up for sale this weekend. Grandmama insists it's silly for her and Grandpapa to rattle around alone in that big place in Snohomish. I suppose she's right, but it won't be easy."

"How does your mother feel about that?" Vida asked, her voice a trifle sharp. "She doesn't enjoy being close to neighbors."

"She'll adjust." Deirdre spoke without inflection, her eyes resting somewhere beyond us.

"I hope so," Vida said. "Good luck. Oh, and do give our best to Beau." We continued along the paved path. I heard the double doors close behind us as Deirdre went back inside the house.

"Ridiculous!" Vida exclaimed when we were back inside the Buick. "Not to mention stupid. Why give up such a lovely place to live with Thyra and Einar Sr.? It doesn't make sense."

"Maybe Marlys wants to install herself in order to inherit the house for herself and Deirdre," I offered.

"No, no, no," Vida asserted. "Marlys wouldn't have had Einar Jr. build her this house away from everybody if she wanted the place on Avenue B. It would make more sense for

Deirdre to inherit the Snohomish house, though she doesn't act as if she wants it. Certainly Thyra won't include Mary Jane in her will, and I doubt that she'd leave the family home to Harold and Gladys. As for Beau, it doesn't matter where he lives—he keeps to his room, so he might as well live in a hotel."

We were back on the highway, passing Alpine Falls. "I'll bet that Deirdre and Davin won't stay with the senior Rasmussens for long," I said. "Maybe Deirdre will get her wish and move to the city."

"The city?" Vida bristled. "Why would she want to do that?"

I never argue the benefits of city living with Vida. She is convinced that a small town—specifically a small town named Alpine—is the only acceptable place to live. Thus I changed the subject.

"You're an infamous liar, Vida," I said with a laugh. "I've rarely heard you spin such a story. And how did you guess that Davin had been in rehab?"

Vida gave a small shrug. "It wasn't difficult. His uncle Harold has had a drinking problem, Einar Sr. was reputed to enjoy more liquor than was good for him, and I've always wondered if Marlys's reclusiveness was due to Demon Rum. I also suspect that Mr. Nichols—I don't recall his first name—may have been a drinker. Perhaps that's what broke up his marriage with Deirdre. If Einar Jr. thought his grandson was beginning to drink heavily—Davin is only seventeen, but that's no hedge against alcoholism these days—then he may have uprooted him from Deirdre's too protective embrace and shipped him off to a rehab center. It had to be that or drugs or even both, but given the family history, I decided it was probably liquor. Naturally, I could be wrong about which vice Davin had acquired, but the point is, the boy had problems, and wasn't a runaway."

"He still has problems," I remarked as we took the turnoff into Alpine. "He acted just a bit strange when you not so subtly inquired as to his whereabouts the night that Einar Jr. was murdered."

"So he did." Vida sighed. "Perhaps he was still staying with his great-grandparents. But that's a big house, and you could easily disappear without anyone knowing. It's the kind of place where you can get lost. In many ways," she added on a somber note.

I really shouldn't have taken the time to go with Vida to the Rasmussens'. We had learned nothing new for our coverage, since Davin's apparent stay in rehab didn't have any viable connection with his grandfather's murder. Indeed, we had ended up with more unanswered questions.

I couldn't dwell on the homicide story. There was the rest of the paper to put together, and less than three hours before Kip MacDuff would start to print. Leo and I finished up the Memorial Day section by three-thirty, Carla and I worked on the front page and the inside, Ginny finished the classifieds, and Vida re-checked her House & Home domain. At five to five, we were ready to roll. After all these years of meeting our deadline, I don't know why I always feel a sense of panic around four-thirty. The paper has always come out on schedule, even when upon rare occasions, we've had a late-breaking item.

"It's a good issue," I said to Leo after giving Kip the thumbs-up signal. "That is, death isn't usually a good thing, but it does create avid readership."

Leo, who had read my story on the remains at the warehouse site, grinned. "Dem bones will have everybody in SkyCo yapping their heads off. You got any guesses?"

"None," I replied. "Vida reviewed all the women—assuming Milo's right, and it is a woman—who had gone missing in the last year, but they were accounted for."

"She might not be from here," Leo said, making a haphazard attempt to put his desk in order. "Those freight riders could be responsible. I hear they almost never get caught. Or someone could have carted a dead body from another town down the pike. If the corpse was naked, then it was either rape or an attempt to disguise the identity. Let's face it, in bigger cities, plenty of people go missing every year. Sometimes their disappearance is never reported."

I knew that was true. The woman might be a hooker, a runaway, a homeless person. "We don't know that foul play was involved," I said. "Milo didn't mention the cause of death."

Leo shrugged. "If you've only got bones, it can be hard to tell. But why dump the body of someone who died a natural death?"

Leo had a point, and in all honesty, I had been assuming that the bones belonged to someone who had been murdered. "I don't blame the Bourgettes for being discouraged," I said, hoisting my handbag over my shoulder. "I'm not sure I'd want to build a restaurant where a corpse had been found."

Leo laughed. "Why not? It could be a marketing ploy. They could have a crime theme, maybe Roaring Twenties gangsters. How much violence has there been in Alpine over the years?"

I found Leo's idea distasteful, and told him so. "Besides," I added, "I think Dan and John are going more for the Fifties diner concept. A simpler lifestyle, innocence, the Eisenhower years."

"Bull." Leo lighted a cigarette. "What was innocent about Ike? You don't send hundreds of thousands of troops to be slaughtered at Salerno and Omaha Beach and Bastogne and all those other hellholes of World War Two because you're innocent. My old man got blinded by a grenade at Monte Cassino. You'd think he'd have blamed the Germans and the Italians, but it was Ike he never forgave. Up until the end, about fifteen years ago, he was a bitter, angry man."

I'd never heard Leo talk about his parents before. The story touched me, and I temporarily forgot about the Bourgettes and the bones and even Einar Jr. "You want to have a drink?" I asked.

But Leo shook off my suggestion with a wry smile. "Can't, babe. I'm meeting with some of the chamber-of-commerce folks. We've got

School's Out, Father's Day, and the Fourth of July issues coming up. Your ad manager never rests. 'Night." He blew me a kiss and was gone.

So was everybody else. I turned off the lights in the newsroom and headed for my car. Then, seeing Milo's Cherokee Chief still parked down the street in front of his headquarters, I changed directions.

Jack Mullins and Dustin Fong were booking a couple of drunks. I didn't recognize the men, who were dirty, disheveled, and kicking at the curving counter with their worn-out work boots. The taller of the two had long black hair and was badly pockmarked; his drinking buddy wore a black-and-white bandanna around his stringy blond hair and had the potbelly that younger men acquire with too much beer.

Always polite, Dustin peered around the two inebriates. "Ms. Lord, are you looking for Sheriff Dodge? He's in his office."

I hesitated, but just then the two drunks burst forth with a foulmouthed indictment of the justice system in general, and Jack Mullins's ancestry in particular.

"Actually," Jack said in his droll manner, "my mother was a quilt maker."

I slipped inside the counter and headed for Milo's office, pausing to knock on the door. "It's me, Emma," I said.

Milo told me to come in. Did he sound resigned, or merely tired? As I faced him across his desk I noticed that he certainly looked worn-out. "You're working too hard," I blurted.

"What else is there to do?" he shot back.

"It's baseball season," I said brightly. "Watch the Mariners on TV."

That was the wrong thing to say. Milo and I had spent many hours curled up on the couch, watching baseball. It was the one thing—besides sex—that we both enjoyed with a passion.

"Don't rub it in," Milo sneered. "I didn't know you were such a bitch."

I'd sat down, and now held my head in one hand. "Damn it, I didn't mean it that way. I'm sorry." I removed my hand and looked Milo straight in the eye. "Are we ever going to get past this?"

"That's up to you." Milo averted my gaze, and stared at one of his NRA posters. His ashtray was overflowing, the air smelled like cigarettes and bad coffee, and his in-basket was about to tip over.

"Okay." I gave him what was probably a phony smile. "Then I'm past it. Can we talk about something else, like business?"

"Go ahead." Milo was stony-faced, and still wasn't looking at me.

"Is there anything new on the bones?"

The Sheriff checked his watch. "It's five-eighteen. Your deadline's passed. Can't you wait until next week?"

A sarcastic response was on my lips, but Milo's version of the baiting game was wearing thin. "Technically, I could. But I want to keep on top of things. Also, I was wondering if you'd determined cause of death."

"The only thing we can rule out is a blow to the head," Milo said, finally looking at me. "The skull seemed in good shape, all things considered."

"There was nothing else at the site, like a spent cartridge, or a knife?"

"Nope. We figure the body was brought there after death."

I figured the same thing. "So what are you looking at? Strangulation, a stab wound, poison?"

"Suffocation's a possibility." Milo popped a breath mint in his mouth.

"You're sure it was foul play?"

"Nope. But whoever it was didn't starve to death, or die of a heart attack. Who'd run around Alpine naked?"

Crazy Eights Neffel, our resident loon, came to mind. But Milo had said the bones probably belonged to a woman, and I'd seen Crazy

Eights in the past couple of weeks, wearing nothing but a bowler hat and carrying a huge stuffed panda into the local veterinarian's office on Alpine Way.

"How soon before you expect to ID the body?" I asked, still keeping my tone cool and professional.

Milo shrugged. "Who knows? There are no dental records."

"Not in Alpine, you mean."

"Not anywhere," Milo said with a grimace. "The deceased had perfect teeth."

"Wow." Bitterly, I thought of all the money I'd shelled out to Dr. Starr and his predecessors over the years. My teeth were very imperfect, but at least I still had them. More or less. "What do you make of that?"

Milo shrugged again. "It happens now and then, though it's usually with young people who've had fluoride at an early age."

"Was this person young?"

Milo chewed the rest of his breath mint, then reached for a cigarette. "Forty to sixty is our experts' best guess. No broken bones. While the teeth were in top-notch condition, they were somewhat discolored. Probably a coffee drinker or a smoker, or both."

I sat back in the chair. "You may never know who it is," I said after a pause. "You're certain that no one in the county has been reported missing in the last year?"

Milo gave me a baleful look. "Don't you think I'd know?"

"Of course," I said. "But not everybody gets reported. I was thinking of rumors, or something about somebody that didn't quite mesh. You know—'My wife went to visit her mother in Kansas. She'll be back next year.' "

"Nope." Milo took a deep drag on his cigarette.

"This doesn't make sense. Have you checked with Snohomish and King counties? What about Chelan and Douglas counties on the other side of the mountains?"

"They've got dozens of missing persons, especially in King County," Milo replied, referring to the area that included Seattle. He stubbed out his cigarette, spilling ash on his desk, then leaned forward. "The next step is to reconstruct the face from the skull. SnoCo is working on that now. We ought to have something by Friday. That's our last resort."

I gave Milo a grateful smile. Maybe he was trying, in his weird, awkward, male-type way, to make amends. "Thanks. What about how long the bones have been there? Can they pin that down?"

Milo gave a nod. "Sort of. At least seven months, no more than ten. I figure eight." The hazel eyes didn't blink as he locked his gaze with mine.

I counted backward. "October," I said. "When the warehouse burned down."

"That's right." The Sheriff leaned back in his chair. "We thought it was kids with leftover fireworks, but that was a guess because a bunch of our local dropouts had been caught at the site twice after the Fourth of July, trying to stir up trouble. We could never prove it, so we didn't charge them. Now I figure it was the killer, disposing of the body."

"Is this for publication?" I asked, inwardly cursing Milo and wondering if it was too late to stop the presses.

"No. That's why I didn't mention it earlier today. I'm guessing." Milo put another breath mint in his mouth. "I've talked to the arson investigators, and they're still not sure what started the fire. They went along with the illegal-fireworks theory because some of that stuff is so powerful it can set off anything that's flammable. But so can a match, if it's put in the right place."

"Like where?"

"Like the victim's clothes, soaked in gasoline."

"And there's no way of telling now?"

Milo shook his head. "Not after the Bourgettes bulldozed the site."

I was silent for a moment or two. "So all we've—" I hastily corrected myself: "—all you've got is the possibility that the recon-structed-skull drawing may resemble someone recognizable."

"So far." Milo didn't look very hopeful.

"May I see it when it comes in?"

"Everybody can see it. That's the only way we can get an ID. We'll put out an APB."

Again, I was silent, trying to think if there was anything else I should ask the Sheriff while he seemed in this more mellow mood. But when I spoke again, it was not of the unknown victim.

"Milo, could we be friends? I think too much of you to be enemies."

Milo's long face registered surprise. "Are you serious?"

"Of course." I folded my hands on the desk, as if I were praying for his understanding. "For years we were good friends. Then, when sex got in the way, everything changed. Can't we go back?"

Milo fiddled with the ashtray, spilling yet more ash on the desk. Then he shook his head, sadly, slowly. "No, we can't. I can't." He paused, rubbed at his chin, and looked away. "I loved you. I still do. Being friends won't cut it. I'd rather stay mad."

Awkwardly, I got to my feet. "Damn," I breathed. "I'm so sorry."

Milo stared at me, hollow-eyed and solemn. "So am I."

The Mariners were playing Minnesota in an away game. I got home in time for the top of the third inning.

No matter who won, I'd feel like a loser.

The next morning, I remembered to make an appointment with Doc Dewey. Since none of my appendages had fallen off and my heart was still beating, the receptionist, Marje Blatt, was able to squeeze me in at ten A.M., June 25. That was almost a full month away, but if my major symptom was crankiness, I could live with it. The people around me were the ones who had to suffer.

Vida was intrigued by the facial reconstruction of the skull from the warehouse site. If anybody could recognize the face that emerged, it would be my House & Home editor.

"Speaking of pictures," Vida said later that afternoon as she leafed through the edition that

Kip had just delivered to us, "Einar Jr.'s portrait looks rather nice after all. Maybe it's the way Leo framed it. The formality makes Einar's pompous aspect more bearable."

A compliment from Vida for Leo was unusual. I was about to insist that she pass it along to him in person when Ginny poked her head through the door to the news office.

"Birgitta Lindholm's on the phone and she's really mad. Emma, can you take line one?"

Carla looked up from her copy of *The Advocate*. "What's wrong with her? She can't have seen the paper. Kip took it to the newspaper shacks less than half an hour ago."

"Who knows?" I sighed, and went into my cubbyhole.

Birgitta, however, *had* seen the paper. Ginny had neglected to tell me that the au pair girl had stopped by the office to pick up a copy. It seemed that she was calling from across the street at a pay phone outside the Burger Barn.

"I am angry," Birgitta declared. "It is wrong to print these words about my privates. I will sue."

"Sorry, Birgitta," I said, resisting the urge to laugh out loud at her phrasing. "The claim you filed is a matter of public record. You have no quarrel with us."

"The claim is record, yes," she responded.

"But not my words with small dark girl. She gophered me."

"What?" I jiggled the phone, thinking we had a bad connection. Then I realized Birgitta meant *badgered*. She'd gotten her wildlife mixed up with her verbs. "I don't think so," I said hastily. "Carla was simply trying to get some facts for her story."

"She snoops," Birgitta persisted.

Not as well as someone I could name, I thought. Birgitta ought to get a dose of Vida. Indeed, that would happen as soon as I got off the phone. There was more to this conversation than met the eye—or ear. "Listen, Birgitta, you should talk to Mr. Bronsky. He used to work for me, and he understands the newspaper business." *Sort of.* "He can explain how we do our jobs."

"You and the short dark person are not nice," Birgitta declared. "You are bad with the visitors."

"That's not true," I said, keeping calm. "Besides, what's the big secret?"

The long silence at the other end made me wonder if Birgitta had left the phone dangling and gone off. At last, she spoke again: "That is what I want to know. *What is the secret?*"

This time I heard the phone go dead.

Chapter Sixteen

AT MY URGING, Vida tore out of the office, heading for the Burger Barn. I watched her through the small window above her desk as she crossed Front Street and rushed past the Bank of Alpine, Mugs Ahoy, SaraLynn's Gift Shop, and out of my line of sight.

Carla folded her copy of *The Advocate* and set it on her desk. "So what's Miss Sweden bitching about?"

"Basically, she feels you invaded her privacy." I gave her a wry smile. "We know better, but she doesn't. Maybe the rules for the media are different in Sweden."

"Maybe," Carla said, wrinkling her nose, "she wouldn't know the rules of the media from a Swedish meatball. Birgitta's just trying to stir up trouble."

I gave her a sharp glance. While she is often distracted, even careless, my reporter really isn't stupid. Her people skills are quite well honed. "Why would she do that?" I asked. "Except, of course, to get her hands on the gold nuggets?"

Carla cocked her head. "To keep anybody else from getting them?"

"I'm not sure I understand," I admitted.

"First of all, she probably didn't want any-body to know about the claim," Carla said, scooting her chair back from her desk, "which they might not have known if she hadn't raised such a fuss Monday when she found out the courthouse was closed for the holiday. Now she's mad at us because we put it in the paper. Birgitta may think it's some sort of antifor-eigner conspiracy."

I uttered a little laugh. "It is, I suppose. It's al-ways that in Alpine, where any nonnative is considered a foreigner. Including us, Carla."

Carla laughed, too. "Weird, huh? I don't know how many people in this town still call me 'the new girl.' "

I nodded. "Same here. Every so often, some-body seems surprised that Marius Vandeventer doesn't own the paper anymore. What's worse, they act disappointed."

Carla patted her abdomen. "When the baby comes, he or she will be born in Alpine. Maybe that'll give Ryan and me more credibility."

"Maybe. But I doubt it." I turned as Vida tromped back into the newsroom.

"Well! I got an earful!" She adjusted her straw skimmer with its festoon of yellow daisies and plopped herself down at her desk. "The girl's not arrogant so much as terrified."

"Of what?" I asked in surprise.

"I don't really know," Vida confessed. "Whatever it is, it has something to do with the
woman named Christina."

"Was she her great-grandmother?" asked
Carla.

"No," Vida replied, still panting a bit. "I determined that much. But Christina had some
connection with Ulf, the great-grandfather,
and apparently was from around here. That's
very puzzling, because there weren't many
women in the area at the turn of the century
when Ulf was allegedly here."

With a thoughtful expression, Carla toyed
with a lock of black hair. "Did you gather that
Ulf gave her some of the gold?"

"I think so," said Vida. "Goodness, it's so difficult to get the facts out of that girl! If that's so,
then Ulf may have been romancing this Christina. Perhaps they were even engaged. Or," she
added in a musing tone, "married."

"That we could check on," I put in. "But
what good would it do? I mean . . ." I threw up
my hands. "I don't know what I mean. Is it
worth the trouble?"

"It is to me," Vida declared. "If nothing else,
I'm . . . curious."

Of course. "Go ahead, see what you can find

out. It would probably be Snohomish County, though. There wasn't much here back then."

"I'll call the courthouse in Everett," Vida said, reaching for the directory. "I'll do it now, while I have a spare moment or two."

"Wait," I said as she began to flip through the government listings. "Why do you think she's afraid? She did say something about a secret."

"It was her manner, the way her eyes darted about," Vida explained without looking up from the phone book. "She was more agitated than angry."

Carla snorted. "That's because you're almost as tall as she is. Birgitta couldn't try to intimidate you."

"I should think not," Vida said, reaching for the phone. "No one ever does."

The county clerk couldn't promise any information before Thursday or Friday. Since the query seemed only a matter of curiosity, I didn't dwell on it. The paper had now hit the delivery boxes, and the usual carping had commenced. Actually, it wasn't quite as usual: I received six calls demanding to know why Einar Jr. rated a full-page photo when he really wasn't a resident of Alpine. Explaining that the portrait was a paid advertisement didn't do much

to soothe our chauvinists. There were twice as
many who phoned about the bones. Could
they belong to Cousin Freddy who went to
Monroe in 1954 and never came back? Was
this the long-lost Aunt Bibba who had
Alzheimer's—though they didn't call it that
then, they just said she was crazy—and wandered off shortly after Nixon resigned? Was it
possible that the remains were those of Goldie,
the retriever who ran away when somebody
shot off a Roman candle too near his tail in
1981?

I was kept on the phone right up until five
o'clock. "Shut it down," I told Ginny. "The
rest of the nuts can wait until tomorrow."
There'd be letters, too, there always were. We
ran the ones signed with verifiable names and
addresses, unless they were libelous or obscene,
and often they were both.

Thursday was a bit of a lull, in terms of our
ongoing stories. There was nothing new on the
homicide investigation, no further word from
Birgitta, and, as expected, nothing on the skull.
The only event of any note was the removal of
the crime-scene tape at the Bourgette property.
I called Dan Bourgette and learned that they
would resume work on Monday. Since he and
John hadn't known how soon the Sheriff
would give them the okay to proceed, Dan was

taking his wife to Victoria, BC, for a long weekend.

About ten-thirty on Friday, Vida heard from the courthouse in Everett. There was no record of a marriage between Ulf Lindholm and a woman named Christina. Vida contemplated calling King, Skagit, and Chelan counties, but I dissuaded her.

"Unless there's some scandal back in Malmö, Sweden," I noted, "we have to assume Ulf returned home and married there."

Vida reflected, fiddling with the big, loopy tie on her frilly pink blouse. "In Malmö? An illegitimate offspring? A bigamist?"

"Maybe. Birgitta did refer to a secret."

"But it must be a secret here, not there," Vida said. "I can't help it, I'm intrigued. Maybe I will call those other counties."

"It'll take forever with King County," I told her. "Give it up. Christina was probably some girl from Monroe or Skykomish or Sultan who caught Ulf's fancy. Maybe Ulf's intentions were honorable, but he had to flee. We'll probably never know. Neither will Birgitta."

Vida showed me her most somber face. "I can't stand not knowing."

"Good luck," I said with a laugh, and started for my cubbyhole just as Mary Jane Rasmussen Bourgette entered the newsroom.

"Emma Lord?" she said, giving me an engaging smile.

"Yes, yes," I said, hurrying to shake her hand. "I've seen you and your husband at Mass."

"I've seen you," Mary Jane responded, her lively dark eyes level with mine. "Can we talk?"

I led her into my office, where the eyes still danced, but the smile faded. "I'm not sure why I'm here," she said, sitting across from me and resting her chin on her fist. "It's just that I'm so frustrated. Why can't people be kind?"

"Any people in particular?" I inquired.

"My relatives," she replied. "They stink."

I had to smile. "You mean the Rasmussens, I take it?"

"You got it. How unnatural is it for a mother not to speak to her daughter for almost forty years? How unfeeling can a woman be?" She paused, and her eyes glistened with tears. "Wouldn't you think that after losing one child, she'd want to make up with one of her two remaining offspring?"

I pictured Thyra Rasmussen in her handsome bedroom, vulturelike, and mean-minded. "Your mother's a very hard woman," I said, no longer smiling.

"You've met her?" Mary Jane looked surprised.

"Vida and I called on her a few days ago. She wasn't very nice, especially not to Vida. But then your mother and Vida's mother had something of a history."

"Mother has a history with just about everybody," Mary Jane said with more than a touch of bitterness. "For years she had nothing to do with my brother Harold. That was when he was drinking. And even later, when he went on the wagon, she treated him and Gladys like dirt. I understand that Einar's wife, Marlys, is a queer duck. I wouldn't be surprised if Mother helped make her that way. But of course I'd never met Marlys until the funeral, and even then, all she did was cry and sort of mumble at me."

"It sounds like Marlys could use a sister," I said. "She must be very lonely now, as well as withdrawn. Maybe you could befriend her." I cringed a little, wondering why I was giving advice to a woman who seemed quite capable of handling her own life.

"You know what?" Mary Jane said, her pretty face very serious. "For years I tried to reconcile with Einar. I even tried asking Marlys to intercede for me. She refused. Oh, she was decent about it, but I got the impression that she wouldn't upset Einar for the world, that she was just plain wishy-washy." She had become somewhat heated, raising her eyes to the low ceiling and grimacing. "There goes the star for charity in my heavenly crown. Sorry."

"She's just plain incommunicado," I said, then explained how Vida had tried to contact Marlys several times. "I realize she's devastated by Einar's death, especially since it was unexpected and brutal. I'm also aware that she's not social by nature. Mary Jane, do you have any idea why she's such a recluse? And what about Beau?"

"I've never seen Beau," Mary Jane said flatly. "He's the same age as our Dan. Deirdre and our Christina were also born within months of each other. You wouldn't know Chris, she and her husband, Jim, live in Lynnwood. Dick and I have seven kids, and they've never met their first cousins or their aunts and uncles." She stopped and blinked at me. "What was the question? I tend to go off on tangents."

I grinned at Mary Jane. "Marlys. Beau. Hiding out in the house on the Sky."

Mary Jane snorted. "I figure Beau is retarded. Einar and my parents would consider that a source of shame rather than a wellspring of grace. When we get shortchanged in this world, we're given the strength to not only overcome the so-called tragedy, but to grow, emotionally and spiritually. My parents and my brother would never see it that way. Their view is always negative, never positive. As for Marlys, maybe she's ashamed of Beau. She feels she failed Einar and her in-laws." She wagged a finger at me. "I'm guessing, mind you. Dick says I have too much imagination."

Since imagination is a quality I prize, I found no fault with Mary Jane Bourgette. Nor could I see much resemblance to either of her brothers. She was dark, about average height, and much more youthful in appearance than what I knew to be mid-to-late fifties. Perhaps she took after Thyra in looks, though I couldn't conceive of Mary Jane turning into a vulture.

"Frankly," I said, "I don't see how you can ever change your mother's mind. Your best bet is Deirdre. Did you know that Davin is staying with her at Einar and Marlys's house?"

Mary Jane jumped in the visitor's chair. "No! You're kidding me! When did that happen?"

I told her about Vida's rehab theory, which Davin seemed to have verified. "He was probably at your parents' house when you went to the funeral reception," I added.

"The Marx Brothers could have been at the house for all I know," Mary Jane sneered. "Dick and I were there about ten minutes before Harold told us that Mother wanted us to leave. I never even got a chance to talk to her, except at the graveside. She acted like I was a smallpox carrier."

"Sad," I said softly. "Maybe sadder for her than you, in the long run." But Mary Jane hadn't come here just to complain about her relatives. I didn't really know her, though it seemed we had hit it off rather well. Certainly she had been quick to unburden herself. "Is there something I can do to help with this mess?" I asked.

"You already have," she replied with a wry expression. "Dick and I haven't lived in Alpine very long. Except for a few people at St. Mildred's we haven't been able to make new friends. And God knows, we're not exactly introverts."

"I've been remiss," I admitted. "It's almost eight years since I moved here, and I haven't knocked myself out to be sociable. Maybe I'm afraid of rejection, maybe I feel a need to keep my distance because I'm a journalist, maybe," I added, "I'm asocial."

"I don't think so." Mary Jane opened her drawstring bag and took out a pack of cigarettes. "Do you mind? Everybody else does."

"No," I said, and feeling in a congenial mood, asked if I might steal one. "I quit every so often," I confessed. "It never quite takes."

"I'm not sure I want to live to be as old as my

mother," Mary Jane said, clicking her lighter for both of us. "It sure hasn't done her any good. Where were we? I lost track again."

"My fault," I said, trying not to inhale too deeply. "My turn for a tangent. I was wondering if you thought I could—"

"Help me," Mary Jane put in. "Here's the situation: Dick and I have a fortieth wedding anniversary coming up in a couple of years. One of the things we'd like to do for it is to present our children and our grandchildren with a family tree. Dick's side won't be a problem—he's got a sister who has been into genealogy for ages. But I don't want to pester her for my ancestors. People are always asking her for favors like that, and it's terribly time-consuming. I was wondering if you had any sources here at the paper." She glanced over her shoulder. "And I don't just mean your files."

Having left the door ajar, I had sensed Vida's presence outside my office, phantomlike and on the alert. I even thought I'd heard her gasp when I asked Mary Jane for a cigarette. But Vida had already admitted she didn't know much about the Rasmussens' background.

"Wouldn't you be better off doing the research in Snohomish?" I asked.

"Sure," Mary Jane responded, "but if my mother found out, she's ornery enough to put up every obstacle she could find. She may be older than dirt, but she still has clout in that town."

"Feel free to talk to Mrs. Runkel, our historian in residence," I said, "though her knowledge is limited. You Rasmussens had no Alpine connection until recently."

"I know," my visitor said. "I didn't expect her to have personal memories." Mary Jane smiled broadly, revealing twin dimples. "But Mrs. Runkel strikes me as having . . . an inquiring mind. I want her to do the research."

It was clear that Vida was torn between flattery and suspicion. She hemmed and hawed, but eventually admitted that her acquaintanceship with *The Snohomish Tribune* went back many years, to the days of Tom Dobbs, and his wife, Vida, for whom she had been named. That was news to me, and it certainly amused Mary Jane.

"You're a natural!" Mary Jane enthused. "You see, this way, my mother won't know what I'm up to."

"It will take some time," Vida said, still wavering.

"I'm willing to pay you," Mary Jane said. "Twenty dollars an hour. How's that?"

"Oh!" Vida looked stricken. "I could never

accept *money*!" Judging from her expression, she might as well have said *filthy lucre*. "Consider it a favor. Or, when your boys open their restaurant, treat me to a free dinner."

"Done," said Mary Jane, and vigorously shook Vida's hand.

"Well . . . yes." Vida had assumed a musing expression. "One thing, Mary Jane. I happened to be passing by Emma's office a few minutes ago, and I heard you mention the name Christina. How is she connected to you?"

"Our eldest daughter," Mary Jane answered. "Do you know her? She doesn't live around here."

Vida shook her head. "No. But I was wondering—is it a family name by any chance?"

"Yes," Mary Jane replied, hoisting the straw bag over her shoulder. "It was my grandmother's name. My mother's mother. She died before I was born."

Mary Jane knew very little about her grandmother, except that her last name was Andersen. Grandma Christina had always been a shadowy figure, referred to by Thyra upon rare occasion. Vida, however, hung on Mary Jane's every word. When our visitor had left, my House & Home editor practically exploded with excitement.

"The gold! Thyra said she inherited all those nuggets and doodads from her mother! Don't you see—Ulf Lindholm may have given some of his treasure to Christina Andersen."

Grudgingly, I agreed. The connection between the nuggets, Ulf Lindholm, and the Rasmussens might not be coincidental. "Mary Jane verified that the gold pieces had been handed down by her grandmother," I said. "In fact, Mary Jane, as the only daughter, was to have inherited them from Thyra. Mary Jane figures that she'll never get a sniff of the stuff because she married a Catholic."

"Yes, yes," Vida said, still agog. "I'm sure Mary Jane was cut out of the will the minute she brought Dick Bourgette home to meet her parents. That is, if she ever had the nerve to introduce him." She sat down at her desk, took off her glasses, and began to rub her eyes in typical vigorous fashion. "Ooooh! Andersen must have been Christina's maiden name, before she married Thyra's father. Why is Christina such a shadowy figure? Do I have time to go to Snohomish today and research *The Tribune*'s files?"

Naturally, it was a rhetorical question. Vida would make the time for her little project. She'd never skimp on her duties at *The Advocate*. I reminded her, however, that Mary

Jane was in no rush. The fortieth anniversary was a couple of years away.

Putting her glasses back on, Vida reached for her swing coat, which she was in the habit of carelessly draping over the back of her chair. "Nonetheless," she said, "it's a pleasant day, and I believe I'll go to Snohomish. Besides, it's almost eleven-thirty, so I'll skip lunch. If you don't see me again today, you'll know why. But if I find out anything truly exciting, I'll call."

Vida might skip lunch, but I wouldn't. Half an hour later I was headed for the Burger Barn.

I never got that far. Down the street by the Sheriff's office, I saw a dozen or more people milling around and waving placards. I covered the two blocks from *The Advocate* at a trot. When I got to Third, the cross street, I could hear the group chanting. "Release Ron," they shouted, marching around in circles.

I recognized most of the protesters: the Peabody brothers, Mort and Ellie Hedberg, Fred Iverson, Richie Magruder, Dave Tolberg, Scott Kuramoto, Sister Clare and Sister Mary Joan, Reverend Nielsen from the Lutheran church, and my own pastor, Father Dennis Kelly. The presence of St. Mildred's two nuns didn't surprise me—they protested everything, including the new four-way stop at Fir and Alpine Way. But Father Den was much more discriminating. Perhaps, because he was black, he'd already done his share of protesting; for the same racial reason, he was careful not to make himself a target on the Alpine civic scene.

It was Father Den who I approached, however. "What's this all about?" I asked, wishing I'd brought a camera.

The priest lowered his crude, handmade placard and smiled somewhat sheepishly. "Some people think Ron's been railroaded. As usual, Sister Mary Joan is rallying support. I balked at first, but my colleague, Pastor Nielsen, convinced me that Dodge might have the wrong man. Ronnie got the fourth grade to make the signs," he added, referring to the principal of St. Mildred's grade school, Veronica Wenzler-Green.

Jack Mullins came out of the Sheriff's office, looking as sheepish as Dennis Kelly. "Father," he said with a tug at his regulation cap, "have you guys got a permit for this?"

Father Den grinned at him. "Sister Mary Joan has the permit. She requisitioned a new filing cabinet last month. I figure she ran out of room from all of her protests. Don't feel she's picking on Alpine—I understand she's been involved in social action from Portland to Vancouver, BC."

Jack seemed resigned, maybe even relieved. "Okay, we can't stop you." He cocked his head at Den. "I don't have to confess interfering with a public display that makes my boss look like an idiot, do I?"

Den shook his head. "Not even the resentment part or that you think your priest *is* an idiot."

"Thanks." Jack's smile was still sheepish. "Go ahead, but if Dodge pitches a five-star fit, don't blame me." The deputy continued on his way to the squad car parked at the curb.

Den turned to me. "Want a placard?"

I grimaced. "No, thanks. Though if you tried hard, you might talk me into it."

Being the lunch hour, the curious had slowed their vehicles to see what was going on at the Sheriff's headquarters. Traffic was backed up for almost three blocks, causing the unenlightened at the rear of the line to honk their horns. Several pedestrians had gathered on the sidewalk, and one of them, Norm Carlson from Blue Sky Dairy, asked the Peabody brothers if he could have a sign.

"Ron drove truck for my dad and me before he got into logging," Norm said with a contemptuous sneer at the Sheriff's front doors. "He's no killer. For once, Dodge has his head up his butt."

Jack Blackwell, who owned the only working mill in Alpine, waved a fist at Norm. "You're full of it, Carlson," he said in an angry voice. "When I had to let Ron go a while back, he punched me out. I wouldn't put anything past that bastard."

"Who wouldn't punch you out, you crook?" raged Norm, referring to Blackwell's slightly less-than-savory personal and professional reputation. "Get the hell out of here, before I split your skull!"

Just as Blackwell charged Norm, who dropped his sign and began beating his attacker on the head, Milo pulled up and jumped out of the squad car. "Hold it! What the hell's going on?" He grabbed Jack while Father Den and Scott Kuramoto attempted to restrain Norm.

"Jeez," I groaned, cursing myself for being caught without a camera. "Where's Carla when I really need her?"

To my astonishment, Carla was running across Third Street. She got down on one knee and began clicking away. Making sure I didn't block her shots, I made an end-around run behind the Peabody brothers and Reverend Nielsen.

"Good work!" I cried. "You're just in time!"

"For what?" she asked, not taking her eye away from the viewfinder. "Is this some kind of major riot or did Sister Ditzwits get bored with her prayers again?"

Since some of the other onlookers were now exchanging heated words with the protesters, Carla wasn't far off the mark. "I'll explain later," I said as Sam Heppner came out of the Sheriff's office.

"Sam!" Milo yelled as he pinioned Blackwell's arms behind him and flung him up against the squad car. "Get this traffic moving! Now!"

Sam, whose mien is usually unhurried, moved swiftly into the street, gesturing for the cars and trucks and sport utility vehicles to drive on. To add to the bedlam, the whistle of a train could be heard as it approached Alpine from the east. The freight's crossing of Alpine Way could stall traffic for up to ten minutes.

Norm Carlson had reclaimed his placard and was lecturing Father Den and Scott about the evil nature of Jack Blackwell. Blackwell, meanwhile, was now talking in semireasonable tones with Milo. Sam Heppner had traffic moving again, albeit slowly. I could hear the warning bells ringing at Alpine Way and Railroad Avenue.

As Carla put another roll of film in her camera, I warily approached the Sheriff. At last, he sent Blackwell on his way, then scanned the protesters.

"Shit," I heard him say under his breath. He started to push through the knot of people, some of whom were calling him a Nazi or worse. I followed the Sheriff.

"Go away, Emma," Milo said, without looking at me after the doors had swung closed behind us.

"Sorry. I have to get a quote." I pursued him behind the curving counter, where Toni Andreas and Dwight Gould stared at us both. "A simple sentence will do. You know—subject, predicate."

"This sucks," Milo retorted, kicking open the door to his office. "Take a hike, Emma."

"That'll have to be a modified indirect quote," I shouted as he slammed the door.

"Protesters, huh?" said Dwight. "We've been watching them through the windows."

"Does Ron know they're out there?" I asked, coming back to the front of the counter.

"Probably not," Dwight replied. "Is Maylene there? I didn't see her."

"No," I answered. "I think this was organized by the nuns from St. Mildred's and maybe Pastor Nielsen from Faith Lutheran."

Toni sighed. "Why can't religious people stick to holy stuff? I saw Father Den out there."

Toni is a member of our parish, though she has more misses than hits when it comes to Mass attendance. "It's called social justice,

Toni," I said. "Frankly, I'm surprised at the amount of strong feeling about Ron's arrest."

"Local boy," Dwight put in before heading off down the hall.

I waited until he was out of hearing range. "What do you think, Toni?"

Toni, whose thinking processes were sometimes in doubt, fluffed up her curly black hair. "Honestly?"

I nodded.

"I think Dodge jumped the gun on this one." Panic surfaced in her brown eyes. "Hey, don't quote me! Please!"

"I won't," I promised. "This is just between us girls. Why do you say that?"

Toni winced. "Well . . . he's been in a majorly weird mood lately. Real short-tempered, crabby with all of us. I don't know how to say this, but when Ron got arrested, it was like Sheriff Dodge was taking out all his frustrations on him. Somehow, I felt he was in too much of a hurry to make an arrest. You know, like he had to prove something. That's not like Dodge. He's usually slow as mold."

"So he is," I said softly. "In any number of ways."

Toni brightened, as any woman would when she suspects even the slightest hint of an intimate revelation. But I didn't know her well enough to make her my confidante.

"How is Ron?" I inquired, anxious to change the subject.

"Okay." Toni shrugged. "Under the circumstances. At first he was mad, then he got depressed. Now he's just majorly worried."

"I don't blame him." After reassuring Toni that our conversation was off the record, I went back outside. The protest was again orderly, though at least two more people had joined it. I recognized them vaguely as college students.

Carla was gone, though Sam Heppner was still directing traffic. With a wave for Father Den, I headed for the Burger Barn. The freight was still creeping through Alpine.

Doubts about Ron's guilt were creeping into my mind.

Chapter Seventeen

BACK AT THE office, Leo was working on an ad for Father's Day gifts from Harvey's Hardware and Sporting Goods. "What next?" he said with a grin. "Dodge gets lynched on top of Mount Baldy?" My ad manager seemed pleased by the idea.

"I'm beginning to wonder if those protesters aren't right," I said in a worried voice. "If Dennis Kelly's parading around with a sign, maybe Ron didn't kill Einar."

"My guess is that Den's out there for the principle of the thing," said Leo, who has come to respect our pastor's good sense and compassion. "Either that, or he wants to make sure those two dippy nuns don't get run over by a couple of Southern Baptists in a pickup truck."

Leo had a point, yet I didn't think that Father Den would get involved in any public display unless he could somehow justify his position. On my way back from the Burger Barn, I'd stopped to get quotes from the protesters who then numbered twenty-six. Richie Magruder, our deputy mayor, and husband of salon owner Stella, thinks with his heart, not his head.

"Ron's a good guy," Richie had asserted. "And Stella says Maylene's not the kind to play around. This whole thing's out of control, if you ask me."

Scott Kuramoto based his reaction on similar "empirical evidence." "I haven't known Ron long, but I enjoy studying people. He doesn't strike me as impulsive or rash. If you work as a repairman, either on trucks or toilets, you need a great deal of patience. This kind of murder doesn't fit the man."

Donald Nielsen, pastor of Faith Lutheran, had concurred. "Ron Bjornson has a good heart. He would never harm another human being. Nor does the evidence—as we know it—support this charge."

Since almost none of the Sheriff's evidence had yet appeared in *The Advocate*, I assumed there were leaks, maybe from Maylene, or Ron himself. As I sorted through my notes, Richie Magruder's name caught my eye. On a whim, I called his wife, Stella, at the salon.

"I've had Milo in here asking about those lipsticks," Stella said in her throaty voice. " 'Midnight Mauve,' it's called. I ordered—or thought I ordered—'Midnight Rose.' Anyway, despite the fact I don't think they look very good on just about anybody unless they've got a Malibu tan, I've sold almost all of them. That happens when you stick a fifty-percent-off sign on a display."

"I suppose Dodge asked who bought them," I said.

"Natch," Stella responded. "I could only remember four or five, and Maylene wasn't one of them."

"She admitted she bought the lipstick," I pointed out.

"Sure she did," Stella said. "But I'm not the only one who rings up sales around here. I do recall Irene Baugh, Heather Bardeen, your Ginny Erlandson, and Amanda Hanson, who's almost dark enough to get away with that shade. Oh, the other one I remember is Cynthia Kittikachorn from the college. With her exotic coloring, it might look very nice."

Cynthia Kittikachorn. Nat Cardenas's secretary, and one of the few people in town who had expressed an anti–Ron Bjornson opinion. "Interesting," I remarked.

"Is it?" Stella sounded dubious. "Got to run, Emma. Ella Hinshaw just came in for her bimonthly blue-hair special. By the way, you're due for a cut. I saw you at that rally or whatever it was that Richie got all worked up about. You don't look so hot."

Only a hairdresser can utter such criticism without hurting another woman's feelings. Or at least suggesting that there's a cure. I hung up, and thought not about my unruly locks, but about Cynthia Kittikachorn's Midnight Mauve lips.

I was still thinking when I heard Vida enter the newsroom. It wasn't quite two o'clock, and I couldn't imagine why she'd gotten back so soon from Snohomish.

"What happened?" I asked, standing in the door of my office.

Vida harrumphed. "Edna Mae Dalrymple is what happened. She was already at *The Tribune*, researching Rasmussens."

"Why?" I asked, leaning on Vida's desk.

"Ohhh . . . You know what Edna Mae's like. Give her an opening for research, and she drives through it like a Kenworth lowboy. Really," she huffed, "we should never have allowed her to get involved."

"I don't think," I said dryly, "it's a question of *allowing* Edna Mae. She doesn't need our permission. Has she found anything?"

"Yes," Vida said with an expression of disgust. "That's why I came back to Alpine."

"And?" It seemed to me that Vida was being rather grudging in her admission of Edna Mae's discoveries.

Vida heaved a sigh. "She tracked down the

obituary of Christina Andersen. She died in 1913."

I stared at Vida. "She must have been very young." Then it dawned on me: "Christina Andersen was her married name?"

Vida shook her head, and a sly look came into her eyes. "It was her maiden name. Christina never married."

At that, both Leo and Carla looked up from their computer screens. "Old lady What'shername's a bastard?" Leo said. "And I thought she was just a bitch."

"Mind your language, Leo," Vida reprimanded. "Yes, Thyra was illegitimate. Edna Mae had also checked the birth records in Everett. Christina was a resident of Scenic at the time, and her occupation was listed as 'seamstress.' In those days that was often a euphemism for prostitute. She undoubtedly plied her trade at one of those wretched brothels along the railroad tracks." She took a deep breath. "And Thyra's father was one Ulf Lindholm of Malmö, Sweden. Now what do you think of that?"

"The secret," I said after we'd all gasped and goggled. "That's what Birgitta is looking for. Her long-lost family. Should we tell her?"

"To heck with her," said Carla. "I wouldn't tell her that it's Friday. She certainly didn't want to tell me anything."

"It wouldn't be right not to tell her," Vida said. "It's strange—no one has ever mentioned Thyra's father. Now we know why." She paused, perhaps wondering how she herself hadn't noticed the omission. "Very well, give me the details about what's going on in front of the Sheriff's office. There must be forty people out there, carrying extremely ugly signs."

I filled her in about the protest. She looked bemused. "Feeling runs very high," she commented. "I wonder . . ."

"Don't we all?" I said, and told her about Stella's lipsticks.

"Interesting," Vida murmured. "Are you suggesting that Cynthia, not Maylene, was having an affair with Einar?"

I shrugged. "It's possible. Who started those rumors about seeing Einar's car at the Bjornson house? It may have been Cynthia, trying to cover her own tracks."

Leo was opening a fresh pack of cigarettes. "Was she ever questioned by Sheriff Dunce Cap about where she was the night Einar was killed?"

I admitted I didn't know. Cynthia hadn't entered the picture until my phone call to Stella.

"Somebody should put a flea in his ear," said Vida. "I'll speak to Billy."

Informing Vida that I hadn't seen either her nephew or Dustin Fong on duty, which meant they were probably taking the night shift, I retreated into my office. It wasn't easy, but I forced myself to work on articles not connected with the murder, the bones, or the gold. The new bridge, which was becoming the old bridge in my mind, required my attention before the next county commissioners' meeting. I checked in with one of the three commissioners, George Engebretsen, who also happened to be a member of the college board of trustees.

George, as usual, was noncommittal. Yes, the residents in the Icicle Creek development area had been promised the bridge for a long time. No, the commissioners hadn't made a final decision. Yes, the neighborhood and adjacent area had formed its own interest group to petition the county to act with all due speed. No, the commissioners weren't turning a deaf ear to the college clique who wanted the bridge near the campus. Yes, there was a problem because the railroad tracks already crossed Highway 2 near the best site for a new bridge. No, the county engineers hadn't come up with another viable site. Yes, the commissioners certainly had the bridge on their agenda. No, there

wasn't any start-up date for construction. Or
for making a decision. Or for getting off their
dead butts.

I remained patient, or at least my telephone
voice did. "That was an awful thing about
Einar," I said after we'd worn out the subject of
the bridge. "I saw you at the funeral."

George, who is in his late seventies, and hasn't
laughed since Alf Landon lost to FDR,
grumped in my ear. "Damned shame. Einar Jr.
and I go way back, to my days at the mill. I
worked over thirty years for Einar Sr."

I recalled that George had been in the logging
business, but I didn't know of his connection to
the Rasmussens. "Did you quit when they shut
the mill down?" I asked.

"I retired two, three years before that, in sev-
enty-nine," George replied. "Back went out on
me. Could have taken a desk job, but I was almost ready to get Social Security. 'Why kill
myself?' I told the wife. Anyways, I ran for
commissioner in eighty. Been on the job ever
since."

The last thing I wanted was to have George
ramble on about his career. "Having been involved with Einar Jr. and his family for so long,
you must have been shocked when he was
killed," I said.

"Shocked is right. People have no sense these days," George asserted. "Then they blame everything on handguns. What's wrong with protecting yourself? Anyways, Einar was stabbed, not shot. You know what kind of crazies use knives."

I was tempted to say *butchers*, but refrained. "How do you mean?"

"Dagos. Spics. Guineas. Chinks. Japs. How many more do you want?" George sneered.

"I was thinking more specifically," I replied. "You know, a particular person."

"Take a look," George shot back. "They're all over the place these days. I see 'em running around the college every time I go out there for a board meeting. And I don't just mean the students."

"Then you mean . . . ?" I let the phrase dangle.

"Start at the top. Got to go. In more ways than one. Prostate's acting up again." George hung up.

I held my head. Was George Engebretsen referring to Nat Cardenas? Cynthia Kittikachorn? Or even Scott Kuramoto? I intended to put the question to Vida, who'd handed over her story about Mary Lou Blatt's trip to Costa Rica. The fact that my House & Home editor had condescended to do the interview was surprising. Mary Lou is Vida's sister-in-law, and the two rarely speak.

Vida, however, was smirking. "Wait until you get to the part where Mary Lou was attacked by a toucan. It must be the only living thing that has a bigger beak than Mary Lou. Of course"—Vida snickered—"Mary Lou's is somewhat smaller now."

The article was more objective than I'd expected, though the accompanying photograph, with a big bandage on Mary Lou's nose, would probably infuriate her when she saw it in print. I made a couple of minor editorial changes, then recounted my phone conversation with George Engebretsen.

"Such a ninny." Vida sighed. "I wouldn't put much stock in what he says. It sounds to me as if his prejudices have carried him away. Besides," she continued with a sly look, "we must inform several people about the Rasmussen lineage." If Vida had been a dog, she would have salivated.

"Who, besides Birgitta?" I asked.

"Your new friend, Mary Jane Rasmussen Bourgette," she said with what may have been a touch of asperity. Vida tends to become jealous of any other woman who lays even the slightest claim to my friendship. "And," she added, with more obvious malice, "Marlys and Deirdre. Don't you think they have a right to know the family history?"

I winced. "Are you sure you have their best interests at heart, Vida? Maybe they already know."

Emphatically, Vida shook her head. "Thyra would never have told any of her children. You heard Mary Jane say that her mother rarely mentioned the grandmother."

I kept a straight face, though I felt like saying that Vida, who'd been eavesdropping, had also heard Mary Jane make that statement. "What about Harold and Gladys?"

"Oh." Vida blinked several times. "Yes, they ought to be informed. For some reason, I keep forgetting about them. Harold and Gladys are forgettable people."

"You take the Lutheran Rasmussens," I said, figuring there was no way to talk Vida out of spilling the beans. "I'll take Catholic Mary Jane. We can flip a coin over Birgitta."

Vida assumed a magnanimous air. "You may have Birgitta. It's only fair."

What she meant was that she would rather drink bleach than call on the Bronskys. We had agreed on the division of labor when Ginny came to my office door.

"Charlene Vickers just stopped by with a big

classified ad for next week," she said, showing uncharacteristic excitement and waving a sheet of paper that looked like a real-estate listing. "Look!"

Charlene, another fellow bridge player and wife of Cal Vickers, the Texaco station owner, had sought relief from empty-nest syndrome by going to work for Doukas Realty. I started to get out of my chair, but Vida snatched the paper from Ginny's outstretched hand.

"My word!" Vida cried. "It's the Rasmussen house on the river! That was quick."

Eagerly, Ginny nodded. "I knew you'd want to know. Gosh, Mr. Rasmussen's only been dead about ten days."

Vida and I were staring at each other. "Probate? Or is it necessary with a surviving spouse?"

Vida made a face. "Not in this state with community property. I believe Marlys can do as she pleases. The question is why?"

"Memories," I suggested. "Einar built her that house, maybe she was happy there, and now he's gone. Deirdre told us that the plan was for everybody to move in with Thyra and Einar Sr. in Snohomish."

"Yes, but so fast." Vida reread the listing, this time out loud. " 'Three bedrooms, two-point-five baths, state-of-the-art kitchen, living room, dining room, family room, office, two fireplaces, triple garage, one-acre riverfront, well landscaped, three thousand five hundred square feet.' The asking price is half a million."

"Too much," said Ginny. "For around here, anyway. I have to proof these ads all the time, so I know prices. I'd say maybe three-fifty."

"Typical," Vida remarked, finally surrendering the listing to me. "The Rasmussens have always been greedy. I'm calling on Marlys and Deirdre right now. And this time I will not be denied by the Widow Rasmussen."

I didn't bother trying to talk Vida out of her mission.It was Friday, it was after four-thirty, and I was about to call it a day. But before I went home, I'd stop by Casa de Bronska. If anyone deserved to know about Ulf Lindholm's connection to the Rasmussens, it was the au pair girl.

Though clouds had descended over the mountains, Ed and Shirley were in the pool. Molly Bronsky had let me in, and when I went out onto the patio, Ed and Shirley emerged, looking like a couple of—dare I even think it?—Polish sausages.

"Hey, hey, hey," Ed called, water dripping from his fat form and small Speedo, "we're just having a couple of precocktail dips."

"How appropriate," I said, then hastily added, "for this time of day."

Mercifully, both Bronskys wrapped themselves in large striped towels. "How about a martini?" asked Shirley, her unnaturally gold curls plastered to her head.

"No, thanks," I replied with a fixed smile. "I came by to see Birgitta."

Ed and Shirley exchanged quick glances. "Didn't she come to the door?" Ed asked.

"No. Molly showed me in," I replied.

"Hunh." Ed sat down in one of the lawn chairs, causing it to creak ominously. "Maybe she didn't hear you ring."

Shirley let out a small squeal of annoyance. "Ed, you can hear that chime in Startup! I wish you'd figure out some way to lower the volume." Turning to me, she seemed unusually provoked. "Either Birgitta is lazy, or she thinks she's too good for us. She told me this morning she wasn't a maid, she was an au pair. Ever since she got this notion about that gold belonging to her, she's been impossible. The next time she threatens to go back to Sweden, I'm going to help her pack."

"Now, Shirl," Ed began, "hold on. When the movie deal comes through, I'm going to need all the help I—"

Birgitta stood on the single step outside of the French doors. "You wished for me?" she asked in a chilly voice.

Ed stammered a bit, but Shirley was still angry. "Yes, we did, Birgitta. Ms. Lord is here to see you."

Once again, I felt insignificant. In the grocery aisle of life, if Birgitta had been a long, luscious cucumber, I'd be a midget dill pickle. But I held my ground as best I could under her withering ice-blue gaze.

"I have some information you've been seeking," I said, grateful that my voice didn't come out in a squeak. "It's about your great-grandfather."

The blue eyes widened and the beautiful face seemed to soften. "Great-grandfather Ulf?" she said in a hushed tone.

I nodded. "Could we go inside?"

"No need for that," Ed all but shouted. "We're all family here. Have a seat, Gitty. Let's break out the Lablatt's. A beer sounds good about now."

"I think it's Labatt's," I said under my breath. "Anyway, it's raining. Birgitta and I'll go into the . . . ah . . . ballroom." I hurried past the au pair girl, assuming she would follow.

Birgitta did, but she obviously knew her employers very well. "My room," she said softly. "It is upstairs, very private, very nice, except for hamsters."

The hamsters, Beavis and Butt-head, belonged to Joey Bronsky, who likes to let his pets roam free. However, I saw no sign of the animals when we entered Birgitta's second-floor room, which, considering Ed and Shirley's propensities, was almost austere.

We sat in matching armless chairs covered in some sort of blue material with big dust ruffles. "Tell me, please, about my ancestor," she virtually begged. "I know the gold is his, and so is now mine."

I decided against warning Birgitta that my knowledge wouldn't necessarily help with her claim. Slowly, carefully, I explained that Ulf Lindholm had been romantically involved with a young woman named Christina Andersen. They had never married, I said, avoiding Vida's suspicion that Christina had been a hooker.

"They had daughter?" Birgitta's eyes had moistened. "What became of daughter?"

"Thyra Andersen married a man named Einar Rasmussen," I said. "They are both still alive and living in Snohomish." I lowered my voice, and dared to reach out a hand to Birgitta. "It was their son, Einar Rasmussen Jr., who was murdered a week ago last Monday."

To my astonishment, Birgitta broke into a broad smile. "Good. He cannot claim gold. This Thyra and the other Einar—they must be very old. Soon they will die, eh?"

"I wouldn't bet on Thyra," I said, and realized from Birgitta's puzzled expression that she didn't understand what I meant. "That is, Thyra is in fairly good health. Mr. Rasmussen is not."

"I must see this Thyra," Birgitta said. "She will be fair. I hear that this murdered man was very rich."

"Thyra," I said distinctly, "is a selfish woman. If you must see her, since she is your kins-woman, don't be too optimistic."

The caution seemed to roll right off Birgitta's tough, beautiful hide. "I will make her see what is right. There will be no trouble."

I had to admire the girl's spunk. Maybe Thyra was about to meet her match. The aged matri-arch and the young au pair were kin, after all. I wished Birgitta good luck and stealthily slipped out of Casa de Bronska. I could have handled an encounter with Beavis and Butt-head, but Ed and Shirley in swimwear was definitely a scary sight.

Dinner was a grilled-cheese sandwich and an apple. I noted the fat red zero on my answer-ing machine, opened my uninteresting batch of mail, turned on the baseball game, and read *The Seattle Times*. It was almost seven when I began to wonder why I hadn't heard from

Vida. Perhaps after her visit to Marlys and Deirdre, she'd gone on to Snohomish, to taunt Thyra Rasmussen.

The Mariners had just made the last out to defeat the Blue Jays in Toronto when my doorbell rang. I assumed it was Vida, stopping to report on her visitations, so I opened the door without bothering to look through the peephole.

It was Milo. Raindrops had dampened his regulation hat and jacket, and his long face looked far longer than usual.

"What's wrong?" I asked as a sudden spasm of fear took hold of my heart.

Milo took one step forward, then stopped and removed his hat. "It's Vida," he said, wiping his brow. "She's been shot."

Chapter Eighteen

I HADN'T HEARD Milo right. The president, the pope, the puppets on *The Muppets* could all get shot, and I'd be upset, but not incredulous. Vida was indestructible, immortal, impervious to accident, disease, or weaponry. The Sheriff had to repeat his information three times before it sank in. I must have staggered, because he put an arm around me and muttered something that sounded like "steady."

"Doc Dewey says she'll be okay," he said at last, steering me into the living room and shutting the door behind us. "Really."

My ears were still ringing as I flopped onto the sofa. "I . . . I . . . What happened?"

Milo stood awkwardly by one of the armchairs, hat in hand. "Take it easy. Do you want a drink?"

I nodded. "Get one for yourself," I called after him.

I heard him in the kitchen, getting glasses, taking down the bourbon and the Scotch bottles from the top shelf above the refrigerator, rattling ice, pouring water, all the familiar sounds that brought back a flood of memories.

By the time he returned to the living room, I was fighting tears. For Vida, for Milo, for me.

"Vida had gone to Einar Rasmussen Jr.'s house on the Sky," Milo began after taking a deep sip of Scotch. "You know the place?" He saw me nod. She got out of the car and was headed up the walk when somebody shot her twice from behind. They got her in the left shoulder and through the hat. As Doc said, she should be fine, but one of her white doves is dead as a dodo." The merest hint of a smile played at his long mouth.

"Jesus," I breathed, my shoulders slumping in relief. "This doesn't seem real. Start over."

Milo sat back in the armchair, also looking slightly more relaxed. "Vida got about six feet from the Buick, and was hit. That's pretty much what happened. She thinks she blacked out. Finally, she crawled to the car and started honking the horn. Nobody heard her, so somehow she managed to get back to the highway."

I remembered the winding road that led to the driveway. It was flanked by vine maples, cottonwoods, evergreens, ferns, and salmonberry bushes. Someone could easily have hidden there. But it was the twenty yards of dirt road that upset me as I pictured Vida staggering, perhaps on hands and knees, trying desperately to seek help.

"Anyway," Milo went on, "she flagged down a guy from Wenatchee in a pickup. He brought her into the hospital here. Luckily, Doc was still at the clinic. He removed the bullet, but she's still in the recovery room."

My personal feelings had interfered with my professional responsibilities. I hadn't thought to ask if Milo had a suspect. When I did, he made a face.

"Not yet. It started raining while Vida was trying to get to the main road. Dwight and Sam have been looking for footprints or some other evidence, but so far, no go."

Thoughtfully, I swirled the rest of my bourbon and water in the chimney glass. "Didn't anybody hear Vida honk the horn? What about the Rasmussens?"

Milo raised his hands, palms up. "They're gone."

"Gone? As in 'moved out'?"

"The house is full of packing crates," he replied. "Dwight and Sam could see them through the windows. There are some other houses off that road, but the dipshits who live there claim they didn't hear any honking. They didn't see anything, either. It may be true.

Their places aren't all that close to the Rasmussens'."

"And poor Vida saw nothing?"

Milo shook his head. "Not that she can recall."

I finished my drink and stood up. "I'm going to the hospital. Vida should be out of the recovery room soon. I want to be there. Have you called her daughters or Buck yet?"

Milo had also gotten to his feet. "I had Toni do that. I wanted to tell you in person."

I felt weak. "Thanks, Milo." Impulsively, I kissed his cheek.

"S'okay," he mumbled, sounding not unlike an embarrassed thirteen-year-old. "You want to ride with me to the hospital?"

I hesitated. Riding there meant riding back. At the moment I wasn't capable of predicting my emotions. "No," I said, going to get my jacket out of the front closet. "You may get a call, and then I'd be stuck. I'll take the Jag."

"Whatever." He put his hat back on and opened the door for me. Then, as we walked through the rain to our respective cars, he chuckled grimly. "The funny thing is, I was about to get hold of Vida when the call came in from the hospital. We got that skull-reconstruction drawing late this afternoon. I wanted her to look at it."

I paused by my carport. "Do you have it with you?"

The Sheriff nodded. "I've got a hundred copies. Want a peek?"

"Sure. Can you bring it in with you when we get to the hospital?"

Milo nodded again. "If Doc's there, I'll show it to him. In fact, I'll post a copy in the lobby."

"Good." I gave him a weak smile and got into the Jag.

Vida's daughter, Amy, and her husband, Ted Hibbert, were already in the waiting room. I saw no sign of their wretched son, Roger, though I must confess to a fleeting vision of him undergoing electric-shock therapy in some shadowy corner of the hospital. In reality, a sadistic Roger would be administering it to some hapless victim. Like me.

"Emma!" Amy cried, jumping up and embracing me. She is as tall as her mother, but not nearly so imposing. "Beth and Meg wanted to come, but I told them to wait," she said, releasing me and squeezing a mangled Kleenex in one hand. "Mom will feel much better tomorrow, and it's Saturday, so that works out better every which way."

Since the other daughters and their families lived out of town, Amy's rationale made sense. When it came to practicality, the trio took after Vida. "Your mother's in no danger, I'm told," I said, shaking Ted's limp hand.

"No, no," Amy replied, her round face and blunt features expressing relief. "Doc Dewey says she'll be a hundred percent in no time. But isn't it awful? All these guns! Why don't people go to one of the gravel pits if they want to shoot target practice? Just look at all the highway signs, full of bullet holes."

Somehow, it had never occurred to me that Vida had been shot by accident. I realized that if it had occurred to Milo, he'd ruled out the possibility. Certainly he'd never suggested such a thing to me. But there was no need to alarm Amy further.

"Your mother's very strong, physically and mentally," I pointed out, seeking safer ground than how or why Vida had ended up in the hospital. "Have you any late word on her condition?"

Amy shook her head. "Only that she should be in her room around nine. It's twenty to now."

For the next fifteen minutes we made innocuous conversation. Or, rather, Amy did. Ted, a tall, thin man nearing fifty, always lets his wife do the talking. I suppose that was the price a man paid when he married a Runkel woman.

"So the teacher said to Roger, 'If you don't

put that pelican down, I'm going to have to . . .' " Amy rambled on while I wondered where Milo was. Putting up facial-reconstruction posters, I figured, maybe not only in the hospital lobby, but on utility poles nearby.

At two minutes before nine, the Sheriff finally joined us. He went through the motions of greeting Amy and Ted, then turned to me with an annoyed expression on his face.

"I checked in with the Snohomish Rasmussens just now," he said. "I talked to the housekeeper, Mrs. Steelman. She told me that they hadn't seen any sign of Deirdre, Beau, or Davin."

I stared at Milo. "Where are they?"

Milo shrugged in disgust. "Who knows? We'll put out an APB. Here," he said with a short sigh, and handed me the drawing. "Look familiar?"

The artist's sketch reminded me of those pencil portraits rendered at shopping malls and county fairs. The face looked sufficiently real, yet there was an eerie quality to it, as if I could actually see the skull that lurked underneath the imagined flesh.

"No," I said, still studying the drawing. The woman was middle-aged, rather pretty, with wide-set eyes and strong-looking teeth. There was no character in the face, however; skeletal remains only show where you've gone, not how you got there.

Neither Amy nor Ted recognized the portrait, either. Doc Dewey entered the waiting room just then to tell us that Vida was in her room and doing just fine.

"Don't wear her out, though," Gerald Dewey cautioned, directing his message more to Amy than the rest of us. "She's still a little woozy. Keep the visit to ten minutes." He smiled, the same kindly expression that his father, Old Doc Dewey, had shown his patients for forty years.

I hardly recognized Vida. She was propped up on pillows, with all sorts of IVs running into her hands. Her usually tousled gray curls were limp, and her skin was very pale. Somehow she looked smaller, thinner, but that wasn't possible. Not even a bullet could diminish Vida.

Clumsily, Amy kissed her mother's cheek, then began to cry. "Oh, Ted!" she sobbed, collapsing against her husband. "Isn't it awful? Poor Mom!"

Vida emitted a noise that sounded like "shush." I patted her hand and Milo waved. Amy took another Kleenex from a box on the stand by Vida's bed and wiped her eyes.

"This is horrible, terrible," Amy rattled on. "Who could have done this? Oh, Mom, I wish *I* had a gun!"

Vida took a deep breath. "Please, Amy. You're distressing me."

Again, Amy flung herself on her mother. I was afraid she'd dislodge the IVs. "Mom! Don't say that! I'd never do anything to upset you! I love you, Mom! I love you so!"

"Yes, yes," panted Vida from beneath the weight of her daughter. "Now, do get up."

Milo was holding a copy of the reconstruction. "Vida, would you mind taking a quick look? We got this back from Everett a few hours ago. So far, no takers."

Momentarily, Vida looked confused. "What? Oh! The skull." She tried to scoot up a bit farther on the pillows. "Oh, dear—where are my glasses?"

Milo looked embarrassed. "They fell off when you got shot. In fact, they're broken. Sam and Dwight have them. They'll bring the frames and your other stuff when they get done searching the Rasmussen place."

Vida scowled, then turned to Amy. "You have a key to my house. Fetch my old pair, with the tortoiseshell frames. They're in the top drawer of my bureau."

Amy started to protest, but Vida waved a finger. "Go. It won't take ten minutes. I must see this drawing."

Amy and Ted left. Milo and I listened while

Vida recounted her harrowing experience at the Rasmussens'. "I didn't realize the house was vacant," she said after Milo informed her about the packing crates. "I didn't get quite that close. Really, it's all so hazy. I wish I could be more specific."

I related my visit to Casa de Bronska. Vida was amused by Birgitta's pluck. "That will save me a trip to Snohomish. I suppose I'll be out of commission for a day or two. How vexing."

Doc Dewey had entered the room. "More than that, Vida," he said with a smile. "I'm not letting you out of here until Monday, at least. And then I want you to take it easy for the rest of the week. Doctor's orders."

"Gerald!" Vida started to rise from the pillows, but immediately fell back. "Dear me! I do feel a bit strange. I suppose it's that anesthetic."

Doc nodded. "I'm about to throw your visitors out. You need some peace and quiet."

Milo produced the drawing. "Doc, take a look. Does this face seem familiar?"

Doc peered at the drawing. "I don't think so. Should it?"

"Probably not," Milo said with a small sigh.

Amy returned alone, glasses case in hand. "Ted's waiting in the car. He insists I shouldn't stay. Here, Mom." She handed the case to Vida.

With effort, Vida removed the familiar tortoiseshell glasses from the case and put them on. "My. These seem strange now that I've gotten used to the new ones. Let's see that picture, Milo."

Doc started to intervene. "Come on, folks, you can't wear Vida out."

Milo held up one finger. "This won't take her any longer than it took you. A yes or no is all I want."

Vida was staring at the drawing. Her jaw had dropped and her hands shook ever so slightly. She moved the glasses up and down on her nose, then pushed the drawing back at Milo.

"Incredible," she said in a stricken voice. "I must be hallucinating."

Gathered around the bed, we all leaned forward. "You know who it is?" Milo asked.

Vida nodded once, her head turned away from us. "Yes." She swallowed with difficulty. "It's Marlys Rasmussen."

Milo started what sounded like a barrage of questions, but Doc Dewey gripped the Sheriff by the shoulder and steered him out of the room. Amy and I knew better than to linger. With shouts of love for her mother, Amy followed me into the corridor.

"Christ," Milo breathed when we were out of hearing range. "Vida must be confused. How the hell could this be Marlys? Didn't you say you saw her at the funeral?"

I, too, doubted the current state of Vida's mental prowess. "Between the anesthetic and the shock, she must be disoriented. Show it to her again tomorrow, when she's had some rest and the anesthetic's worn off."

Milo didn't respond. We were walking through the now empty waiting room. He kept silent until we were out on the street.

"I'm all mixed up," the Sheriff said suddenly. "No—maybe I'm just the world's biggest dumb shit."

It was dark, with the rain softly falling on Milo's hat and my uncovered head. I tried to study the Sheriff's face under the wide brim. "Why do you say that?" I asked.

He turned his head, gazing down Pine Street toward the library and the senior-citizen center. "Maybe I'm the one who's confused." Unexpectedly, he grabbed me by the upper arms. "Am I screwed up?"

"Probably," I replied. "Most of us are."

"Shit." He dropped his hands, again looking not at me but at his surroundings. "Ron Bjornson didn't shoot Vida."

"So?" My own confusion was growing. "The

person who did isn't necessarily the one who killed Einar."

Milo shook his head. "Vida was shot at Einar's house. Now you're saying that Birgitta Whatever-her-name-is has a connection to the Rasmussens. The gold, maybe even the bones, they may all tie in. And none of it has jackshit to do with Ron Bjornson."

As a native Puget Sounder accustomed to our soft rain, I never use an umbrella. If Vida was going to be off the job for a while, the last thing I needed was to catch cold. "Milo, let's go someplace and have a drink. How about the ski lodge?" I suggested.

"The Venison Inn is closer," he said. "I've got to get back to the office. Dwight and Sam should be there pretty soon."

I didn't argue. We got into our respective cars and drove the three blocks to Alpine's only real watering hole in the downtown section. During the four minutes that it took to get there and park, my mind was in chaos. Why was I having drinks with Milo? Why was he leaning on me when, for the past few months, he practically spat at me on sight? Why did I feel sorry for him when he had been so blasted ornery?

I'd told him I wanted to be friends. This was friendship, hearing out the other person's troubles. It was possible that we were taking a tentative step toward resolving hostilities. The problem was that I didn't know if it was a step backward or forward.

Oren Rhodes and the regulars at the Venison Inn pelted Milo with questions about Vida. Naturally, her shooting had become the evening's hot topic. The Sheriff answered tersely, but made it clear he wasn't in the mood for idle chatter. And of course we received our share of curious stares. No one had seen us as a couple since last October.

Milo didn't speak until Oren had delivered our drinks. "You got motive, you got opportunity, you got a weapon," the Sheriff said as he set his cigarette down in the ashtray. "You got a guy who's been on the edge for a while because of his job situation, you got a wife who people say is screwing around with the victim. The guy can't pinpoint his whereabouts, maybe he even lies to cover his ass because he did something dumb that makes him look guilty. Then you got about four thousand people in town, another couple of thousand out in the county, and even more over in Snohomish, pressuring you for an arrest because the victim was a big shot. Let's face it—most homicides aren't premeditated. Wife gets pissed off at husband, beans him with a golf club, two drunks mix it up in a bar, one puts out the other's lights. Maybe that's the problem—I see the obvious answer. And God knows, jealousy is always one hell of a motive." He retrieved his cigarette and took a deep drag. "Where did I go wrong?"

I'd been wondering, too. Yet I had no concrete answer. Milo wasn't one to jump to conclusions. Where indeed had he gone wrong?

"It's not the case itself," I finally said. "It's how you perceived it. You wanted to appease the public. Not as voters, because you don't have to be elected to your job since the new legislation was passed last November. But you felt pressured. Einar Rasmussen Jr. was, as you said, a big shot. The problem is, he wasn't a native. By arresting a genuine local boy, you alienated Alpine. When it came right down to it, Einar wasn't as big as Ron. Einar was"—I paused at the irony—"from Snohomish."

Milo revealed his own chauvinism by not betraying even the slightest of smiles. "Maybe you're right. The big question is, was I wrong to arrest Ron? That's what's driving me nuts."

"I can't answer that," I admitted. "Public opinion doesn't mean Ron's innocent."

"Yeah, right." Milo cradled his drink. "Now, with Vida getting shot, everybody's really going to be up in arms. Except for certain locals, who would've liked to shoot her themselves because she's pissed them off," he added, finally exhibiting a touch of humor.

"Why would anyone—seriously—want to shoot Vida?" I said. "Her daughter Amy thinks it was an accident."

"That's possible," Milo allowed. "We've got our share of nuts who cruise Highway 2, taking potshots at whatever catches their warped fancy."

"But," I said dryly, "you don't believe it."

Milo sighed. "I don't know what to believe anymore. I'd be an even bigger jackass than I already am if I didn't consider it likely that whoever shot Vida may have also killed Einar."

"Einar wasn't shot."

"Doesn't matter. Murderers use whatever's handy."

"But why?" I persisted, then had a sudden brainstorm. "To keep her from getting to the house?"

Milo's sleepy eyes opened wide. "Could be. What—besides those packing crates—was in Einar's house that the perp didn't want found?"

I didn't know. "You'll have to get a search warrant. Did Dwight and Sam talk to the Rasmussens in Snohomish?"

Milo shook his head. "Out of our jurisdiction. I've asked the SnoCo Sheriff to check them out. The know-nothing neighbors by

Einar's house said they hadn't seen any cars in the driveway for a couple of days."

Vida and I had been there Wednesday. Deirdre hadn't spoken as if the move were imminent. Obviously, it had been. "What if Vida's right?" I asked, thinking of Marlys's inaccessibility.

Milo frowned. "You said you saw her at the funeral."

I took a deep breath, asked Milo for a cigarette, and tried to explain: "We saw someone we assumed was Marlys. Thinking back, it could have been anybody. She was swathed in veils and a long coat. She stayed within the family circle at the grave site, and all of them were in the screened-off mourners' room at the church."

Milo still looked skeptical. "The rest of the Rasmussens would know if it was Marlys."

"Yes." I puffed away on the cigarette, feeling a bit decadent. "But they'd also band together to keep a secret. Thyra would see to that. As far as I can tell, she still rules the family with an iron hand." Suddenly I remembered my previous cigarette of the day, with Mary Jane Bourgette. I recounted how Mary Jane had approached her sister-in-law at the cemetery and Marlys had only mumbled something incomprehensible. "Don't forget, Mary Jane hasn't seen Marlys for going on forty years. She might not recognize her without all those veils and the hat."

"Weird." Milo finished both his drink and his cigarette. "I've got to stop by the office." He paused. "You want to come along?"

I was startled. "Sure. I'll meet you there."

The Sheriff was standing, putting his hat back on. "You know something?" he said in a wistful voice. "What I really wonder is if I was trying to appease the public or trying to please you."

I stubbed out my half-smoked cigarette. "Please me?" I shook my head. "Maybe you were trying to show me."

"Show you?" Milo seemed puzzled.

I gave the Sheriff a wry glance. "Show me up."

Milo didn't respond.

The Sheriff's deputies were wet, dirty, tired, and out of sorts. Dwight said they'd found all sorts of junk between the highway and the Rasmussens' front yard.

"People are frigging pigs," Dwight declared. "They drive through all this beautiful country and toss everything out the car window except their kids."

"We couldn't get lucky and have the Rasmussens live by one of the marshy areas along the river," Sam complained. "Rain or not, we might have found a fresh, clear footprint. As it is, we found about two dozen, including deer and cougar tracks. There're plenty of fishermen, hikers, and wildflower gatherers, especially this time of year, even if it's against the law."

"The river's kind of slow in there," Dwight noted. "Fishermen come up toward the highway because there aren't any good holes and they don't want to get yelled at for walking through people's front yards."

"We're already getting casts of the prints made," Sam put in. "Most of them look like men's shoes."

We were standing inside the counter area, with Milo resting a foot on the edge of Toni Andreas's empty desk. Dustin Fong was handling the phones and I guessed that Bill Blatt was out on patrol. No doubt Bill was checking in frequently to keep abreast of his aunt's condition.

"First thing tomorrow," Milo said, "we get a search warrant for the house. What about tire tracks along the highway?"

Dwight and Sam exchanged sullen looks. "You know the road, chief," said Sam. "There's an actual shoulder in that stretch. You could pull over anything but a big rig and it'd fit on the pavement."

Milo swore under his breath, then scowled. "That's the point. Why pull over?"

I understood what Milo meant. "There's about a quarter mile of straightaway in there," I said. "If you were driving through, you could see a car turn in the road to the Rasmussen place."

Milo and the three deputies were all looking at me. "So," Dwight drawled, "you just happen to be coming along and you see Vida's big Buick pull off the highway and you decide to stop and shoot her?"

I was unfazed by the implied criticism. "It's not as haphazard as that. You might be headed for the same destination. Or maybe you just left."

Milo scratched his head. "Vida doesn't remember seeing another car, parked or otherwise."

I thought about the way Vida drove: she was a real rubbernecker, especially in town. She'd definitely notice another vehicle in the vicinity. But given what had happened to her, would she remember?

"Maybe," Milo suggested, "there wasn't any vehicle."

We all looked at each other. Certainly that

was possible. But what did it mean? Unfortunately, I had no answer.

The next morning, I stopped in at the hospital shortly after nine. I'd already called to check on Vida's condition, and had been told she'd spent a restful night. From my own, admittedly limited, sick-bay experiences, that meant that she hadn't fallen out of bed, been attacked by wolves, or set fire to her hair. There is no rest in the hospital, with nurses and orderlies parading in and out of the room every twenty minutes—except when you need them.

Vida looked much better, however. She was sitting up on her own, her color had returned, and the familiar tortoiseshell glasses made her appearance seem almost normal.

"Such a fuss!" she exclaimed. "You'd think I'd been blown up by an atom bomb! I've told them to screen my calls. Eleven people have already phoned this morning. I scarcely got through breakfast."

Even as we spoke, a deliveryman wearing blue jeans and a metallic leather jacket arrived with two big bouquets. Under Vida's guidance, he placed the flowers on the windowsill. "Marje Blatt, my niece," she said, opening one of the accompanying cards. "How sweet." She paused, reading the other card. "The Runkel contingent. Lovely glads, so many colors. I can never get the chartreuse ones to winter."

I'd settled into one of the modular plastic chairs. "Have you remembered anything else about yesterday afternoon?" I asked.

Vida made a sour face. "Not really. What I do recall has come into focus, but there's not much I can add. I saw no one, heard nothing, didn't notice any cars or trucks where they shouldn't be. Still, I'm sure of one thing—that is definitely Marlys Rasmussen's face in that drawing. Those remarkable teeth—didn't I tell you she had a wonderful smile?"

I nodded. "Perfect teeth, no dental charts. But," I went on, growing serious, "who pretended to be Marlys at the funeral? And why kill her?"

"Marlys *and* Einar," Vida replied grimly. "The question becomes, who wanted to get rid of them both? Who benefits? The obvious answer is Beau, Deirdre, and Davin. Harold and Gladys to a lesser extent. But don't forget the Bourgettes. And," she added with a dark look, "Birgitta Lindholm."

"But if that was Marlys at the warehouse site, she was killed before the fire last October," I pointed out. "Birgitta arrived in Alpine less than a month ago. Plus, she claims not to have known about the connection between herself and the Rasmussens."

Vida examined the dressing on her shoulder. "So she says. The word *claim* seems to apply to Ms. Lindholm in many ways. What if she had been here before? What better way to come back than as an au pair to the Bronskys?" My House & Home editor made a face. "Ugh. There *should* be a better way, but Birgitta might not have known of it."

The deliveryman reappeared with another batch of flowers, including a large white azalea. "My, my," she murmured after reading the cards, "people are so very kind."

"You have lots of friends," I noted. "And relatives."

"Relatives." Vida grew thoughtful. "How strange. Everything in this case seems to be family-oriented, though it certainly didn't look that way in the beginning. It was all about Ron and Maylene, and seemed to center on the college. Then there was Mr. Yoshida and the nuggets, but even that was a blind. It's the Rasmussens, everywhere you look. So typical."

"I wonder if Milo will release Ron," I mused.

"Perhaps," Vida said. "If I were Milo, I wouldn't wait until the real killer is found."

"Milo won't like admitting in public that he

was wrong," I said. "Ron intends to sue the county."

"Very embarrassing." Vida nodded. "But Milo will do the right thing."

A chunky nurse with rosy cheeks and graying black hair stepped into the room. "Bath time," she announced. "Shall I bring the rubber ducky?"

Vida looked horrified. "Good heavens! This doesn't sound at all dignified. Couldn't you wait a few minutes? I have a visitor."

The nurse, who I recalled was a Peterson or a Petersen, glanced at her watch. "It'll be at least a half hour. I'm going on break."

"Then go, Constance," Vida commanded. "I haven't done much to get dirty. And do spare me the duck."

I asked Vida who was taking care of Cupcake in her absence. As usual when Vida isn't at home, Amy took over the household duties. "Roger is going to mow the lawn." She beamed. "So responsible, so conscientious, such a hard little worker."

If Vida was going to sing Roger's praises, I decided I might as well leave. "I'll be back later today," I promised. "I'll let you know what's going on with Milo. Maybe the SnoCo Sheriff will have talked to the Rasmussens. I hope whoever questions them has a copy of that drawing."

On my way out, I stopped around the corner of the hallway by the nurses' station, which was temporarily vacant. I realized that Milo hadn't said anything about the bullet that had wounded Vida. Maybe he'd told her the caliber and what type of gun might have fired it. I decided to go back and ask her.

I was just turning around when I heard the scream. It was coming from down the corridor, and I was sure it was Vida.

Chapter Nineteen

As I TORE around the corner I saw Doc Dewey running after someone at the end of the hall. Doc was a good ten feet behind his prey, and came to a sudden stop when he reached the stairway exit.

"Goddamn it," Doc yelled as he gave the door a fierce kick. "The sonuvabitch locked it! Quick, somebody! Press the alarm!"

Two nurses, an orderly, a cleaning woman, and three patients had erupted into the hall. My first thought was for Vida. I ran into her room and found her gasping against the pillows.

"Vida!" I cried. "Are you okay? What happened?"

"Man," she wheezed, trying to raise trembling hands to her throat. "Flowers." Vida was still gasping.

I didn't know what she was talking about. Her face was crimson, the bedclothes were in disarray, and the dressing on her shoulder was pulled partially off. My own hands were shaking as I tried to give her some water. One of the two nurses I'd just glimpsed in the corridor rushed into the room.

"Mrs. Runkel!" she exclaimed, pushing me out of the way. "Hold on. Doc will be here in just a second."

The next few minutes flew by in a blur. Alarm bells rang, people ran up and down the hall shouting, Doc came chugging into the room to take over. I made myself small, quivering next to the closet. Then I heard sirens approaching, no doubt Milo or one of his men. It wasn't an ambulance; I can tell the difference.

"Okay," I heard Doc say. "We've got something in the IV to relax you, Vida. You'll be fine, though you may have a sore throat and neck for a couple of days." He squeezed her hand. "Don't even think. It's going to be okay."

Timorously, I moved away from the closet. "What happened?" I repeated, this time to Doc, whose usual unruffled appearance was in wild disarray.

He guided me out of the room, closing the door and leaving the nurse with Vida. "Jesus," Doc moaned, looking none too steady himself. "That was the damnedest—excuse my language, Emma—but I never . . ." He pressed his fingers against his temples. "I was coming up to make my rounds," Doc said, speaking more slowly. "I'd used the stairs instead of the elevator. I usually do, the hospital's only two stories, but that's about all the exercise I get most days.

I entered the ward and decided to check on Vida first, even though she's in the middle of the floor." He gave me a knowing look. "She *is* special. Anyway, here was this guy leaning over Vida. I thought at first he was hugging her, but she screamed, and I realized he was choking her. I grabbed him and we wrestled around, then he broke loose and ran down the hall. I tripped or stumbled or some damned thing, and didn't catch him before he tripped the lock on the stairway door. Damn, damn, damn. I could have had him."

"Who was he?" I asked, feeling bewildered by this latest turn of events.

Doc shook his head. "I didn't recognize him. I could describe him, though. Sort of."

Jack Mullins came rushing up to us. "You okay, Doc? How about Vida?" Receiving assurances, Jack relayed what information he had: "The guy got away, probably on foot. Dot and Durwood Parker were coming out of the senior center down the street. They saw somebody in a leather jacket hightailing it down Pine. They just thought he was in a hurry, and didn't notice where he went."

"A leather jacket?" I echoed. "The delivery-man had on a leather jacket." Vida had croaked the word *flowers*; now I knew what she meant.

Doc and Jack both stared at me. "What deliveryman?" asked Doc.

"From Posies Unlimited, I suppose. He came in twice." I cursed myself for paying more attention to the flowers than to the bearer.

Doc shook his head. "Delphine has deliveries dropped off at the desk," he said, referring to Delphine Corson, Posies Unlimited's owner. "The orderlies or the volunteers bring them up later."

I frowned at Doc. "Then why didn't the nurses notice him?"

Doc looked upset again. "I suppose they thought he was a visitor. Or maybe they didn't see him. They get busy with patients or filling out charts and don't always notice things. Crazy Eights Neffel came in last week with a beaver wearing an argyle sweater. Nobody saw Crazy Eights until he went into the women's rest room."

"We'll keep looking," Jack said. "Dodge is on his way. We got hold of him just before he went to search the Rasmussen house."

"I should have caught that bastard," Doc said in chagrin. "I should exercise more. I'm out of shape. Maybe I should ride a bicycle, like the college kids."

There was nothing I could do for the time

being, so I left. I was getting into the Jag when Sandford Clay hailed me from across the street.

"What's all the commotion?" he asked.

I gave Sandy an abridged version of the latest attack on Vida. Naturally, he was aghast. "Who would want to do in Vida? She's an icon." He shook his head in dismay. "I won't bother Dodge with my little discovery right now."

"What's that?" I asked politely.

Sandy uttered a little laugh. "It's the dangdest thing. Want a look?"

"At what?" I was growing a bit impatient as the rain started to come down harder.

"That chest. I found something startling in it this morning."

I couldn't resist. The Clemans Building, which houses Sandy's office, was across the street from the hospital. I accompanied the assayer to the third floor, where he took the chest out of his safe.

"I came in this morning to tie up some loose ends," Sandy explained, opening the lid, but leaving the nuggets at the bottom. "Then I got to thinking about that Swedish girl who said the gold belonged to her. Just for the heck of it, I got the chest out and gave it a really thorough going-over. I should've done it before, but I hated to tamper with the chest. Even with some exterior damage, these McFarland cases are a collector's item." Gingerly, he inserted a letter opener in the gauzy lining of the lid. "You see?"

Several yellowed pieces of paper lay behind the lining. "Wow," I breathed. "What is it?"

"See for yourself." Sandy carefully removed the papers and handed them to me.

The handwriting was cramped and old-fashioned; the awkward English was difficult to understand. But I could read the signature, which had been written with a flourish: Ulf Lindholm, Malmö, Sweden. The date was November 3, 1908.

The gist of the letter was that Ulf had saved the life of Kenzo Yoshida, a railroad worker and amateur miner. Yoshida had discovered a large quantity of gold near what had then been called Wellington and was now Tye. A pair of unscrupulous men whose names were given only as Cap and Axel had tried to kill him and steal the gold. Ulf had rescued Yoshida and hidden him in one of the ovens that the Greek workers had dug into the mountainside to bake their favorite breads. In gratitude, Yoshida had given half of his treasure to Ulf before fleeing to safety in Seattle. But the would-be thieves and murderers sought vengeance. It became

Ulf's turn to go on the run. He planned to hop a freight and head east for New York, where he would use some of his nuggets to pay his passage home. Several ounces of gold had been entrusted to one of the Greeks to deliver to the love of Ulf's life, Christina Andersen. The remaining share was to be buried for Ulf, awaiting his return to America.

"For some reason, Ulf never came back," Sandy said with a wry little smile. "Maybe he found another love in Malmö."

"Birgitta's claim is solid," I said. "She has not suffered the Bronskys in vain. But she'll still have to cope with the Rasmussens."

Sandy looked puzzled. "How is that?"

I explained about Edna Mae Dalrymple's genealogical research. Sandy whistled softly. "The girl won't get any of that gold from Thyra Rasmussen," he said. "I hear she's a real pistol."

I agreed. "Of course Birgitta isn't entitled to their share, only what you have here." I tapped the chest. "I don't know how Christina earned her living—or Ulf's gratitude—but she was going to have his baby. Thyra was born the following spring."

"Fascinating," said Sandy, caressing the chest. "This job can take some interesting twists and turns. Gold, silver, precious gems, antiques— I enjoy working with them. But it's the stories behind the objects that make my work worthwhile."

"Mine, too," I said.

Sandy Clay planned to notify both the Sheriff and Mayor Baugh as soon as possible. I tried to imagine Birgitta's reaction when she learned that the nuggets were hers. There would be no squeals of excitement, no jumping for joy. She would behave calmly, coolly. Birgitta expected to get the gold. If not in name, she was a Rasmussen in spirit.

When I got back to the Jag, Averill Fairbanks approached me.

"Emma," he called. "Got some news."

Was I never going to leave Pine Street? The last thing I needed was another nutty sighting from Averill. "Can you call it in Monday?"

"Won't keep." He leaned his stubby body against the Jag's bonnet. "I been trying to tell Vida, but that mule of a woman won't listen. It's about them prospectors."

I was trapped. "What prospectors?" I asked, my voice weary.

Averill rubbed at his nose. "Where they're mining. You know—the old firetrap that burned down a while back."

"The warehouse?" Something flitted through my mind, something to do with Averill, something pertaining to gold. A snatch of Robert Service, a hint of the Yukon. "Are you talking about the nuggets that were found after the fire?"

"Ah . . ." Averill looked uncertain. "Maybe. Maybe not. I'm talking about the guy who was digging before the fire. Only he was burying something, now I come to think of it."

Impulsively, I grabbed Averill's arm. "Was this just before the fire? Maybe the same night?"

Averill's forehead creased in concentration. "Might have been at that. Was it 'round about Halloween?"

Not having been in Alpine at the time, I couldn't remember the exact date. "A week or so before, maybe."

"Hm-mm." Averill nodded slowly. "Sounds right. He had one of them moon-walking machines with him."

I let go of his arm, though I felt like shaking him. Fact and fiction mingled so closely in Averill's account that I was struggling to tell the difference. "Do you know who it was? Doing the burying, I mean? Was it President Cardenas from the college?"

Averill shook his head. "Not this time. That was way back, him and some high mucky-mucks from Olympia."

I gritted my teeth. The groundbreaking ceremony, no doubt, almost two years earlier. "Who did you see last October?" I asked, pessimistic about getting a sensible answer.

"It was one of those Pluto guys," Averill replied. "You can always tell 'em by their coats."

"Coats?" I repeated.

Averill nodded some more. "Sure. They're made of plutonium."

I gave up the idea of questioning Averill further. Maybe I'd gotten all there was to get. Milo could take over from here, as soon as he had time.

I figured the Sheriff wouldn't stay long at the hospital except to query staff. He'd been headed for the Rasmussen place. I'd meet him there. I, too, was curious about the house.

It was pouring as I headed down Highway 2. Our May weather was behaving more like November. Usually it was pleasant in May, dreary in June, with summer finally arriving in July. El Niño was playing its tricks.

After turning off the highway to reach the Rasmussen house, I drove down the dirt road. There was no sign of Milo. It wouldn't be smart to park my car where Vida had left the Buick. Reversing, I took a right-hand turn that led to the other houses along the river. The split-level in front of me looked deserted.

Perhaps the owners had gone into town. I parked the Jag as far off the drive as possible, to allow room for another vehicle. The road into the Rasmussen property was concealed by trees. With the rain pounding on the car's roof, I might not be able to hear Milo pull up. Getting out of the Jag, I walked to the fork in the dirt road. What was taking Milo so long? Over an hour had passed since I'd left the hospital.

A noise from somewhere off on my right startled me. A twig had snapped. I froze in place, but saw nothing. A deer, perhaps. I tried to relax.

After ten minutes I forced myself to make a decision: Should I go back to Alpine and find out why Milo hadn't shown up? Or, since I hadn't seen anyone lurking about, should I take a quick peek at the house?

Curiosity overcame caution. Through the rain I went, head down, but ears alert. I reached the driveway safely. Sure enough, I could see the packing crates through the windows. The kitchen, which Vida and I had viewed before from this same vantage point, was swept clean of belongings. Certain that Milo would show up at any minute, I went around to the rear of the house, which faced the river.

A flash of lightning hit just as I turned the corner. The thunderclap followed almost immediately, which meant the storm was close by. I pulled my jacket over my head and saw the river flowing past the backyard.

But it was more than a garden. While rosebushes and a few small fruit trees had been carefully planted, there was also an eerie little plot. Small crosses protruded from the dark earth, with cedar shakes bearing hand-carved names: Dolly. Red. Peepers. Candy Man. Fluff.

It appeared to be a pet cemetery, and it made me flinch. The Rasmussens hadn't lived here very long. How could they have so many animals die on them?

Lightning struck again, then the inevitable thunder. I shuddered, and started back for the front of the house.

"Hi." The figure standing ten feet away was that of a youngish man wearing blue jeans and a metallic leather jacket. My first reaction was that I'd never seen him before in my life, but I had. He was the deliverer of flowers to Vida, and the man who had tried to kill her. Twice.

I had to think fast. "Are you here to look at the house? It doesn't officially go on the market until Wednesday."

The man in the leather jacket looked momentarily perplexed. He was in his thirties, slender, about average height, with thinning fair hair, and soft features that looked as if they hadn't worked very hard at life.

His hesitation impelled me to rattle on. "The ad will appear in this week's *Advocate*," I said, trying to figure out how to get around him and reach the Jag. "It's a wonderful property, plenty of square footage, river view, three bedrooms . . ."

Three bedrooms. Suddenly I knew who this man was, I knew what had happened to Marlys, to Einar, and what was about to happen to me. "Call Doukas Realty," I said, scooting around him.

Three bedrooms. Deirdre had implied that everyone in this house had a separate room. That accounted for her, for Davin—and for Beau. But not Marlys, who didn't need a bedroom because she'd been dead for six months.

"Hold it." His voice, like his features, was very soft.

I turned, aware that my attempt at a smile probably looked sickly. "Yes?"

"You're not a Realtor." Again, that soft voice, as if it hadn't had much use over the years.

I shrugged. "I didn't say I was. That's why you should call—"

He moved swiftly, like a snake, barring my way. "You were here before, a couple of times, with that old bat with the birds on her head. You were at the funeral with her, too. What are you doing here?" The soft words conveyed more menace than if he had shouted.

My brain was turning to mush. "I . . . I saw the ad, before it goes in the paper. This is a wonderful house. I wanted to have a look. I might buy it myself."

He shook his head. "You're snooping. Like your friend."

I took a deep breath. "You won't sell this place if you treat potential buyers so rudely. It's overpriced to begin with, Beau."

His head jerked back. "You don't know me."

" 'Do you know Beau'?" I said, quoting the catchphrase that had gone 'round the area for years. "I do now."

"So what?" The words stayed soft, but there was a sneer on his face. "Don't you think my little cemetery is worth an extra fifty grand? Everything I ever loved is there."

My only hope of escape was distraction. I wouldn't run for the Jag. I'd have a better chance heading for the highway, where I could flag someone down.

"I saw all the little signs," I said, forcing my voice to sound normal. "What were they, Beau? Dogs? Cats? Hamsters?"

"Cats," Beau replied, taking another step

closer. "Persians, Siamese, Manx. All sorts of cats. They were beautiful. But they don't live long."

Deirdre had taken out an ad for a lost cat named Fluff. But since then, Fluff's grave had been marked with a sign, like the other cats that Deirdre had implied were runaways. They weren't. They'd been murdered, by Beau. I closed my eyes in horror, imagining what this grotesque man had done to those animals—and to his own parents.

"No, they don't," I agreed. "You should have gotten a parrot. They live longer than humans. By the way, where's your bicycle?"

When Beau glanced over his shoulder, I ran. Around the corner I chugged, past the kitchen, the dining room, the living room. I heard him call softly behind me, still not raising his voice. Did he have the gun? Maybe not, or he would have displayed it before this.

But he was right on my heels as I raced up the drive. By the time I reached the dirt road, he was almost upon me. Another flash of lightning lit up the sky and then the thunder rumbled so close that I wondered if the house had been hit.

I felt his weight on my back, pushing me to the ground. He didn't have the gun; he would go for my throat. I writhed beneath him, hunching my shoulders to protect my neck. I think I screamed, though I'm not sure. But I know I heard Beau let out a terrified yelp. Suddenly he released me, and I rolled over to see why. Maybe Milo was standing in the road, his sidearm at the ready.

There was no Milo nor any other human. What I saw through the rain was a cougar on its hind legs, teeth bared, and forepaws raised. If Beau's cry had been of terror, the shrill sound of the big cat was a series of surreal shrieks and growls. I felt paralyzed, but Beau started to run toward the house.

The cougar pounced. Beau was dragged to the ground. The animal, with its small head and sleek gray body, must have been six feet long. He attacked almost methodically, and Beau's anguished screams could barely be heard above the next clap of thunder. I couldn't watch, but neither could I shut my eyes as the cougar mauled Beau and the storm raged around us.

Suddenly the savagery was over. Beau didn't move. The cat sat back on its haunches, licking blood from its paws. Only then did I realize I was next. Why hadn't I escaped to the Jag? I started to sob as my foolishness sank in.

The cougar never looked my way. With lithe, graceful movements, it slunk past the house. Then it turned the corner and disappeared.

Milo pulled up in the Cherokee Chief. As he got out it was obvious he didn't see Beau at first. "Emma, you idiot," he called, "what the hell are you doing here?"

I couldn't speak. Feeling sick, I gestured at the mangled body in the driveway. Milo stared, then drew his weapon.

"Who the hell is that?" he demanded, edging closer to Beau. "Jesus! He's one dead mess! How the hell . . . ?"

I still couldn't speak, but at least I could move. Avoiding Beau, I grabbed Milo's arm and mutely led him to the rear of the house. The cougar sat at the edge of the little cemetery like a sentry.

"Cats," I finally croaked. "Beau's cats."

Milo seemed bewildered. The cougar still didn't look at us. The animal continued sitting there, perhaps communing with his fallen brethren. Milo had raised his gun, but now he holstered it. Apparently he understood something that I didn't.

"Let's go," Milo said, his voice hoarse. Roughly, he put an arm around me and steered me back up to the road. "How'd you get here?" he asked as I buried my head against his chest in order to avoid seeing Beau.

"My car's over there," I said, muffled. "Off the dogleg."

"Can you drive? I've got to stick around."

I nodded. The Rasmussen property was to our rear, so I raised my head. "I'll be okay in a bit. I need some time."

Still with his arm around me, I led Milo to the Jag. "Beau Rasmussen killed his parents," I said.

"What?" Milo was taken aback.

"That was Beau back there. The cougar killed him because he killed all his cats."

"You better not drive," said Milo, skepticism writ large on his face. "Come on back with me to the Chief."

I started to protest, but was ignored. Milo all but shoved me headfirst into his vehicle, then came around to the driver's side. He began radioing in the information that there was a dead man at the Rasmussen house, apparently the victim of a cougar attack. Then he sat back and waited for me to collect myself.

"Okay," he said after several minutes had gone by. "Your color is almost normal. Tell me, if you can, who that is in the driveway back there. All I know is that the guy's dead."

I gave myself a good shake, sending raindrops flying all over the front seat and dashboard. "He's Beau Rasmussen, the man nobody ever saw. He was crazy, and don't ask me to get specific, though I'd guess he was bipolar. That's why his parents never let him out of the house. Imagine Thyra Rasmussen suffering the indignity of a grandson who'd create havoc in the real world."

"I've never met Thyra Rasmussen." Milo still looked dubious.

"I have. She's a dreadful woman." I took a deep breath. "I suppose Beau got to the point where he resented his parents, where he believed they were keeping him prisoner. Marlys hardly ever left the house, either. She probably didn't dare. She must have seemed more like a prison warden than a mother. Beau had reached his mid-thirties without ever having had any personal freedom. I figure he finally snapped last October, and killed Marlys. He was used to burying things. You saw his cat cemetery. But he could hardly bury his mother in the backyard. So he brought her into Alpine, buried her at the old warehouse, and set the place on fire."

"This is all conjecture." Milo's long mouth set in a firm line.

"No." I paused to make sure my thought process was staying unscrambled. Rain ran down the windshield, which was beginning to fog up inside. "There was a witness. Averill Fairbanks saw Beau bury Marlys."

"Averill Fairbanks?" Milo was justifiably incredulous.

I nodded. "He told me this morning. Oh, he wouldn't have made a very good witness on the stand, but he definitely saw Beau. Averill said he was burying something, and that it was probably right around the time the warehouse burned down. Averill described Beau as wearing a plutonium coat. Plutonium is a silver color, I believe, which would describe Beau's metallic leather jacket, especially by moonlight. Averill also mentioned a moon-walk machine, or something like that, but I suspect it was Beau's bicycle. He'd no doubt transported his mother on it after he killed her. Beau probably never had a driver's license, since he rarely left the house. My guess is, he went by bicycle. I'll bet you'll find one over in the woods by the highway, and that's why Vida never saw or heard a car. Neither did I. And who'd notice him on his rare forays into town? With all the students around here now, we've got people on bikes all over the place."

The rain thrummed on the Cherokee Chief's roof. Milo was beginning to look less skeptical, though hardly convinced. "Why kill Einar Jr. six months later?"

"Maybe Einar—who wasn't a bad man, just a

self-centered one—couldn't go on living with his son's guilt. Einar must have guessed what had happened to his wife. But we've got Thyra to reckon with. First, she had to hide some sort of serious head case. Then he killed. She must have been frantic. Thyra must have warned Einar that the truth must never get out."

Milo was rubbing his long chin. "So Beau was afraid his dad would give him up. Why kill Einar at the college? Why not at home, like Marlys?"

"Too risky. Remember, when Marlys was killed, only Beau and Einar were living here." I waved in the direction of the Rasmussen house. "But Deirdre moved in recently. She might put up with Beau impersonating her mother—maybe she thought he was just doing it for some kind of morbid stunt—but she'd balk at murder. There was also Davin to consider."

"Deirdre had to know," Milo said.

"That Beau was a killer? Maybe she did, and that's why she took off with Davin. I don't blame her. She was probably afraid for their lives."

"She had a reason." Milo grunted. "But what about Scott Kuramoto? I thought they were a duo."

"They may be. But can you see Scott married

into that family?" I countered. "He wouldn't want it, the senior Rasmussens would hate it. Let's call it a fling. Lonely people do strange things."

Milo's hazel eyes were fixed on my face. "They sure do."

I didn't want to get sidetracked. "I came to the Rasmussen house because I thought you'd be here with the search warrant. Where were you? I almost got killed."

Milo looked indignant. "I was with Vida. Do you think I'd leave her alone for a third attack? I had to wait for Bill Blatt to relieve me. What was the deal? Why try to kill Vida?"

I had to smile. "Vida's reputation almost did her in. Thyra must have learned that Vida had come calling on Marlys, more than once. The old witch knew that Vida's persistence—and curiosity—could pay off. I think Thyra gave Vida more credit than was due, but of course there was that ever-present fear of being found out. The Rasmussens had lived with that for most of Beau's life. It must have eaten at Thyra like a cancer. Knowing that Beau had already killed, I suspect she told him to get rid of Vida. Like the rest of them, he danced to her tune."

Milo leaned back against the driver's seat. The storm had passed over, and the thunder was now a distant rumble. "Jesus. What a family.

They even fed on each other." Jerkily, he turned back to face me. "So what the hell happened today?"

I explained about the pet cemetery, then about Beau's arrival. "We heard of cougar sightings at the edge of town," I said. "I don't understand it, but that big cat went right for Beau, and completely ignored me. Thank God."

Milo gave a nod. "Animals are like that. Especially cats. They're protective, they sense danger to their species. And sometimes they seek revenge."

Milo's upbringing had made him familiar with all forms of wildlife. I'd watched him fish, but I'd never seen him hunt. He had lowered the gun on the cougar, because he respected the animal's grief. I respected Milo's understanding.

A squad car and an ambulance were arriving behind us. I hesitated. Should I wait to see what happened? But for once, my personal needs overcame my professional duties. Milo could tell me what went on. I had to get away from this place of horror.

"I can drive now," I said, opening the door. "You have to wait here, right?"

Milo hesitated. "Yeah. I'll wait here."

For a moment, I stared straight into his eyes. "I'll be at the hospital with Vida. I'll wait there."

"Okay."

I went out into the rain. When I drove past Milo on my way out, he was still waiting.

"Ooooh!" Vida was punishing her eyes again, distraught because she hadn't been in on the denouement. "You behaved so recklessly! You might have been killed! Why couldn't you use *sense*?"

"I already explained that I was sure Milo was there—or would be coming very soon. Anyway, you're the one who got shot and almost strangled."

"That's different." Vida put her tortoiseshell-framed glasses back on, then smiled wickedly. "I can't help it, I would love to be a little mouse in the corner when they tell Thyra about Beau. At last, that nasty woman will get what she deserves."

"Actually," I responded, "she's every bit as much of a killer as Beau. Her manipulation of the family and her obsession with keeping up appearances helped turn him into a murderer. She, too, has blood on her hands."

Vida scowled at me. "Yes, yes, of course she

does. I'm not talking about *that*." She paused, clearing her raw throat. "I meant my mother's gourds."

Ron Bjornson, relieved but belligerent, was released from jail Monday morning. On Friday, after the story of Beau's death and the carefully worded statement from Milo that the Rasmussen case was closed, Einar Sr. killed himself with his shotgun. I had written and rewritten the article at least six times, to avoid a libel suit. But the inferences were there: the late Beau Rasmussen had killed his parents.

If Einar Sr. had no longer been able to endure the web of evil which entwined itself around his family, Thyra was unrepentant. She wouldn't talk to me, but she'd issued a statement which all of the local papers picked up, including *The Advocate*.

"When a family becomes prosperous and prominent," she had said, "there are always envious parasites who try to bring them down. Lies, rumors, and unfounded allegations are their tools. We have had our share of undeserved tragedy, but we shall persevere and maintain our status in the community."

Vida, who was out of the hospital, but confined at home for another week, had no comment. She was still savoring what she considered a personal victory over Thyra Rasmussen.

It was a subdued, haggard Deirdre who was the most willing to talk to me. She came into the office the following Monday, after her grandfather's funeral.

"Davin and I are moving to Seattle," she said, almost in a whisper. "I don't care what I have to do to get work. I could never stay with Grandmama, and Davin needs a big support network for his drinking, which he can get in a big city. I don't belong around here, anyway. I've never liked small towns."

I smiled, a bit sadly. "Belonging is a tough concept. I'm not sure I belong in Alpine. And I know that even after all the years I've been here, the locals *know* I don't belong. I guess it comes to where your heart feels at home."

"I never felt at home with my family," Deirdre declared, her usually soft features strained and hard. "Beau and his horrendous problems got all the attention. That's why I married Jerk-off when I was so young. I had to get away. Then I came back to this." She made a sharp gesture with one hand. "Beau was what they used to call manic-depressive. My parents took him to doctors when he was younger, but they didn't have as many medications then. Later Grandmama put a stop to more sophisticated treatment. She insisted Beau was fine, just moody. My mother did her best to get him to take some kind of medicine, but as he got older he became more rebellious. If that's the word for his kind of madness." She spoke with great bitterness.

"Did your father tell you that Beau had killed your mother?" I asked.

Deirdre shook her head. "He said she'd just gone off, she couldn't take being Beau's keeper anymore. I almost believed it. But I immediately sensed the tension between my father and Beau. I knew what had happened. Then Dad was killed, and I was sure I was right. I thought I'd go mad myself when Beau decided to dress up as Mom at Dad's funeral. It was horrible."

"But you wouldn't tell?"

"No. I couldn't, then. I was too upset. And I was afraid for Davin. Can you imagine what a nightmare this has been since I moved in with Dad and Beau? That house—I'd like to give it away."

"Not at that price," I noted.

Deirdre snorted. "That was Beau's idea. He wanted to live with Grandmama. He knew she'd take care of him. I think they were kindred spirits."

It was Deirdre who enlightened me about the

woman Einar had been seeing on the sly. She was Cynthia Kittikachorn, not Maylene Bjornson. Scott Kuramoto knew about the affair, and thought that Cynthia and Einar had gotten together briefly just before his appointment with Carla at the RUB. Cynthia, afraid of getting in trouble with Nat Cardenas, had spread rumors about Maylene even before the murder.

Deirdre left my office around five. I was bringing dinner in for Vida, which meant a stop at the Grocery Basket's deli. As I drove down Front Street, Milo hailed me from the curb. Almost getting rear-ended, I pulled around the corner and waited for him to join me.

"I solved the Bjornson problem," he said, looking more cheerful than I'd seen him in a long time. "I hired him."

"What?" I started to laugh.

Milo was leaning through the Jag's side window. "You got it. By cutting out some of the overtime the deputies are working, especially behind the desk at night, we can afford Ron. He's used to working graveyard, so that won't bother him. He can do some of the handyman stuff around the office, even repairs on the patrol cars."

"That's brilliant," I said. "So no lawsuit."

"Right. Ron's pretty pleased. He gets benefits, too, as a county employee."

"Wonderful." The smile that had lingered
from the laugh felt frozen on my face as a sudden silence grew between us.

"You want to catch the Mariners on TV
tonight?" Milo finally said. "I'll make dinner at
my place. I owe you one."

"You don't owe me anything, Milo." The
smile was gone. "Anyway," I said, trying to
make my voice sound light, "I'm taking dinner
to Vida. Some other time, okay?"

Milo ducked his head under his regulation
hat. "Tomorrow?"

"Call me in the morning before I leave for
work, around seven-thirty."

"Okay." The Sheriff sounded a little uncertain. He stood up, leaving me to stare at his
midsection.

I wished I could have seen his face. I hoped
he couldn't see mine.

After dinner and a long visit with Vida, I
went home to my little log nest at the edge of
the forest.

There were no letters in the mail, no calls on
the answering machine. I considered phoning
Milo. But I didn't.

As I was finishing my second cup of coffee around seven-forty the next morning, the phone rang. I started to reach for the receiver, then stopped. It rang again.

And again.